LOVE FOUND

Uriel's heart stopped beating. His jaw dropped open.

He couldn't be seeing what he was seeing in that moment. He *couldn't* be feeling what he was feeling. Not now. Not here, in a *bathroom*—after two thousand years. Maybe he'd slipped in the rain outside and hit his head.

No, that was impossible. He was relatively invincible. Being hit on the head would do nothing to him but make him a little cranky.

She was really standing there before him. She was real; he could see her, hear her—he could even smell her. She smelled like shampoo and soap and lavender.

Jesus, he thought, unable to refrain from letting his gaze drop down her body and back up again. She was everything that he had ever imagined she would be, from her tall, slim body to her long jet-black hair, and those indigo blue eyes the color of a Milky Way night. Her skin was like porcelain. Her lips were plump and pink and framed perfect, white teeth. She was an *angel*.

She was his archess. And she was . . . *scowling* at him?

AVENGER'S ANGEL

A NOVEL OF THE LOST ANGELS

HEATHER KILLOUGH-WALDEN

A SIGNET ECLIPSE BOOK

SIGNET ECLIPSE

Published by New American Library, a division of
Penguin Group (USA) Inc., 375 Hudson Street,
New York, New York 10014, USA
Penguin Group (Canada), 90 Eglinton Avenue East, Suite 700, Toronto,
Ontario M4P 2Y3, Canada (a division of Pearson Penguin Canada Inc.)
Penguin Books Ltd., 80 Strand, London WC2R 0RL, England
Penguin Ireland, 25 St. Stephen's Green, Dublin 2,
Ireland (a division of Penguin Books Ltd.)
Penguin Group (Australia), 250 Camberwell Road, Camberwell, Victoria 3124,
Australia (a division of Pearson Australia Group Pty. Ltd.)
Penguin Books India Pvt. Ltd., 11 Community Centre, Panchsheel Park,
New Delhi - 110 017, India
Penguin Group (NZ), 67 Apollo Drive, Rosedale, Auckalnd 0632,
New Zealand (a division of Pearson New Zealand Ltd.)
Penguin Books (South Africa) (Pty.) Ltd., 24 Sturdee Avenue,
Rosebank, Johannesburg 2196, South Africa

Penguin Books Ltd., Registered Offices:
80 Strand, London WC2R 0RL, England

First published by Signet Eclipse, an imprint of New American Library,
a division of Penguin Group (USA) Inc.

First Printing, November 2011
10 9 8 7 6 5 4 3 2 1

For Fran,
who really is an angel now

ACKNOWLEDGMENTS

With deep, heartfelt thanks to:

My husband and dearest friend, who inspires me, advises me, has faith in me, gives me hope, keeps me going, and holds me tight. I would be nowhere without him.

My daughter, who tries so very hard to let me write even though she really just wants to be with Mama.

My parents, who never stopped believing in me.

My brother, who always asks how my writing is going.

My dear friend Mary, whose reviews and advice keep me honest.

My dear friend Meagan, for giving me the rare time I need to pen my words.

LSU's Religious Studies Department, for fostering within me a deep love of all things eldritch.

Erotica Republic, for their immense help and invaluable feedback.

Bob Mecoy, who gave me a chance.

My wonderful agent, Robert, the miracle worker who makes magic happen.

My editor, for her invaluable insight.

And my überprecious "sources": Susan Stewart, Bruce Officer, and the myriad of willing, friendly storytellers in Scotland.

INTRODUCTION

Long ago, the Old Man gathered together his four favored archangels, Michael, Gabriel, Uriel, and Azrael. He pointed to four stars in the sky that shone brighter than the others. He told the archangels that he wished to reward them for their loyalty and had created for them soul mates. Four perfect female beings—archesses.

However, before the archangels could claim their mates, the four archesses were lost to them and scattered to the wind, beyond their realm and reach. The archangels made the choice to leave their world, journey to Earth, and seek out their mates.

For thousands of years, the archangels have searched. But they have not searched alone. For they are not the only entities to leave their realm and come to Earth to hunt for the archesses. They were followed by another. . . .

CHAPTER ONE

2,000 years BCE

The archangel Michael gripped the rock in his right hand so hard that his fingers left imprints in the stone. His jaw was clenched, his eyes shut fast against the pain coursing through his veins. The woods were sparse this far north and the ground beneath him grew colder and harder as the strength was sapped from his inhuman body.

His brother, the archangel Azrael, transformed as he was to a predatory creature, had his fangs embedded deep in the side of his throat, and with each pull and swallow, Michael experienced a new and deeper agony.

"Az . . . that's enough," he ground out, hissing the words through gritted teeth.

I'm sorry, came Azrael's hesitant reply. He didn't speak the words, but Michael could hear the genuine regret skating through his brother's mind. Azrael had yet to pull out—to stop drinking him down.

Not for the first time, Michael knew he would have to use force. He picked up the rock that his fingers grasped, and after another grimace and wince of pain, he slammed the stone into the side of Azrael's head. His brother's teeth were ripped from his neck, tearing long gashes in his flesh as Azrael toppled to the side, catching himself on strong but shaking arms.

"Az," Michael gasped, dropping the rock to cup his hand to the side of his neck. "Az, I'm sorry." He slowly rolled over, propping himself on one elbow as he attempted to heal the damage. Light and warmth grew beneath his palm, sending curative energy into his wound. But Azrael's head was still down, his long sable hair concealing his features from Michael's sight.

"Az?"

"Stop, Michael. I can't bear it."

Michael felt the healing complete itself, heard his heart beat steady within his body and closed his eyes. His brother had an incredibly beautiful voice. And yet now it resonated with despair.

Michael let his hand drop and sat up the rest of the way. He opened his eyes again and looked upon his brother's bent form. "This pain you're going through can't last much longer," he said softly.

"A single moment longer is too long," Azrael whispered. Slowly, and with what appeared to be great effort, his tall dark figure straightened. He raised his head to meet his brother's gaze and Michael found himself once more staring into eyes of glowing gold, eerie and mesmerizing, in the handsome frame of Azrael's face.

"Kill me," Azrael said.

Michael steeled himself and shook his head. "Never."

If any one of the four archangel brothers could have summoned the will to kill the other, it would not have been Michael or even Azrael, but rather Uriel. He was the Angel of Vengeance. Only Uriel would be capable of comprehending what it would take to smother empathy and reason and love long enough to deal the final blow Azrael begged for.

But Uriel was not with them. He and their other brother, the archangel Gabriel, had been lost in their plummet to the Earth two weeks ago. The four archangels had been separated and scattered, like dried and dead leaves on a hurricane wind. Michael had no idea where the others were, much less what they might be going through.

He knew only that he had gone through a transformation as he'd taken on this human form. Michael was not as powerful as he'd been before their descent. The nature of his powers was the same, more or less. But the scope of those powers had diminished greatly. He was able to affect only what was immediately around him, and for only a relatively short period of time. His body grew weary. He knew hunger. He often felt weak. He had changed drastically.

But not as much as Azrael.

As the former Angel of Death, Azrael's change was different from Michael's. It was darker. It was much more painful. It was as if this new form were steeped in the negative energy he had collected during his seemingly endless prior existence. As the reaper in the field of mortal spirits, Azrael had taken so very many lives. There was a weight to that many souls, and they carried him down with them now. His altered form bore the fangs of a monster, a sensitivity to sunlight that forced him to hide in the shadows of night. Worst of all, it demanded blood.

Always blood.

"Please, Michael." Azrael's broad shoulders shook slightly as he curled his hands into fists and the powerful muscles in his upper body drew taut and pronounced. His skin was pale, his hair the color of night, his eyes like the sun. He looked like a study in contradiction as he gritted his teeth, baring his blood-soaked fangs. "Don't make me beg."

Michael got his legs beneath him and stood. He backed up against one of the few trees in the area and had opened his mouth to once more refuse his brother's request when Azrael was suddenly blurring into motion.

Michael's body slammed hard against the tree's trunk and the living wood splintered behind him. He was weaker than he'd been several minutes before; blood loss drained precious momentum from his reflexes. Though he was able to heal his wound, he was not able to replace the blood that Azrael took from him.

He'd been here before. He and Azrael had been here every night for two weeks.

Michael didn't know how long he would be able to engage in this nightly battle with his brother. Azrael was very strong. Even half-crazed with pain, he was most likely the strongest of the four of them. The monster that he had become was eating him up inside. It was devouring the core of his being, leaving him an empty shell.

Life was different on Earth. There had been no discomfort before this. No hunger. No thirst. These sensations were novel to Michael, but whatever discomfort he was experiencing because of his new, more human form, Azrael was obviously suffering a thousandfold. His transformation was brutal and it was killing him.

But Michael wouldn't give up on him. Not now—not ever. With great effort, he shoved Azrael off him and prepared himself for another senseless battle with his brother and best friend.

Somewhere, Uriel and Gabriel were most likely struggling as well; either with themselves, or with each other. Or with both. Michael had to find them. He *had to find them*, and bring the four of them back together. They were on Earth for a reason. They had come in order to find the women, the soul mates, that the Old Man had created for them. They'd come to Earth to find their archesses. And they didn't stand a chance at finding their archesses until they found one another.

Worse, Michael knew that they hadn't made it to Earth alone. He knew the four of them had been followed. Samael was the one archangel they had reason to fear. He had always been stronger than Michael, and at one point, he had been the Old Man's favorite. But that was a long time ago and now, due to his jealousy over the archesses, he had come to Earth to find the women for himself.

Over the years, Samael had proven himself to be a charismatic, cold, calculating, and wholly dangerous rival.

Michael didn't know what would happen if Samael got to the archesses first. He had no idea, in fact, what would happen if he and his brothers found them, as they were meant to. All he knew for certain was that he wasn't willing to leave this to chance. Each archess was too important. Michael and the others had experienced loneliness for too long. These women would be the end to that. They meant everything.

Time meant everything. Michael gritted his teeth, narrowed his gaze, and rolled up his sleeves. Azrael came at him like lightning, and like thunder, Michael met him halfway.

CHAPTER TWO

He'd been warned, hadn't he? Again and again and again . . .

The archangel Uriel blew out a sigh and ran his hand over his face. Then he clenched his jaw and looked back out the limousine window. He watched, distractedly, as the car passed several shop windows decorated in larger-than-life movie posters of the blockbuster *Comeuppance*. It was late afternoon on Saturday and the town was small; the shops were closed. But the posters were still larger-than-life. He flinched when his own ice-green eyes stared back out at him from a backdrop of crumbling castle walls, lightning-marred skies, and beautiful costars that hung on his well-muscled arm.

"Christ." He looked away and sank farther down into the leather seat.

"You'd better not let on to Gabriel that you're regretting this in any way, because he sure as shit won't let you live it down." Across from him, Max Gillihan, Uriel's agent, sat with crossed legs and a knowing smirk, his own dark brown eyes glittering from behind his wire-rimmed glasses. As usual, he wore a three-piece business suit in muted colors and his brown hair was cut short and styled neatly. He smiled, flashing white teeth. *"Ever."*

"Tell me about it," Uriel mumbled under his breath.

He was more than aware of what his brother would think of his newfound sense of regret. Especially since

Gabriel had repeatedly warned him against taking on the world of fame and fortune, shaking his damned raven-haired head and touting his counsel in his deep Scottish brogue. He'd warned against becoming too well known and having his face plastered to the sides of buildings. The archangels were immortal; they didn't age. What kind of fake disaster was Uriel going to have to fabricate in order to keep the world from noticing that he hadn't grown any older in decades? Gabriel was right, as much as Uriel hated to admit it. Forget that he was drunk when he had doled out his unwanted advice. Whether he was sober or not, Gabriel was never wrong.

And that irked Uriel to no end.

"You shouldn't be regretting it anyway, Uriel. Hell, you're Christopher Daniels and he's a big movie star now," Max told him, using Uriel's stage name.

Uriel's right brow arched in that irritated way that drove women crazy on the big screen. "And I care about that *why*?" he mumbled.

Max threw back his head and laughed. "You cared plenty enough a year ago, when you signed the *Comeuppance* contract."

Uriel crossed his arms over his chest and looked away. It was as good as admitting defeat.

Again, the man across from him chuckled, this time adding a head shake. "Two thousand years and you never get any credit. Give yourself some now, Uriel. You're an *archangel*, for Christ's sake. You're *supposed* to be in the limelight." He paused for effect. *"Right?"*

"You sound like Samael when you argue like that," Uriel muttered.

"I bet I do. He may be a royal pain in the ass, but you have to admit he's got great business sense." Gillihan's smile never wavered. The man was multitalented. He was Uriel's agent, and he was also their guardian. As a guardian, he was a very old, very wise man, despite his wrinkle-free face and the youthful glint in his chocolate-brown eyes.

Uriel shook his head. He felt strange in that moment—displaced. He was an archangel—or he had been many years ago. Give or take a century, two thousand years ago, he and his brothers had given up their positions with the Old Man and elected to come to the mortal realm in order to find the one thing they lacked in their own realm—a mate.

Being an archangel was a gift and a curse. They were the favored ones, closest to the Old Man, and together, they had all of the power in the universe. The Old Man had created his archangels as perfect male specimens. But a male naturally desired a female. And because there were no female archangels, they each felt a gaping loneliness that nothing seemed to fill.

So two thousand years ago the four favored archangels, Michael, Gabriel, Uriel, and Azrael had been gathered to speak with the Old Man. He'd told them that as a reward for their continued loyalty, he had created for each of them the most precious gift of all: a female mate.

These he called archesses. Uriel closed his eyes as his memories turned dark. He and his three brothers had never had a chance to claim their archesses. Before they could accept them, disaster struck and the women were lost—scattered on the winds of Earth.

The archangels decided to go after them.

They'd thought it would be easy. They were archangels, after all. Nothing had ever been difficult for them. But decades passed and centuries crawled by and the four brothers found no trace of their archesses. Instead, they found themselves trapped in bodies that were more human than archangel. They experienced human emotions and felt human agony. After a while, they found that just the struggle to survive the human condition was a constant distraction from their search for their archesses.

Michael was the first to make his stand in the human world. He was the warrior among them and had joined every army, had fought in every war, and had volunteered for every dangerous job humanity required: spy, fighter pilot, rebel. He had moved from village to village, town to town, and city to city, leaving friends behind as time passed and it became clear he wasn't aging. Life was hard, but as the years went on he had assimilated, along with his brothers. Michael was now a police officer in New York City.

Gabriel, the former Messenger Archangel, had lived in Scotland off and on since his arrival on earth. He possessed an affinity for the land and its people, but he, too, needed to be exceedingly careful with the passage of time. Every twenty years or so, he regrettably departed the land of the Thistle and was away for some time. He was on one of those breaks now and working as a firefighter in New York City, not too far away from Michael.

Azrael, the former Angel of Death, didn't keep to any particular place on Earth. His existence was even more difficult than that of the other three brothers. At first, they hadn't understood what had happened to Azrael when they all came to Earth and were transformed. His form had been altered in a cruel and painful manner. But now the archangels knew what to call his transformation. They knew what he was. He'd been the first, in fact—the first vampire.

As such, he visited a different city every night. He stayed in the shadows; he fed and he moved on. He never killed when he fed. He drank from abusive drunks and addicts, evening out the score for the humans they would have harmed, and he was never hurt by the taint in their blood.

For centuries, Azrael had kept to this pattern of constant movement. However, in the last few years, he'd changed his behavior somewhat. Now when he wasn't sleeping or drinking from some unsuspecting mortal, Azrael was onstage, dressed in black leather and a black half mask. That was the costume he used when he performed his music, hiding part of his face from the prying eyes of his millions upon millions of screaming fans.

Azrael was the Masked One, lead singer of Valley of Shadow, an immensely popular rock band that had taken the world by storm ten years ago. He had always had an amazing voice. It was mesmerizing, literally, and it had propelled him to the top of the charts in no time flat.

Occasionally, Az was approached by someone who recognized him for what he was. A rare individual would sometimes come forth, knowing that Azrael was a vampire and desperately wanting that vampirism for themselves. Seldom did Azrael oblige. However, once in a while, he felt the choice to turn a mortal was the right decision. He would feed from that individual a certain number of times—and the change would take place. Over the course of thousands of years, even a seldom-granted request will add up. Whether he approved or not, vampires now roamed the Earth, claiming Azrael as their father.

Uriel, for his part, had never really felt that there was a niche in the mortal realm he could comfortably fill. He'd once been the Angel of Vengeance. He had once punished the plethora of evildoers that the Old Man had created and unleashed upon the world. Along with the conception of humans had been the making of various animals and creatures. Some of these creatures had come to be known in the mortal realm as demons, devils, ghouls, and goblins.

When he'd resided in the archangel realm, it had been Uriel's task to seek out these creatures and the humans who joined them. But now that he was on Earth . . . it wasn't as easy to tell the monster from the human. And punishing them was no longer his task anyway.

He still knew right from wrong. He still hated evil and felt the need to protect innocence. But finding a way to do so on the mortal plane was not easy. It hadn't taken Uriel long to tire of his role as human assassin for the troublemakers in human history, as sharpshooter in war after war, as a sniper, as a double agent, as a killer. In the end, he'd realized that he was tired of being Uriel. He wanted to be someone else for a while. And so he'd answered a casting call pinned to the wall of a coffee shop in California. After all, acting was all about pretending to be someone you weren't.

And now here he was, in a limousine on his way to a signing because he'd suddenly become as popular as the Masked One. The movie, *Comeuppance*, had been so overwhelmingly successful, they'd turned it into a book and now the cast members were signing copies of it all over the country.

Outside the car window, the blur of buildings passing by slowed down and the car pulled to the right, gently rounding a corner into a drive. Overhead, a built-in speaker came to life.

"We're here, Mr. Gillihan."

Max sat up a little straighter and nodded at Uriel. "All right, here's the deal. The bookstore said there would be a pull of two to five hundred people today—"

"Here?" Uriel was certain his expression matched his emotions. He was an actor, after all, and expression was everything. "In this Podunk little town?"

"There are teenyboppers everywhere, Uriel," Max explained calmly. "When it comes to you and your fake set of fangs, they'll come out of the woodwork if they have to *eat* their way out."

"Nice visual."

"I know, isn't it?" Gillihan laughed again.

The limousine slowed to a stop and thunder rolled over the top of the car. Uriel frowned. A storm was coming? He hadn't sensed it, and usually he could. He must have been incredibly distracted not to notice.

"I told Nathan to pull to the back of the store to give us a little time to prepare before we head in," Gillihan continued, suddenly all business again.

"Did you hear that?" Uriel asked, interrupting him.

Max frowned and then blinked. "What? The thunder?"

"Yeah," Uriel replied, peering out the window at the gathering darkness as he pulled on his leather jacket. "Did you notice it coming before?"

Max seemed to consider this for a moment. He glanced out the window and his brow furrowed a little more. "Actually, no. But this is the Southwest. These things come up out of nowhere and all of a sudden." He shrugged as he pulled a few new pens and a file folder filled with photographs out of his briefcase. "I grew up down here."

Uriel rolled his eyes. Max Gillihan hadn't "grown up" anywhere. He'd simply *existed* for two thousand years. But, for some strange reason, he always waxed nostalgic when they visited a new location, and insisted that he'd been raised there.

"In a place not too far from here, actually. Called Lovington. It was a crap-smudge on the map thirty years ago, and it's even less than that now," Gillihan continued, shaking his head as he effortlessly doled out the lie. "But I remember the storms. Blew the roof off our house one summer." He handed the pens to Uriel and turned in his seat to signal to the driver.

"Wait." Uriel held up his hand. Gillihan paused, his brow arched.

Uriel felt uneasy. Something was off. This was supposed to be just another signing. . . . And yet something told him that it wouldn't be. "I'm not ready yet."

Max's gaze narrowed and he sat back in the leather of the opposite seat. "You'd best get ready, my friend. Because it's going to be a long night."

Uriel blew out a sigh and ran a hand through his thick brown hair. "That's what I'm not ready for."

Eleanore Granger glanced up when she heard the thunder. She'd known the storm was coming. She smiled to herself. She *always* knew.

She glanced back down at the gathering crowd beyond the front doors of the store and couldn't help the out-and-out grin that lit up her face. "They couldn't have picked a worse day, could they?" Within minutes, the rain would be falling. Everyone outside would get soaked.

It was probably wrong that the thought gave her a thrill of satisfaction. But she was tired and she was frustrated and she was sort of sick to death of seeing *Comeuppance* posters in every store window from here to Timbuktu, interviews with all the cast members on the news, and new fashion designs in department stores that mysteriously resembled what the characters wore throughout the film.

And all because the main characters were attractive.

A jet plane carrying 236 passengers had gone down over the Pacific last week and the news slot that covered the horrific story was composed of a single live hour, and a revisit that night and the next morning. Meanwhile, the handsome visage of Christopher Daniels, the actor who played Jonathan Brakes in *Comeuppance*, seemed to be plastered nonstop on the fifty-inch plasma TV screen above the fireplace in the café of the bookstore. Whether in movie trailers, on interview shows or in news clips, he seemed to have been there for two weeks straight.

He was up there again, in fact. It was late Saturday afternoon and *Denna's Day* was airing their interview with the star. Yes, he was gorgeous. Ellie had to admit as much, though she did so *only* to herself. The actor was quite tall and trim and broad-shouldered and his thick, dark hair was slightly wavy where it hit the collar of his shirts and jackets. His nose was Roman, his chin strong but not too strong, and whether clean-shaven or darkened by a shadow of stubble, his face forced a double take.

It's his eyes, Ellie thought distractedly.

Those *eyes*. Christopher Daniels had eyes of the lightest green she had ever seen. She had thought they were contact lenses when she'd first seen them on the big screen. But interview after interview, it was clear that the eye color was his own. Ellie had dreamed about those eyes a few times. Not that she would willingly share this information.

He was most certainly a stunning man. His voice was smooth and he moved with a nearly unnatural grace. Ellie had to force herself not to gaze at his pictures when she passed them everywhere—on store windows, the sides of buses, in Walmart.

Were the women of the world truly that desperate for a pretty face? Including herself? Since when did a handsome man trump a tragedy in the news? It was crazy.

Ellie refused to play into that craziness. At least when she was awake.

The walkie-talkie on the customer service desk a few aisles away came to static life and someone in the stockroom asked her if she was there. Eleanore finished shelving the books she had with her and strode to the desk to pick up the walkie-talkie. "I'm here, Shaun. What's going on?"

"The bigwigs are here. But they pulled up to the back door instead of the front door. You want me to tell Dianne or Mark? What should I do?"

"Um . . ." Eleanore thought for a moment. Why would they have pulled up to the back? Were they hiding for some reason? Did they need to talk to a manager? "Give them a minute, I guess. Maybe they just need some time to get ready. If they're still back there in five, we'll tell Dianne."

"Oh my God!"

Eleanore jumped and turned to face a group of three girls who were standing at the entrance to the science fiction aisle behind her. One of the girls was pointing at Eleanore.

"I heard you! Christopher Daniels is here, isn't he?"

"What? No, I—"

"I heard that guy on the other end, Shaun! He said that they were pulled up by the back door!" The girl's voice dropped to a very loud, conspiratorial whisper and she turned frantically to her two companions. "Oh my God, guys, we can head to the back of the store and see him before anyone else does!"

"Wait!" But before Eleanore could even contemplate stopping the trio, the girls were off like Abercrombie-armored rockets, weaving through the store to the front door while trying not to draw too much attention to themselves.

"Crap." Eleanore pressed the talk button on the walkie-talkie and put her hand on her hip. "Shaun, do me a favor?"

"Sure, babe."

"We've got a threesome of Brakes Flakes racing toward Christopher Daniels's limo. Can you head them off for me, please?"

Shaun managed to click the talk button on his handset in time for Eleanore to catch his laugh. "I'll see what I can do."

"Thanks." She put the radio back on the desk and ran a rough hand through her hair. "Shit." She squeezed her eyes shut tight. Then she picked up the phone at the desk and addressed her boss. "Dianne, I'm afraid I need to head back to help Daniels. There's a group of fans racing through the store."

It was clear from her heavy sigh that Dianne wasn't pleased. "No kidding. The kids in front just noticed, and there are more heading back there now. I'll get someone to cover for you temporarily. Hurry and help Shaun," she replied and hung up.

Eleanore whirled around and left the customer service desk to head toward the exit beyond the bathrooms, but just as she was passing the women's restroom, the distinct sound of someone retching stopped her in her tracks.

Oh no, she thought. *Someone's sick.*

The sound came again, this time followed by the low whine and sniffling sounds obviously made by a child.

Eleanore's heart broke. Not only was the person sick—she was just a kid.

"Crap," she whispered. *Double crap.*

She glanced once toward the locked back door and then down at the key that hung on a lanyard around her neck. She had a choice to make. She could go and save Christopher Daniels from his fans and, in turn, save the bookstore from any resulting reprimands, and hence, save herself from losing her job.

Or she could go and save the child instead.

As Eleanore pushed on the swinging door to the women's restroom, she realized that there had really been no choice to make, after all.

Uriel stared out the window at the falling rain. He sighed. One of his given powers was that he could forecast the weather; he could accurately determine what the sky was going to do a good while before it actually did it. However, today the storm had come without warning.

Which left Uriel a bit befuddled. Perhaps he was more distracted than he'd realized. He had to admit that he'd been busy. Filming for the second movie had been nonstop and trying. Promotional interviews for the first movie took up the majority of whatever time was left. Add to that signing autographs and answering fan mail and finding dates for red carpet events . . .

"Shit," he suddenly swore under his breath.

"And here I was hoping that you were just about to tell me that you were finally ready to go in and lie down in the bed you've made for yourself." Gillihan sighed. "What is it now?" He still sat back against the opposite seat, his legs crossed, his hands resting casually on his perfectly creased trousers. He arched one brow and waited for Uriel to answer.

"I have to find a date for Thursday night." He had a "gala" in Dallas to attend that night.

"Ask one of the multitude of women who come to your signings."

"I'd rather not." Uriel shook his head. "It feels wrong—like I'm pitting my fans against one another or something."

"Oh, listen to yourself." Gillihan rolled his eyes.

Uriel cocked his head to one side, his green eyes sparking with warning.

Gillihan sighed again. "You and your brothers are more trouble than you're worth. You *wanted* this, remember? You swore you had to have it." Max leaned forward, placing his elbows on his knees. "I bet you don't even remember why you were sent down here in the first place." He shook his head and gazed at Uriel over the top of his glasses.

Uriel frowned. "To Texas?"

Max shook his head. "Earth, genius. A few piddly thousand years go by and you all get so mired in what it means to be human that you take your very existence for granted." He paused and considered something. "Except, perhaps, for Michael. He rides the other end of the spectrum and takes himself too seriously."

"I haven't forgotten," Uriel told him firmly. And it was true. He *hadn't* forgotten why he and his brothers had been given humanlike forms and allowed to reside on Earth two thousand years ago. It was just that they had been looking so long without finding any sign of even one archess that they'd gotten to the point where they just didn't think about it most days.

That was all.

"The least you can do is quit your whining and get on with your increasingly meaningless existence without giving me any more trouble," Gillihan told him flatly.

Gillihan's words were abrasive, and they were meant to be. But Uriel knew that, deep down, it wasn't the guardian's fault. He'd been down here for as long as Uriel and his brothers had and it was simply too long for anyone to go without accomplishing something and gaining a sense of fulfillment, no matter how immortal he may be.

"I'm sorry, Max," Uriel said softly.

Gillihan blinked. He sat up straight, and then blinked again. "You are?"

"You're right." Uriel shrugged and slapped his hands on his jeans in a gesture of defeat. "What have I got to complain about? Chicks dig me. I should be happier than a pig in shit." He smiled that smile that had women swooning in the aisles. "That *is* what they say down here, right?"

Max laughed. "It's what they *used* to say, mostly. But close enough." He shook his head and turned in his seat to reach his arm through the opening between their cabin and the driver's seat. Just as he was signaling for Nathan to head back around to the storefront, a shrieking sound drew his attention to the windows.

Uriel looked too. And then his eyes grew very wide. "Is that what I think it is?"

"I'm afraid so," Gillihan replied.

"They're blocking the exit," Uriel said, his tone laced with shock.

There was no time to formulate a plan. He could either stay inside the car indefinitely and wait for the cops or escape from the car and run. *Fast.*

Uriel threw open the door of the limousine and bolted out of the backseat. Behind him, he heard Max calling, but he ignored the guardian and headed directly for the bookstore.

Later, and in retrospect, he would realize that heading *toward* the bookstore instead of *away* from it was, at the very least, a bizarre decision. Especially considering that the throng of teenage girls now racing toward him like a medieval village mob was coming from said store.

However, there was little thought involved. The girls were coming around the corner from the front of the store, which gave him a clear shot at the back door. It was mostly instinct that propelled Uriel across the lot to the locked back exit of the establishment. And it was superhuman strength that then allowed him to wrench the door open against the lock and rush inside.

He sensed that the alarm wanted to go off. He used his powers to silence it and pulled the door shut behind him, making sure to yank it in tight enough that it warped a little and held.

The girls outside reached it just as it shut and their fists pounded furiously on the metal of the barred exit. They were getting soaked out there. He was more than a little damp himself.

He wondered if they were also hurting one another as they shoved toward the door. He sincerely hoped not. But whatever was happening, the sheer number of them suggested that the door wouldn't hold for long. All they had to do was work together and it would come open.

Uriel passed the restrooms on his left and strode toward the science fiction section of the store just beyond the exit foyer. There, he stopped and grimaced. Another mass of girls, nearly as large as the first, was grouped around the front of the store. There must have been a hundred of them. . . . Maybe more.

The door behind him creaked and then scraped.

Uriel thought fast and ducked into the women's restroom. Once inside, he closed his eyes, pressed his back to the wall beside the door, and listened. The exit door of the bookstore gave way beyond and he could hear the group of girls rush into the hallway. They raced by, their Converses squeaking with rain water on the linoleum tile.

"You have to memorize a script to act, and the movie you starred in was also turned into a book, so I assume that you can read."

Uriel's eyes flew open to find a woman and a little girl standing a few feet away, beside the door of the first stall.

"I was obviously wrong," she continued. "Because you've mistaken the women's restroom for the ridiculously famous sex symbol restroom—which is next door."

Uriel's heart stopped beating. His jaw dropped open.

He couldn't be seeing what he was seeing in that moment. He *couldn't* be feeling what he was feeling. Not now. Not here, in a *bathroom*—after two thousand years. Maybe he'd slipped in the rain outside and hit his head.

No, that was impossible. He was relatively invincible. Being hit on the head would do nothing to him but make him a little cranky.

She was really standing there before him. She was real; he could see her, hear her—he could even smell her. She smelled like shampoo and soap and lavender.

Jesus, he thought, unable to refrain from letting his gaze drop down her body and back up again. She was everything that he had ever imagined she would be, from her tall, slim body to her long jet-black hair, and those indigo blue eyes the color of a Milky Way night. Her skin was like porcelain. Her lips were plump and pink and framed perfect, white teeth. She was an *angel*.

She was his archess. And she was . . . *scowling* at him?

He frowned.

The door to the bathroom had shut firmly behind Christopher Daniels, and he clearly had heard what she'd said, but he still just stood there like he was frozen and Eleanore could not figure out why. "Mr. Daniels, is there something I can help you with?" Eleanore asked.

She had to admit to herself that when Daniels had first entered the women's restroom, she'd been taken completely and utterly by surprise. First of all, he was even more handsome in real life than he was in his plethora of press photos. And that wasn't supposed to be the case at all. Wasn't there supposed to be loads and loads of makeup involved? Tricks of the light? In real life, didn't actors have acne and scars and wrinkles and undyed roots for miles?

In real life, an actor's eyes didn't seem to *glow* the

way they did in the movies. But Christopher Daniels's eyes did. It was nearly eerie, they were so intense. They instantly called to mind the dreams she'd had of him. It was always his eyes she saw just before she woke up. All of the pictures he had plastered across the nation didn't do them justice. His eyes were the color of arctic icebergs, so very, very light green that they seemed . . . more than human. They were incredibly beautiful.

She was standing in a restroom, face-to-face with a famous actor who was, quite literally, the most attractive man she had ever seen. And yet he was looking at her as if *she* were the gorgeous movie star instead.

And so she was more than a little surprised at herself when, instead of feeling faint and falling all over him like all of the other girls in the world seemed to do, her first instinct had been to stand up to him. For what, exactly, she had no idea. For coming into the girls' restroom, she guessed. Of all things! What kind of crime *was* that, exactly?

Eleanore's subconscious mind knew the truth. She wasn't mad at him for coming into the wrong restroom, of course. She was mad at him for being who and what he was. Gorgeous—and famous. It was an old brain kind of thing.

He was obviously hiding. That was clear. And from the sound of the giggling schoolgirls beyond the door, she would wager a guess that it was his *fans* he was hiding from. The nerve! First, these guys fight tooth and nail to climb their way into fandom and then they balk at being loved by the masses.

What was up with that?

Meanwhile she'd forgotten Jennifer, the little girl she'd come into the bathroom to help in the first place. But Jennifer had clearly noticed Daniels as well. Her hand slipped out of Eleanore's own as she spoke up. "Miss Ellie made my stomach feel better!" she chimed in, completely out of the blue. "I was throwing up, but she touched my tummy and made it stop."

Eleanore paled. *Oh no,* she thought. *Be quiet, be quiet, be quiet—don't say any more!*

"Which is a good thing," Jennifer went on, nodding emphatically, "because the throw up made me want to throw up some more." Jennifer was only about five, but she wasn't shy. She grimaced and seemed to want to push the memory away with her little hands. "It was *so* gross."

Eleanore felt herself blanching further. She pulled her gaze off the famous actor and looked at the wall. She needed to compose herself. She needed to get a handle on the situation—take control.

Finally, she rolled her shoulders and looked back up at him.

She blinked. He was still staring at her in abject fascination. That *was* fascination, wasn't it? Not amusement? Maybe he just thought she was mental. . . .

"Mr. Daniels, I'm going to find Jennifer's parents and then I would be happy to announce your arrival over the intercom, if you'd like—"

Daniels pushed himself off the wall and stepped toward her. His motorcycle boots made a heavy thud on the linoleum floor. It sounded dangerous. A warm, erotic warning thrummed through Eleanore's body.

"You're the reason it's storming," he said. "Now it makes perfect sense."

Eleanore's world tipped on its axis, and fear gripped her. Her vision began to tunnel. "P-pardon me?" she asked. Her voice sounded hollow to her own ears.

What is he talking about? He can't know.

She almost shook her head against the possibility. She thought about taking a step back, suddenly needing space. But there was a tiny hand in hers, squeezing tight, and she couldn't escape.

"You're a man and this is a girls' bathroom," little Jennifer said.

Christopher Daniels glanced down at the child. Jennifer's nose was scrunched up and her gaze was reprimanding. The actor seemed to be considering the girl for a moment and then he looked back up at Eleanore.

"Ellie," he said softly.

Eleanore swallowed hard. Her mouth and throat had gone dry. "It's—it's Eleanore," she stammered. And then, realizing that she'd just given out her name and that perhaps she shouldn't have, she looked away from him and shook her head. "Mr. Daniels," she tried again. "Excuse me. I really do need to find Jennifer's parents. She's just been pretty sick."

She brushed past him to push open the door and as she did, the air seemed to thicken around her; it suddenly felt cloying and confusing. It took forever to get by the actor; she could feel him watching her as she came near and he made virtually no move to get out of the way. His nearness was electrifying and disarming, his body tall and hard and very real. Time seemed to slow down as she opened the door and stepped out into the store.

But once she was past him, she walked as quickly as she could with a five-year-old tethered to her arm, which wasn't very fast at all. She heard footsteps behind her and glanced back to see that Daniels was following her. He kept pace easily, a small, determined smile playing about his lips.

Christopher Daniels is behind me, Eleanore thought. *The famous actor, Christopher Daniels, is behind me! He's probably looking at my ass.* She tried not to groan out loud at that thought. As if it mattered!

She wasn't sure what her bottom looked like from his vantage point; she never bothered with the mirror that much in the morning. And she was nearly as horrified by the fact that she *cared* what she looked like to him as she was by the fact that he seemed to be *looking* at her. Was he looking at her butt?

Of course he's looking at my butt, she thought. *He's a guy! That's what they do!*

She berated herself for the internal monologue of

Clueless-worthy concerns and once more wondered what he'd meant by his storm comment. Did he know that she'd caused the storm? If he did—how?

There's no way, she thought. *He must have meant something else.*

Eleanore stopped beside the customer service desk and bent to whisper into Jennifer's little ear.

"This is our secret, okay?" she said, hoping against hope that the child would catch the urgency with which she made the request.

Jennifer looked up at her and then glanced over at Daniels, who was leaning against a bookshelf a few feet away, his arms crossed over his chest, his expression both bewildered and amused. Then she nodded and smiled up at Eleanore, and Ellie's fear dropped down a notch.

Eleanore straightened and picked up the phone at the customer service desk. She saw Daniels peek over the racks at the crowd by the front doors. A woman dressed in a suit with a name tag glanced nervously at her watch and then stood on her toes as if to look for someone. They were wondering where their star was.

There was a tall man in a suit with them. He was pushing his way through the women—and a few men—to the front of the store. Eleanore wondered vaguely who he was, but let it go as she made a "lost child" announcement over the intercom to get the attention of Jennifer's parents.

When she'd finished, she put the phone back in its cradle and turned to face a harried-looking couple who instantly knelt before Jennifer to console her. Jennifer's mother scooped her up into her arms and with a quick thank-you to Ellie, they were on their way out of the store.

Now Ellie turned to face Daniels, who was still leaning against the bookshelf, watching her. In the next split second, he straightened from the shelf, closed the distance between them with two purposeful strides, and pinned her to the customer service desk, one strong arm braced against the counter on either side of her.

Eleanore inhaled sharply and her heart did a somersault in her chest.

"I have to go to a big party Thursday night. Come with me," he said. He was so close, his breath whispered across her lips—it smelled of licorice and mint.

"W-wha . . ." she stammered. Then she dry swallowed and tried again. "What?"

She heard a faint cracking sound and glanced down to see that his grip on the desk behind her had tightened. She turned back to face him and watched as his gaze flicked to her mouth and back.

"Ellie," he said, as if testing her name out on his tongue. "Here's the thing," he continued softly. "I need a date to a big promotional party in Dallas. A gala. I don't know anyone in Texas. You were kind enough to let me hide in the women's restroom." He smiled an incredibly charming smile. "And I appreciate it," he added. "So I would be honored if you would consider being my date next week on Thursday."

Eleanore took a few seconds to digest this. There was a part of her that simply couldn't believe her position at that moment. She was being cornered by Christopher Daniels, against her own customer service desk, and asked out on a date. But despite the impossibility of it all, she knew she wasn't dreaming. This felt too real.

He was so *big*. So tall and . . . he looked hard—everywhere. And his nearness was doing strange things to her. He smelled good. The leather of his jacket and whatever aftershave or shower gel he'd used were a heady, highly tantalizing combination. There wasn't an ounce of him that wasn't pure masculinity, from the set of his jaw to the smooth, determined sound of his voice.

"You're not answering," he said, once more glancing at her lips as he'd done before. He seemed to be leaning in closer now, and Eleanore was finding it more difficult to breathe. "Does this mean you're considering it?"

Christ, I'm falling for this jerk. I've barely met him and I've already got it bad.

She tried to swallow past a spot in her throat that had gone dry. She wondered then, as she gazed up into those impossibly colored eyes, how many women he'd done this to lately. He was good at it.

He's an actor, she told herself. *Of course he's good at it.*

That was a sobering thought. She blinked and felt her own gaze harden. He seemed to notice, because something flashed in his eyes and his gaze narrowed in response.

"You're serious," she said in a low voice. "You don't know anything about me and you want me to just agree to go out on a date—in another city—with you."

"I know enough," he told her plainly. "And yes. I want you to go out on a date with me." He paused and then added meaningfully, "Very much so."

She stared back at him for several more heartbeats, and then, before she realized what she was doing, she had the customer service desk phone to her ear and was pressing a button behind her on the carriage.

Daniels seemed as surprised as she was and only watched as she put the speaker to her mouth.

"Attention guests! It is my pleasure to announce to you all that the star of the evening, Mr. Christopher Daniels, is here with us now and is making his way to the front of the store to begin signing autographs for all of his much-appreciated fans."

The sound of cheering rose from the front of the store and spread through the aisles. Daniels glanced up, not moving from where he had her ensnared between his arms.

Eleanore glanced behind her to catch frantic movement at the front of the store.

When she turned back to face him, it was to find Christopher's jaw tensed and his teeth clenched in obvious irritation. But his ice-green eyes returned to Eleanore's face and once more trapped her gaze in his. He took a deep, calming breath and seemed to ponder the situation.

Then he smiled and straightened, stepping away from the desk. Eleanore stayed where she was and watched him warily. For a moment, his eyes flicked to her neck, her shoulders, and back up again. She could have sworn she saw a troubling indecision cross his handsome features. He looked as if he were tempted to grab her, throw her over his shoulder, and abscond with her.

"It was a pleasure to meet you, Ellie," he said instead, locking gazes with her a final time. "I'll be seeing you again soon."

With that, he turned and strode down the aisle toward the front of the store.

Eleanore was too stunned to move. She watched him go, and as he disappeared, she listened. The ecstatic greetings started up almost immediately. They were crazy about him.

And now she could see why.

He asked me on a date, she thought. *The gorgeous, famous movie star from* Comeuppance *asked me on a date.*

A part of her wanted to be thrilled at the thought. But there was another part of her that knew better. It was that other part that had forced her to cut their exchange short by announcing his arrival. Because *that* part of her had a feeling that Christopher Daniels was not who he pretended to be. Not just on the screen—but in real life.

He knows something, she thought.

She didn't know how it was possible; even the very idea was unfathomably weird. But somehow, Christopher Daniels seemed to know that Eleanore had caused the storm. He'd told her as much. *You're the reason it's storming,* he'd said. She was willing to bet a dollar that he even suspected her healing powers after Jennifer's untimely exclamation in the bathroom.

And now he also knew her name and where she worked.

Several more long, tense seconds passed and Eleanore's body finally relaxed a little and she slumped against the desk. She closed her eyes and ran a somewhat shaky hand through her long hair.

Life had just gotten a little too interesting for her taste. Maybe it was time to move again.

CHAPTER THREE

She could have stopped the rain from hitting her if she'd wanted to, or if she'd even thought of doing it, but neither was the case as Eleanore ran from the back—and broken—door of the store to her car, which was parked in the rear lot. She hurriedly beeped the lock, jerked the door open, and slipped inside, slamming and locking the door behind her. There, she sat in the seat and stared at the back edifice of the place where she worked. She wondered whether she would ever see it again.

The darkness pressed in on the windows of her car. Christopher Daniels had been signing autographs for hours. It was eight o'clock and the store would close at eleven. She wondered where he would go then. To his hotel? Where *was* his hotel?

A multitude of questions were chasing one another through her head at that moment—all of them unanswerable. She blew out a big sigh and laid her forehead on the steering wheel. Then she closed her eyes.

If she left, this would be the thirteenth time she'd moved in the last four years. She was beginning to have dreams about houses that were bizarre amalgamations of the different places she'd lived, various styles and cultures all lopped together like some sort of leaning, precarious Dr. Seuss dwelling. They were always fragile and rocked a little in the wind.

And they made her feel that way, too. Fragile.

"What am I going to do?"

Was Christopher Daniels worth another move? Did he really pose some kind of threat to her? Even if he did somehow know that she was the one who had caused the storm and even if he had figured out that she could heal, it wasn't Daniels himself she was afraid of. It was the fame that came with him. He was forever being followed, always in the public eye. If he brought this kind of attention upon her, it could be disastrous.

Eleanore blew out another sigh and squeezed her hands into fists. She could call her parents. But if this really was the beginning of yet another dangerous situation, then her mother and father would be better off not hearing from her about it. She didn't want to get them involved anymore. They'd earned the right to keep out of it. And it would do them some good to believe that their daughter had finally found a place where she could reside peacefully.

God knew that they'd done their own brand of time with her. When she was little, she'd spent kindergarten in three different cities before her parents had realized that they were going about things the wrong way and decided to homeschool her with the help of highly paid tutors. It was difficult back then because she was far less careful about what powers she used and when she used them. And kids like to brag. That was part of it. The other part was that, when she was little, her powers were still developing, and she'd often discovered them accidentally.

And that was always a scene.

Like the time when she was five and had begun placing things in the cart at the grocery store, even though her mother had told her she couldn't have them. Lots of children did this, of course. But not many use telekinesis to do so.

And when she and her parents had gone camping— and she'd sent the flames from the campfire out into the surrounding brush with no more than a thought. She'd wanted to see the fire dance. It would have been disastrous if her parents hadn't recognized what was happening by that point and talked her into bringing the fire back under control.

Doing a rain dance with her stuffed animals and actually making it rain was a bit of a scene as well since she did it every day for a week in order to water the wildflowers she and her mother had planted.

Eventually, her parents got used to her surprises—more or less—and chalked them up to the wonder that was their ever-changing daughter. But that didn't mean that raising her was easy for them.

Eventually, they began to fear that their daughter's special abilities might be noticed by someone powerful—and maybe not so nice—who would want to use her for their own gain. After a while, they realized someone was indeed after her, but they didn't know who. They would return home to find locks jimmied. Strange vehicles with illegally dark windows would idle at the ends of alleys. They had their suspicions; Ellie's gifts were extremely attractive. Were these people government agents? A terrorist group? There wasn't enough evidence to support any of their guesses. The thought of their daughter being used by someone who would take away her freedom to make her own choices and live her own life was too horrible for them to bear. So regardless of whose attention Eleanore had unwittingly gained, avoiding any further attention became an overriding precaution that wound up ruling their lives.

They moved around frequently, never remaining in one place for very long. They kept Eleanore out of the public school system. They taught her to live cautiously and to always be prepared to have to leave at any given moment.

Now the rain pelted the roof of Eleanore's car, steering her thoughts toward a similarly rainy day ten years ago. She had been fifteen and fully engrossed in the 3

Doors Down video "Kryptonite," which had fast become her favorite that year. Suddenly, her father was bursting into her room and tossing her jacket to her.

Strange vehicles had been spotted by friends around the neighborhood. Eleanore's parents were convinced that their worst fears were coming true and someone was coming to take her from them. And so it was with a strange and numb resignation that Eleanore had quickly pulled her "escape" bag out from under her bed, swung it over her shoulder, and followed her parents out the back door of the house and down the mud-soaked alley to the backyard of an unoccupied house on the same block.

Her father kept a car parked in the abandoned house's garage. It was a gray SUV with dark tinted windows and out-of-state license plates. It would have made the perfect, nondescript getaway car if it hadn't been for the dogs.

When the animals heard her family making haste down the alleyway in the rain, they did everything they could to draw attention to them. The barking was loud and furious. Eleanore couldn't make out their furry bodies through the slats in the wooden fences, or she would have used her telekinetic powers to slam them into one another. Anything to shut them up.

Within breathless seconds, a white van pulled up at the end of the alley and two men got out. Eleanore remembered one of them starkly. He wore a tight gray T-shirt over massive muscles and black army fatigues. In his right hand, he carried a needle. The wet metal glinted menacingly in the gray light of the rain.

She did manage to yank the needle out of his slippery grip and send it flying with her powers. But then her father wrenched her to the side and shoved her through an opening in a gate in the alleyway. They half dragged her through the yard, and in the distance, she heard men shouting. She heard the sound of tires tearing at wet asphalt and gravel.

She and her parents made it to the garage and her mother pushed her down on the floorboards of the backseat just as her father muscled the garage door open.

Eleanore's memory became fuzzy after that. She remembered that the car started up and she was slammed from side to side. There was a lot of sound—violent and chaotic. Glass breaking. Metal chinking like the sounds dishes make in a dishwasher.

And then darkness.

Eleanore came to understand on that day just how dangerous her abilities were—and realized fully just how much trouble they caused her parents. No, raising her wasn't easy for them.

But fortunately for her, they accepted her powers as a part of her and loved her anyway—endlessly and deeply and unconditionally. Jane Granger swore up and down that her daughter had some purpose on this planet and that it would make itself known when the time was right. Walter Granger was a bit more on the scientific side of the argument and wondered whether his wife shouldn't have had so much artificial sweetener while she'd been pregnant with Eleanore. Either way, though, they were okay with it.

Her father was a professor, and professors went wherever universities were hiring, so it was easy for him to move around the country. Her mother was an attorney in her own practice, so she was mobile as well. And the two of them working together were affluent enough that they were able to protect their daughter with a fair amount of efficiency, which Eleanore had been well and truly grateful for on that fateful day.

It was a given that Eleanore would never be able to use any of her homeschooled education for a career that required her to stay in one place. Hence, she was damn lucky that her family was wealthy enough to provide her with an ever-full emergency fund.

Eleanore thought of this now as she listened to the

sound of the rain pelting the top of her car. She wondered if she would have to use that fund in order to escape one strangely determined, dangerously handsome Christopher Daniels.

None of her abilities would help her with this particular problem. They were no good when it came to keeping her from being found out. That was the curse part of the gift—as Adrian Monk would put it. She could do loads of very impressive things, yes. But each of them was *so* impressive that she couldn't really do them at all. Because when she did, she gave herself away.

As she possibly had done tonight. With the storm. And the little girl.

So now she had another choice. Leave? Without a two-weeks' notice or any indication of where she was headed? Or stay . . . and take her chances with the incredibly hot actor who cornered her in the bookstore—and might be the one who was about to give her away.

She blew out a sigh and lifted her head to stare out the windshield. "I can't do this anymore." She shut her eyes again and shook her head. "No more." She made her choice then and there, in that moment, as lightning flashed in the distance and thunder once more rolled over her car.

Whatever danger Daniels might or might not pose, she would face it and figure it out. It wasn't that she was opposed to moving out of Texas. That wasn't it—at all. It was that she was tired of running altogether.

The next time she picked up and moved, she wanted it to be because she liked the place she was moving to. Not because she was desperate or afraid. Besides, she might be wrong about the actor. Maybe he *hadn't* put two and two together and figured out that she'd healed Jennifer. And maybe his comment about the storm was existential. Maybe she would never even see him again and he'd just been toying with her.

Asshole.

With that liberating thought, Eleanore shoved the

key into the ignition and turned on her car. As she drove, she willed the storm away, and within a few minutes, the clouds dissipated and a few stubborn stars reclaimed their places in the heavens.

When she got to her apartment, she parked under her assigned awning and headed up two flights of stairs to her door. Then she went inside, shutting and locking the door behind her.

Down below, in the quiet courtyard, a tall figure slid his hands into the pockets of his expensive trench coat. He nodded once, to himself, and then strode through the grass and out into the parking lot without making a single discernible sound.

Uriel was going crazy. He was certain of it. For two thousand years, he'd managed to keep his wits about him, through disease and famine and wars and a world culture that was changing so rapidly, it literally boggled the mind. He'd taken it all in stride and tried to remind himself that he was there for a reason. And a good one.

It was more difficult some days than others. He'd learned the hard way that being down amidst the pain was a hell of a lot different from experiencing it from up above. Up there—*out* there—he'd been disconnected. Detached and withdrawn. Truth be told, he'd always wondered why humans whined as much as they did. Apathy was the way of the archangels. How can one possibly empathize with something that they possessed no means of feeling themselves?

But once they were living with the humans, all that had changed. Uriel had felt anything but apathy when he'd helped pull bodies out of floodwaters or when he'd walked alongside Michael as the poor man had tried to be everywhere at once when the plague had killed so many, or more recently when he'd handed out bread and cheese in government lines.

And he sure as hell wasn't feeling it now.

Right now, he was anxious and frustrated enough

that he actually contemplated calling his brothers to help him get out of this signing. He'd already been there for hours—and from the look of the line of fans, he had hours to go. He would be there right up until the damned store closed. Now that he'd found his archess, he was wasting precious time.

When he looked up from yet another "Best wishes" and spotted Max in the crowd, he signaled the man over and asked the next person in line if he could just have a moment. The girl nodded and smiled, probably feeling just as anxious as he did at that moment.

Gillihan moved to the table and then met Uriel on the other side.

"Well?" Uriel prompted.

"Her full name is Eleanore Elizabeth Granger," Max supplied.

"Is she okay?" Uriel asked.

"She got home safe," Max told him, whispering as he turned his back to the crowd. "And I have her address."

"So get me out of here. I need to see her again."

Max considered this a moment. "I know you're anxious. It's understandable. But I highly recommend waiting until morning. She wasn't in the best mood when she left here and if you go knocking on her door tonight, you'll most likely frighten her half to death."

Uriel's gaze hardened. "You want me to *wait*?" The thought was more than distasteful for him.

Max sighed, shrugged off his coat, and pulled off his glasses to pinch the bridge of his nose. "Yes, wait. We can have Azrael watch over her tonight if you're worried about her."

"Why would I be worried?" Uriel's no-nonsense look had intensified, his eyes now sparking with warning.

Max's eyes widened defensively. "I don't know."

"What aren't you telling me, Max?"

Max shook his head and gave up. He pulled Uriel a little farther from the waiting crowd and lowered his voice. "It's just a feeling I have. I saw the interior of her apartment through her windows just before she arrived. It's rather minimalist. As if she's the type who doesn't like to be tied down. I think the girl scares easy." He shrugged. "Which is why I suggest you wait until morning."

Uriel sighed heavily, turned way from Max, ran a frustrated hand through his hair, and then put his hands on his hips. He turned back to Max. "It's also why I probably *shouldn't* wait."

"You can't go into her apartment, throw her over your shoulder, and expect to have any kind of lasting relationship with her."

"She's my archess. This should be easier."

"Nothing is easy, Uriel. Especially nothing that counts."

Again, Uriel sighed. "Fine. At least get me out of here so I can speak with my brothers about this."

Max looked from him to the line of fans waiting to get his signature. Uriel knew what he was thinking. Normally, Max would demand that Uriel face up to the life he had chosen and see it through to the end. It was part of his job as guardian—making sure the boys behaved. However, this was clearly different. Eleanore Granger was the entire reason Uriel was here on this planet to begin with.

"Very well. Just this once." Max adjusted his glasses and went on. "And since you'll be speaking with him anyway, have Azrael track Samael's current location. I'd like an idea of how far ahead of the game we are."

Uriel was reaching down and pulling his jacket from the back of his chair before Max had even finished speaking. "I'm out of here."

Behind him, he heard a sharp intake of breath. He turned to see the girl who was next in line clutching her book tightly to her chest. Her cheeks were red and her eyes were shiny with unshed tears.

Oh, Christ, he thought. *I'm such a bastard.*

He forced a warm smile to his face and reached a hand out to take her book. "One more," he said softly.

The girl blinked and swallowed audibly and then she, too, smiled. "Thank you so much, Mr. Daniels. This one's not for me; it's for my niece. She's thirteen and has strep, so she couldn't be here."

Uriel glanced up at her, and, as he often did when faced with news that surprised him, he scanned her soul for any trace of a lie. It was something all archangels could do if they thought to concentrate on it; it was a little like possessing a sixth sense. He studied the woman closely and found that she was being genuine. And he really was the biggest bastard in the world.

"It's my pleasure," he told her sincerely. "What is your niece's name?"

As Max Gillihan prepared to make excuses for Christopher Daniels's sudden departure, Uriel penned a heartfelt get-well wish and slipped a photograph of himself in between the pages of the autographed book. Then he handed the book back and thought of Azrael, the archangel with fangs and glowing gold eyes.

"Don't let the vampires bite," he told the girl. "They really do exist, you know."

The layout of the archangels' mansion had changed many times over the years, as the tastes of the men who lived within it seemed to alter according to boredom, convenience, and style preferences. It could look like anything, really. It had been sent down along with their guardian, Max, when the angels had first come to Earth in search of their archesses. It was a living space and a transportation device rolled into one. Its superdimensional properties allowed travel through its doorways as if it were a teleporter, which allowed them to go nearly anywhere at any time they desired.

However, just as the archangels had been separated during that first descent, Max and the mansion were lost on the wind and it wasn't until many years later that the five of them and the mansion were reunited.

At the moment, the four brothers were gathered in a

relatively small, utterly normal-looking kitchen that sat just off a likewise normal-looking living room. The archangels all preferred their living space on the more modest side these days. Having been around for as long as they had, they already felt as if they'd literally seen everything.

Uriel had given them each a buzz on his cell as soon as he'd left the signing and, through the use of the mansion and its magical properties, they'd all managed to head home right away. Any of the archangels could call up a portal to the mansion from anywhere in the world, so long as they were standing before a door. It didn't matter what kind of door it was. Even a car door or the door to a refrigerator would work.

"All right, so we're all here," Michael said as he sat forward over the table and laced his fingers together. He was a tall man and his muscles stretched the material of his T-shirt taut across his chest as he leaned forward. His blond hair was probably a touch long for what they preferred on the police force, and it curled across his forehead. As with all of the archangels, his chin was strong, and his sported a five-o'-clock shadow. His blue eyes were the color of clear sapphires.

Michael glanced at the black-haired man at the head, whose gold-flecked amber eyes glittered beneath the lamplight. Azrael met his gaze and held it easily. He was the opposite of Michael in many ways. Though Michael was tall, Az was taller by several inches and his hair was black as pitch and quite a bit longer. It fell well beyond his shoulders. His face was clean-shaven and pale—a stark contrast to the darkness of his hair.

"Even the Masked One has afforded us the pleasure of his happy-go-lucky presence," Michael said in a sarcastic tone. He turned back to Uriel. "So spill. What's the big news?"

"I found her." Uriel could hold it in no longer. He loved the stunned expressions that crossed his brothers' faces in that moment.

It was unnaturally quiet in the kitchen for a few seconds. And then, in a voice so resonant and charismatic that it had won him millions of screaming fans worldwide, Azrael spoke up. "You're speaking of your archess." His amber eyes began to glow.

The other three looked over at him. Michael's gaze narrowed and he turned back to Uriel. "Is he right? Are you talking about your archess?"

"Yes." Uriel pulled out a chair and spun it around, lowering himself gracefully into it and lacing his arms over the back. "I knew her the moment I saw her." Uriel briefly closed his eyes, recalling his first impression of the archess. Dressed in jeans and a bookstore apron, she'd appeared to him as a shining beacon clothed in a thin veil of normalcy. To him, everything about her was otherworldly. "She's beautiful. Stunning, really," he told them. "I caught her healing a little girl in the restroom at a bookstore."

At this, his brothers straightened and he caught them glancing at one another knowingly.

He smiled, unable to prevent himself from feeling proud of Eleanore. "She has a kind heart." He turned to Azrael. "Max wants you to find out what Sam's doing right now." Azrael was the only one among them capable of performing a scry to determine the whereabouts and actions of an individual. In fact, there was much Azrael could do that the other brothers could not. His altered form was often as much a gift as it was a curse.

Michael sat up and took a deep breath. He ran a hand through his thick blond hair and shook his head. His eyes were wide. "I can't believe this. After so long, for one of us to actually see our mate is like . . ."

"A bloody dream?" Gabriel piped in.

Uriel glanced at him, as did the others. Gabriel was the quintessential tall, dark, and handsome. Whereas Azrael's appearance was stark and otherworldly, Gabriel's was down-to-earth, approachable, and laid-back. He was what more than one woman had termed "imminently fuckable." His physique more or less matched those of his brothers—tall and well built. But he had a careless air about him, a Colin Farrell kind of vibe that hinted at sensitivity and then killed with practiced charm.

With one hand, Gabriel slowly turned a bottle of beer on the tabletop. His other lay casually in his lap. His silver eyes were stark against his handsome, tan face. That was one thing the four of them had in common, among a few other, less obvious traits: their eyes were supernaturally stunning.

"I'll believe it when I see her," Gabe said, his Scottish brogue not quite so heavy now since he'd had only half a beer. He was a strong and handsome man, but at the moment he looked tired.

Uriel wondered if Gabe had had a rough day. But he didn't let his concern keep him from shooting his brother a dirty look. On the big screen, that look would have caused women to put their hands to their chests. But Gabriel, for his part, just smirked and took another swig of his beer.

"She's real," Uriel said. Without taking his green eyes off his brother, he added, "And she's mine."

Gabriel's silver eyes flashed. "Is that a challenge?"

Uriel bared his teeth.

"Enough, you two." Michael's voice boomed across the kitchen. "With brothers like you, who needs enemies like Samael?" He shook his head and then gazed once more across the table at the most enigmatic of his brothers.

"And speaking of Sammy," he said, "Max is right." Michael nodded at Azrael. "We need to know where he is right now and what he's doing."

Azrael cocked his head to one side and studied his brother. Then he looked at Uriel. "You remember that the scry is two-way, I assume."

Uriel nodded. He knew.

"Bloody hell." Gabriel rolled his eyes. "If Joe Black

over here scries on the bastard, then Sam'll know some-thin's up." He shook his head. "No' a good idea." The brogue was deepening.

"What do you propose, then?" Michael asked calmly.

Gabriel shrugged. "We protect her ourselves until she decides to join with *Lifestyles of the Rich and Famous* over here." He gave Uriel a sideways, meaningful glance. "Or whoever it is she chooses."

Uriel was up and out of his chair in the next instant, and Gabriel followed suit, both men moving with blinding speed. But before the two of them could meet, Michael was standing between them, one hand on each of their chests. Uriel could feel his heart pounding beneath his brother's palm.

"I said, that's enough." Michael spoke through clenched teeth, his blue eyes glowing dangerously. Then he turned to Gabriel. "You know that isn't how this works, Gabe. We will each recognize our archess. Your saber-rattling is inappropriate right now. Don't forget that your own archess is still out there somewhere," he warned. "And Uriel has a taste for vengeance."

Gabriel glanced back at Uriel.

Uriel smiled. It was one of those wholly unkind smiles that made people shiver deliciously in movie theaters around the world. And it was filled to the brim with unspoken promise.

Behind them, Azrael stood, slowly pushing his chair out so that it scraped against the tiles beneath it. The other three turned to face him.

He was already taller than the others, but his penchant for black somehow made him appear to tower over them. His long, wavy black hair was the calling card of the Masked One. On the stage, the singer remained masked to millions. No one but his brothers—and Max—knew who he really was.

"I've done the scry," he said softly.

Michael's hands dropped from his brothers' chests. "Already?"

Azrael stepped away from the table, his black combat boots resounding loudly on the tile as he made his way from the kitchen to the living room and the double glass sliding doors that led beyond. "It turns out that our guardian's concern is warranted," he told them as he used telekinesis to unlatch the lock and open the doors before him. "The easiest way to find honey is by following the bees. Samael keeps as much of an eye on us as we do him. He already knows who and where Miss Granger is, and he's planning to collect her as we speak."

"What?" the three of them asked at once.

"And Max is coming up the front drive," Azrael finished before he stepped out onto the balcony and gazed down three floors to the massive courtyard below. He turned and nodded once at the others. "Give him my best. I'm going to find breakfast."

With that, Azrael smiled, flashing sharp white fangs. Then he dissipated into a cloud of gray smoke and was lifted onto the wind, where he disappeared entirely into the darkening night sky.

"Bloody showoff," Gabriel muttered.

Michael shook his head and manually slid the doors shut again. Uriel silently agreed with Gabriel. Azrael was certainly the most . . . *interesting* of the four of them and he'd obviously gotten used to flaunting the theatrics he displayed onstage.

Michael turned to face them and sighed. "We're about to have a fight on our hands, boys."

Uriel gazed out the double glass doors behind him and into the black unknown beyond. The green in his eyes grew dark. "So be it."

Samuel Lambent, better known as Samael to a certain crowd, slowly rose from his massive desk and paced to the floor-to-ceiling windows behind him in his opulent office. The windows reflected his image back at him—a tall, sleek man in an extremely expensive gray tailored suit. Ash white–blond hair brushed the collars of his shirt and coat and a platinum wristwatch gleamed in the overhead lights. From a nearly painfully handsome face, charcoal-gray eyes gazed indifferently down at the world that continued to bustle sixty-six floors below. His reflection smiled a small, pleased smile that bespoke of intense charisma—and a touch of cruelty.

An archess, he thought. *Finally.*

The first of four.

Life was about to get a hell of a lot more interesting, wasn't it? At that, he gave a full-fledged grin, flashing straight white teeth.

He'd felt Azrael's obnoxious tickle of an intrusion, but he'd been expecting that, of course. Samael had men, both human and otherwise, working as informative agents all over the world. They were good at what they did; Samael never had to wait on his intel. And as soon as he had received word from one such agent that Uriel had located his soul mate, he'd been waiting for that scry.

The issue now, however, was how much time he would have to act before the archess accepted Uriel as her mate. With that thought, he turned and picked up the manila file folder that had been laid upon his desk. With long, dexterous fingers, he flipped the folder open and peered down at the photograph.

"Eleanore Elizabeth Granger," he whispered aloud, his dark gray eyes sparking red at their centers. "A lovely name for a lovely creature," he added.

Of course, he knew everything about her now. He hadn't chosen his earthly profession lightly. He was the founder, president, and CEO of the largest media company in the world. At the heart of media was information; and he was its king. Over the years, he had amassed enough power through its deep, multitudinous channels that he could now glean knowledge about anything he wished—or *anyone* he wished—at a moment's notice. Any intel he could not gain through these normal channels, his agents quickly discovered on the side.

He continued to gaze at the woman's photograph. Her parents and friends called her "Ellie." He laughed at that, the sound melodious and deep. If anyone had heard the chuckle, they would have been entranced. He had an intoxicating voice, the likes of which had only ever been matched by one other being on Earth. The Masked One, also known as the archangel Azrael, possessed a powerful voice as well, but it was deeper than Samael's. The Masked One had a voice that sounded like a foreboding premonition. Like a fire—welcoming yet dangerous.

Like death.

Samael's, on the other hand, sounded like seduction.

Samael tossed the folder back onto the desk and turned toward the windows once more. Then he pulled a slim, silver phone from the interior pocket of his expensive gray suit. He flipped it open and his hand glowed momentarily. He placed the phone to his ear and waited. It picked up after the second ring.

On the other end of the line, Uriel said nothing. The handsome movie star had learned long ago that it was best to let the bad guy speak first.

So Samael smiled and indulged him. "You have a choice to make, my friend."

Uriel remained silent, but Sam could feel the archangel's anger even across the distance. He wasted no time. "Give her up or lose her altogether." He chuckled as he thought of young Eleanore and the drastic way in which her life was about to change. "Time is short." He closed the phone again and repocketed it.

"Mr. Lambent?"

Sam turned to face the young man in the doorway.

"Your jet has arrived, sir. And your car is waiting."

Samael nodded, picked up the file folder, and followed the young man out of his office.

Uriel stared at the phone in his hands and could feel his green eyes glowing.

"Well, we knew that was comin,' didn't we?" Gabriel said. He brushed past Uriel to make his way to the marble staircase landing. Michael followed him. They'd both watched him take the call.

Uriel continued to stare at the phone. Then, very slowly, he flipped it shut and repocketed it. He'd never felt so angry.

"Max, any news?" Michael asked as he descended the stairs to meet the guardian at the bottom.

Uriel paced to the landing and peered over the railing. Max Gillihan was just shutting the front door behind him, three stories below. With a blast of superhuman strength, Uriel leapt over the balcony railing, dropped the three stories to the marble foyer below, and crouched to absorb the impact as his boots slammed down. He turned to Max. "He knows."

Max paused, his eyebrows raised. "I'm assuming Samael contacted you."

"Uriel just got the call," Michael told him.

Max glanced at Uriel, noticing the glowing eyes. He sighed heavily. "I see." He shook his head and stepped past Uriel to make his way up the stairs and back into the kitchen. "We don't have much time, then." He glanced over his shoulder at Uriel. "What did he tell you?"

"To let her go or lose her altogether," Uriel repeated. He could hear the grating wrath behind his words.

"He wants her for himself, doesn't he?" Michael suggested, his tone tight. He and the others followed Max up the stairs.

"It stands to reason," said Max. "It's why he followed us down here all those years ago." He pushed through the swinging doors to the kitchen. "But that's better than wanting her dead straightaway."

"How the bloody hell do you figure that?" Gabriel asked as the three of them followed their guardian to the island table and took seats to watch Max proceeded to make himself a sandwich.

"If Samael wants someone dead, they end up dead in

short order," Max told them, setting the mayonnaise and mustard out beside two slices of whole wheat bread. "If he, instead, plans to seduce her, then . . . well—"

"He's fair good at that too, isn't he?" Gabriel said.

"Gabe's right. We still don't have much time," Max said. "There is little Samael excels at more than seduction."

Uriel watched Michael's expression of worry deepen. He knew his own eyes were shooting daggers. He was pissed and didn't bother hiding it. Samael's track record with the ladies included nearly every famous beauty that had existed in the last two thousand years of human history. Wars had been started in the aftermaths of his seductions.

"We'll ask Azrael to watch her tonight," Michael assured him. "If Sam goes anywhere near her, we'll know."

"It's time you had this, then," Max said.

They all turned to the guardian to watch him pull a single gold bracelet from the inside pocket of his suit jacket. He placed it gently on the counter in front of Uriel and then returned to his task of making a snack. They all gazed at the bracelet and a hush fell over the trio.

The archangels recognized the bracelet even though they hadn't seen it in thousands of years. The gold wreath was one of a group of four. The Old Man had given them to Max long, long ago, when the archangels had first decided to come to Earth to look for their archesses. There was one bracelet for each of them.

The bracelets were meant as added protection against the plethora of preternatural, spectral, psychic, fairy, ghostly, and otherwise unpredictable—and dangerous—creatures the Old Man had created along with the humans that inhabited the mortal realm. The archangels could most likely have handled anything they encountered on their own, but the Old Man was indeed fond of his four favorites. The bracelets possessed the magic to lock a being's supernatural powers within his or her body, thereby rendering that being more or less power-less.

If Max, the bracelets, and the mansion hadn't been lost to the archangels during their descent to Earth two thousand years ago, Michael would have been able to slap one of the gold bands on Azrael. It would have trapped both his archangel and his vampire powers within himself and given him the breathing space he needed to cope with his change. As it was, however, Max and the archangels hadn't found one another for quite some time after their descent. And Azrael had been smothered in both need and power, ruled entirely by the turbulent magic coursing through his veins.

But since nothing supernatural had seriously threatened them in centuries, they hadn't seen the bracelets in as long. It had been thousands of years since those first tentative steps upon the mortal realm, and the archangels hadn't had need for the bracelets for the last several hundred. It had been a while since any other supernatural creatures had put in an appearance, so the archangels had more or less forgotten about the bracelets.

After a few moments, Uriel cleared his throat. "What are you suggesting, Max? That I use this on Eleanore?"

Max stopped what he was doing, placed his hands on the counter, and sighed. "Play nice first. But realize that, if she even believes you in the first place, she may not take kindly to the idea of being created solely for the satisfaction of another being—much less a male. What will you do if she decides to continually blast you with lightning?"

Uriel didn't have an answer to that.

Max continued. "Remember that Samael is about to make a move. You need to protect Eleanore from him. You need to bring her here to the mansion. If she doesn't come willingly, you won't have any choice but to take matters into your own hands." He glanced at the bracelet and nudged it closer to Uriel. "Think of this as a precaution. As a plan B."

Uriel stared down at the gold band. It was a stunningly beautiful piece of jewelry. But the most impressive thing about it was the intricacy of the magic woven within it. Once donned, only the one who placed the bracelet on a being's wrist could remove it. Otherwise, the being was bound to wear it always.

He wondered, as he reached down and fingered the bracelet with tentative fingers, what Ellie's reaction would be if he used this on her. If she was already against the idea of being his archess, then trapping her powers within her body probably wouldn't warm her to him any.

But like Max said—it was a plan B. And Samael did pose a threat.

"Right," he said softly. Then he lifted the bracelet and placed it in the front pocket of his jeans. If the way Ellie had stood up to him in the bookstore was any indication, his archess was almost as likely to slap this on his wrist as he was to get it on hers.

CHAPTER FOUR

At around ten o'clock, Eleanore finished showering and eating and sat down at her desk. She logged on to her computer and signed on to her IM server. Then she waited for Angel to log on to the chat box on her end; when she saw her initials, she began typing.

> E: You wouldn't believe who's here right now, signing autographs in my store.

> A: Okay—autographs? I'm officially on the edge of my seat!

> E: Christopher Daniels.

There was a long pause while, on the other end of the connection, Angel obviously processed the news.

> A: You're shitting me.

> E: lol Nope. I've been off work for two hours, but Mister Jonathan Brakes is probably still there, wondering which of his adoring fans he can sink his teeth into for dinner. Or would it be breakfast?

> A: I have never been more jealous of you than I am right now.

> E: I thought you hated that movie.

A: Oh, I do. With a passion. Am I the only one creeped out by the thought of someone several hundred years old going after someone who's barely twenty??? Talk about robbing the cradle. But Christopher Daniels is freaking HOT. Did you get to talk to him at all? Get his autograph?

Eleanore gazed down at the screen and smiled a wry smile. She'd more than spoken to him.

E: You know how I am. I wasn't really interested in an autograph.

A: You're kidding me! You WORK there, for crying out loud! You could have at least shown him where he was supposed to park his mega-fine ass!

E: I did do that. Sort of.

A: Oh? Explain.

Eleanore hesitated.

A: Now!

She laughed at the screen and shook her head. There was no way she could tell Angel exactly what happened, of course. Not with the storm and the little girl and all that. After six years of communicating electronically, she felt she knew Angel better than she knew herself, and she was closer to her than she'd ever been to anyone in her life. They were best friends, of a sort, though they had never met nor had so much as a phone conversation. They both hated talking on phones and had sworn it off right at the start. They'd met in a chat room for a vampire romance novel and hit it off.

There were days when Eleanore was certain that she could tell Angel anything. She seemed to empathize with everything that went on in her life—except for the magical power thing, which Angel didn't know about because Ellie had kept it hidden all these years. If Ellie told Angel the truth, then Angel would be just as burdened with keeping her secret as she was.

Eleanore continued to stare at the screen, biting her lip as she did so.

A: You there?

E: Yeah, I'm here. Sorry. Just thinking.

A: About Daniels?

E: Sort of, but not really. More of a general spacing out, I guess.

A: That's my Ellie.

E: What's it like in the North Pole right now?

Angel lived in Minnesota and as far as Eleanore was concerned, it had to be one of the coldest places in the world.

A: Cold. White. Caught the change of subject, btw. Nice try. I still want all of the juicy details about vampire boy.

E: Okay. Fine. The truth? He asked me out on a date.

It took a minute for the reply to come back this time.

A: He what?

E: He asked me out. To some sort of event on Thursday. But I turned him down.

A: He what?

E: Very funny. You heard me the first time.

A: He what what?

Eleanore laughed.

A: Okay, now I know you've gone around the bend. I can't freaking believe Christopher Daniels asked you out. I really can't. And you turned him down. I'm leaving the computer now to go and scream into my pillow. My eyes are turning green.

The chat box grayed out and Ellie smiled, shaking her head once more. She closed down her e-mail program and pushed away from the desk. It was time for bed. And she had a strange feeling her dreams would be interesting. At the very least.

When Eleanore put the coffeepot in the fridge and the carton of soy milk on the coffeemaker the next morning, she finally had to admit to herself that she hadn't gotten nearly enough sleep. It was Sunday and it was a good thing she didn't have to go in to work that day, because her dreams had been plagued all night with images and flashes and impressions of Christopher Daniels. It wasn't the first time she'd dreamed of the actor. It was just the first time the dreams had been so vivid that she'd had to kick off all of her covers in order to breathe.

She shook her head, pinched the bridge of her nose where she felt a headache coming on, and tried again. Soy milk in the fridge, coffeepot on the coffeemaker. Flip the switch.

Nothing happened.

"No, no, no, not now." She bent and eyed the electrical outlet to make sure it was plugged in. It was. The coffeemaker was old; it had been in its death throes of late so she'd taken to heading to Starbucks for her caffeine fix. She just really didn't feel like getting out of her pj's at the moment.

She tried the switch again, and again nothing happened. "Come on, girl. Don't die on me yet. Please—just one more pot. Just this morning, come on." She tried coaxing the coffeemaker as she flipped the switch a few more times, but it was unresponsive.

Ellie sighed and let her chin drop to her chest.

There was a knock at the door. Her head snapped back up and the alertness she'd been trying for all morning slammed into her. No one ever knocked at her door, and certainly not this early in the morning. She stood motionless in front of the coffeemaker, listening intently. There was no sound beyond the door; no voices to give the visitor's identity away.

Ellie knew she was being cowardly, but she couldn't help it. She knew that if she stayed still long enough, whoever was there might go away.

The knock came again, this time a bit more persistent and solid.

Ellie squeezed her eyes shut, swore under her breath, and headed toward the front door. Whoever had come to call better not be offended by the fact that she was in her pj's. Not that they had any right to be offended, paying her a visit this early and without warning.

Ellie slid the peephole cover back and peered through.

Christopher Daniels stood on the other side of the door, a large paper cup of coffee in each of his hands. He was standing in profile, his gaze trained on something in the distance, but after a few seconds, he straightened and turned toward the peephole.

He smiled and mouthed "Good morning" as if he could see her.

Ellie's world tilted a little.

Oh my God, she thought.

There was no way Christopher Daniels was on the other side of her door. It was unbelievable enough that the famous actor had managed to find her home. That he had cared to look for it in the first place was even more surprising. Unless . . . Was it possible the interest in her he'd shown at the bookstore was genuine?

Questions spun in her head. She thought of the way he'd mentioned the storm and how Jennifer had slipped on her secret. Either he was being sincere about his interest in her—or he wanted to get close to her because of her powers. The only reason he could have for wanting to do that would be so that he could turn her over to someone else—someone with the intent of abducting her and using her abilities for their own gain. Someone who had been chasing her across the country since she was fifteen.

She had to admit that the scenario seemed more than unlikely. Daniels was rich and famous and had no reason to be working for some covert operation. But she couldn't get a handle on him. He'd really thrown her for a loop.

"Coffee's getting cold," he said from the other side, his voice coming through clearly.

Eleanore ran a hand through her hair, fisted it there, turned in place as if she were going to walk away, and then faced the door once more. She was the embodiment of indecision.

"I know I'm a good actor," Daniels said, "but I'm really not a vampire. I promise if you let me in I won't bite."

Ellie blew out a sigh, rolled her eyes dramatically, and then unbolted the door. She popped it open and glared at him. Her glare faltered, though, at the sight of him unhindered by the glass of the peephole. He was so tall. His long-sleeved thermal shirt was pushed up to his elbows, exposing strong forearms. It drew tight across his broad chest as if painted over the expanse of hard muscle there.

A small gold band of a bracelet was wrapped around his left wrist; it bore intricate designs and seemed to fit him perfectly. Distractedly, she wondered how he'd gotten it on. His jeans were just as form-fitting as his shirt and called far too much attention to the long, lean power encased there.

His dark brown hair was slightly damp from the cold November morning and curled against his forehead in thick waves that begged to be touched. She caught a whiff of him, like soap and cologne, and felt herself instantly flush. The scent of coffee came next, erasing what was left of her scowl.

Suddenly she felt ridiculous standing there in front of the famous Christopher Daniels in nothing but pj's and a nasty expression. Her gaze slipped from his impossibly green eyes to the coffee in his hands. Curls of steam rose lazily from the sip holes, beckoning her. She suppressed a moan and turned a slightly apologetic look on the actor.

"Okay," she said with a small shrug and a smile, "which one's mine?"

"This one," he said, holding one of the cups out to her.

Eleanore took it and her fingers brushed against his as she did. Sparks of energy thrummed through her fingertips, into her arms, and then raced across her chest. It was far more intense than it should have been and Ellie froze in place at the contact. Neither of them said anything; finally, she cleared her throat and turned the cup around in her hands. "How did you know what I like?"

"I saw your drink on the desk at the bookstore," he said softly. His voice sounded tighter than it had a moment ago. His green gaze had darkened and his attention had focused on her like a pinpointed laser beam. "I would be fine with just having coffee on the front doorstep, but I'm afraid that if you don't let me in soon, we'll have to contend with people coming up here to ask me for autographs."

Even as he said this, Eleanore caught the distant sounds of teenage girls giggling below in the courtyard. She stepped back through her doorway and invited him in. "Say nothing about my state of dress or my lack of furniture and I might let you stay longer than it takes me to down this coffee," she warned him.

Daniels stepped past the threshold and into Eleanore's apartment. She watched him with some trepidation as he glanced around, taking in their surroundings. Ellie's apartment wasn't exactly cheap; it was in a better part of town and somewhat gated. Plus, hers was a corner suite with a fireplace, which not all of them had.

But she never spent much on furniture. It seemed pointless to her to waste money on something she might have to leave behind at any given moment. There was always a chance that the people around her would begin to notice she was different. And then it would be time to pick up and go, so she was always ready.

She wondered what Daniels, the famous and very wealthy movie star, would think of her minimalist decor. He probably had a mansion.

"Have a seat in the living room and I'll go change," she told him.

She walked into the kitchen and pulled a mug down from one of her shelves. Then she tried to steady her hands as she poured her coffee from the paper cup he'd handed her into the mug and popped it into the microwave. She took a deep breath and returned to the living room, where he was still standing beside the couch, taking it all in. She brushed nervously past him and made her way down the hall to her bedroom.

Ellie shut the door behind her and hurriedly pulled off her pajamas. Then she pulled on a pair of jeans and a T-shirt and quickly ran a brush through her hair.

When she returned to the living room, it was to find Daniels standing before a pair of plywood shelves she had put together and placed in one corner. One shelf held all of her CDs. The other contained hardback and paperback books.

He was reading the titles of the books when he glanced up at her entrance.

His head turned and his gaze instantly pivoted to her once more. Eleanore felt her face and ears grow hot.

The hint of a smile began to curve Daniels's lips. "You like Valley of Shadow," he said, holding up one of her

CDs. An image of a cemetery covered the front and in the center of the graveyard stood a single man dressed in black, half of his face hidden by a black mask. "Fan of the Masked One?"

"Who isn't?" she replied with a faked shrug of nonchalance. "He has the voice of an angel." It was probably pathetic, but she was so inexperienced at flirting, she was grateful to have something else to focus his attention on.

Daniels stared at her intently for a moment and then smiled a slow, enigmatic smile. "You'll get no argument from me," he said as he turned and slid the CD back into its slot.

Ellie watched as the muscles in his back and arms bunched invitingly with every CD he removed and replaced. The *schlick-schlick-schlick* sound of their shuffle filled the air in the room with a tense kind of static. In that moment, she was struck with the surreal realization that Christopher Daniels, tall and gorgeous and replete with hard-cut muscles, was actually in her apartment and appeared to be honestly interested in what she liked.

What were the chances?

She cleared her throat. "I'm going to get my coffee," she told him. She had backed up a step to head for the kitchen when Daniels stopped what he was doing and turned around to face her.

The green of his eyes was so piercing and intense in that moment, she nearly gasped. Instead, she lifted her hand, almost protectively, and found her fingers lightly brushing the hollow of her throat. "Your eyes are so green," she said before she could stop herself. Her blush deepened, inflaming her face. *Stupid!*

Christopher's grin was intensely pleased. "They get that way."

She felt like an idiot. With a good amount of effort, she forced herself to pull her gaze from his and focus on his coffee cup. "Does yours need warming up?" she asked. Her eardrums began to hum with the sound of blood rushing through them and her voice sounded hollow.

He glanced down at the paper cup he'd placed on the coffee table. "No." He looked back up at her, capturing her eyes with his. "Thank you. I'm good."

She nodded and hurriedly spun around. Once she was in the kitchen, she leaned against the refrigerator and tried to catch her breath. Her heart was thrumming wildly in her chest; she could feel it beating frantically at the pulse points in her wrists and temples.

Good God, what the hell is he doing to me? She rolled her eyes and bit her lip hard. *Get a hold of yourself, Ellie,* she mentally scolded. *He's just a human being, just like you, just like everyone. He's just a guy. So calm the hell down!*

A few minutes later, she had gotten herself under enough control that she could face him again. She returned to the living room holding her steaming mug with both hands. Her fingers were fidgeting around the porcelain, but at least it kept them busy.

"You're a fan of manga, too," he said with a nod to the plethora of colorful trade paperbacks on the shelf.

She smiled nervously. "I've taken to reading newspapers backward."

"Poe?" He gestured to the black leather-bound tomes.

"I do love Poe."

"And vampires."

At this, she froze. Daniels smiled a "got you" smile and turned to gesture to the title of the nearest paperback book. "*Slave to a Vampire: An Erotic Compilation of Stories About Vampires and the Brides They Claim,*" he read aloud.

Eleanore's blush was back and as furious as ever.

Daniels sat down on her couch and pulled a single magazine from under the picture book on her coffee table. On the cover was a photograph of him as Jonathan Brakes—fangs, glowing eyes, and all.

Ellie shrugged noncommittally and stubbornly plastered an innocent expression on her face. "I got that magazine for the article on Tim Burton," she said in a matter-of-fact tone.

Daniels's brow arched. He glanced down at the cover and searched for Tim Burton's name. It wasn't on the cover. She knew that already. He opened it and searched the table of contents. Ellie shifted from one foot to the other, trying not to let her embarrassment show. Burton's article was on page twenty-three. "I'm surprised you knew it was in here," Daniels said. "What with all of this eye candy in the way."

Eleanore said nothing to that. Instead, she took another sip of her coffee and tried to hide her face behind her mug as she did so.

On the couch, Daniels opened the magazine up to his own article, which was easy, since the magazine had been opened to that page so often it now did so automatically. Daniels shot her another knowing glance and Ellie felt like sticking her head in a hole. Then he began reading. "Christopher Daniels came out of the closet today when he announced to the world that he has a crush on his costar, Lawrence McNabb, the tall blond actor who plays Daniels's enemy in *Comeuppance*."

"It does not say that!" Eleanore exclaimed, coming forward to put her coffee mug down on the table in order to snatch the magazine from him.

He was faster, though, and moved it to the side so that she nearly fell on top of him. She barely managed to brace herself on the arm of the couch, and she caught his wicked grin when she only just prevented herself from landing in his lap. "So you *did* read it," he said.

Eleanore hastily straightened and crossed her arms over her chest. That did it. She had been nervous as it was, but his teasing had now put her on the defensive. "What are you doing here?" she asked him. "And how did you find me?"

Daniels dropped the magazine on the coffee table and leaned back to drape his arms over the back of the sofa. Ellie's gaze flicked to his thick arms and then flicked back to his face. She couldn't help it. He hadn't missed it, though, and his smile broadened.

"The truth?" he asked.

"It's usually preferable," she said tightly.

He nodded and leaned forward, resting his elbows on his knees and lacing his fingers together. His gaze never left hers. "I had my agent track down your address. I just needed to see you again."

She felt her brow furrow. "Do you always track down your dates this way?"

He smiled a winning smile. "You're not my date. You turned me down, remember?"

She mulled that over. It was true enough.

"I also didn't know how else to meet you," he admitted then, with a sigh. He leaned back once more into the sofa and shrugged. "If I return to the bookstore where you work, everyone will recognize me and you'll end up on the cover of *People* magazine. Call me crazy, but I had this impression that you wouldn't appreciate that kind of publicity."

Ellie blinked. Then she looked away. She was caught off guard by this small confession. He couldn't be more right, of course, but she wondered how he knew. Was it that obvious? Or did it have something to do with the storm? With her healing little Jennifer?

The questions were back again. They were always there, it seemed.

Suddenly, she felt very weary. "Fair enough," she finally said and sat down in the love seat opposite him. As she sat, the light caught the gold band on his wrist and reflected off it.

She frowned a little and cocked her head to one side. "That's an interesting bracelet. Where did you get it?"

Daniels looked down at his wrist and seemed to think very carefully before answering. "I've had it for years," he said. "It was passed down to me from my father. It's supposed to be magic."

Her interest was piqued now. Being that she could

call lightning from the skies and control fire, magic—or rather, *power*, at least—was something she happened to know a little about. "Oh?"

Daniels looked back up at her, once more trapping her gaze in his. He considered her in silence for several tense moments and then licked his lips. "The writing on the outside tells a tale," he explained. "The bracelet was made by God for his four favored archangels. The magic in the wreath possessed the ability to bind a magical being's powers within their body." He paused and looked back down at the bracelet as he slowly turned it over. "At least, that's how the story goes."

Eleanore glanced at the beautiful gold band again. She'd always loved a good tale of fantasy and magic. "What kinds of beings?" she asked. And then she added, "What kinds of powers?"

Something dark flashed in Daniels's eyes and he suddenly seemed to be seeing Ellie all the way down to her core. "You name it," said softly. "Vampires, werewolves, angels, and demons. Take your pick."

Ellie frowned. "Why would an *angel's* powers need to be bound?"

Daniels looked down at the band on his wrist and chewed on the inside of his cheek; she could see the slight indentation as he did so. He was mulling something over. Finally, he looked back up. "Angels are like humans in that they're unpredictable," he told her. "You never know when one might turn on you for no good reason." He smiled a rather cryptic smile and shrugged.

"Which archangels are his four favorites?" Ellie asked next. She wasn't feigning interest for his sake. She really wanted to know.

"Michael, the Warrior Archangel," he told her softly. "Uriel, the Angel of Vengeance; Gabriel, the Messenger Archangel; and Azrael," he finished, his tone dropping a touch, "the Angel of Death."

Eleanore spent several seconds too many trapped in that verdant gaze and then managed to rip her eyes away long enough to once more study the etchings engraved on the bracelet. She wasn't a religious person, but she was familiar with the names, of course. It was impossible not to be, especially since she worked in a bookstore.

However, something about the tale didn't make sense. It felt . . . incomplete. She supposed it didn't really matter. Fiction and fantasy were like that.

Finally, realizing that she hadn't said anything in too long, she blinked and pulled her gaze away to stare at the coffee table. "If it was meant for archangels, then how did you end up with it?" she asked, playing along with the story.

Daniels waited a beat before replying. "Just lucky, I guess."

Ellie glanced up at him. He easily held her gaze. She swallowed, squared her shoulders, and asked, "Why did you want to see me, Mr. Daniels?"

"It's Christopher," he said.

She didn't humor him by repeating the question and he smiled at her obvious stubbornness.

"I was blown away by you last night," he told her. "And you turned me down. Naturally, I had to try again."

"Try what again?" She didn't say "Mr. Daniels," but she also didn't say "Christopher." Stubborn, indeed.

"Go out with me," he demanded softly, leaning forward again to pin her with what was one of his more potent and famous gazes. "Tonight. I don't want to wait for the gala on Thursday. Just let me take you out tonight." He spread his hands out before him in a pleading and placating fashion. "Give me one single night of your life, Ellie. Would it really be so bad?" Eleanore sat very still on the couch for several long beats. Christopher Daniels was asking her out again. She couldn't explain this sudden fascination the actor seemed to have with her. Was she really that attractive? Couldn't he have anyone in the world that he wanted?

Why her?

When she didn't reply right away, Daniels leaned back against the couch and draped his arms once more over the backs of the cushions. He studied her silently and inquisitively, but there was a tension to him as well. His muscles were flexed and his calm—even his breathing—seemed forced. The air around him felt . . . impatient.

Ellie considered his request. The truth was, she very much wanted to go out with him. But anywhere he went, he would be trailed by an entourage of agents and bodyguards and fans. That was too much publicity for her.

She was going to have to turn him down.

She slowly pushed herself up from the couch, and he watched her rise. Standing up afforded her a little height over him and that gave her the will to go on. She managed to clear her throat. "You're a vampire, Mr. Daniels," she said, deciding that staying within the realm of make believe was more comfortable to her at that moment than reality. "I never trust vampires."

Something intense flashed in the green of Daniels's eyes. His tone was low. "Never, Ellie?"

Several beats of silence followed.

"What are you afraid of?" Daniels leaned forward, taking his arms off the back of the couch. "Afraid I'll bite?" He paused for effect. "Or that I won't?"

Ellie blanched. She could feel the blood drain from her face.

"Or maybe you'd prefer something different?" he hedged. "Perhaps something from the pages of *Slave to a Vampire*?" He stood and strode to the shelf where the paperback had been stowed. He pulled it free from its stack and began sifting through the embarrassingly dog-eared pages.

Eleanore felt that she would die right then and there. She couldn't let him read what was in that book. Especially the pages she'd folded the corners down on! She lunged forward, scooting around the coffee table as he began so casually glancing over the words she had masturbated to a hundred times.

But as she went for the book, intent on yanking it from his grasp, he moved it out of her reach, turned to face her, and slipped his arm around her waist. Electricity shot up her spine. Time blinked, the world spun, and he had dropped the book to fist his fingers in her long, thick hair. In the next instant, he was forcing her up against him with a strong hand at the small of her back. Her breath left her and the world dropped out from under her when he closed the distance between them, his mouth claiming hers with a determined fierceness that was unlike anything Eleanore had ever imagined. Not in her wildest dreams could she have fathomed a kiss like this.

She couldn't help but give in to it. He tasted too good—like white wine and licorice. His presence, tall and hard and dark above her, was making her so dizzy she was positive she was going to pass out.

He was demanding. He was delicious. She was in heaven.

There was a knock at the door, but it was far away and barely real. Christopher's hand spread across her back, trapping her as his other hand slid beneath her hair to cup the nape of her neck. The gentlest pressure there ensured that she not break his kiss. As if she was going anywhere....

The knock came again, and this time Ellie stilled against him.

"Miss Granger, are you awake?" a woman called from the other side of the door. "I thought you'd be off today," she continued, a little strained so that she could be heard through the door, "so I waited until this morning to bring your renewal papers by."

Christopher's grip on her didn't let up, but he did end the kiss, slowly pulling away. She opened her eyes to look up at a gaze that had gone from jade to striking emerald, pupils expanded like those of a cat before it pounces.

"I'll pick you up at eight," he whispered against her lips.

Ellie's breathing was ragged, but she felt a little better when she noticed that his was as well. His grip on her back was nearly bruising, it was so tight. She could feel a tremble there in the immense strength of the arm that held her.

Without waiting for a reply, he stepped back and his arms slipped from her body. The cold immediately came in to fill the space where he had been and Ellie fought not to shiver.

Christopher watched her for several more beats, his gaze scorching. And then he turned away and strode to the front door. Eleanore watched as he opened it to reveal a very surprised landlady on the other side.

Patty Jensen stared up at Daniels with a mixture of awe and vague recognition. She was obviously taken at once with his attractiveness. But then she frowned, just a little, and as Daniels nodded good morning to her and brushed past her to head down the stairs and leave the complex, Jensen turned to Eleanore. "Was that—"

"Nope," Ellie replied, coming to take the forms from Jensen's hands. "Nope, it sure wasn't."

CHAPTER FIVE

It took Eleanore two showers, with a trip to the gym in between, for her to expend even a small amount of the nervous energy that Christopher's kiss had charged her body with. She had never kissed a man before. Growing up, she'd never been in one place long enough to have a boyfriend. And now that she was on her own, she hadn't slowed down any. One glance at her sparse living quarters was testament enough to that.

Christopher Daniels was her first.

She had nothing to compare him to, but if her current frazzled, oversexed state was any indication, he was a good kisser. A very, very good kisser. Like, *The Princess Bride*, five best kisses ever kisser.

She couldn't wait to tell Angel about it. Of course, she also knew that she *shouldn't* tell Angel about it. After all, bragging about this kind of thing was what teenage boys did, not grown women.

She laughed at herself as she finished towel-drying her hair and headed into her office to sit down at the computer. The time at the bottom of the screen read 7:12 p.m. She had a little while before Daniels would show up if he was serious about taking her out. She had no way of confirming the date, as she didn't have any method of reaching him.

Ellie pulled up her e-mail account, confirmed that Angel was online, and opened a chat box.

E: You're not going to believe what happened today.

A: Hey, girl! What happened? Something good, I hope.

Ellie was about to reply when she heard the sound of a Harley roaring up the lane beside the apartment complex. Eleanore knew that Angel loved motorcycles; she went nuts over the silhouette of a man on a bike. Ellie was pretty sure that the *real* reason the girl liked Christopher Daniels was that in *Comeuppance*, he'd ridden a Triumph.

The bike drew nearer and Eleanore let her fingers play over the keyboard.

E: Hold on—hog going by. Sounds like magic.

A: Oooh! Quiet moment of respect now commencing. . . .

But as Eleanore read, she frowned. There was a skidding, swerving sound, distinct and chilling. And then that brief heartbeat of silence, the kind that occurs right before something goes very wrong.

The sound of a crash in the night is electrifying. It captures your attention, no matter what you're doing. It shoots through your body like a steel rod and activates the scenery of your imagination. The sound of the accident was like the crunching of full tin cans beneath a steamroller, and it instantly iced Eleanore's blood.

She was up and out of her chair before she fully realized what she was doing. Her body moved on autopilot—through the office door, through the living room, and then through the front door of the apartment, which she barely realized she'd opened using telekinesis.

When she stood on the landing outside, she turned toward the street, automatically searching for any immediately visible signs of wreckage or mangled bodies. However, she saw nothing but the slight sheen of the blacktop in the reflected light of streetlamps above. The night was silent.

Had she imagined it? Maybe she was more tired than she'd thought. But then something blinked. Red. White. Red.

A taillight, she thought. She raced down the stairwell, taking the steps two at a time. Distantly, she wondered why she was the only one to have heard the crash. It wasn't that late at night. Shouldn't there be other lights going on behind the windows of neighboring apartments by now?

Eleanore hit the bottom landing and rushed toward the parking lot and the street beyond. There, she stopped and peered in the direction from which she'd seen the blinking light. The street was empty, and there was no noise save for the buzzing of the streetlights, the harsh sound of her breathing, and the whimpering of a chocolate Labrador retriever who sat beside a toppled, crunched, and riderless motorcycle.

Eleanore's heart leapt into her throat. She willed her legs to move once more. The November night was cold. All she wore was a thin pair of yoga pants, a white T-shirt, and a pair of sheepskin Warmbat boots.

The taillight continued to blink on and off, but there was no sign of the person who had been in the motorcycle's saddle. There was a ditch a few feet away, its deep recesses lost in shadow. Stomach knotted with fear, Ellie crept to the lip of the ditch and looked down. In the vague darkness of the shadows below was a long figure wearing what appeared to be leather. He was instantly recognizable as a man—tall, lean, and broad shouldered. At first glance, none of his limbs were twisted at odd angles. But his helmet was missing.

A black puddle was spreading from beneath a shock of longish, unruly white-blond hair. Eleanore couldn't see his face. He was lying on his stomach. As she skidded down the cement slope, unconsciously grateful for her boots, she realized that she didn't *want* to see his face. It could be gone, after all. If he hadn't been wearing a helmet at all, it was likely that he was dead.

She reached the bottom and then crouched beside him, heedful of the ever-expanding crimson-black puddle. Her long, slim fingers checked at his wrist for a pulse.

There wasn't one.

"Oh God, no . . ." She felt herself beginning to panic and heard it in the rising pitch of her voice. She knew she had to get his heart beating first, before anything else. She could heal his wound easily enough, but if he had lost too much blood, his heart would give her trouble. She couldn't make a heart beat if there was nothing for it to pump.

Eleanore placed her hand palm-down as gently as she could on the man's leather-clad back and closed her eyes. She felt the heat in her hands and she knew that the magic was working when she also felt herself grow weaker.

She urged his heart to beat first and then quickly concentrated on his head wound. *Too hard*, she thought distractedly. The wound was more difficult to mend than it should have been. She healed one separation to find something wrong underneath; layers and layers of misfiring synapses and broken connections and internal bleeding. It was a head injury of the worst kind.

This is wrong, she thought, her teeth clenched in frustration. It shouldn't have been this hard. It was as if his body were fighting her, damaging itself on purpose in order to make things more difficult. Healing someone always drained her to some extent, but this one had her careening toward unconsciousness.

Eventually, the body under her hand stirred and slipped from beneath her, but by that time, she was utterly wasted. She started to fall forward and caught herself on the man's shoulder just as he rolled over and looked up at her. His eyes were the color of a charcoal storm, speckled with flecks of platinum that looked like both diamonds and steel. The storm deepened beneath her and Eleanore found herself entranced.

He sat up and shifted so that he held her exhausted body in his gloved hands. She had no choice but to let him; she was weak beyond speech or movement.

My God, she thought in stunned silence as she stared up at him.

His face was undamaged, and it was the most incredible face she had ever laid eyes upon. His fair skin and fine, absolutely perfect features reminded her of an anime character, especially when paired with his white-blond hair and incredibly tall, muscular physique. He had to be a model. Maybe a movie star.

He looks like an angel, she mused as the Earth shifted beneath her.

Her vision was tunneling. As she slipped beneath that warm, black blanket, she thought she caught the hints of a smile at the corners of his perfect mouth.

Cruel, she thought.

And then there was nothing.

There was something wrong. Uriel glanced at the grandfather clock again: 7:13. He turned and paced through his quarters and left his wing of the mansion to rush down the stairs to the main area below.

Michael was there, preparing to go to work; on his uniform, he wore the gold bar of a lieutenant, but they knew that he would soon be making captain. Though he used a different name and background information each time, Michael quickly worked his way up through the ranks of every precinct he went to work for. But the fact that he never aged and was never seriously hurt even though he was often shot at made his choice of professions a difficult one. Max was sometimes called in to wipe memories, as he had the time that Michael took several bullets to the chest.

In the end, Michael would quit his job under the

pretense of wanting to run the family business or travel the country in a Winnebago. Uriel had little doubt that the archangel cop would soon be quitting again; he'd been with the NYPD for fifteen years now and hadn't aged a day.

It struck Uriel as strange that he was still there; he thought Mike was supposed to be at work an hour ago. He was running late for his shift, apparently. Maybe he was trying hard not to get that promotion.

Gabriel was just getting back in; the fact that he was still damp from a shower at the station house was evidence that he'd been in the thick of another fire that night. However hard it was for Michael to be a cop, it was worse for Gabriel, the firefighter. You could fake the near miss with bullets. Fire was another thing altogether. It was vicious and unpredictable and always left scars.

Now Gabe sat on one of the couches, silently pulling on a dark bottle of beer.

Uriel passed both brothers by without a word and headed to the kitchen. He looked at the clock on the microwave: 7:14.

He gritted his teeth and ran a nervous hand through his thick hair. He felt on edge. He was anxious and restless and impatient and it was understandable; time was passing at an insurmountably slow rate. He needed to see his archess again. He needed to hold her, touch her—*take* her.

But there was something else, too. He couldn't put his finger on it, but it felt a little like there were guard dogs in his brain, and right now they were barking up a storm.

"I'm going," he said as he left the kitchen and strode across the living room to where his leather jacket hung on the coatrack.

Michael looked up and caught his gaze. "You'll be almost an hour early. She won't be ready." He shook his head in warning. "Women hate that."

"She'll get over it," Uriel muttered as he grabbed his keys and pocketed them.

Gabriel had been silent on the couch, but now he leaned forward, put his empty bottle on the coffee table in front of him, and stood. "I'm going with you."

Uriel stopped and looked up. Their eyes met; their gazes held.

"You aren't the only one who can bloody well feel it," Gabe told him, going for his own jacket.

"Christ, I knew it," Michael muttered, taking his hat off and joining them beside the coatrack. He looked down at his uniform, there was a flash of white light, and suddenly he was dressed in street clothes. "I'm going, too."

"I'll meet you there," said Azrael from where he was emerging at the archway that led to his wing of the mansion.

All three brothers turned to watch him pull on a long black trench coat, every ounce of his six-foot-five frame radiating the dark charisma that was the Masked One.

Now Uriel understood why Michael hadn't left to go to work. All of his brothers had been in tune with him enough to know that something was bothering him—that something was wrong.

He nodded his thanks to each of them and then turned toward the mansion door. Luckily for the archangels, the mansion was really no more than a temporal spell of sorts; a portal through the magical building's doors could be opened to any other door anywhere in the world. Uriel opened the door and stepped through to find himself coming out of an apartment a block down from Eleanore's.

The night was cold and dark and almost unusually quiet. Azrael flew ahead of them while they jogged down the street, and Uriel was grateful for the vampire's speed. The closer they got to the complex, the more Uriel was certain something wasn't right. By the time he reached the stairs that led to her second-floor apartment, he was taking them three at a time and practically flying himself.

The three brothers came to Eleanore's door to find it ajar. There was silence beyond.

"Az?" Uriel called.

"Come in, Uriel. We've been waiting for you."

It wasn't Azrael's voice that greeted him from the other side of the open door. It was Samael's.

Uriel pushed the door open to reveal Samael seated in the same spot that Uriel had been sitting in a few hours earlier. A tall man in a dark blue business suit was standing dutifully beside him.

Azrael was standing across the room, leaning against the wall, his arms crossed over his chest. He shot Uriel a warning look, his gold eyes flashing, and then turned his gaze back to Samael.

"Where is she?" Uriel asked angrily, stepping into the apartment.

"Honestly, Uriel, can you think of nothing more original to ask?"

"I've got one for you," Gabriel growled, coming in behind Uriel, his own silver gaze glowing like ice. "Where the *fuck* is she, you scaff bastard?"

Samael chuckled, the low sound deep and rumbling. "Now, now. This is no way to greet a guest who's come with good news."

Uriel waited, wondering how long he would have to stand there before he could rip off the fallen archangel's head.

Samael casually unbuttoned the top button of his expensive charcoal-gray suit jacket and adjusted his tie. "Your archess is safe and, thus far, untouched. I've come to offer you an accord," he said, with every hint of nonchalance. "I propose a bargain."

"Of course you do," Michael said. His tone was as low as Samael's. And, at the moment, just as deadly.

Samael went on as if Michael hadn't spoken. "It's simple enough. I wager that I can win the heart of our lovely Eleanore before you can, Uriel. The stakes are these," he said, as he leveled his powerful gaze on Uriel and pinned him to the spot. "I win, and not only is the archess mine, but you agree to serve me for all time. You win, and of course, the archess is yours."

The room was silent for what seemed a short eternity. Michael cocked his head to one side and frowned. "I'm sorry. I'm sure I didn't hear you right. I could have sworn you just proposed a wager that there's no way in hell we would accept. Would you mind repeating yourself?"

Samael's smile broadened. He looked down at his hand and appeared to study his perfect manicure. "She has already fallen for me, Uriel." He addressed his next words to Uriel alone. He glanced up at the green-eyed man who had once been the feared and notorious Angel of Vengeance. "I can have her in a day. No more." He let his hand drop to his side and straightened. "And you've no way to get to her." He shrugged. "You don't even know where she is." His smile was back. "Do you?"

"I'd wager she's in your bed," Gabriel ground out through clenched teeth.

Uriel chose that moment to strike, but his brothers were no fools. It took all of a heartbeat for Michael and Gabriel to come forward and wrap their arms around Uriel's strong form. Azrael whirled through the room, his body seeming to mist under the speed with which he moved. He stopped between Uriel and Samael.

"He has Eleanore," Azrael said, spearing Uriel with a golden gaze. "Remember that."

"Oh, I dinnae think he'll be forgettin' it anytime soon," Gabriel muttered, his grip on Uriel's thick, banded arm very, very tight.

"Of course, you can try to take her from me, Uriel,"

Samael continued, as if nothing had just transpired. "But good luck convincing her you're in the right—and I'm in the wrong." He cocked his head to one side and his gray eyes glittered. "Especially when you bring the bracelet into the scenario." He shook his head. "I doubt she'll appreciate the lovely gift once she knows the truth."

"Get out." It was Michael who spoke then, his voice a mere breadth above a whisper.

Samael's eyes cut to the tall, blond archangel who had once been the Old Man's favorite so long ago. His charcoal gaze began to glow. The look they exchanged was of the most pure form of hatred. Masked by the sheerest facade of calm.

"Very well." Samael nodded once. "I've said what I came to say."

He stood and moved to the front door of Eleanore's apartment, the man in the blue suit following on his heels. In the doorway, Sam turned and his gray eyes pinned Uriel one last time. "The ball is in your court."

With that, Samael's form melted into the darkness behind him. He and his servant vanished and the apartment was once more free of his ominous presence.

Eleanore came awake in a pleasant daze, her limbs deliciously heavy, her body languid, her mind strangely at ease. But the feel of the mattress beneath her was different; it was foreign to her. The air felt unfamiliar. She slowly blinked her eyes open. *Where am I?*

She could sense that it was freezing outside. It was a hard November freeze that would kill what remained of the farmers' crops and the last, stubborn roses that clung to untended vines across the town. She could always sense these things, so she knew it to be true despite the warm, white comforter draped across her.

Slowly, she sat up; the sleepy succor her body was wrapped in made her feel luxurious and easy, like a cat taking a stretch after a long nap. Again, she blinked. Her short-term memory was blurred, but miraculously, she wasn't afraid. She should have been. This, she knew. And yet . . . she couldn't seem to be bothered.

"Where am I?" she asked out loud, taking in the opulence of the massive master bedroom suite she found herself in.

A hearth sat nestled into the opposite wall, flanked by carved granite and marble. It crackled pleasantly, the fire within it the perfect height and warmth. The flames sent dancing light across the marble floor and its thick rugs. The pile of the rugs was high, inviting bare feet. There were tapestries on the wall, each depicting something ancient and mysterious. There were unicorns and dragons and there was text written in languages she didn't comprehend. The air felt clean, free of dust, and scented with something she couldn't quite put her finger on. A kind of flower? A spice? It was intoxicating and made her feel even more relaxed.

There was a large oak door in the wall adjacent to the fireplace and upon it now was a gentle knock.

Eleanore wondered who could be on the other side, and when she did, she remembered everything that had happened that night: the motorcycle accident, the mad dash across the street, the fight to save the victim's life.

She remembered passing out—and looking up at an angel's face right before she had done so. She sat up a little straighter, ran a nervous hand over her hair, and glanced around at the bed and the room. *It must be his*, she thought, and she wondered how she had gotten there.

The gentle knock came again. Eleanore cleared her throat and called, "Come in."

The door opened, swinging slowly inward. Filling its frame was indeed the impossibly beautiful angelic rider. "Good evening," he said. His voice was so perfect that it sent shivers through Eleanore's body. She hastily suppressed the moan that threatened, absolutely forbidding herself to give this total stranger the satisfaction.

His dark eyes were glittering with secrets and his lips were curled in a gorgeous, incredibly sexy smile. He easily strode across the room to stand beside the bed and she gazed up into his charcoal-gray eyes.

Oh crap, Eleanore thought. *I want him. And I'm probably one of a million women he's had in this bed who wanted him just as badly.*

"Where am I?" she asked.

He was handsome, but he was a stranger. And she was alone and in his bed.

"You're at the home of a doctor who has been out of the country for some time; I'm renting the house," he said softly.

He was wearing tight, worn blue jeans and a form-fitting dark gray long-sleeved shirt that matched his eyes. Both the jeans and the shirt clung to his incredibly tall, trim, and muscular body. She could actually see the muscles rippling beneath the somewhat thin fabric of his clothing.

"I hope you'll forgive me," he told her, glancing at the yoga pants and shirt she still wore. "I'm afraid I bled a little on your clothing. However, I thought you would most likely prefer changing yourself." He gave her a sheepish grin then, and it was utterly disarming.

She blinked and glanced down at herself. He was right. She was still fully dressed and there were bits of dried blood here and there. She was entranced by him and he was far too handsome for anyone's good, but he'd been chivalrous. She had to give him that.

"What's your name?" she asked.

"Sam," he told her simply. Then he bent to sit on the bed beside her and her heart leapt into her throat. He raised his hand and gently cupped her face. She was helpless to pull away. In fact, she felt frozen to the spot as he tenderly brushed his thumb over her cheekbone and studied her as if she were just as beautiful as he was. "And you are Eleanore."

Her heart rate thrummed madly. "How—how do you know?"

"A long time ago, I made it my job to know everything." He smiled a mischievous smile. "I've gotten rather good at it." He chuckled.

When he removed his hand, Eleanore felt slightly strange. A little bereft. But his smile filled the tiny void and she found herself relaxing once more.

Wake up, Ellie, her inner voice warned.

She knew nothing about this man. Not really. She knew he was rich—that much was obvious from her surroundings. You can't rent a fully furnished house with marble floors and tapestries unless you're loaded. She also knew he liked motorcycles.

"Sam what?" she asked. The least she needed was a last name.

He chuckled again and there were more delicious shivers. "Lambent."

Eleanore thought about the name, which sounded familiar. "You mean like Samuel Lambent, the media mogul. . . ." *What a coincidence*, she thought. *I'll have met two famous, gorgeous men in one week.* But of course this was a different Sam. Lots of people had the same names. And the extremely wealthy, extremely famous Lambent didn't come to small towns in Texas. She was pretty sure he lived in Chicago.

"I won't keep you." He sighed, his smile almost sad now as he changed the subject. "I'll provide you with fresh clothes and a ride home. And I promise that your secret is safe with me. But"—he paused, his eyes darkening—"I would ask that you allow me to see you again." She watched as his pupils expanded.

She was nearly trapped in that look of growing hunger until she realized, suddenly, that he hadn't denied it. He hadn't denied being Samuel Lambent.

"Oh my," she whispered. "You *are* Samuel Lambent."

For a long, silent while, Sam just stared at her.

And she stared back.

Finally, he nodded. "Yes." He sighed and shrugged, pushing off the bed to stand once again. "I'm sorry I kept it from you."

She swallowed hard, looked him up and down, and realized she recognized him now. She'd seen profile pics, snapped hurriedly, in magazines and newspapers. He never gave interviews, so the photographs were of poor quality. But there was the tall, strong build. There was the shock of white hair. They sure as hell didn't capture his insane handsomeness.

"Why *did* you keep it secret?" she asked. Why was he so secretive in general?

"I suppose I'm nearly as used to hiding as you must be." This he said with a lowered head and a meaningful look through the tops of his charcoal-colored eyes. She knew damned well what he was referring to. She had saved him, so he obviously knew she could heal people. And he must realize that a power like that was too valuable. He knew she must always be on the run.

And, of course, in the back of her mind, she wondered whether she would have to run from him as well. And whether it would do any good to run from one of the wealthiest, most powerful men in the country.

Eleanore looked away. "Frankly, I doubt it." What could he possibly have to hide that was as bad a secret as hers?

Sam slipped his hands into the pockets of his jeans. "You don't think so?" he asked.

She glanced up at him. He was looking at the floor, his gaze contemplative. He turned away from her to walk to a plush overstuffed chair beside a folded screen on the other side of the room. He gracefully sat down and then pinned her with his powerful gaze once more.

Eleanore was instantly arrested. His expression was painfully intense. She fidgeted and sat up straighter to swing her legs over the side of the bed. She still felt weak, but not uncomfortably so.

"In truth, there are people that I'd rather not have knowing where I am."

"You're hiding from them?"

He nodded.

"Why?"

He didn't answer. He just smiled a small, secret smile and the glint of his eyes told her that an answer wouldn't be coming anytime soon.

"It's really that bad?" she asked, bewildered.

His smile turned rather nasty. "You have no idea."

Again, he stood and this time he strode all the way across the room to the door. "I'll have some clothes brought up for you," he told her as he pulled the door open and turned to face her. "There's a light meal waiting downstairs; I know you must be hungry." He smiled a tender, gentle smile. "Healing people obviously takes a lot out of a person. I'm indebted to you." He paused long enough to let this sink in.

Eleanore blushed and looked away.

"When you've finished, I'll be happy to give you a ride back to your apartment."

She nodded. Then he opened the door, stepped out into the hall, and closed it behind him, leaving her alone.

Out in the hall, Samael stopped and ran a shaking hand through his white-blond hair. Then he lowered his hand and looked at it.

This is unexpected, he thought. *I'm trembling?*

She was getting to him. Her nearness. Her perfection. Knowing what she was and what she meant—it was too much. He couldn't stop thinking about how she might feel.

And she was so *good*. She's been created as a mate for an angel—and yet here she was, her own woman, replete with her own thoughts and morals and her own lifetime to back them up. She was her own person.

She no more belonged to Uriel than Samael had belonged to the Old Man.

It was strange for him to realize all of this. He'd never thought so much about one human being before. It was making him feel . . . *off*. Not quite himself.

Samael moved down the hall to the top of the marble staircase.

"Jason, where is Lilith?" he called down to the young man who was walking through the foyer below, a cell phone to one ear.

The man immediately disconnected the call and pocketed the phone. "I'm not certain, my lord. But I will find her for you right away."

Samael nodded once, and then descended the stairs. Jason met him at the landing.

"Do you mind my asking how our guest is doing?" Jason inquired. He was a handsome young man with brown hair and blue eyes. As he had been when he was with Sam in Eleanore's apartment, he was once more dressed in a very expensive blue suit. He appeared tall, though not as tall as his master. He was also fairly well built.

There was the air of wisdom and silent obedience about him that utterly belied the youth in his handsome features. He waited patiently as Samael glanced once back up the stairs and then turned to face him again.

"She's beautiful," Samael whispered. "And precious." He frowned then, and stared at something unseen, somewhere in the vicinity of the marble ground. "I believe I have her trust. And I'm fairly certain she'll wish to see me again." He looked back up and met Jason's gaze. "Any word from lover boy?"

"Not yet, my lord. But soon, I've no doubt."

"No." Samael smiled and shook his head. "Nor do I."

Eleanore sank into the fine leather of the passenger seat and tried not to fidget. Everything was happening so fast and it was all so unbelievable, she didn't really know what to make of it.

First, Christopher Daniels. And now Samuel Lambent. Two extremely big people in one very small town in two extremely short days. It was a little overwhelming.

Eleanore closed her eyes and leaned her head back against the headrest of the luxury vehicle. It smelled nice in here. Like well-oiled leather, new car scent and gentle, wafting cologne.

Money, she realized. *This is what real money smells like.*

She'd always thought her family was well off, but there was something subtly different about this. Maybe it was the fact that none of them had ever driven a Bentley.

"I apologize if I've made your life even more complicated," Sam said suddenly.

Eleanore opened her eyes and turned to gaze at him. *Jesus, he's beautiful*, she thought. His profile was straight out of a manga comic. So perfect. The gold watch on his left wrist glittered momentarily under a passing streetlight and Eleanore shook her head, allowing it to fall back against the headrest once more. "You've made it more interesting, that's for sure," she whispered.

He chuckled, the sound sending delicious rivulets of pleasure through Eleanore's body. *How does he do that?*

"I'm about to make it even more interesting," he said then, his voice dropping to become even quieter.

Eleanore stilled. She watched him as he turned to glance at her. "I'm sorry, Eleanore, but I wasn't lying when I told you I make it my business to learn everything I can about people I deal with. And I know about your association with Christopher Daniels."

She blinked and frowned, not sure how to feel about that. "What about him?"

Sam's grip on the wheel tightened and then loosened again. She saw the tension riding up his arms and into his shoulders. He took a deep breath and let it out slowly as he surveyed the streets outside. "He isn't what he seems to be."

That's mysterious, Eleanore thought. *Okay. Elaborate, please.*

"What do you mean?" she asked out loud.

At that, Samuel Lambent turned and fixed Eleanore with a hard gaze. "Let's just say you and I aren't the only two in the world with something to hide."

CHAPTER SIX

Uriel glanced up from where he sat in the wooden chair before the dark windows, their curtains pulled back to reveal the blackness of the earliest Monday morning hours beyond.

Michael felt the archangel's green gaze and turned to meet it. Uriel's tall figure was framed by the night behind him. His expression was eerily calm and yet a touch too determined for Michael's tastes. He'd never seen his brother like this before. Uriel had been named the Fire of God in closed quarters. The name was spoken in hushed tones by those who knew they'd done wrong. He was justice cloaked in shadow; the one whom guilty men feared seeing when they looked over their shoulders. The Angel of Vengeance had an indomitable will. An eye for seeing souls. And a sword that was sharp and quick and merciless.

And yet Michael had still never seen him like this.

He couldn't quite tell what he was thinking. He was just . . . stark. Stoic. Scary as hell.

The two angels simply stared at each other, neither speaking. Michael wondered how long it would go on when Uriel finally stood, gracefully, slowly, and strode through the room toward the halls and bedrooms beyond.

He was headed toward his wing of the mansion. Michael was worried; Samael's challenge still hung over them unanswered, and Uriel was impulsive. He stood to lose too much. His archess was all he'd ever really wanted. Michael was certain that if Uriel was given the chance, he would try to contact Samael and take him up on his deal. But he couldn't leave the mansion without Max at least knowing about it. The guardian was intricately tied to the magical building; he always knew what it was doing.

Michael took a deep breath and released it slowly. The situation was unbearable, but Uriel couldn't be allowed to barter with the Fallen One. Not under any circumstances.

Uriel moved through the halls wrapped in an utterly belying calm. His mind had been made up from the get-go. And when he'd felt the envelope in the pocket of his black leather jacket, he'd known it was from Samael.

All he needed now was some privacy.

He reached his quarters, entered his room, and shut the door behind him. Then he paced to the fireplace, waved a hand over the hearth, and gazed into the flames that suddenly erupted into existence. They crackled and glowed and provided enough light for him to read the small envelope that he then took out of his pocket.

It was light gray, with a charcoal-colored seal. The image embedded in the seal was of a pair of angel wings. A note had been hand scrawled on one side of the envelope: "Do not break this seal." It was a half-warning. Uriel was very familiar with those. The Old Man had been quite fond of them and Uriel had been assigned to dole out the justice to all who disobeyed them.

In essence, they were warnings without reason. In whole, it should have read, "Do not break this seal . . . unless you have business with Samael."

Which he did.

Uriel swiped his thumb beneath the seal and broke it. The fire beside him leapt higher, filling the room with a red-orange radiance that grew until it was all-encompassing.

He was a bit surprised at first—but the surprise faded fast. He didn't bother placing his arm over his eyes. Instead, he faced the fire, gritted his teeth, and waited. The blaze engulfed him, painless but warm and bright enough that if he had been human, he would have been blinded for life.

It receded after a few seconds and Uriel was no longer in his master bedroom.

"Ah, so you've decided to join us," Samael said from where he stood beside a liquor tray, pouring himself a Scotch on the rocks. The room Uriel stood in seemed to be a study, as opulently designed and decorated as everything else Samael surrounded himself with.

"I wouldn't go so far as to say that just yet," Uriel muttered.

Samael laughed and turned to face him. "Can I offer you a drink?"

Uriel said nothing. His gaze flicked from Samael to the tall, handsome man who was standing calmly against one wall. He had dark brown hair and blue eyes and was dressed in a fine Italian suit. "Jason," he said in cool greeting.

Jason's azure eyes glittered, flashing malign intent.

"You knew what you were doing," Uriel told him.

"Said the avenging angel with the apathetic sword arm," Jason shot back, his tone still calm, but his gaze shooting daggers.

Samael watched the two with interest. He arched a brow and returned his glass to the small table. "Perhaps it would be best if we got down to business."

"I have some terms of my own," Uriel stated as he turned to face the archangel he and his brothers called the Fallen One.

Samael calmly gestured to the small gray envelope that now rested, open, in Uriel's hand. "By all means. Name them and they will appear on the document."

Uriel glanced down at the envelope. Then he pulled the white sheet of paper out from its interior and deftly unfolded it. It was blank. But he knew it wouldn't remain so for long.

"I imagine you'll want equal face time with the archess," Samael suggested, his own charcoal eyes shining with devious light. As he spoke, words of deep black ink, written in a language only vaguely known eons ago, appeared upon the page in Uriel's hand. "And, of course, an extra day or two to undo what damage has already been done," Samael added.

More words appeared on the page.

Uriel fought the urge to crumple it in his irritation. But, though he allowed the document to remain intact, his grip tightened and his teeth began to grind. He looked up and leveled the blond archangel with a withering gaze. "I want a hell of a lot more than that," he said. "I want your promise that if I win, you will stay away from the others."

That seemed to catch Samael by some small amount of surprise. He paused and considered Uriel's words. "I assume that by 'others' you mean the other archesses."

Uriel noticed that no further writing had appeared on the page. He smiled a rueful smile. "Don't tell me you're afraid, Samael."

Samael shrugged nonchalantly, apparently completely unaffected by Uriel's saber rattling. "More concerned, really, than anything else." He paced around Uriel to the fire that blazed in the hearth across the room. There, he leaned over it, bracing his arms on the mantle as he gazed into the flames. "You're playing with actual people here, you and your brothers. Real souls, real women, with lives of their own." He straightened again and turned to Uriel. "And if they choose to reject any of you, I doubt you'll give them the option. Freedom is not a choice for an archess, is it?"

"And you plan to save them from us—is that it?"

Uriel asked, a look of utter disbelief on his handsome face.

Again, Samael shrugged. He smiled but didn't answer. Instead, he changed the subject. "I can understand your reticence in signing, Uriel. After all, I'm far better at this than you and your brothers. I can see your need to protect the claims on these souls that you believe you've staked."

"You won't bait me, Samael. Michael, maybe. Gabriel, certainly. But me?" Uriel shook his head.

"Of course not," Samael agreed readily. "The Angel of Vengeance can't be fooled so easily into behaving in any form of rash manner."

At this, Uriel bristled, but he kept his visage calm. "Those are my terms, Samael. Accept them or there will be no bargain."

"Oh, there needn't be a bargain, Uriel," Sam said as he strode across the room toward the beryl-eyed archangel. "It matters little to me. Eleanore Granger can be mine by tomorrow night, with or without your blood on that document," he promised. "I simply can't pass up an opportunity to get a little something extra." He stood before Uriel, the two angels head-to-head, toe-to-toe, and he peered deeply into his enemy's eyes. "The Angel of Vengeance would make a very beneficial addition to my staff," he whispered. "That is the only reason I have proposed a wager at all." He shook his head once. "Otherwise, the archess is almost assuredly already mine."

Uriel gazed long and hard into Samael's stormy eyes. He thought of Eleanore Granger healing the child in the restroom despite the risk to herself that it posed. He recalled the way she smelled—like soap and lavender. He saw her eyes, so deep and indigo blue, their pupils expanded with desire.

She had wanted him. Nearly as badly as he'd wanted her. There was no denying that. It was this mutual desire that made Uriel confident he had a solid chance with her. If Samael backed off, Uriel might be able to undo whatever damage the Fallen One had already done.

He was good, Samael. Very, very good. With no more than a glance, he'd coaxed devout queens from their kings and launched battles that saw thousands dead.

Uriel took a slow, deep breath, composing himself before he spoke. Finally, he said, "I want a week alone with her. And you keep your lies to yourself."

"I would never dream of lying to a woman." Samael grinned, perfect white teeth flashing. "It isn't my style."

The contract grew warm in Uriel's grip. He looked down to see that the entire page was now covered in the black ink lettering. There were two lines drawn at the bottom. One for Samael's signature. The other for his.

The Fallen One snapped his fingers and a pen appeared in his hand. At the same time, the giant polished oak desk that was against the wall a moment ago was suddenly directly beside them. Samael snatched the contract out of Uriel's hand and placed it on the table.

Then he turned back to Uriel and held up the pen. It was a clear crystal fountain pen. It looked as though there was no ink in it. "I suggest you read it over very carefully before you put pen to paper," the archangel told him. "My contracts tend to be binding."

Uriel's gaze flicked to the pen in his hand and then to the contract on the table. He read it over, knowing full well that it most likely did no good to be careful. There was no such thing as safety when dealing with Samael. His grip on the document tightened when he saw that the clause he had requested regarding the other archesses had been left out. Samael wasn't giving an inch. But there was nothing he could do about it.

When he'd finished, he turned back to his rival. "You first."

The Fallen One arched a brow and then faced the table. With an expression on his beautiful face that gave away absolutely no trace of emotion, Samael placed the tip of the pen to the inside of his wrist and pressed hard.

The metal slid into his vein and the pen filled with the deep red liquid.

Uriel forced himself to remain calm as he watched the most powerful archangel in existence sign his name in blood on the first of the two lines. When Samael had finished, the pen magically emptied itself once more—and the Fallen One held it out for him. He didn't say anything; just waited for Uriel to make his move.

Uriel took the pen, and without hesitating, he pressed it into his own vein. The pain was far greater than it should have been, but then he had expected as much. Samael would pass up no opportunity to cause him, or any of his brothers, agony.

He never gave the fallen archangel the satisfaction of knowing how much it hurt. He simply placed the pen to the line and signed his own name. When he'd finished, he handed the pen back and waited.

He didn't have to wait long. Both pen and contract vanished. "I'll see you in a week, Vengeful One," Samael said softly. "Until then"—he smiled, raising a glass of red wine that Uriel hadn't seen him retrieve—"good luck."

Samael took a sip of the wine, and then he and his servant and the study they'd been standing in were gone. Uriel was back in his room, in the mansion. And the inside of his wrist was throbbing.

"You have to be on live television in less than an hour, Uriel. You can cancel, of course," Max told him, with faked nonchalance. "However, you'll then have to explain to Jacqueline Rain and the half of the world that watches her why you changed your mind and ruined her show with absolutely no warning whatsoever. Then there will be inquiries. Most likely, far too many for our particular comfort level."

Uriel shot Max an utterly exasperated look and again ran his hand through his hair. He was pacing back and forth across the foyer of the mansion and had been for the last twenty minutes. It was Monday afternoon and Jacqueline Rain was queen of Monday afternoons. This interview had been set up long ago and there was no way to cancel it. His mind was feverishly working, formulating the beginnings of a plan, and every interruption to his thoughts felt like a needle jammed through the pincushion of his mind.

Cars were waiting for him outside. The press had apparently gathered in the blocked-off street outside of the studio. Max's cell phone had been ringing so often and so loudly, the guardian had been forced to switch it off.

The world was waiting for him.

And he had less than six days to win the heart of his soul mate.

"You've made a deal with the Fallen One," Michael remarked from where he leaned against the banister, his well-muscled arms crossed over his chest. "I hope you have a plan."

Uriel had to hand it to the archangel. Michael was disappointed in him; that was a given. But the man was also intelligent and wise enough to know that berating Uriel at this juncture would do no one any good.

"I'm working on it."

Max stepped in front of him then, blocking his return progress across the marble floor of the foyer. "I'm sorry, Uriel," he said sternly. "But we have to go." He gave the archangel a no-nonsense look and added firmly, "Now."

Uriel took a deep breath and nodded. In truth, he was ready. He knew what he was going to do and he hoped, desperately, that it would work.

He turned to Gabriel, who was leaning casually on one of the many side tables that lined the foyer. "Gabe, I need you to do me a favor."

Gabriel uncrossed his own thick arms and straightened, his silver eyes coming to life. "What, then?" he asked. He and Uriel had their differences and none of them would argue that fact. But Gabriel knew good and well that this wasn't a time for petty disagreements or grudges. His brother's eternal freedom, as well as the safety of an archess, were both at stake.

"Make sure that Eleanore's watching channel fourteen at three o'clock today."

Gabriel nodded once. "That I can do." Archangels had the ability to manipulate ordinary, everyday things such as the channels on televisions or radios, the temperature of a fridge or a microwave, whether or not an air conditioner would work, and so forth. It was a power that felt a little like using a remote control or taking the elevator when you had perfectly good legs, so it wasn't one they used very often. However, it would come in handy today.

Uriel turned back to Max. "All right, let's get this over with."

Max nodded and led the way out of the mansion to the drive beyond. Right now, their ability to transport through a door in the mansion to any proximity they chose at a whim was certainly going to come in handy. If they hadn't been capable of such a feat, Uriel never would have made it to the studio on time. It was in California and they were in Texas at the moment.

"I hope you're at least learning a lesson in all of this," Max muttered as they ducked into the limousine and closed the door behind them.

"Don't worry, Max," Uriel replied as he took his seat across from him. "If not, I'm sure the other three will learn from my horrid mistake."

"Got another one, General."

"Let me see it." Kevin Trenton stepped forward, an apparently young man wearing army fatigue bottoms, combat boots, and a tight black T-shirt over his well-honed muscles.

He rested his palms on the desk on either side of the technician in front of him and gazed, with stark blue eyes, at the image on the computer screen. The map's center pulsed with the red glow of another recorded flux.

He was getting closer. He had mapped these anomalies all over the world and at first they had appeared random. But now . . . Now there was a definite pattern to them. They seemed to be centered on none other than the same extraordinary young woman that he had been watching for the last twenty years.

If this map was correct and these fluxes were any indication, he would be able to pinpoint her location—and the location she would soon be traveling to—with enough accuracy to trap her once and for all.

"Get the major on the phone. I want to speak with him privately."

"Yes, sir."

Kevin's eyes narrowed on the screen as if he were gazing at Eleanore Granger and not an electronic map. "You can run, little Ellie. But you can't hide." He smiled then, shaking his head. "Not for long, anyway."

Eleanore kept looking over her shoulder. The aisle was always either empty or occupied by a browsing customer—no wealthy media mogul motorcycle hunks. No Hollywood movie stars. Just her and the clientele. So why was she so nervous?

Because I've stepped into the Twilight Zone, *that's why*.

She closed her eyes for a moment and rested her forehead against the philosophy books she'd been reorganizing. She had a headache, but trying to heal herself of a headache would make her even more tired than she already was, and she knew from experience that it was best to save her energy in case something much more important arose. Like broken bones or heart attacks or little girls throwing up in the restroom.

So she'd taken some ibuprofen and, because she'd had no appetite, she'd taken them on an empty stomach. And now she had a fairly annoying case of acid indigestion to boot.

She sighed and tried to think of something positive to take her mind off the discomfort. She didn't have to wait long for a distraction.

Once more, over the hearth in the café, the giant plasma screen was powered to life. Janet Gomez, the woman who worked behind the counter, had the remote control in her hands and was glaring at it with what appeared to be frustration.

"This thing isn't working. The screen won't shut off," she muttered to herself.

Eleanore smiled, picked up another stack of books, and turned back toward the philosophy aisle. As she did, Janet apparently gave up and began flipping through the channels. Eleanore stopped to watch as faces and sounds whizzed past on the screen, until a very familiar face appeared and Janet instantly paused in her channel surfing.

"... Mr. Daniels, you're returning to the Southwest after the show to finish a bit of shooting for the sequel to *Comeuppance*, if I'm not mistaken."

Christopher Daniels, looking sexy as ever in a black T-shirt and jeans that did nothing to hide the tall, strong body beneath them, nodded. "Yes, that's right."

"And you'll be attending the Red Carpet Gala in Dallas on Thursday, I presume." It was Monday and Jacqueline Rain, the highly popular daytime talk show host was leaning forward in her chair.

Again, Daniels nodded, adding a brilliant smile.

"Have you got a date?" Rain asked, grinning suggestively. "It's only three days away."

Eleanore nearly dropped the books she was holding.

Daniels hesitated before answering, and the live audience, unseen to the cameras, very loudly encouraged his reply. He laughed and shook his head. "I can't say just yet."

Rain turned to the audience and shrugged helplessly. "What can I do, ladies? He's not talking!"

The audience laughed and the women cheered.

When they'd settled down a bit, Rain turned back to Daniels. "Well, I'm so sorry to say that we're coming to the end of our time here with you—"

Rain was interrupted by a tremendous uproar of boos and disappointed moans from her live audience. She turned a sympathetic smile upon them and laughed at the camera. Daniels had the amazing grace to blush.

The noise died down and Eleanore put down the books and began moving down the main aisle, her eyes unaccountably glued to the screen. The other employees and customers in the near vicinity had stopped what they were doing and found themselves watching as well. Daniels was a very charismatic man.

"I thought you didn't like him?" Janet sidled up next to Eleanore and nudged her with her elbow.

Eleanore felt heat creep up her neck. She shot Janet a begrudging look and shrugged what she hoped translated to nonchalance. "I never said I *do* like him."

"Yeah right." Janet rolled her eyes, a small smile tugging at her lips. "You're all talk."

On the screen, Jacqueline Rain turned back to Daniels and repeated what she had been saying before the outburst. "As I said, Christopher, I'm afraid we're just about done. But you mentioned earlier that there was something you needed to do before the show was over?"

"Yes." Christopher nodded, his green eyes glittering beneath the lights. "There is. Thank you."

Jacqueline sat back in her large leather chair and gestured for him to proceed.

Eleanore watched, in strange fascination, as Christopher turned directly toward the camera and gazed into it. The camera man zoomed in and the actor's beautiful features filled the screen, his eyes uncannily stark and intense.

She honestly felt, in that moment, that he was watching her, personally. It was ridiculous, wasn't it? But she could have sworn that he could see through the camera and across the miles—and that he was pinning her to the spot with that gaze.

"I'd like to ask a favor of one Eleanore Granger, the lovely bookstore angel who likes Valley of Shadow and Edgar Allan Poe."

What?

There was a beat of silence that must have been felt around the world.

And then Eleanore blinked. That wasn't right. There was no way he'd just said her name on national television. She seriously had him on the brain if that was what she thought she'd heard.

The audience suddenly "ooohed" and Jacqueline Rain chuckled, grinning broadly. "Eleanore Granger?" she repeated.

"Yes."

"Holy mother-flipping Jesus," Janet whispered beside her. "Is he talking about you? Did he just call you out in front of millions of people?"

Eleanore felt the blood rush from her face, a cold-and-hot mix of emotions washing over her. She experienced something like staggering shock, outright disbelief, a slightly numbing fear, and even unabashed gratification as the other employees began to gawk at her. The few customers around them took this as a cue and realized who she was. Then they too began to stare.

"Eleanore—Ellie." He said her name softly, enticingly, and very personally. "Will you do me the honor of accompanying me to the Red Carpet Gala on Thursday night?"

Again, the audience in Rain's studio cheered, and this time there was a definite nervous energy about them. Jacqueline Rain appeared delighted beyond imagination at the turn of events; it meant more publicity, of course, and that was always a good thing.

"Oh my God . . ." Janet whispered.

Eleanore shook her head. Her jaw was slack, her eyes wide.

"Girl, how many bookstore angels can there be by the name of Ellie Granger?" Janet turned toward her, grabbed her by the upper arms, and looked her in the eyes. "You must have made some kind of impression when he was here Saturday," she said, her expression stunned and her head shaking in disbelief.

Eleanore still couldn't talk. She just barely managed a shrug, and because Janet was holding her arms, it wasn't much of a shrug, at that.

"You have to go with him!" said Cynthia Washington, who had joined them in the café. Cynthia was a self-proclaimed "Brakes Flake." To her, Christopher Daniels was perfection—a god. There was no denying a god. "You absolutely have to accept the invitation," she reiterated breathlessly.

The café broke into a murmur of agreement, the customers and other employees wholeheartedly encouraging her to accept.

Eleanore looked from them back to the screen. The camera had left Daniels and was panning out over the audience, some of whom had very hastily created makeshift signs of loose-leaf paper and bolded text on cell phone screens. They all read, "Ellie, say yes!"

"Mom, calm down. It's no big deal—"

Eleanore fingered her right temple and squeezed her eyes shut. She'd never been more tempted to heal a simple headache before. It was fast becoming something more than a simple headache. Her mother and father were on the other end of the line, each with their own phones and both speaking at the same time.

"Honey, this is too much publicity. How did this fellow even meet you?" her father asked her.

"Walter, it was bound to happen eventually. I mean, think about it! It's not like our daughter is unattractive! Anyway, it doesn't matter how it happened; we have to deal with it now."

"Katherine, let her answer my question without interrupting for once—"

"I wouldn't have to interrupt if you'd stop drilling her with questions."

"Mom, Dad, seriously. You need to breathe. I'm okay, all right? Nothing has happened to me."

"Not yet, sweetheart. But before long, someone is going to snap a photo of you on their cell phone and your picture will go very, very public." Her mother sighed. "They found us once before, Ellie...."

Eleanore's stomach knotted, her headache instantly thrumming to full throttle. "I know, Mom." She wasn't going to forget. Not ever.

They fell into a temporary silence then, each of them trapped in memory.

Finally, her mother spoke up again. "I think you should contact Christopher Daniels's agent and tell him right off the bat that you want nothing to do with him. Then come up here for a month or two and let things calm down. We're secluded here," Katherine Granger reminded her. "A cabin in the woods, far from prying eyes."

"I hate to admit it, sweetheart, but your mother might be right about this. I know what a damper it's going to put on your social life." Her father sounded sad, and older than his fifty years. "But, though we both want you to have friends, this is just too public. This is too big. We need to phase you out."

Phase me out? Eleanore's brain was buzzing. It was spinning and sliding and dancing and nothing made sense anymore. She had run from who she was her entire life. It was harder than it would seem to have to keep a very, very low profile. It was incredibly difficult never being able to go to an actual university, never going into veterinary medicine as she'd wanted to—never dating or making lasting friendships in any one place because she was constantly afraid she might slip up.

Now, despite everything she'd endured and every precaution she'd taken, the world had found her and spotlighted her. And she had to run again.

"I have to go, guys. I'll call you later tonight."

"Honey, wait—"

Eleanore hung up and powered down the phone. Then she turned and threw the cell phone across her living room with all the strength she could muster. It hit the far wall, put a dent in the plaster, and then tumbled to the carpet.

She straightened and peered at the remarkably tough electronic device and then turned to gaze into the fireplace. The flames crackled and spoke to her in a hissed, ancient language. She tried to calm down; a crackling fire usually did the trick. But it was harder this time.

Images of that experience ten years ago coasted through her mind's eye. There was the danger, the needle, the noise and chaos, and overriding it all, the fear of separation from her parents and everything solid and real in her life.

Her parents were right, and that was the worst of it.

Eleanore was admittedly frightened, but she was also very angry. How *dare* Christopher bring that kind of attention upon her? How could she have trusted him? Let him into her apartment?

Kissed him?

Oh, she was definitely mad. And, then again, there was another emotion riding her frayed nerves at that moment, sending her dancing dangerously close to emotional overload. She was upset and scared, but she also kept seeing those jade-colored eyes. And that tall, rock-hard body. She thought of the way he'd pinned her and bruised her lips with his kiss as if he were a man gripped by desperation. She'd felt as if only she could save him.

Despite her fury, her body responded to the thought. Every time she imagined any part of him or heard his name or saw his picture on a poster, she grew flushed. Anxious.

Wet.

"Oh, crap," she muttered, running her hands over her face as she slid down the wall to sit on the carpet.

I'm in so much trouble.

She wondered, suddenly, how long it would be before some gossip magazine or newspaper or even news-channel reporter made it to her front door. It wouldn't take long to find out where she lived now that they knew her name and where she worked. That was what the Internet was for. And the media was relentless.

Media . . . Eleanore frowned as a thought occurred to her. Samuel Lambent was a media mogul. Hell, he probably owned every stupid paper and magazine and news channel that might decide to come and question her over the next few days.

I could go to him, she thought hesitantly. *I could ask him for a favor. After all, I saved his life.*

He could protect her from the media—make her invisible to them.

But, as quickly as the thought entered her mind, she roughly shoved it away. "No," she told herself firmly. "I'll deal with this myself." Her mother was right. She needed to nip this in the bud right away. But she wouldn't go through Christopher's agent. She would go through the movie star himself.

She imagined he would probably get in touch with her personally before Saturday. She had no way to contact him, after all, so the ball was entirely in his court. And when he did contact her, she would give him a piece of her mind. Best to face things head-on. Right?

No, Ellie. You need to run.

The thought whizzed through her mind like a firefly on a moonless night. It was bright and it was sudden and it was impossible to ignore. It was also probably true. But she ignored it anyway, stood back up, and strode through her apartment toward her bedroom. It was time for a long shower and a dreamless sleep.

*   *   *

From his perch outside her bedroom window, the former Angel of Death watched the woman sleep. She was beyond lovely; her eyelashes were so long that they brushed her cheeks. Her hair shimmered in the moonlight, and her smooth skin was pale and perfect.

Her chest rose and fell in slow rhythm. She was under deep.

Azrael had been sent to watch over her after Uriel's little public display that afternoon. He watched a vein pulse in her neck, blue in the moonlight, inviting in its innocent offer.

Azrael smiled a slow smile and shook his head. Uriel was a very lucky archangel.

CHAPTER SEVEN

Traffic was bad this morning, even for a Tuesday. It took Eleanore a full twenty minutes to get from Frankford to a block from the Starbucks on the corner of University and Eighty-second Street. That was virtually unheard of in a town the size of hers.

Luckily, she had been up early, dreams of Daniels once more rousing her from sleep. So it hadn't been as difficult as it normally was to shower, get dressed, and hop in the car for a coffee run before opening the store.

That last block before Eleanore was finally able to pull into the lot and join the masses of SUVs and pickup trucks waiting in the drive-through was as slow as Christmas. The light took forever to change; it took so long she actually thought it was broken. The drivers were being rude, not allowing anyone to make left turns. The sun was just beginning to peek over the horizon, and its harsh rays were blinding people who were already squinting from lack of sleep.

It was one of those mornings.

As Eleanore let her MINI Cooper idle in the long line, she rolled up her windows and pressed a few buttons on the CD player. The music poured over and around her and she momentarily closed her eyes.

She'd almost managed to relax when she heard the scream of tires burning on rubber. It was a sudden, terrifying sound that ripped through Eleanore, silencing the music, the hum of her motor, and her own dizzying thoughts. For the second time that week, she felt herself moving in slow motion, weighed down by the dreadful knowledge that bad things were about to happen.

And they did.

The burning scream continued for devastatingly long seconds and was joined by another, second screeching cacophony. Eleanore turned in the thick, molasses air to watch through her window as a pickup truck veered to the left, bumped the curb going way too fast, and then flipped, rolling over a white sedan and then slamming into an SUV in the right lane.

Across the intersection, more cars skidded to unsteady stops, their bumpers crunching, the telephone pole coming down to smash a parked car beneath it.

It all probably happened in the course of seconds. But in Eleanore's eyes, it looked like lifetimes. Several of them. Births and childhoods and marriages and careers and retirements—there in one instant and gone in the next. It was the kind of accident that people looked on with muted horror because they knew that people had been hurt, and most likely killed.

It was with a strange resignation and a detached awareness that Eleanore realized she'd left her car. She was running across the parking lot and toward the intersection. She couldn't feel the ground beneath her feet or hear anything past the rush of blood in her ears. Her body moved of its own accord, as if she were trapped in a dream and watching herself from above.

The closest vehicle was the white sedan. Its roof was caved in and the old man behind the wheel was trapped between the metal above him and the seat below him. But Eleanore knew that he was all right. It was an instinctive and natural thing with her. She had always been able to read people for injury and illness. The man was terrified and he'd wet himself. But other than a few scratches from the glass, he was unharmed.

Her sense of unease grew, however, when she vaulted

over the hood of the sedan, ignoring the scrapes it caused to her own flesh, and ran to the second vehicle that had been caught in the fray.

The SUV.

"Oh God. No, no, no, no . . ." She was speaking and barely realized it, hearing her voice from far off—high pitched, desperate, a cry and a sob and a whisper of pleading.

There was a child in the backseat. Very young . . . But the car seat she was in was crushed beneath her, and the door had been shoved into the side of her small, delicate body.

She was unconscious and drenched in blood, as was her father in the front seat. The driver's side of the entire vehicle had been viciously crumpled inward. She sensed broken ribs and internal bleeding. She sensed concussions and a ruptured organ and a heartbeat that was steadily slowing. Slowing . . .

With a cry of determined alarm, Eleanore reached her arm through the shattered back window, placing her palm against the toddler's bloodied head. In flashes of pain and disorder, she recognized the injuries within the girl's body, noting that it was indeed the child's heart that was giving out. There wasn't much time.

Something was happening up ahead. He could sense it before it went down—a thrumming kind of hum in the air that vibrated his spine and set his teeth on edge. He found himself leaning forward in his seat until Max looked over at him from the opposite seat and frowned.

"Is there something wrong?"

"Yes," Uriel replied. His green gaze was trained in the far distance, at some point blocks away, where there seemed to be some kind of traffic jam. A crowd was gathering around an SUV.

Awareness shot through him like a bolt of electricity. "Max, it's Eleanore!"

*   *   *

Eleanore was unaware that she was being watched. All around her, people gathered, some calling 911, others pointing, still others using their cell phones to take photographs that would later become grisly accounts of life and death on the streets of Texas.

A few were tending to the relatively uninjured woman in the pickup truck that had initially caused the wreck. The police would later find that she'd been texting when the light had changed; she hadn't looked up in time to see the cars in front of her slow and stop.

Still other bystanders were trying to calm down the panicking elderly man in the white sedan. But no one came near Eleanore. Instead, they looked on with wide eyes and spoke to one another in hushed tones.

. . . Her hand is glowing. . . . No, I swear. I'm not shitting you . . .

. . . Holy fuck—is she? She is! She's healing that little girl!

. . . I swear to Christ, I'm not seeing this; you wouldn't believe me. . . .

. . . Take a picture!

Eleanore heard none of it, was aware of none of it, and only saw the body beneath her touch and felt the soul that clung to it in desperation. She focused on her little heart first. She willed it to keep beating, promising it that she would give it the blood it needed to keep up the fight. Then she mended the gash in the girl's liver. Next was the punctured lung; she had to move the ribs back in place and mend them in order to make it work.

As she concentrated, Eleanore grew weak. The wounds were fatal, as they had been for Samuel Lambent. There was so much damage, so very much to make right.

Several seconds and twenty eternities later, she pulled her hand away and slumped against the side of the car. Wearily, she noted the people around her. They were blurred though, half there and half not, less substantial to her than the dying man in the front seat.

The girl's father.

I won't let you die. . . .

With renewed determination, Eleanore pushed off of the crumpled metal and turned toward the front of the car once more.

Dad was hanging in there. But he was losing a lot of blood. If she didn't heal him soon, he would lose too much. Sirens wailed in the distance. But it was such a far, far distance. . . . Eleanore reached in and placed her right hand over the man's crushed chest. Ribs were broken. A lung was punctured here, too. Several vertebrae were knocked out of place.

It took her forever to heal him. She felt as if she were shoving a five-hundred-pound boulder up a muddy forty-five-degree-angle slope. Finally, she felt the last rib click into place and the man's life stabilize beneath her touch.

Her legs gave out from under her then, and the world tipped on its axis. She could hear the people gathered around and understood what they were saying, despite the fact that the sentences were melded together. She could see their faces—dangerous strangers, looming above her and all around her. She knew it was over now.

All of her running. All of her hiding. It would end this morning, on this street. They would come and take her away and drug her up to keep her from fighting, and she would live out the remainder of her life strapped to a hard bed with bleached sheets and the scent of antiseptic in the air.

"Please . . ." She meant to say, "Please don't take me away," but her vocal cords gave life to only the one word. It was all they could manage before they, too, gave out.

Had she killed herself? She wondered this, as she closed her eyes against the flood of reality. She'd never saved two lives like this. She'd never healed so many horrible, horrible wounds.

I went too far, she thought, as she felt strong arms lift

her from the pebbly ground and clutch her to a hard chest.

Warmth enveloped her. There was the smell of leather, and there was someone breathing softly against her ear.

"You're safe, Ellie. Rest. I have you. You're safe. . . ." Fingers gripped her tight; bands of steel held her firm. She knew she was being moved, and quickly. But she was so exhausted and so far gone that she could no longer keep oblivion at bay.

It won, in the end, that dark nothingness to which the helpless go. Whatever would happen would happen. She could only pray—and sleep.

With a surge of mind-blowing possessiveness and protectiveness, Uriel shoved his way through the crowd to his soul mate, who was now lying on her back in the road, her beautiful blue eyes closed against the madness around her.

She had healed the little girl and her father. He knew it as if he had watched it himself. She had been in the right place at the right time and had witnessed the accident. And the archess in her had leapt to the fore in order to protect those who were not as powerful as she was. She drained herself, placing herself in the public eye and in extreme danger in order to save two innocents from certain death. And the people around her repaid her kindness by ogling her, snapping photographs, and filming her on their cell phones.

A few of them snapped photos of him now as well. *Christopher Daniels!*

Uriel bent over his archess and scooped her up into his arms. She was so light—it was as if her power had literally drained her of substance. He whispered to her, trying to console her slight form, and as he did, he felt hot tears stinging his eyes. In a show of righteous anger that he had no ability to control, Uriel turned to face the onlookers once more.

His emerald eyes were glowing bright with the wrath

coursing through him. His teeth bared, he straightened to his full height and bellowed into the crowd, "Get *back*!" His order was unnaturally loud, carrying over the din of confusion and amazement that the intersection had become.

In the next instant, and out of a clear blue sky, lightning struck a parked vehicle in the black lot on one corner of the intersection. Thunder pierced the sky, drawing shrieks of surprise from half of the people in the streets. Others ducked, shielding their heads protectively as another bolt hit the top of a building, eliciting a second peal of thunder that rocked the earth beneath their feet and bellowed in human eardrums.

The crowd began scrambling back away from Uriel, whose eyes were lit with an eerie and unnatural fire. On the sidewalk across from him, a limousine pulled up and skidded to a loud halt. But the sound of its tires squealing against the pavement was drowned out when another bolt of lightning struck down and the people scattered in fear.

Uriel rushed toward the car with Eleanore in his arms and the door was opened for him before he reached it. He ducked into the back and Max stepped out onto the sidewalk.

Uriel laid Eleanore out on one of the seats and turned his burning gaze on his guardian. "Deal with them," he growled.

Max Gillihan swallowed and nodded. He had never seen Uriel like this. And the errant lightning was a new thing; Uriel could not normally control the weather. It was all disconcerting, but Max had little time to think on it. Human minds needed to be cleansed of their recent memories. Cell phones and cameras needed to be wiped. Conversations had to be traced and dealt with.

That was part of his job.

So Max slammed the car door shut and nodded to the limo driver, who pulled away without further ado, leaving the guardian to his arduous task.

*   *   *

The sun coming up over the lake in Chicago never failed to take Samael's breath away.

It was something he never would have known, nor would have been able to appreciate, from where he used to reside, in a place where the sun never set to begin with.

But without night, there could be no day. And it took a human existence to understand such a thing. Samael knew that this was why the Old Man would never fully be capable of empathizing with the people who lived and breathed on his planet. He was too far removed from them; his hands were too clean, dusted off with finality long, long ago.

Now, from the sixty-sixth floor of the Willis building, which most people still called the Sears Tower out of habit and a grudging respect, Samael could believe that he had made the right choice. Right here, right now, with those pink-purple-orange reflections gleaming off of the water and the blood-sweat-and-tears creations of man—it was easy.

Samael took a deep breath and let it out slowly. He closed his eyes as the first beam of light hit his window, warming it from the outside. He placed his palms against the glass and absorbed the heat, needing it as much as did the human world down below.

"My lord?"

Slowly, and with quiet, slightly irritated deliberation, Samael lowered his hands and turned around. He and his "staff" were alone on their floor today. Otherwise, Jason would not have addressed him in such a manner.

"What is it?"

"You'll want to see this, sir." The handsome young man held a folder in his hand. It looked a lot like the manila folder that had held Eleanore Granger's personal information. Jason strode forward and held it out for his master.

Samael took it and opened it to the first page. He was met with the photograph of a young woman gazing at him with hazel eyes that nearly glowed in a tanned, smiling face.

"This photograph was taken in Brisbane, Australia, two days ago," Jason told him as Samael absorbed the woman's beauty, his fingertips tracing over the rich brown curls that cascaded to her shoulders and behind her back. "One of Darion's men snapped it, my lord—after watching the woman heal an injured surfer."

Samael's head snapped up, his charcoal-gray eyes darkening. "Did anyone else see this?"

"No, sir." Jason shook his head once. "Darion was not in his human form and the surfer was unconscious. She pulled him out of the water, tended to him, and ran from the scene. Darion and one of his men followed her throughout the remainder of the day until they took this photograph that night, as she was dining with friends."

Samael thought this over. His dark eyes were glittering with untold machinations. He looked back down at the pages in his hand, reading her name. "Juliette Anderson," he whispered.

The second archess. Like Eleanore, she, too, was strikingly beautiful. They were nearly as different as night and day in hair color and complexion. But there was a likeness to them as well. It was incredibly subtle, whatever it was; he couldn't quite give name to it.

"I wonder," he said then, running his hand over her photograph once more, "who *she* belongs to."

It was with a slow and highly unsettled uncertainty that Eleanore came rising back into consciousness. Her eyelids were heavy, but there was light behind them. Not a blue light or a muted light, as one would find in a hospital room or under fluorescents. This was sunlight.

That's a good sign, she thought meekly.

She concentrated on listening then. She expected to hear buzzing sounds, like the flickering of halogen bulbs. She expected the jingling of keys on chains or the melodic, muted tones of people pressing the buttons on code keypads. But there was none of this. Instead, there was the gentle crackling and popping of a fire in a hearth. And there was warmth.

And the feeling that she was being watched.

Eleanore turned her head and opened her eyes. Her vision was blurry, but through it, she saw the fuzzy outline of a face and body beside the bed. It leaned forward and a lock of her hair was gently brushed from her forehead.

"Take it easy," he said. "You're safe here, Ellie. I won't let anyone hurt you." The figure moved back again and she heard the creaking of a wooden chair beneath him. She recognized his voice this time when he added, "Rest as long as you need to." He sighed and she saw him run a hand through dark brown hair. "God knows you've earned it."

Though she couldn't see it clearly, she knew that his brown hair was thick and a little too long to be conventional. And she also knew that his eyes were green; the kind of ultra light green that was next to impossible to get without contacts.

And if she hadn't felt as if she had been run over by a Mack truck, she would have sat up in that bed right then and there and decked him.

"You asshole . . ." she whispered, her voice a hoarse scratching of what it had been earlier that morning. She swallowed, blinked, and forced herself to go on. "You had no right . . . selfish . . . spoiled . . . überbrat . . ." She breathed the last part, the effort utterly and completely wearing her out.

Christopher Daniels was still beside the bed. She blinked a few times as his figure came increasingly into focus. She wondered what he was thinking.

His beautiful form sharpened and cleared just as he threw back his head and laughed heartily, deep and full, the sound like a salve on Eleanore's body and soul. It soothed away her fear and somehow smoothed over the rougher parts of her indignant fury.

She frowned, watching him, bewildered by the fact

that she was so fascinated with the sound of his voice and the warmth that his nearness afforded her.

Finally, he straightened, lowering his head, his smile lighting up his face the way it did on the silver screen. But *this* smile was just for her. And his green eyes sparkled with emotion that was not faked; he wasn't acting now.

"You're absolutely right, Ellie. I should not have done what I did." He seemed to ponder something for a moment, silent and contemplative. Then he asked softly, "Will you consider forgiving me?"

Eleanore licked her lips and whispered, "Too tired to forgive you."

"I think I can do something about that," he said then, and stood. She watched as he moved away from the bed and two other men stepped forward. She blinked and frowned.

They were extremely handsome, both of them. One had black hair and gray-silver eyes and looked as though he spent a lot of time outdoors; he was tan and scruffy and had a five-o'clock shadow. The dark tone of his skin caused his eyes to stand out with such severe intensity, they seemed to almost glow in the handsome frame of his face.

The other man had wavy blond hair and very, very blue eyes. They looked like light, clear sapphires as they gazed down at her.

Two more men with impossible eye color. Goose bumps rose on her flesh and she was helpless to stop the flush of a blush that warmed her neck and cheeks. She wanted to shake her head at the circumstances; they were just too improbable. But she was too weak. What the hell *was* this, anyway? These kinds of men didn't really exist. Was this some kind of gorgeous actor convention? Was Richard Armitage in here somewhere, too?

"Eleanore, my name is Michael," the blond man explained softly as he took Christopher's seat and leaned forward.

Tall, dark, and handsome stood beside him and nodded a greeting. "I'm Gabriel," he said, watching her closely. He had the slightest Scottish brogue that curled the edges of his words with an ancient sort of elegance.

Very gently, the blond one placed his hand on Eleanore's exposed arm. For some reason, though he was a complete stranger, she didn't want to pull away. His touch didn't frighten her. It was warm and comforting and as inexplicable as it seemed, Eleanore *trusted* him.

"This is going to be hard for you to accept at first, but you aren't the only one in the world who possesses the ability to heal others," he told her. His tone remained calm, his voice even. He spoke slowly and waited for her to process his words. "I can do it as well," he said, flashing white teeth in a humble smile.

Eleanore didn't know what to say to that. Obviously, the cat was out of the bag on her abilities. She wondered how much damage had been done. All of those people—all of those cell phones . . . and the little girl and her father. Were they okay? Had it been worth it?

Beside her, Michael closed his eyes and Eleanore felt her arm heat up under his palm. For a half second, she was afraid that it would heat up too much and that she would get burned. But instead of building, the heat spread—up her arm, across her chest, up her neck, and down through her stomach and into her limbs.

She closed her own eyes and exhaled, allowing her head to roll to the side as Michael's healing magic did its job. She could feel her strength returning to her. It was like being uncovered and lifted from the grave after being buried alive. She had never been on the receiving end of this kind of power. It was wondrous. She almost wanted to get hurt again just so that she could keep feeling it.

Gabriel laughed, and Eleanore vaguely noticed that his chuckle was as charismatic in its deep timbre as Christopher Daniels's was. "I think the lass is feelin' a wee bit better."

"Are you an actor, too?" she found herself asking, as

if she were intoxicated and there was no filter for her thoughts.

Gabriel's eyebrows shot up, his expression at once bemused and disgusted at the insinuation. "No, lass. But speakin' of actin'," he said as he turned to shoot Christopher a pointed look.

Michael looked up as well and Eleanore glanced from one to the other, waiting.

Michael nodded. "I think that it's high time you two had a long talk." He stood and stepped away from the bed, the muscles in his tall form rippling beneath his jeans and T-shirt just as Christopher's always did.

Eleanore took it as a cue. She put her arms beneath her and sat up in the bed, at once marveling at how easy it was to move. Only seconds before, she'd been nearly positive her own heart would soon stop beating from sheer exhaustion. Now, however, she felt she could sign up for a marathon and make it at *least* half of the way through. And running wasn't even her thing.

She removed the covers and swung her feet over the side of the bed. Now that she was no longer horizontal, she could see the vastness of the room. It resembled Samuel Lambent's rented home in its grandiose size and the fine quality of its decor. The fireplace was marble, the walls were hung in fine Renaissance art, and the marble floors were covered in thick plush rugs, all done in muted, tasteful tones.

Christopher was back beside the bed now, kneeling so that they were at eye level. "How do you feel?" he asked quietly.

Eleanore looked down at him and a dangerous thought flashed through her mind.

The one called Gabriel cleared his throat. "Uh, Uriel, I would no'—"

Eleanore didn't notice that Gabriel had called him by another name. She wasn't paying Michael or Gabriel any attention at all, in fact. Her hand was balled into a fist, her gaze quickly narrowing. At the moment, all of her focus was on one thing and one thing only.

With every ounce of rejuvenated energy she possessed, Eleanore brought her right arm back and drove it forward into Christopher's jaw. His head snapped to the side and he toppled backward, away from the bed.

With renewed vigor and the delightfully jubilant impression that something in her world *finally* made sense, Eleanore stood up. She was not at all weak or unsteady.

"You wanted to know if I would forgive you?" she asked lightly, feeling an honest-to-God spring in her step as she bounced on the balls of her feet and gazed down at the handsome man who was gingerly rubbing his chin. "Well, of *course* I will," she chimed, smiling sweetly at him.

Michael, who was obviously trying as hard not to laugh as Gabriel was, held up his hands in placation when Daniels glared up at the two of them. The blond man's lips pressed together in a tight smile that held back his apparent amusement. He shrugged helplessly. "Gabe tried to warn you, man."

CHAPTER EIGHT

There are several different ways that one can react when faced with news that is either highly improbable—or incredibly bad. You can scream and cry, or laugh at a really high pitch while you simultaneously hyperventilate. You can also refuse to believe it outright and, in extreme cases, shut down altogether.

Unless you're a woman who has the ability to command lightning, move objects, and heal chicken pox.

"Prove it." Eleanore sat back in the wooden chair at the table and crossed her legs. She folded her arms over her chest and waited patiently. Healing was one thing. She'd been able to do that since she was two.

But the things these men were claiming were farfetched on a good day. And it hadn't exactly been a good day. They'd told her, quite bluntly, that they were archangels who had come down to Earth two thousand years ago in order to find their "archesses," who, apparently, were their female angel soul mates. That, in and of itself, was quite a good story.

In addition, they claimed that they each had more or less the same powers except that Michael was able to heal wounds and Azrael was able to do a *lot* of things the others couldn't. This seemed sort of a strange twist to their tale, but they wouldn't elaborate and apparently "Azrael" wasn't there to speak for himself.

They claimed supernatural strength, telekinesis, a

vague control over the elements, the ability to forecast weather with absolute accuracy, and a talent for speaking, reading, and writing any language in the world. On top of that, they claimed they were able to use weapons in ways human warriors could only dream.

The men in front of her looked to one another, thrown off by her request.

"I'm waiting," she said, shrugging and arching her brows.

"Okaaay ..." The man whose name she'd always thought was Christopher Daniels, but who now claimed he was the archangel named Uriel, narrowed his gaze in consideration and shoved his hands into the pockets of his jeans. He shifted his booted feet and cocked his head to one side. "What exactly did you have in mind?" His starkly colored eyes sparkled in the firelight.

He's still incredibly sexy, she thought, *whatever the hell his name is.*

She remembered his kiss, began to blush, and quickly looked at the floor. "Well, I don't know." She shrugged again. "Can't you sprout wings or something?" Gabriel laughed in that deep voice of his, and Eleanore shot him a sideways glance. "Well, can't you?" she reiterated.

"No' exactly." Gabriel shook his head.

"We gave up those forms when we came down here," Michael told her.

"How convenient," Eleanore deadpanned.

The men looked at one another, seemingly helpless until Eleanore sighed heavily. "Look, it's not hard. Just show me."

"Christ," Gabriel swore, shooting Uriel a dirty look. "If my archess wants you to dance the bloody jig, you'd better sodding well do it," he told him flatly. Then he turned and, without warning, he reached his right arm out toward the fire in the hearth.

In answer, it leapt to sudden life and proceeded to shoot forward a good twenty feet from the fireplace, drawing an alarmed squeal from Eleanore. She leapt from the chair she was in, instinctively preparing to either run or exert some paranormal control over the fire should it start to spread, but she was saved the trouble when the fire suddenly froze into solid ice.

Eleanore stood stock-still and stared at the wondrous sculpture of nature. It crackled much like a fire would, and shimmered where it hovered a few feet above the marble floor, a column of frozen water that had grown out of its elemental opposite.

She had no opportunity to comment on the display of Gabriel's power, however, as the task slipped from one brother to another within a split second and Uriel took up the reins. He raised his arms at his sides and every piece of furniture in the room, including the chair Eleanore had been seated in just a few seconds ago, rose steadily from the ground and then began spinning slowly above their heads.

Eleanore stared, open-mouthed, at the display. She could move objects, too, but she'd never tried so many objects, or anything heavier than a chair. Using her powers tended to drain her badly.

Uriel smiled, cocked his head to one side, and the furniture spun faster and faster until it became a blur of leather and textile. When it stopped, it had transformed. The love seat was now a fainting couch. The couch, a divan.

There were several beats of stunned silence. And then Uriel set the pieces back down on the marble floor.

Eleanore looked on with wide eyes as Gabriel and Uriel then turned to Michael. He shrugged and smiled at Eleanore. "You've already seen some of what I can do," he told her in a friendly tone, reminding her that he had, in fact, healed her. "Do you believe us now?"

"I think that's enough, boys," a voice suddenly said from the archway that led to the foyer and the exit to the mansion beyond.

Eleanore recognized the man who had spoken as

Max Gillihan, who she knew was the agent to Christopher Daniels.

Uriel, Eleanore corrected herself.

Eleanore's gaze narrowed on Gillihan as he pulled his glasses from his face and tucked them into his front suit pocket. He made his way to a large overstuffed leather chair and sank into it, crossing his legs at the knees.

"Miss Granger isn't buying it."

"Buying it?" Eleanore asked, instantly bristling from the man's tone.

"Oh, you believe well enough that these men have powers—much like you do, Miss Granger. But that isn't why we're here, is it?" It wasn't a question. Eleanore knew what he meant. He meant that she accepted their abilities because she, too, had those abilities and it was therefore hard for her to ignore that such things were possible.

It was the claim that they were angels—*archangels*, no less—that she wasn't buying.

"Miss Granger, I know why this is hard for you to accept."

Eleanore pinned the agent with a hard blue gaze. "Oh?" she asked, getting somewhat irritated now. "And what part do you play in all of this, Mr. Gillihan?" He was an agent for a movie star. What did he have to do with this, exactly?

"Max isn't just my agent," Uriel told her, as if he could read her thoughts. "He's our guardian and has been for thousands of years."

"Yes," Gillihan continued, his tone gentle, his voice quiet. Then, as if to brush the subject under the rug, he went back to what he was saying. "And the reason this is hard for you to accept is because if you believe that Uriel and his brothers are angels, then it means that you must make the next logical leap and accept that you, too, are an angel. An archess, to be precise."

"Now, listen." Eleanore gritted her teeth and pointed

at the man. "Let's just get one thing straight right here and now, shall we?" She took a deep breath and shook her head. "I'm no angel," she told him flatly. "You have *no* idea what kinds of things I have done in my life. You have no idea what kind of person I am. This is preposterous." She shook her head again and threw her hands up in the air.

Then she closed her eyes, weighing her words. "I can see that you're all very special. Hurray for you that you can do the things you can do. But I don't like being lied to. My life is complicated enough, and frankly," she said, her tone lowering meaningfully, "I don't believe in angels."

"I don't blame you," Max said matter-of-factly. "The world you live in bears too many battle scars. There is too much unexplained pain and loss and even I will admit as much."

Eleanore frowned, her gaze narrowing. "What's that supposed to mean?"

"Nothing," Max said. "I just understand where you're coming from. But that doesn't change the fact that Uriel, Michael, Gabriel, and Azrael are archangels—and so are you."

Eleanore's hands curled into fists, her teeth grinding in irritation. "I'm *not* the kind of person that ..." She fished around for the right term, growing more frustrated by the second, until finally, she gave up and simply pointed up. "That *He* chooses to make into an angel. Believe me. I'm just a human. And not a very good one at that."

"Not one of us is going to believe that for a second, Ellie," Uriel said from behind her. She hadn't realized he'd moved to stand so close beside her. She spun around to face him, her blue-black hair flying around her as her dark gaze met his. He was smiling a very slight smile. Like his brothers, he wore tight clothing over well-developed muscles, which she could see moving gracefully beneath his long-sleeved thermal tee.

How fucking distracting.

"What the hell would you know?" she asked him, trying to keep her tone calm and her attention off his body.

"I know that you risked your own life to save two strangers this morning," he told her. "You'd have to be a very tricky bad guy with a good imagination and a really complicated plan for you to have fit that scenario into your design."

"Anyone with my ability would have done the same," she said, shaking her head wearily.

"Bullshit." Uriel's gaze narrowed. "If there's anything I know about humans, it's that most of them are assholes. I've spent enough time punishing the worst of them to be well aware of that."

Eleanore frowned, confused. "Punishing them?" she asked, finding that her voice had dropped in volume.

There was a brief but heavy silence, pregnant with untold secrets. And then Michael cleared his throat from where he was leaning against the mantle of the fireplace. "Uriel used to be the Angel of Vengeance."

Eleanore blinked. She felt strange and disconnected. As if she'd been catapulted none too gently into some bizarre dream. "The Angel of Vengeance?" she asked. She'd never paid much attention to Christian mythology, so she was thrown by what she was hearing. She heard herself speaking but wasn't sure whether she could be held responsible for her words at this point. "As in flaming sword, justice, smiting the sinners—stuff like that?" Her voice was nearly a whisper now.

Uriel said nothing. His eyes were glowing again.

Glowing, Eleanore realized, as if lights had been switched on behind them—unnatural and beautiful and oh, so wrong.

The archangel nodded at last, admitting the truth. And, in that instant, Eleanore knew that it was all true. *All* of it. "You . . ." She felt dizzy. She closed her eyes and ran her hand over her face, trying to cool it off. The world had become a confusing, chaotic, senseless, feverish carnival ride and Eleanore wanted off. "You mean to tell me that you punish people—you strike them down or whatever it is you do ... but you never ... *help* them?"

No one answered her. She looked up at Uriel and then at Michael. And then at Gabriel and at Max. She met their eyes, one at a time, as she said, "Women are raped over and over again in Sudan, you know." Her tone had dropped; her voice had become quieter. "Children—they're just little girls." She remembered reading the articles and the images their words had called up. "They're raped and beaten and tortured and then shot to death or sliced to pieces with a machete. Some are cooked and eaten." She swallowed hard, forcing down sudden bile. "And the men who do this go unpunished. ..."

She shook her head and looked back at Uriel. "And where are you while all of this is happening? Oh, right. You're on TV. Talking with Jacqueline Rain. You're on the big screen, flashing fake fangs for teenyboppers in Hollister jeans and Hot Topic T-shirts." She laughed, the sound harsh and cold even to her own ears. "You're fucking famous," she accused. "The Angel of Vengeance is famous."

"Eleanore, there's something you need to understand—" Michael began, but Eleanore saved him the trouble of continuing. She spun on the blond archangel and fixed him with a look that she knew reflected all of the righteous wrath she was feeling in that moment. "And *you* ... Which angel were you, Michael? Don't tell me you're *Michael*—as in *the* Michael? Wow. And here you are in this gorgeous marble mansion when tornadoes and hurricanes are killing children, and cancer and AIDS are running rampant, and things like religion and race are breeding wars that never end. Why is that? Don't have a magic spell for those things, Michael?" It wasn't really a question. And wisely, Michael didn't try to answer it.

"No. Of course not." Ellie shook her head resolutely

and closed her eyes, both weary and desperate to convince herself of what she was saying. "Because if you did, surely you would have used it by now."

"We never had those abilities, Eleanore," Michael told her. He had straightened, pushing himself off of the wall, and now there was a good deal of calm influence behind his words. "Even before we were given human form, we were anything but omnipotent." He looked at the floor and shrugged helplessly. "It's something that people have never understood."

Eleanore wasn't placated in the least. If anything, his words made her angrier. "What you're all telling me is that angels are really nothing but holy parlor tricks?" she said softly. "Beautiful and bright and sort of flashy— but utterly fucking useless?" She whispered the last bit, turning in place to meet each of their gazes as she quietly but firmly put the accusation out into the open.

It was a challenge, of sorts. She wanted them to tell her she was wrong. She was daring them—practically begging them—to prove otherwise.

But none of them could accept such a challenge, because in the end, she knew she was right. Whatever their reasons, they had failed to save the world from the evil within it. And they would lose.

"I'm no angel," Eleanore repeated. "I am *not* one of you."

Though she had yet to raise her voice, she was clearly disgusted now; Uriel could feel her ire making his skin cold and his face hot. He felt like a starving man looking down into the water to watch a giant fish sniff at the worm on a hook—and then turn and swim hastily away.

He was losing her. He would never win her back now; she was slipping from his grasp. Because she hated him. She hated *all* of them. And from her perspective, she had every right to. Hell, he couldn't blame her either.

Uriel stuffed his hands into his pockets, his lips pressed into a grim line. He felt the bracelet then;

smooth metal caressed his fingertips. He closed his eyes as his heart rate picked up and his stomach did a flip. There was always that. As a last resort. If Ellie chose to fight them on this and refused to stay at the mansion, she would be easy pickings for Samael. He couldn't let that happen.

And speaking of the Fallen One, Uriel couldn't even begin to tell her about Samael until she at least accepted who she was. The one depended upon the other.

Eleanore finally lowered her head to rub her eyes. After a long pause of silence, she whispered, "I want to go home."

"It won't be safe for you there," Max told her. "I may have missed someone at the site of the accident this morning and we mustn't forget the broadcasted message that Christopher Daniels sent out." Here, he paused and shot Uriel a pointed look.

"Hey, she said she forgave me for that."

Gillihan rolled his eyes. "I'm afraid that in any case, you're better off remaining here until we can determine the best and safest course of action from this point on."

Again, Eleanore was silent and, not for the first time since knowing her, Uriel found himself wishing that he'd possessed Azrael's ability to read minds. He wondered what she was thinking.

Finally, she sighed and her shoulders slumped. "This is all just too much. . . ."

Max was up and out of his seat in a flash. He strode toward her, his expression one of deep understanding and concern. "I know, Ellie," he said as he came to stand before her and offered her his hand.

She looked up at him and, for some reason, she took it. Uriel was impressed but not surprised. Max just had that way with people. . . .

"We will figure this out," the guardian told her gently, giving her hand a squeeze. "In the meantime, we can have whatever you need brought from your apartment to the mansion."

"I need to call my parents," she mumbled. From the tone of her voice, she sounded numb. It was a sort of soft monotone, without inflection; a distracted kind of muttering, done only as a vocalized reflection of some troubled internal thought.

"Of course," Max said, giving her one final squeeze and gently letting her go. He looked up at Uriel. "I had her car brought here and placed in the garage. Her purse and phone are in the passenger seat."

Uriel nodded. "I'll get them." He pulled his hands out of his pockets. "Ellie," he said softly.

She turned to face him and he saw the confusion in her eyes. It was coupled with weariness and doubled by disbelief. She was nearly in shock. He frowned and very gently cupped the side of her face with his hand.

She instinctively closed her eyes at his touch, and hope blossomed inside of Uriel. It was a start.

"Would you like to come down to the garage with me? Get some fresh air?" he asked. He recalled the tubs of Ghirardelli cocoa on her kitchen shelves. "And we can stop in the kitchen on the way out; I can make you some cocoa."

Eleanore gazed up at him and he waited with bated breath for her reply. Finally, she nodded. "Fresh air would be good."

And cocoa, he added with a smile. *I bet I had her at cocoa.*

Samael glanced up from behind his desk at the tentative sound of a knock at his door. He knew the knock well; he'd heard it, in its different forms, for thousands of years. Except for when it wasn't a knock, but a slow and anxious peek behind the flap of a tent. But that was another world and another time.

"Come in, Lilith."

The door opened to reveal a petite woman in a wool skirt, warm tights, knee-high leather boots, and a button-down silk shirt. A pair of reading glasses hung on a long string of beads around her neck. Her dark brown hair was neatly pulled back into a low ponytail that shimmered under the office lights. Her skin was smooth and held a youthful glow, but her dark eyes were ancient.

She stopped inside the office, gazed at Samael for a long, silent moment, and then slowly closed the door behind her. Then she cocked her head to one side and said, "You wanted to see me."

Samael sighed heavily and sat back in his chair. "I need you to do me a favor."

"Another one?" she asked quietly, almost sadly. "This behavior of yours is self-destructive, Sam."

She was the very embodiment of contradiction, Lilith. She should have been as bitter and as angry as he was. More so, in fact. She had been the first of the Old Man's creations that were thrown out, tossed down, and forgotten. When it happened, all of those eons ago, the moment had marked the dawning of Samael's ultimately damning epiphany.

That the Old Man was not, in fact, *all* he pretended to be.

But that was another issue altogether. Lilith should have been filled with righteous wrath and a desperate desire for vengeance. Instead, she busied herself with reading and traveling and learning—and perpetually worrying about Samael.

It was confounding.

Samael thought for a moment before he sat back up in his leather office chair. "This is different."

"Oh?" Lilith asked as she came forward and took a seat in one of the similarly lined chairs on the other side of his desk. She crossed her legs and placed her hands in her lap. "If this is different, then it doesn't involve a contract, of course. And it wouldn't have anything to do with your brothers." She blinked a few times, to convey a faux innocence, and waited for him to reply.

A muscle in his jaw twitched and his gray gaze narrowed. "They're not my brothers."

"They're more yours than mine."

"That's not saying much."

"We all have the same father, do we not?"

Samael leaned forward and laced his hands together on the desk. "Will you do me the favor or not?"

Lilith sighed and pursed her lips. It was an oddly endearing gesture. She was a very attractive woman with porcelain skin, fine bone structure, and a delicate frame, though she always chose to dress conservatively, caring more for comfort and function than appearance. The effect was one of cuteness to a nearly painful degree.

She waited a long while before speaking. Finally, with a tone that reflected a weariness she must have felt deep, deep down, she asked, "What do you want me to do?"

"I'm in Hogwarts," Eleanore murmured when they passed yet another corridor that shouldn't have been there. The mansion was immense and didn't seem to be tied to the laws of physics. It just went on and on.

"You get used to it," Uriel told her, the corners of his lips curling into a self-deprecating and entirely attractive smile.

When they reached the garage door, he turned to face her and Eleanore found herself growing nervous. She was alone with Christopher Daniels again. She'd been nervous enough when he was just a movie star. But now he was also an angel.

"Listen," he said softly. "I really am sorry for what I did to you on national television." He shook his head and laughed low. "I was so desperate to see you again, I seriously wasn't thinking clearly." He paused and asked, "Will you allow me to make it up to you?"

"You really are an archangel?" Eleanore asked.

Uriel blinked. "I was. I'm not sure what you'd call us now." He shrugged. "Two thousand years on this planet will do strange things to a man. We've changed."

"In a good way or a bad way?"

He squinted a bit as he considered how to answer

that question. And then he shook his head. "We're just different. Some good, some not so good."

Eleanore processed that and took a deep, cleansing breath. The hot cocoa had helped a lot. He'd made it perfectly, with tons of tiny marshmallows.

"Ellie, please accompany me to the gala on Saturday?" He asked the question so suddenly and so softly, she wasn't sure at first that she'd heard him correctly. But the look on his handsome face was one of such earnest hope, it seemed to surpass anything he'd ever pretended to feel on the big screen. A lot of women would have killed for him to look at them that way.

"Would I have to buy a new dress?"

"I don't care if you go in hot pants and Rollerblades," he said with a smile. And then his green eyes flashed with something mischievous. "In fact, that might not be such a bad—"

"And would you be picking me up?" Ellie interrupted quickly to change the subject.

He chuckled. "Of course."

Eleanore paused and swallowed hard. The next question was the only one that really mattered. "And would you be able to . . . to deal with it if something happened?"

Uriel frowned. He leaned in, just a little. "Like what, Ellie?"

She loved it when he said her name like that. He'd never called her anything else and it sounded perfect coming off of his tongue.

"I don't know . . . like SWAT teams and helicopters and handcuffs and men in white lab coats with needles full of tranquilizer?" She shrugged and tried to smile, but it had happened to her before and the images running through her head were very real and they scared her very much. She lowered her head and looked at the floor.

Uriel gently took her chin between his fingers and raised her head until she met his gaze. His green eyes had hardened, pinning her to the spot beneath their weight. His tone lowered further. "Ellie, talk to me. Did someone hurt you?"

Fragments of images flashed in her mind's eye: rain-soaked skies, mud puddles, barking dogs, and needles. She shivered and at Uriel's very determined, worried expression, she sighed in resignation.

And she told him everything. Then and there, in the hall outside the garage in his magnificent, magical mansion, Eleanore told him the story of her life, her powers, and the strange men who had hunted her family down. She told him about her narrow escape when she was fifteen, about how she was always on the move, and much to her horror, she found herself sharing how lonely she sometimes felt. Friendships were long-distance. Relationships with the opposite sex were nonexistent.

She'd only ever had a crush on one boy, Kevin, when she was fifteen—and that had never gone anywhere because she'd had to leave her home before she'd even had the chance to speak with him in person.

Uriel was the only man she had ever kissed.

And though she tried to stop herself, she actually told him as much. As she admitted this final, damning bit, she choked back a sob and willed her eyes to stay dry. He touched her arm and she shivered; the feeling was electric. She felt exposed in front of him now and couldn't bring herself to meet his gaze.

But the thought of him kissing her was chasing away her bad memories. His nearness beside her was like standing next to a sexual furnace. She felt not only vulnerable, but suddenly expectant. Hopeful.

For the second time that day, Uriel cupped her chin and tilted her head, forcing her to look at him. She gasped when she saw that his eyes were glowing as they had when he'd lifted everything in the room with his telekinetic powers.

He looked like an angel now, supernatural and powerful. She could easily imagine wings at his back. Those glowing green eyes held her in place as surely as his arms could have.

"Ellie, I won't allow anyone to harm you. Not now. Not ever." He shook his head once. "Do you understand?"

Eleanore managed a nod. Barely.

Then Uriel released her chin and placed his hands on the wall behind her, trapping her against it; she stepped back into the hard surface and could go no farther. Her eyes flicked to his lips and back again. He was so close. . . .

"I know you don't understand it fully yet and I know it will take some time for you to accept, but you and I are . . ." He paused, as if searching for the right words. "You were made to be protected by me," he finally told her. "There isn't a force on Earth that can get through me when you're standing on the other side." He shook his head, lowering it to stare at her through those unnatural, determined eyes. "I promise to keep you safe," he swore. "Always."

Eleanore's head swam. He smelled so good; he always smelled so good. Like the leather of his jacket and that perfect, masculine spiced soap or deodorant. He was filling her senses, leaving no room for thought.

Again, she swallowed hard. She was suddenly having some difficulty breathing. But something niggled at her consciousness. There was something left undone, unsettled, floating in vagueness and ambiguity.

She had always possessed a hard stubborn streak and it came into play now. Just as it seemed he might kiss her—and, God did she want him to—she rallied all of her strength and forced herself to straighten. With some effort, she squared her shoulders, reached up, and placed her palm against his chest.

He smiled a wry smile and glanced down at her hand. *God, he feels good. . . .*

She could feel the muscles beneath her touch, hard and coiled and strong—waiting, like magic untapped.

Christ, I can't concentrate. . . .

She closed her eyes and said quickly, "I need to get something straight." She spoke in a rush, as if she might not get the words out if she didn't do it all at once. "You said that I was created, along with three others like me, and then we were tossed to the wind—and landed down here. Just like that?"

She opened her eyes again and let her hand drop. It was hard to do. Her fingers immediately missed the feel of him. But she clenched her teeth and forced herself to push onward. "And then you chose to come after us? Just like that? There's nothing more to the story? I mean, why were we thrown out like garbage in the first place? Are we . . ." Here, she paused, shocked at how much the next words hurt her to say. "Are we *mistakes*?"

Uriel's eyes widened. He instantly shoved off of the wall. "*God*, no."

Eleanore gasped as he grabbed her arms and drew her to him, his entire form now radiating an intensity that hadn't been there only seconds before. His glowing green eyes sparked orange fire as he shook his head. "No, Eleanore. Absolutely not. You are . . ." His gaze trailed over her eyes, her cheeks, her lips, her blue-black hair, and then returned to her eyes. The space between their lips was suddenly like that space between Adam's fingers and God's on the Sistine Chapel—charged, electric, so small and yet too big at the same time.

"You're *perfection*," he told her, his voice no more than a whisper. "In every sense of the word."

"Then why did I get thrown out?" she whispered.

Uriel frowned, and she could see the wheels spinning behind those gorgeous eyes. There was something else there—something he wasn't telling her.

"What is it?" Eleanore asked, needing to know.

"It's complicated." He shook his head, just a little.

His jaw set, and for a moment, Eleanore thought he was going to keep it from her.

But then he let out a breath though his nose, and closed his eyes. "But you were honest with me, so . . ."

His tone was one of such weariness and defeat, it was clear to Eleanore that he would rather have talked about anything else in that moment than what he was about to say.

He opened his eyes and stepped back, just a little, letting his arms fall from where they had trapped her against the wall. "My brothers and I were not the only archangels," he began. "There were others. One, in particular, had been the Old Man's favorite since his creation. Then Michael came along and—" He paused, as if unsure of how to phrase his words. "In a way, Michael took his place. There was a lot of mistrust. Some of the angels didn't feel the Old Man had his head screwed on right anymore. Dissention caused rifts and separated us into factions."

Uriel's gaze traveled to Eleanore's hair and he gently lifted a lock of it to slowly rub it between his fingers as he spoke. "One day, the Old Man pulled the four of us aside and told us he had a gift for us. He showed us four stars in the sky. They burned brighter than the others. He told us there was one for each of us. Our soul mates— our archesses." Uriel released her hair and ran a hand through his own. "We've existed for so long and"—he smiled a small, strangely wry smile—"we're all male. We were lonely beyond belief."

Eleanore did as he said and imagined such a world. She couldn't help but do so. And as it always did when faced with something sad, her empathic heart hurt for him.

"The Old Man had decided to reward us for the loyalty we'd always shown him by creating these female angels just for us." He gently cupped her cheek and brushed his thumb along her cheekbone, warming her to her core. "So that we would no longer be lonely," he added softly.

Uriel blinked, frowned, and looked at the floor now, as if lost in the darker parts of his memory.

"As we were standing there, the archangel who had fallen out of the Old Man's favor came up behind us. His name was Samael. He was not alone. And he demanded that the Old Man create archesses for him and the other archangels. He was like that—always wanting anything anyone else possessed. It was his idea of fairness." Uriel sighed. "When the Old Man refused, there was an uprising. Your safety was threatened. To protect you, he decided to hide you by sending you out of our realm and into this one."

Uriel looked up at Eleanore.

"The four of us decided we wanted to come after you. It had never been done before. No angel had ever fallen to Earth before. We had no clue what would await us here." He shrugged. "But the Old Man granted our wishes and we left. We thought it would be a lot easier than it was. Unfortunately, your souls were scattered and we had no idea where to look. Our communication with the Old Man was completely cut off; we haven't been able to contact him in two thousand years. It's like we entered an entirely different universe. For all we knew, the four of you could float in limbo for eons or you could be born and born again and we would miss you by chance." He shrugged and shook his head. "It's amazing to me how little we understood about the human realm before experiencing it for ourselves. Even the Old Man had no clue." At that, he paused and frowned. In a softer voice, he said, "Sometimes I think he still doesn't."

Eleanore was silent as she digested this. She should have felt overwhelmed, but aside from her initial anger earlier, she felt strangely . . . calm. It would explain so much. Why she had always been different. Her ability to heal. It even made sense, suddenly, that she'd never really minded her lack of any kind of boyfriend. Men were always vaguely interesting to her, but when she had to pick up and move, they were the least of her concerns.

And now she knew why. They weren't meant for her. Uriel was.

That explained her fascination with him from afar.

Why she dreamed of him and read his articles and even sat through his movie just so that she could peer into his green eyes.

"You ... seem okay with this," Uriel said. She looked up at him to find an almost painfully hopeful expression on his handsome face. "Are you?"

Eleanore smiled a small smile and shrugged. "You know, I think I actually am." She believed him. She believed Max. She was an archess and Uriel was her soul mate. It was an amazingly peaceful realization. As if she'd had a scratch she couldn't reach her whole life. And now it no longer itched.

"Who's doing your job now that you're no longer the Angel of Vengeance?" she asked softly. It was something that she'd been wondering since he'd first admitted as much.

"No one. Humans don't need angels to do their work any longer. Not that they ever did. Humans have amazing imaginations and their capacity for punishing one another far outdoes anything I ever came up with. In the end, revenge finds its own way, as does everything else we once delivered to the world."

Ellie said nothing. She couldn't disagree with that.

Uriel took her by the upper arms, squeezing gently. "Are we okay?" he asked, his eyes no longer glowing.

She shrugged and offered him a confused but friendly smile. He smiled back, looking relieved.

Then he turned away from her and opened the door to the garage. A vast, echoing darkness yawned open beyond, and he stepped into it. Eleanore blinked while her eyes tried to adjust and she hesitantly followed him in, looking around as she did so. The garage door was solid but for severely tinted windows punctuated by thin slats of clear glass that allowed very small beams of sunlight into the vast garage. The windows were most likely tinted to protect the paint jobs of the vehicles inside. Something hummed electrically in the blackness and something else *tink*ed in mechanical rhythm.

Machinery of some kind. She heard Uriel run his hand over the wall, and turned to find him searching for the light. He found it, flipped the switch, and the fluorescents popped to life above them. The garage came into sudden, flickering view. Eleanore stopped in her tracks and stared.

Uriel disappeared into the row of vehicles and she lost sight of him. "What *are* all of these?" she asked, her tone filled with wonder. The closest "car" to her was by far the most bizarre, and barely recognizable as something that moved—it was the wheels that made her believe it was some sort of transportation device. Otherwise, it looked like something from the middle ages. Its wheels were huge, its "carriage" was nothing but a gigantic flat wagon, and the entire contraption was connected to a massive conical tank with one giant tube sticking out of it.

Eleanore slowly moved toward it and placed her hand on the carriage. "What the hell is this thing?"

"It's technically the first automobile ever invented," Uriel told her, his voice carrying over from somewhere deeper within the garage. "It was designed in 1335 by a man named Guido da Vigevano. He was also a doctor and a good friend of Michael's."

A friend of Michael's . . .

It hit her then, in that moment. How truly old Uriel and his brothers were. It was one thing for someone to tell you that they were immortal. It was another to be standing a few inches away from proof to that end.

Eleanore moved away from the vehicle and stared down at her hand. She'd just touched the very first automobile ever made. How many people could say that? "Does it work?"

"Not without help," Uriel replied, suddenly standing next to her once more.

Eleanore jumped and spun to face him. She hadn't heard him come up beside her. He smiled. "And these other cars?" She gestured to the long row of vehicles that seemed to progress from oldest to newest in one solid line of history.

"All invented or owned by people we've known throughout the years. Michael loves anything with wheels, so most of them are his."

"I see." Eleanore looked from the 1335 vehicle to the next, which appeared to be a massive tricycle with steam pipes and vents all over it. After that came a recognizable steam engine, albeit a small one. Then something resembling what she would have identified as a Model T. After that, it was one long line of smoothed-out angles, better paint jobs, less wood, more leather, rubber, and chrome.

Eleanore left the ledge where she was standing and walked in front of the line of cars until she was standing before an early-model Harley-Davidson. "Michael likes motorcycles, too?"

"Like I said—anything with wheels."

Eleanore had to smile at that.

Samuel Lambent would love this, she thought.

Someone cleared his throat behind them and Eleanore and Uriel turned to see Michael and Gabriel standing in the doorway to the garage.

"What do you think?" Michael asked, pride clear in his features.

"I think you're a heck of a collector. I know someone who would probably pay top dollar for this one." She gestured to the Harley.

"Oh?" Michael asked, somewhat amused. "It's not for sale. But out of curiosity, who?"

"Samuel Lambent," Ellie replied without thinking.

The garage fell into silence around her and she looked up to see each of the men staring at her, somewhat stricken expressions on their handsome faces.

"What?" she asked, wide-eyed.

Gabriel looked up at his brother. "We need to tell 'er about Sam."

Eleanore turned from him to Uriel, who glanced at

her and then glanced away, as if he couldn't meet her gaze.

"She's already met him, Uriel, and you know she's gotten the wrong impression of him," said Michael.

"Who?" Eleanore asked, unable to stop herself. "I've got the wrong impression about who?"

"Samuel Lambent," Gabriel answered, before Uriel could.

"Enough, Gabe. I'll handle this."

"All right, then, but best make it soon; the weesack's obviously made 'imself out to be a bloody hero."

Eleanore turned to face Uriel once more and found her hands on her hips. "What the hell is going on, Christopher?" She corrected herself with a quick shake of her head. "I mean Uriel." It was going to take some getting used to, no matter how attracted to him she was.

"You two leave." Uriel leveled his brothers with a hard, meaningful look. Michael shrugged and left right away. Gabriel returned the dark gaze with one of his own, nodded once to both of them, and then followed Michael out, closing the door behind him.

Finally, Uriel turned back to Eleanore and sighed. "I'm sorry, Ellie. They're right. We need to talk about Samuel Lambent."

CHAPTER NINE

"What about him?"

"He's not what he pretends to be," Uriel said.

"Did you get my things from the car?" she asked, quickly changing the subject and turning away from him to stand on her tiptoes and gaze down the long line of vehicles. Presumably she was searching for her own MINI Cooper. But clearly she was uncomfortable with the subject of Lambent and didn't want to discuss him. He wondered why.

Uriel stared down at Eleanore's head and frowned. "Ellie, you need to listen to me right now. What I'm trying to tell you is very important."

He moved forward to take her arm and turn her back around, but as he stepped toward her, the sun's thin rays at the slats in the windows of the garage shifted and a stream of it hit his eyes. He squinted against it, instantly irritated, and pulled back.

Then he frowned again. That was weird.

"Ellie, please turn around and talk to me."

"I can't see my car from here—it must be behind that SUV down there." She started off along the row of cars once more, and he was forced to follow her. Instinctively, he turned his face away from the light at the windows, not even realizing he was doing so.

She was moving quickly and he could feel his irritation rising. "Eleanore, Samuel Lambent is not just a me-

dia mogul, and I know you think he's a nice guy. . . ." He
flinched when the sun hit his eyes once more, but gritted
his teeth against the pain. "But you couldn't be more
off," he finished through a clenched jaw.

Eleanore ducked in between two of the vehicles to
her left and Uriel hurriedly went after her. "Ellie, his
name isn't actually Samuel. It's Sama—"

Sharp pain shot through his right eye and into his
skull, immediately lancing everything from his brain to
his stomach with agony. He instantly stopped, and once
again acting on instinct, turned away from the windows,
clutching at his gut as he ducked behind the large SUV
beside him. He crouched low and closed his eyes. The
pain eased, and as it did, he noticed that his breathing
was ragged. Heavy.

What's happening to me . . . ?

This wasn't normal. He rarely felt pain, and when he
did, it was either fleeting or an injury, in which case, Michael would heal him and that would be that. This was
different. Something was definitely wrong.

"Here it is!" Eleanore called from several cars down.

Uriel ignored her and concentrated on his body. The
inside of his left wrist was throbbing. Beneath the buzzing of the lights overhead, which were suddenly louder
than before, he also discerned the faint sound of something splashing.

Drip . . . drip . . . drip . . .

He tried to steady his breathing and listen more
closely. Then he looked down to see small, bright crimson splashes on the polished concrete of the garage
floor. Each flower of dark red was a tad larger than the
previous one. As he looked on, another flower joined
the bunch. And then another.

They were coming from his fingertips. Slowly, he
turned his hand over. Streams of bright red had streaked
across his palm and down his fingers. He followed their
trail to the now-stained cuff of his long-sleeved thermal
shirt and then roughly shoved it farther up on his arm.

His wrist was bleeding. The wound was small but deep; it was the piercing he'd given himself with Samael's blade-tipped pen. He'd thought it healed—apparently not.

"Eleanore!" He raised his head and rested it against the grill of the vehicle behind him. He closed his eyes and waited for her reply.

"Yeah?" She was farther away now.

"Please . . ." *Come here,* he thought, wanting her near. Needing her near. "You need to know the truth!" he told her, even as the pain was back in his head and it wrenched the breath temporarily from his lungs. He swallowed hard several times, choked down bile, and continued. "Samuel Lambent is one of u—"

That was as far as he got before the real torture kicked in. There was a ripping sound from inside his skull and blood erupted in his mouth. He cried out, unable to stop himself, and slammed his head against the SUV's radiator cover. His gums bled and throbbed in an anguish unlike any his long existence had ever known. With a bewildered, horrified fascination, Uriel felt his canines elongating from behind his tongue.

Oh God, he thought. *Azrael! Help me!*

He was now petrified with the absolute knowledge that a transformation had come over him. His fear for himself was bad enough; his fear for Eleanore was greater. She was in this garage with him—somewhere—and the hunger that was now dawning within him and yawning awake scared the hell out of him. He could smell his blood where it continued to gather in his palm and spill over onto the garage floor.

And he could smell hers as well.

There was only one man he could think of who might be able to help. Only Azrael possessed the ability to hear him. But it was daylight and the Masked One would be confined by the sun to his quarters under the mansion.

Despair sliced through Uriel. He gasped for breath

beneath the onslaught and cried out again, using all of his mental capacity. There was nothing else for it.

AZRAEL!

"Uriel?" Eleanore's voice came tentatively around the cars several vehicles down. "You okay?"

She can sense something is wrong. He knew it was part of who she was—her ability to heal. He knew that now; as he knew with dreadful certainty that if he didn't get away from her as soon as inhumanly possible, he was going to hurt her.

When he'd sworn to her that he would never allow anyone to harm her, he hadn't considered that one of the people he might have to protect her from was himself.

Az. Please help me.

And then he heard Azrael's voice in his head. *I'm sending the others, Uriel. Try to remain calm.*

His brother's tone was tranquil and controlled, but forceful in the way it carried through Uriel's mind and echoed in the chambers of his consciousness. It instantly filled him with hope. They were on their way.

At the same time, he heard Eleanore's footsteps drawing nearer. "Uriel? Where are you? Are you okay?" She was more worried now and moving quickly from vehicle to vehicle. He could smell her drawing nearer . . . She smelled like . . . like . . .

Oh fuck.

She smelled like sex and dinner and satisfaction and heaven and he was in agony, his insides in knots, his body on fire and frozen at once, his fangs now fully developed and his gums throbbing. His vision had turned slightly red and everything in the room was entirely too bright. His head felt as if it would explode.

Explode . . .

Unless he sank his fangs into Eleanore's throat and drank her in. Her blood would stop his pain. It would end this torture. He knew what he was becoming now.

He'd played the part on screen enough to recognize the symptoms. He had no idea how it was happening or why, but he was becoming a vampire.

And he needed Ellie. . . .

"Ellie, I'm here," he whispered, croaked, and called to her.

In turn, her footsteps changed direction, breaking into a run as they neared him. He looked up as she came around the corner.

"Eleanore, get back!"

The door to the garage was slammed open on its hinges to bang noisily against the adjacent wall. Eleanore stopped in her tracks and stared at Gabriel, Michael, and Max Gillihan. They were rushing toward her.

As if in slow motion, she looked down at Uriel. Eyes red as fire gazed back at her, freezing her in her tracks. His handsome face had gone pale, his hair was longer and darker, his lips were parted to reveal the cruelest set of fangs she had ever seen. They were white as the moon, long, sharp, and faintly bathed in his own blood. His body was shaking, trembling with unholy need; she could feel his pain and knew what was going on in his body as she always knew when looking upon the suffering. His hard muscles were even more pronounced than normal, and a deep, throaty growl was emanating from the recesses of his throat.

Eleanore couldn't scream. She couldn't even gasp. All she could do was stand there and stare through wide eyes as the monster who had only moments before been an archangel rose from his crouched position and leapt toward her.

Everything happened very quickly then; time seemed to pick up speed and momentum so that each event blurred by in rapid succession: Uriel's transformed features rushed toward her face; someone was shoving her roughly, his hand slamming into her chest with such force that it knocked the wind from her lungs; she went sailing backward to violently smack into one of the garage walls, banging her head against the concrete and her hip against a large metal tool chest as she dropped to the ground, stunned.

There was a roar—and then a growl . . . some screaming, things breaking. Shattering? Eleanore blinked lazily; the world was out of focus and sound was distant, like an echo.

She was scared. She was also very sleepy. But worst of all was the nausea. It came fast and furious, like it did with a migraine, and Eleanore tried not to retch. It took her a half second more before she was closing her eyes again and summoning all of her strength to heal herself. She knew it was her head. She knew it as if she could see the injury from a doctor's vantage point. She saw the concussion and the blood pooling beneath her skull and she concentrated on that—and on the nausea it created.

Just as the nausea ebbed and Eleanore was again resting back against the wall to exhale with new weariness, she felt breath on her cheek. The garage had gone eerily quiet.

She opened her eyes. Uriel knelt before her, his hands pressed to the wall on either side of her, trapping her there. The irises of his eyes were burning red; she could actually see the movement of flames within them. He bared his fangs and a deep, low, predatory rumble surrounded them both like thunder.

Eleanore swallowed hard, her heart rate kicking up a few hundred notches. *What the hell is happening to him?* Once more, her life had been plunged into mad chaos. "Uriel," she said softly, trying desperately to find the strength to reason with him. Self-preservation was kicking in. She could feel a little of her power still there, but she'd used a lot healing her concussion. Still, if she needed to, she could move a few objects—maybe aim for his head. "Please don't hurt me," she whispered. "You promised."

She gazed up into those eyes and felt lost. The world around them melted away into a monochromatic background. *He's a vampire.* It was irrational and impossible, but there it was. He had become the Jonathan Brakes of America's imagination. He'd become the vampire, the darkness, the hunger.

It suits him, Eleanore thought. It was one of those crazy, senseless thoughts that raced unhindered through a person's mind when they teetered on the precipice of madness-inducing fear.

He's beautiful. He's going to kill me, but he's gorgeous.

The corners of Uriel's mouth turned up then, offering the slightest, cruelest smile.

"I can read your mind now," he told her, his voice deeper and more seductive than it had been before. *Can you hear me, my love?*

She was startled that he could make his own thoughts heard in addition to being able to read hers. His laughter echoed through her mind, low and rumbling and erotic. And Uriel's eyes sparked, his pupils suddenly expanding to nearly engulf his red burning irises.

Eleanore wasted no energy screaming. Instead, she focused as she never had before, noticing several things in quick succession. The back of Uriel's leather jacket was smoking. There was a thin beam of light from the slats in the garage windows trained on him from behind. There was a motorcycle a few feet away from them both.

And then Eleanore concentrated every ounce of remaining power she possessed and willed the motorcycle behind Uriel to rise from its resting spot and rush, full-speed, toward the darkly tinted garage windows. She sent it flying as fast as she possibly could and hoped it would hit the glass hard enough to shatter it.

It did.

The garage door shook violently in its casings as the motorcycle slammed into the metal, denting it beneath its chrome weight. The glass instantly exploded, splintering into a million tiny fragments of crystal and flowering outward in shimmering shards of destruction. The sound must have given Uriel pause, for his smile was gone and his pupils instantly shrank to normal size, revealing once more his red and burning irises.

And then the light streamed freely through the windows and Uriel was ducking, rolling, rushing for cover behind the SUV he'd been crouched beneath moments ago.

Eleanore squinted against the sudden sunlight that flooded the garage, and then she scanned her surroundings, searching for the other archangels. Michael was pulling himself up from where he'd apparently been thrown against a far wall. His chest was covered in blood.

Eleanore's gaze left his form and traveled to Gabriel's seemingly broken body where he lay, facedown, a few yards from Michael. The back of his head was bloodied; it matted his dark hair and stained his neck and right arm. A familiar terror raced through her when she realized that she hadn't the strength remaining to bring a full-grown man back from the brink of death. But when he, too, began to stir and push himself up off of the ground, relief flooded her system.

Max Gillihan was nowhere to be found.

Eleanore looked down at Uriel once more. He was safely sequestered in the shadows behind the large vehicle and currently spearing her with hard, hungry eyes.

She started beneath that gaze; there was such determination behind it, it bordered on hatred. But there was pain in those eyes as well. She would always be able to recognize such a thing. And despite the obvious danger he posed as he crouched there and branded her with that gaze, she was hurting for him. By all logical reasoning, she barely knew him. And yet—he was everything. She couldn't stand to see him suffer.

Uriel . . . she tried, thinking that she could more effectively reach him through her thoughts. *Uriel, I don't know what's happening to you, but we can figure this out together. I want to help you.*

The low growl was back, deep and resonant as thunder.

Please trust me, Uriel. She began speaking rapidly in her mind now, trying to distract him from his pain and hunger; she could almost feel it herself, the way she always did with those in pain. *I know something strange is happening—something unnatural. I know you've become a vampire. But I trust you.* She plunged on, hoping at least some of it was getting through. *We have to fix this; you owe me a gala on Thursday.*

"Eleanore, get away from there," Michael called to her, his voice much weaker than it had been before. She glanced in his direction to find him doubled over, his arm wrapped tightly around his bleeding midsection. He hadn't healed himself yet, and because she had grown up with the same healing ability, she automatically assumed that it was because he didn't want to waste his power in case he needed it for something worse later.

When she turned back to Uriel, it was to find him with his head down; he was no longer gazing at her. His eyes were closed, his hands curled into fists at his temples.

Uriel? she whispered mentally.

It hurts . . . came the weak, raspy reply. Even in her mind, he sounded agonized.

The sun? she ventured.

Everything. The sun, his empathic voice continued, *the hunger* . . .

"We need to get him inside!" Eleanore turned to Michael, and then to Gabriel, who was now standing on two unsteady legs, bracing himself against the far wall. They both looked at her as if she were certifiable.

"Please!" she called to them. Her legs were shaking beneath her. She felt nearly as tired now as she had after healing the little girl and her father at the accident that morning.

Gabriel closed his eyes and ran his hand over the back of his head. He flinched, hissing through clenched teeth. Then he opened his eyes again, now a glowing, molten platinum, and leveled them on Eleanore. They startled her, forcing a step back.

"First, tell 'im to put on the fucking bracelet!" Gabriel shouted harshly, coughing after he did so. Blood appeared on his lips.

Eleanore frowned and turned back to Uriel. *The bracelet?* she asked him, forcing the mental thought into his head.

Smart . . . keep me from . . . using my powers, came his agonized reply. Uriel lowered his hands, unclenched his fists, and shoved his right hand into the front pocket of his jeans. When it came back out again, his fingers clutched the thin gold bracelet that he'd been wearing when he'd been in her apartment. It shook in his trembling grasp and he flinched when it reflected a stray beam of sunlight, as if to magnify its cruel potency.

No way, Ellie thought. It was true? The story he'd told her about the bracelet—it was all true? It was really magical? If what he'd told her was true, it would bind all of his supernatural abilities inside of his body. It would render him powerless. She remembered how she'd been confused as to why an angel would need its powers bound. He'd given her that enigmatic smile and a shrug.

Now she knew. Angels were not necessarily always angels.

She watched as he lowered the bracelet to his left wrist and touched it to his flesh. On contact, the gold wreath evaporated in another display of bright light and then reappeared, seamlessly wrapped around his arm.

And that answers the question of how he got it on, she thought.

He dropped to his hands and fell forward. At the same time, both Gabriel and Michael erupted into motion, rushing forward to grasp their brother by the arms, one on each side of him. Eleanore stepped back out of the way as they lifted him from his kneeling position.

Instantly, a ray of light struck his left hand and the left side of his neck and he bellowed in pain. They dropped him as he ducked down, trying to cover the redness that had appeared in a line across his neck and the back of his hand.

"Here!" Max was back and running from the entrance of the garage to where the three of them crouched down behind the black SUV. He was carrying what looked like a thick leather tarp. He didn't hesitate in tossing the black material over Uriel's smoking form. Michael and Gabriel instantly wrapped it around him tighter and then, with a nod to each other, they once more attempted to draw him out of the Bronco's shadows and across the garage. This time, there was no howl of agony and the team was able to move quickly.

Outside the broken garage windows, the sky began to darken with storm clouds. No one but Eleanore noticed. The weather had always reflected her emotions. Now was no different. She was torn by both fear *of* Uriel and fear *for* him and the sky was likewise torn between light and building darkness.

As the two men ushered their brother back into the mansion, Eleanore hung back. She felt like a vessel composed of bewilderment and adrenaline. Just when she had come to accept that Uriel was an archangel and she was his archess—just when she thought she might actually be okay with the fucked-up events of the last few days—he'd changed on her.

He'd become something else. She wasn't sure what to

do now. She wasn't sure what to think. She was numb—in shock. She was more than a little confused.

Max turned as the brothers went past and gently took Eleanore by the arm. "Are you all right?" he asked, leading her to the door as well.

She nodded. Then shook her head. "What happened to him?" she asked. Her voice was higher pitched than normal.

Max's brow furrowed with concern. "I don't know," he told her. "Let's get you inside."

She turned to go with him, but then suddenly stopped short. "W-wait," she said, shivering violently. Shock was setting in. Max must have noticed it and recognized it for what it was because he shrugged off his coat and draped it over her shoulders.

"D-did he know s-something like this was going to happen?" Her teeth were chattering now, as if she'd just gotten out of a cold swimming pool. "I mean . . . he h-had that bracelet on him, right?" Ellie looked up at him. "He t-told me what it does. Why was he c-carrying it if he didn't kn-know this would h-happen?"

Max Gillihan visibly paled. He blinked behind his glasses and looked away, taking a slow, deep breath. "It's complicated," he told her. "Come inside, Eleanore. You're not doing so hot. I'll make you some coffee or tea."

An idea came slamming into her in that moment, broadsiding her as if she'd crossed the street against traffic. "Oh my G-god. It was m-meant for me, wasn't it?" She knew it was true, even as she said it. Uriel hadn't known this was going to happen; he hadn't known he would turn into a vampire, for whatever bizarre reason. He'd been carrying the bracelet to use it on her. Because she was an angel. An archess.

Max closed his eyes and put his hands on his hips, his lips in a thin, grim line. He thought long and hard about his response before he replied. Then he said, "Like I said, Ellie, it's complicated." He sighed defeatedly and his shoulders dropped. "The bracelet was only a precaution. We had no idea how you would react to learning what you are. Most women these days would rage at the idea of having been created for a man."

He was trying to reason with her, but she was only half hearing him now. *I'm not safe here,* Ellie thought. It was an irrational, shock-induced thought and it whiz-banged through her mind like a pinball. *First they're angels and so am I and now Uriel is a vampire and I know they were going to use that damn bracelet on me....* She continued to shiver, but her focus sharpened and her gaze narrowed. *I can't trust these men. I can't trust Uriel.*

Max opened his eyes and studied her expression. "There's much to explain, Eleanore, and I'm sorry that it's all coming out like this. It couldn't have gone worse. But if you'll give us a chance, we'll make it right." Max turned and headed for the door of the garage. "Please come with me and I'll see that you get warmed up."

He stopped in the hall when he realized she wasn't following him and turned to face her. Eleanore swayed just a bit on her feet, but she managed to meet his gaze. And then she called the lightning forth from the skies.

She knew exactly when to duck and cover her ears.

The white-hot electricity snaked through the garage windows, not rising from the ground as it was supposed to, but birthed from some unknown spot in the sky and out of her single-minded will for it to exist. The path of its heat seared the air behind Eleanore as she dove for the ground, covering her head in desperation. The backs of her fingers and knuckles singed as it passed through. Somewhere overhead, it blasted through the wall and Eleanore knew that it had taken a direct route through Max Gillihan on its way.

She didn't bother to roll over and look at him after the thunder had ceased booming. Instead, she pushed herself to her hands and knees, shook her head to clear it, and then shoved herself to her feet. Only then did she bother to look.

Gillihan was lying on his stomach, facedown, and there was a black scorch mark on the back of his button-up shirt. Near his unmoving fingers lay a gold bracelet. Eleanore instantly recognized it. It was another bracelet exactly like the one Uriel had just used on himself.

Bastard, she thought. *He was going to use it on me. Smart man. It would have saved him a lightning bolt.*

With that thought, she bent down, retrieved the bracelet, and pocketed the item. Then she turned to hastily make her way across the garage toward the window that the motorcycle had shattered. She used a nearby pickup truck for leverage and grabbed hold of the windowpanes, hoisting herself up. She sliced her palms as she did so, but she barely noticed the pain. Once up, she planted her left boot firmly on the window-pane and then vaulted herself over the ledge and out into the yard beyond.

It was lucky that she'd pulled this trick while still on the first floor. The grass she landed on was thick and wet. The air was dense with moisture, as if it had just seen the passing of a summer storm.

Eleanore straightened slowly and looked around. The road in front of the mansion was deserted and un-paved; the mud was fresh and deep; a storm had defi-nitely come through. Puddles of water littered the messy street in depthless potholes.

She turned and glanced up at the building she had just escaped and was shocked to find herself staring at the door to an old, weathered barn. There was no man-sion in sight.

Eleanore gaped for a few seconds, utterly befuddled. At last, she shook her head, decided to chalk it up to yet another supernatural impossibility, and turned back to-ward the dirt road.

The land across the street was undeveloped and

dense with scrub brush, Russian thistle, and low-lying trees that were more thorn than leaf. Foliage was like that in West Texas.

Eleanore wasted no time in sprinting across the long, manicured lawn of the mansion . . . or barn. The desert air was cold and damp in the post-rain twilight and she was already beginning to feel its chill through her clothes. Temperatures dropped drastically at night in Texas. She needed to get into town, find a phone, and call someone for help before she got hypothermia.

Too bad her car was stuck in the garage in the mansion. Wherever the hell that was.

She knew she needed to act before the sun went down, because something told her that when it did, Uriel the vampire would not be in pain any longer. And she was willing to bet he would come after her. The look in his eyes had more than assured her of that much.

"Holy fuck, what happened to you?" Gabriel asked.

Max pushed off the wall of the archway that led to Michael's bedroom and removed his hand from his mouth where he'd been holding a white handkerchief against his lip. It was stained with blood. "I was struck by lightning."

Gabriel frowned and then craned his neck to peer around Max's still-smoking body. "Where's Granger?"

"She's escaped."

Michael slowly stood from where he had been seated beside Uriel's semiconscious form. The archangel-turned-vampire was spread-eagled and manacled, thick chains trapping his arms and legs to the head- and footboards of a metal-framed bed.

"What do you mean she's escaped?" Michael asked.

Max tossed the handkerchief onto the bedside table and then froze when Uriel's eyes snapped open and his head turned toward him.

"You're bleeding," Uriel said. His voice was not his

own. It was still eerily deep and held a strange echoing quality. His eyes also still burned a bright, fiery red.

"Indeed," Max said softly. He watched his charge with a wariness that he was not in the mood to exhibit at that moment. He was feeling rather sore and burned out just then. Literally.

Pieces of his suit shirt and trousers were missing in dark, smoking patches and his hair was also rather darker than it should have been. If he'd been human, he would have been dead, of course. As it was, however, his recovery was taking a tad longer than he liked.

"Your girlfriend zapped me with one billion volts of electricity. I'm afraid I bit my tongue in the process."

Uriel said nothing. He simply continued to pierce Max with those burning eyes until Max could take no more and turned away. He addressed Michael instead. "She's afraid of us now. She used the last of her power to hit me with the lightning and then took the bracelet I had been about to place on her. She ran out the broken window of the garage."

"She cut herself," Uriel said then, drawing everyone's attention. The angel-turned-vampire was staring up at the ceiling now. "You got some of her blood on you when you were looking out the window, no doubt."

"It's Sherlock Holmes, the bloody undead," Gabriel muttered, his eyes wide.

He, Max, and Michael exchanged glances, and then Max waved them toward the open door that led to the hall beyond. They got the hint and followed him out. Once outside, they closed the door behind them even though each of them was well aware that if Uriel truly had become a vampire, it would do little good.

"You were going to bind her?" Michael asked, right off the bat.

"She knew about the bracelet; I imagine Uriel blabbed. And she figured out that he was carrying it to use on her. She was in shock and I didn't trust her to react rationally any longer. With good reason, apparently," Max explained.

Michael and Gabriel said nothing.

Max changed the subject. "I know what happened in the garage. The contract that Uriel signed must have had some kind of stipulation within it—a hidden clause, if you will—which prevented him from speaking about Samael."

"I'm sure he read it before he signed," said Michael.

"That's why I suggested it was *hidden*," said Max.

Michael ran a frustrated hand through his hair and Gabriel swore under his breath.

"Therefore, when he began telling Eleanore the truth, he also began to change," Max explained.

"I'll say this for the bugger. 's got a fucking good sense of humor."

Max nodded and took a deep breath. "What did Uriel do with the contract after he signed it?" he asked Michael.

Michael shook his head and shrugged. "He said that it disappeared."

"I was afraid of that. I'll have to go and retrieve a copy. Luckily, I happen to have such jurisdiction when dealing with Samael." Max straightened and added, "Until then, you two will need to watch over him closely. Azrael had to go under again after wrenching us all into action. When he awakens, have him take over for a bit. He'll know far better than you will how to deal with one of his own kind."

"I think it's fairly easy to tell that he's hungry," Gabriel suggested.

"Yes, and what do you propose we do about it?" Max asked.

Gabriel shrugged and shook his head. "I'm only saying."

"We'll figure it out," Michael said. "Now, what about Eleanore?"

"She took off somewhere around the outskirts of the

town she lives in, as far as I could tell," Max remarked. "The mansion repaired itself almost immediately after her departure and it has shifted since then. It must have known that she wanted to go home, so it took her there." He paused and considered his next words before he said, "I think the best man for tracking her down would be Azrael. It'll be night soon. No one is better at finding prey in the dark than he is."

Michael and Gabriel digested this in wary silence. It was a long while before Michael sighed heavily and nodded. "Go get the contract, Max. Find out what the hell is going on."

CHAPTER TEN

When life is uncertain and you find yourself repeatedly on the run, you learn to take certain precautions. You make plans. If you think you might be stuck somewhere suddenly, without any money, you invest in a piece of jewelry that you can pawn at a moment's notice. Then you formulate a plan that includes the procurement of transportation, food, and lodging.

Long ago, Eleanore made sure to leave a standing account at Western Union and memorize the pickup number. Then she'd strategized what her next moves would be so that she now knew to use library computers, Craigslist, and taxicabs.

Eleanore was furiously planning her next moves even as her feet pounded through the mud beneath her. Her body grew increasingly cold on the outside and increasingly hot from within. If she'd had any of her powers left, she would have made the sun shine—but she was tapped out and night was moving in anyway.

As it was, she knew she'd be lucky if she reached a phone before someone from the mansion managed to locate her. As she ran, she struggled with the notion of contacting her parents. It was her instinct to turn to them. They had always been there for her and were the only people in the world she wholly and purely trusted. However, she wasn't certain she wanted to involve them in this mess. And she wasn't even sure that she truly needed them.

She had a diamond on a long chain around her neck, given to her by her mother for just such an emergency situation. She wore it hidden beneath her shirts and had been sporting it for so long that she normally forgot it was even there.

She knew to use a public computer to find a local car for sale within her price range. And she knew to use taxis or public buses and aliases as she was transporting herself through town on these different emergency errands.

She might not need to call her mother or father. Uriel had told her about their mansion and its magical ability to transport people across vast spaces, and all of the Southwest looked pretty much the same with its scrub brush, dirt, and flat lands, so she couldn't be certain whether she was in the right state or not. But if she *was* somewhere close to home in Texas, then she could do this on her own. On the other hand, if she was on the other side of the state, or worse, in Arizona or New Mexico, then there was too much ground to cover before daylight; she would never make it home before . . .

Eleanore pushed the image of Uriel and his fangs from her mind. She suddenly felt so tired. She didn't know whether she entirely trusted herself to think clearly enough to keep from getting caught this night.

She didn't even know what had happened back there. It was so freaking confusing. She only knew that Uriel was more than he'd claimed to be and that the look in his eyes when he'd peered down at her in the garage had been life-threatening.

He listened to me, though, she thought erratically. *He listened to me when I spoke to him telepathically. Whatever was happening to him, he tried to calm down for me. . . .*

She didn't know why that was important. She was simply terrified and that was about all she could discern at the moment. Her stomach was cramping with hunger, her feet and hands were cold, she was more than a touch thirsty, and her side was stitching. It was hard to contemplate reality and a deeper truth when you felt like crap.

Up ahead, the dirt road became gravel, and just where the atmosphere misted with fog around the edges, Eleanore could make out the beginnings of paved tarmac. She headed in that direction, hope blossoming inside of her.

Azrael gazed down at the man chained helplessly to the metal bed before him. There were dark, deep circles beneath Uriel's closed eyes and his lips were pale and drawn.

"Time is not on our side. He must feed soon or he will die," Azrael said softly. "He's already far gone." In truth, he looked good and dead already, but Azrael knew otherwise.

"What do you mean?" Michael asked, coming up beside him. "I know he looks bad, but isn't that just the vampire thing?"

"A vampire must feed every night or he won't survive," Azrael told him. "And he was awake during the day. You have no idea how taxing that is; if he doesn't consume human blood very soon, there will be no saving him." He wasn't entirely certain that even that was enough to save him.

"You've got to be joking," Gabriel grumbled, running a hand through his pitch-black hair. Nearly all traces of his accent were gone now; it changed according to his mood and the gravity of the situation. "He's going to bloody die?" he asked, gazing steadily into the fire.

Azrael knew his brothers well. He recognized the pain in Gabriel's slumped form. He and Uriel had never gotten along very well. And yet he would wager that they were the closest, deep down, of the four of them. Azrael was the black sheep of the bunch, and close to none of them. Michael was the born leader of the crew and tended to set unreachable standards. Uriel and Gabriel were on an even footing and always had been. They could empathize with each other, and though it made it easer for them to fight, it also made their bond stronger. You always hurt the ones you love the most.

He contemplated what had to be done. He knew that Eleanore was out in the coming night alone, and that he needed to go after her. But far more pressing, at the moment, was obtaining sustenance for the newly created vampire dying before him.

He would have to go hunting on Uriel's behalf. None of the other angels would understand this, nor would they be able to bring themselves to such a task. It was up to him.

Azrael nodded once and prepared to take his leave of them.

But then he smelled her. It was a distinct scent, soft and warm and subtle. There was a tentative aspect to it, as much as there was to her character. Vampires eventually detected such notes and learned to unconsciously assign such characteristics to the things that they smelled, as an individual's scent became as much a signature of who they were as the lines of their face or the sound of their voice. So he was not at all surprised by the gentle footfall at the door behind them.

"I may be able to help you," came the voice of a woman.

The others turned, and Azrael joined them in looking upon the slight, petite form of Lilith where she stood in the doorway, one hand braced casually against the frame.

The road had, indeed, solidified beneath her feet and, fifteen minutes later, Eleanore was wholeheartedly thanking the couple that had given her a ride to the nearest grocery store.

There was a phone booth against the wall on one side of the parking lot.

Eleanore stepped inside the store and took a few minutes to warm up. She bought the nearest thing to a protein bar she could find and downed it with a bottle of Dasani water. Once she was semicomfortable again, she borrowed a piece of unused receipt roll and a pen from the nearest cashier and returned to the phone booth. She pulled the very thin phone book out of its shelf and stared at the name on the cover: Rockdale.

It sounded vaguely familiar. It was in Texas, but the problem was, she could have sworn it was nearer to Austin than to where she lived. It would take her ten hours to get home by car.

Eleanore tried to remain calm. "This state is way too effing big," she mumbled under her breath. She hurriedly thumbed through the phone book, scribbled some notes on the back of her paper, and then went back inside to return the cashier's pen.

Now she had the address and hours of a local pawn shop and a taxi was on the way to pick her up. She also knew the address to the only Western Union office in town. She wasn't sure how much money she would need to purchase a used car without so much as giving a real name, but it would probably take most of what she had readily available to her.

When she'd finished folding up the paper, she shoved it into her pocket and her fingers brushed the smooth metal of the gold bracelet she'd stolen at the mansion. She blinked.

She pulled the bracelet out and turned it over in her hands. It shimmered in the quickly fading sunlight. It was really quite an extraordinary work of art. The etching and detailing in the bracelet were so tiny and wrought so perfectly that it would seem only lasers could have etched the design. . . . But she knew it was too old for lasers. It practically radiated an ancient air.

It was also gold. With a start, Eleanore realized that gold was one of the best conductors of electricity and that it should have melted when she'd struck Gillihan with the lightning bolt. At the very least, it should have singed her fingers when she reached down to pick it up.

But it had been cool to the touch, and it was utterly unharmed.

Eleanore gazed down at the bracelet a few moments more, feeling raw inside. This bracelet must have belonged to one of the other brothers. She wondered whether Michael and Gabriel had been planning on using their bracelets on their archesses as well. Max said it was a precaution; that they had no idea how an archess would react to the news of being made for another being. But to her it was more than that. If a woman wasn't allowed to be angry or rally against what she felt was an injustice, then she was no more than a prisoner.

This felt like a betrayal of trust. More than anything else, it was that shady duplicity that hurt. More than anything that had been done to her, it hurt that Uriel had been willing to use his bracelet to take away what she was and render her powerless against him. To take away her freedom and her choice.

That really, really hurt.

Eleanore blinked back tears and repocketed the bracelet. She took a deep, cleansing breath, made her way out of the booth to lean against the wall of the grocery store, and let her head fall back to close her eyes.

"Lilith," Max uncertainly greeted the young—yet *very old*—woman and took a few steps forward. "What brings you here?"

Azrael could see that the guardian wanted to go to her. His feelings over the centuries had not changed. But he remained where he was, poised between the archangels and the woman known in their circle as the Dismissed, and waited.

It was a while before Lilith replied. Finally, she lowered her hand and entered the room. She was dressed as she always dressed, conservatively and simply. She wore only a silk button-down shirt, a knee-length business skirt, stockings that were most likely gartered, and heels. The reading glasses she sometimes carried on a chain around her neck were gone and her hair was down.

Few humans knew the true story of Lilith. Eons ago, nearly before the onset of time itself, Lilith had been created as a female companion for the first mortals the Old Man placed on Earth. Those mortals were considered by many archangels to mark the beginning of the Old Man's degeneration. The archangels thought the creation of man was a poor decision. Lilith was worse. Freshly formed, she'd been given an ultimatum: serve man or suffer dire punishment. Like all mortals, Lilith had been born with a mind and will of her own. She was fiercely strong, and she defiantly refused the Old Man's orders. As a punishment, she'd been sent out into the vastness of the mortal realm with nothing but the ability to suffer mortal death—and then awaken once more to her mortal, yet immortal, form. She died a thousand deaths in those first years from starvation, disease, and murder.

Her petite frame should have housed a soul both horribly bitter and perhaps a touch insane. However, she was neither. Lilith was a pillar of strength and perseverance, patience, and pardon.

Azrael thought of this now, as the woman slowly, gracefully, made her way across Michael's massive master bedroom until she eventually stood at the foot of the large iron-framed bed and stared down at the man bound to it.

"You would expect no different, of course," Lilith said then, turning to face Max with a sad smile and a small shrug. "But for what it's worth, I bring an offer from Sam."

At this, the company of angels and their guardian said nothing. After several long seconds, and with determined calm and composure, Max finally took a deep breath and asked, "What is it?"

"Uriel will die if he doesn't feed, and at this point, he will need more than human sustenance."

At once, Max turned to Azrael. "Is this true?"

"It's possible," he said. It had already occurred to him, in fact. On the one hand, a very healthy human with a lot of blood might just save Uriel. But he had been up during the day, leeched by those hot, bright hours. And he had been burned by the sun; such things were more lethal to a vampire than cyanide to a mortal.

Max turned back to Lilith and she went on. "I offer my blood to him in exchange for an amendment to the contract."

Max's jaw tensed; Azrael could see the muscle twitch. Beside him, he heard Michael's heart rate speed up. And behind him, he could smell the adrenaline suddenly pouring into Gabriel's bloodstream; the former Messenger of God was incredibly angry. Azrael wondered how long Gabe would be able to hold his temper before he decided to do something rash.

"What kind of amendment?" Max asked.

"Upon completion of Uriel's feeding, Samael wishes to be allowed to again meet with the archess." Her tone was both weary and apologetic. "He basically wants to break his forbearance a day early." She cocked her head to one side and waited for an answer. It was clear from her expression that she was not the proud bearer of such a request. She was simply the messenger. Azrael wondered whether Gabriel could at all sympathize.

"Let her do it," Azrael said then, and all eyes were on him. He knew that it wasn't what they wanted to hear. He knew they expected him to think of something else; he was the vampire, he was the one who should have known how to get out of this situation. But the hard truth of the matter was, vampirism was not a gift. It was called a curse for a reason. There was no easy way around the hard edges of it. And Uriel was dying.

As it was, his heartbeat was barely discernible.

"Do it." He turned to Lilith, knowing that his gold eyes were now glowing with determination and resolve. "Do it before it's too late."

Lilith squared her small shoulders and nodded. She looked so fragile there, beside the bed, as she resigned herself to her duty.

Azrael prepared himself to stop his guardian should Gillihan decide to interfere, which he could imagine the man absolutely wanted to do. But Max surprised him by keeping his distance. He was tense and he was angry; Azrael could tell that much easily. But he remained where he was, wisely deciding not to do anything that might endanger Uriel.

And as Lilith sat beside Uriel on the bed, pulled her thick dark hair from one side of her neck, and exposed the long, slim column of her throat, Azrael's eyes continued to burn.

He, too, had yet to feed for the night.

It took only a gentle nudging and urging for Uriel to open his own glowing red eyes. He took one look at Lilith and at the pale, taut flesh that she offered him, and the chains holding his wrists pulled tight as he sat up in the bed. If he hadn't been wearing the bracelet that trapped his superhuman strength within his body, they would have snapped.

At once, Michael and Gabriel were mobile, both of them coming forward to try to stop Uriel from whatever it was he planned to do. But Max held up his hand and Azrael moved forward to unlock the chains. Then he turned to pin both Michael and Gabriel to the spot with hard eyes.

"Leave him," Max told the men. "He won't hurt her. He can't," he added softly, his voice dropping to a whisper as he turned back around to watch.

Azrael could not afford himself the same luxury. Instead, he stepped back from the carnal scene and turned toward the window that had been covered in heavy drapes. He strode toward it and tore the drapes open, revealing a deepening night beyond. Azrael deftly clicked open the latch and lifted the window, allowing a cool breeze to waft into the room. It carried with it the faint scent of honeysuckle.

In stoic silence and without a farewell, he allowed his form to mist and evaporate and then shot out through the open window into the waiting darkness.

Eleanore pushed away from the wall and scanned the parking lot, looking for any sign of yellow that would signify that the taxi had arrived. It had been at least five minutes since she'd called. But as she stepped off of the curb and onto the asphalt, her hand shielding her eyes from the streetlights coming on, she began to notice something. It felt like teensy pinpricks on the back of her neck and a fluttering in her stomach.

She was being watched.

Eleanore set off across the lot, the feeling growing stronger. She stopped in between a blue Jetta and a yellow Jeep Wrangler and slowly turned in place, her gaze scanning the far corners of the lamp-lit parking lot.

She stopped when her eyes met those of a tall brown-haired man with green-blue eyes. He was wearing a black trench coat over dress clothes. The tips of his black leather shoes were shiny beneath the reflected lamplight. The man lowered his head a touch and peered at her through the tops of those strange eyes—and then he raised his hand to his ear and his lips began moving, almost imperceptibly.

An earpiece, Eleanore thought. *He's communicating with someone. . . . Oh no . . .*

Eleanore tried to calm the frantic beating of her heart as her gaze pulled away from his and continued around the lot. Another man, just as tall and striking, dressed similarly, stepped out of a windowless white van parked at the edge of the lot. She watched him extend his arm so that it was slightly hidden behind his coat and the shadows afforded by the still-open door. But something within his gloved grip glinted evilly.

A needle. There was no mistaking that wicked gleam of metal.

Eleanore's stomach lurched, the world growing static-like and numb around her. Flashes of her childhood played before her mind's eye. A mad dash down a rainy alleyway, another white van, a man with a needle ...

He, too, raised his other hand to his ear and began communicating. Both men were watching her steadily.

Eleanore swallowed hard, tasting bile. She could remember only one other time in her life when she had been so frightened. Not even in that mansion, watching Uriel turn into a monster—not even then had she been as terrified as she had been that night when she was fifteen. And as she was right now.

This was her very worst fear.

They knew about her now. They'd found her *again*. And they'd come to collect her. Max Gillihan had been right; he'd missed someone at the accident site. Someone must have gotten pictures of her—or video. Footage of her healing two people with nothing more than her bare hands.

Oh God, oh God, oh God. She needed to concentrate. *Focus,* she thought. *Focus, goddamn it! Two on the left of the parking lot.* She forced the observation through her brain. But the right exit was empty. She saw no one beneath the lights and there were no strange cars parked on that side.

With a burst of energy she hadn't known she possessed, Eleanore broke into a run toward the opposite end of the parking lot. Her boots pounded the ground beneath her, her long legs eating up the distance with efficient speed.

But as she neared the wide drive that accessed the street in front of the store, a black SUV skidded to a halt before it, swerving violently to bump the curb. Its black shining paint streaked brightly beneath the streetlights, bringing Eleanore to a sudden, violent stop. The SUV came to a screeching halt and blocked the exit directly before her.

Eleanore gasped and backpedaled, knowing all too well who was hiding behind the illegally dark-tinted windows. She didn't have to wait long for a confirmation as the door to the SUV swung open and a man who could have been a carbon copy of the other two spoke loudly enough into his earpiece that she could hear him this time.

"She's right here; we have her."

Eleanore didn't wait. There was no more rational thought processing involved. She simply spun in place and broke into a sprint directly toward the trees on the other side of the parking lot. She felt no pain, no weariness, nothing but adrenaline-induced numbness as she hit the mass of black thornbushes and trees. Her arms shielded her face as her long legs carried her through the closest break in the wicked foliage and into the dark and treacherous wilderness beyond.

Once through the thicket, she didn't slow. She kept running. She ran, ducking beneath branches she noticed milliseconds before they would have taken out her eyes. She ran and ran, jumping over stubborn puddles that would have soaked her clean through.

She ran.

"That's enough."

Uriel glanced up at his guardian over the smooth plane of the neck in which his teeth were still firmly embedded. The pain had subsided. It had been racking him with a pure, undistilled severity unlike anything anyone could have imagined. It had been torture—hell. He'd never known a body could hurt as much as his had. The only way to deal with the pain had been to shrink from it and hide within himself.

And then, just as he'd become resigned to sinking into a final oblivion, he'd smelled an offer of blood. Food. Sustenance. Salvation.

The scented knowledge had wrenched him from his semiconsciousness with a knife-hard jolt, once more infusing his changed form with the hunger that was literally killing him.

A single glance had located the woman—he knew her, somehow, but was too far gone to acknowledge the fact. All he could smell was the blood. All he could hear was the pulse in her veins. It roared in his eardrums, called to him and taunted him.

Nothing could have stopped him—neither the chains around his wrists nor all of the armies in hell—from taking what he needed from her.

And so he had.

"I said that's enough." Max's tone was hard now, forceful in its authoritative edge.

Uriel blinked, realization flooding him. He tasted the saltiness on his tongue, felt his fangs in her throat. And he knew what he had done.

Slowly, so as not to harm her any further, Uriel pulled his teeth from her neck and eased away from her. Max was instantly bending and lifting the unconscious form into his arms.

It was Lilith. He could see that now.

Oh God, what have I done?

Dread coursed through his veins as surely as the blood he had taken from her. Max quickly stepped away from the bed and strode across the room to the open door. He took Lilith with him, hugging her tightly to his chest. She was so small in his arms, so tiny and frail.

What have I done?

"I know wha' you're thinkin'. But you did wha' you had to do," Gabriel told him from where he stood at the foot of the thick metal bed.

"Concentrate now on Eleanore," Michael added. He stood from the seat he'd been occupying and approached the bed.

Uriel slid to the side and braced his arms against the mattress, pushing himself up as well. He was still fully dressed; his brothers had not wanted to touch him once he'd been restrained.

"Where is she?" he asked, feeling his strength returning tenfold.

"She escaped from the mansion, remember?" Michael asked, narrowing his gaze as he looked his brother over. His expression was worried.

But Uriel remembered. He'd scented her on Max. She'd vaulted through a window—a broken window. And lightning? Yes ... He had smelled the scorched and bitter scent of both flesh and clothes that had been set on fire. He remembered everything now.

His gaze unconsciously hardened as he thought of it.

She'd run from him. And he couldn't blame her one bit. And yet ... the thought of her running from him made his blood hum to liquid life in his veins. It literally heightened his senses as if preparing him for a hunt. He could feel his eyes begin to glow; there was a sharpening in his vision and a new strength in his limbs. And his fangs were still there.

"She's hurt," he said, recalling the sweet siren song of her own special blood.

"No' so hurt she can't run," Gabriel said. "That's a good sign."

"She's not alone. Azrael has gone after her," Michael continued.

Gabriel came around the bed and pulled his black leather jacket from the back of a wooden chair a few feet away. "Right," he agreed, his tone dark and low. "He bloody has at that." He slid into the jacket and straightened his collar, spearing them both with those molten platinum eyes. "Bu' then, so has Sam."

CHAPTER ELEVEN

For the second time that night, Eleanore's hopes rose suddenly, spiking hard when she could make out the flat, shimmering plane of paved tarmac up ahead through the trees. She drew nearer and came to the wet, black asphalt to see that it bordered the wrought-iron gates of a cemetery.

You've got to be kidding me. She almost laughed at the Gothic irony of the situation. *Running for my life through a graveyard. Perfect.*

The paved ground simply served as a makeshift driveway. In both directions on either side of the establishment, the woods—thinned out though they were by a dawning winter—were endless and twisted. It would be an arduous, if not impossible task to make her way through them. She had no choice but to go through the graveyard.

She scanned the burial ground, took in the crooked crosses and crumbling headstones, and then slipped through a small opening in the gate left by the rusted lock and chain.

There were no fresh graves within the cemetery. It was old and worn and overgrown with now-leafless vines. The stones were cracked; some simply acted as beds for weeds and vines that had long since made their rooted claim on the weathered names and dates. From the state of some of the sun-bleached plastic flowers laid upon the stones and covered with rain-splattered mud, Eleanore wondered whether the cemetery had been forgotten altogether.

It filled her with a deep sense of sadness to walk between the markers, viewing the etched carvings one after another. The older they were and the more worn the dates, the younger the dead. One pair of particularly small and tilted stones bore the dates of children—a brother and sister—who had died merely a year apart. When she studied the dates, she realized the first had died while the mother was pregnant with the other.

Eleanore could not run through this hallowed ground. Time was pressing in on her, the sun had already gone down, and the temperature had already dropped dramatically.

But the souls that had been left here beneath her feet pulled at her, clutched at her, and forced her into a state of reverence and respect. The dates on the stones begged to be read, the names noticed and whispered aloud. The dead wanted to be recognized. Whether they'd been there for one year or a hundred. By the time she reached the other side, the etchings were no longer discernible and mist had fully enshrouded the hallowed ground.

The night was complete and upon her. Eleanore stood at the iron cemetery gate and wrapped her hands around the rusted metal bars. She would have to climb to get out on this side. She gave the gate a quick shake to test for sturdiness, and it held. Then she took a deep breath and, to gather her strength, she rested her forehead against the metal, closing her eyes.

"They are speaking to you."

Eleanore jumped and spun around to face the source of the deep, melodic voice. A tall man stood there, five yards away, dressed in black from head to toe. His long raven hair reminded Eleanore of her own; the color blended seamlessly with the sable material of his jacket. His eyes, however, were stark and gold as the sun. They nearly glowed in the frame of his pale, handsome face.

At once, Eleanore was petrified. She could not even ask him what he was talking about. Her mouth was instantly dry. This was the stuff of nightmares. A cemetery, a deserted road, a stranger who was undoubtedly ten times stronger than she was. One who barely looked human.

"The dead," he said, with a slight nod to the nearest headstone. "The ones who stay behind. They always speak, but mortals never hear them. You're different, though. They can sense that. It's why you walk with respect through these grounds, isn't it?" He spoke softly, yet his voice resonated with an easy charisma in the hollowness of the night. And it sounded vaguely familiar. . . .

He stepped toward her then and shoved his hands into the pockets of his black jeans. It was a casual gesture, done perhaps to put her at ease.

She tried to ask him what he wanted. Her lips parted and her tongue moved, but no sound whispered past her teeth. She was too frightened. The night had held too many unsavory surprises. She'd most likely worn herself out in her mad dash through the tangled woods.

Her back was pressed against the cold metal of the gate; its rusted edges cut into the damp material of her hooded sweatshirt. She wondered whether the protein bar she'd eaten would provide enough energy to call another bolt of lightning from the damp sky.

"I won't harm you." He smiled a small smile and she could have sworn there was something predatory about it. But it was dark and she couldn't quite tell. "I'm here on my brother's behalf," he said.

What brother? she tried to ask him.

Finally, she was able to make some sound. "Who—" Her voice broke, cracking in dryness. She swallowed, half coughed, and tried again. "Who the hell are you?" she finally croaked.

"I'm Azrael," he told her calmly and continued to draw closer. "Uriel is my brother." His long legs ate up the ground very quickly, despite his easy, unhurried pace. And she could go nowhere.

She remembered them mentioning Azrael. He was the brother who hadn't been at the mansion when she was there but who apparently had more power than they did. Looking at him now, she could believe it.

"Which angel"—she swallowed hard, nearly coughing again, her throat was so dry. She fought past the uncomfortable tickle and finished—"are you?"

At this, he stopped in his tracks and something sparked in those unearthly amber eyes. He glanced at the cemetery around him and then looked back at her. He said nothing, but he didn't have to. She knew.

"You're the Angel of Death." She felt numb even saying it.

Azrael nodded slowly, and Eleanore was once more struck with a familiarity. There was something—*rock star*-like—about him. He reminded her, in that moment, of Lestat.

Eleanore blinked. Then her eyes grew wide. She put her fingers up, blocking out the top half of his face. It was a dead match. "You're the Masked One," she whispered.

He raised his head again and his gaze sparkled. He smiled.

Eleanore didn't know what to make of this new development. It seemed everyone in Uriel's little "family" was famous. She was getting used to it, and a touch jaded. But above all, she was still scared.

"Look, I need some time to figure this out," she told him, clearing her throat to go on. "I don't want to go anywhere with you right now, s-so don't even ask." She glanced down at his booted feet, which took another step toward her. "And you can stop coming closer, too," she added. "I don't care how famous you are." She shook her head. "I don't trust you."

"Wise girl," came another voice.

Eleanore jumped a little against the metal bars holding her in place and turned to see Samuel Lambent calmly step out of the shadows of the more tangled and forgotten area of the cemetery. He was dressed in a suit tonight, one that was charcoal gray and perfectly tailored. The vision of him was surreal in this haunted and ghostly setting.

Azrael turned to look as well, though he did not seem at all surprised. His expression didn't change. His gold eyes simply glittered in the misty darkness.

"So many people have run afoul after trusting that particular angel." Samuel nodded toward Azrael.

Eleanore's brow furrowed, her eyes wide. *What the hell?* What was Lambent doing here? How did he know that Azrael was an angel? What the bloody banks was going on?

She was beginning to feel like she'd been caught by those men in the parking lot after all and shot full of tranquilizers. This was some sort of drug-induced dream. The cemetery, the fog, the Masked One—and Sam.

Except that she was in too much discomfort for this to be a dream. She was so cold. Her legs hurt. Her lungs hurt. Her skin stung where branches and thorns had torn through her clothes and sliced her open.

"It's not a dream, Eleanore," Azrael told her gently.

Sam chuckled. His white-blond hair brushed his shoulders. It looked fine as feathers and starkly bright in the surrounding darkness. There was a light behind his dark gray eyes now, adding to the surreal quality of his appearance.

"S-Sam?" she muttered, feeling stupid. Why couldn't she talk right? Is this what real terror did to a person? Exhaustion? Was she in shock?

"I'm sorry, Ellie," he told her. "Things were not supposed to go this far."

"She isn't yours, Samael," Azrael said then, his tone quiet but laced with undertones of malice. "Why will you not accept this?"

Samael? thought Eleanore. *Did I hear that right?*

"Not yet." Sam shrugged and smiled a broad smile. "And I stress *yet*."

I have to get out of here, Eleanore thought then. She could feel that something extremely bad was about to go down. It was a vibration in the air around her, a buzzing sensation in her blood.

"Can you feel them, Azrael? Those whose ancestors you brought to this place know that you walk among them. They are restless." Samuel chuckled again, clasping his hands easily behind his back as he slowly paced to a place somewhere between Azrael and Eleanore. He glanced at her and there was genuine amusement in his crackling silver gaze.

"Enough," Azrael said. He spoke without anger and without any real force, but his voice carried across the darkness with incredible beauty. He also sounded weary. Genuinely weary. "Speak the truth, Samael. For once in your ungodly existence."

At this, Samuel Lambent threw back his head and laughed heartily. The sound was as deep and rumbling and beautiful as the voice of Azrael.

Eleanore was simply bewildered. She would have given almost anything at that moment to be transported somewhere safe and bright and free of men altogether.

Sam stopped laughing and turned his piercing gaze on her. It took her breath away to be suddenly under such a weight.

"*Anything*, Eleanore?"

Eleanore blinked. *He read my mind. . . .*

"Say nothing to him, Ellie!" Azrael commanded from where he stood. His gold eyes were now blazing bright as fire. They reminded Eleanore of Uriel's brilliant frozen gaze as he'd looked upon her in the garage only hours ago. "Do not speak, and guard your thoughts well," Azrael told her. Something in his golden eyes held a very real warning.

She looked from Azrael to Samuel, and in her mind she replayed her meeting with the wealthy media mogul. She thought of the motorcycle crash and his injury that had been uncommonly difficult to mend. And now here he was. In a cemetery on a dark night, when he shouldn't have been able to find her at all.

Eleanore suddenly found herself doubting Samuel Lambent. *Samael,* she thought. Azrael had called him Samael. Was he the same Samael Uriel told her about in the mansion? The one who had caused her and the other archesses to be lost to the archangels all of those years ago?

Sam cocked his head to one side and studied her very carefully. He turned to face her fully, spearing her with eyes that were abruptly and unexpectedly unnerving.

"Who, then, shall you be taking counsel from on this night, Eleanore?" he asked her slowly, softly. There was danger in that gaze, but there was something else as well. Pain? He smiled a small, self-deprecatory smile. "Death or the 'Devil'?"

That's it, thought Eleanore. Her creep-out-o-meter had just pretty much exploded.

The tombstones were heavy enough to do damage to a human if slammed into one telekinetically—but she was no longer so sure Samuel was human. And she honestly didn't feel that she'd yet regained the strength it took to call lightning forth from the skies. Not that it would stop either of the men with her.

As worthless as she knew it would be, the only recourse left to her, despite everything, was to run. She spun around and grasped hold of the metal bars of the gate behind her, bringing her legs up with the intent of vaulting over it.

But it was Samuel Lambent's tall, suit-clad form gazing steadily at her from the other side that stopped her short. She hadn't seen him move, of course. And it should have been impossible for him to be standing behind her at one moment—and then be standing thirty feet away, outside of the cemetery the next.

"Running will do you no good," he said as he came

toward the gate from the other side. He said it matter-of-factly and looked down at the ground as he walked. He was a gorgeous man in an expensive suit merely contemplating a fact, nothing more.

Eleanore instinctively let go of the rusted bars and stepped back from the metal barrier that now seemed so utterly flimsy.

Sam paused where he was and casually unbuttoned his suit coat. He shoved his hands into his pant pockets. "Running will only weaken you, Ellie," he said with a shrug. Another few lazy steps forward and he sighed heavily, nearly closing the distance between himself and the gate. When he finally reached it, he looked up, caught her eyes with his, and peered all the way into her soul.

In no more than a whisper, he said, "I promise you that you will need all of your strength once I get you alone."

The air around Eleanore shifted with an unnatural wind. It whipped at her hair and blew debris into her eyes just as she was shoved roughly backward and went flying across the cemetery to land on her back on a patch of grass and mud several yards away.

Eleanore lay stunned for a moment, listening to the shriek of bending, wrenching metal and the violent crunch and splinter of wood. And then she rolled over and pushed herself up onto her elbow, using her other hand to shove her long black hair out of her face. But arms came around her then, strong bands of steel that hauled her backward across the ground and against an equally hard body.

Self-preservation kicked in and Eleanore went into overdrive, fighting furiously in her captor's grip. But the fight did no good and it didn't last long before her captor was twisting her arm behind her, and she was contemplating the lightning once more.

"Zap me and you'll get yourself, too. Be a good girl and hold still."

She recognized that voice. It was Jason something or other, Samuel Lambent's personal assistant.

Despite the fight-or-flight reflex pouring adrenaline into Eleanore's blood, she was beginning to feel well and truly spent. Exhaustion was creeping in around the edges when metal cuffs were snapped onto her wrists and Jason's arms came around her once more.

She couldn't move. There was nowhere for her to go. Jason held her tight as she peered across the cemetery to where two men were fighting, their tall forms locked in mortal combat. Each had a hand around the other's throat. The air was charged with lightning, and it wasn't Eleanore's doing. There was also a deeper darkness to the night around them. It was more cloying, colder and blacker. It seemed to linger in patches and moved as the two struggling figures moved. It followed them, welcoming its honored guests, laying out its shadows for them to tread upon and draping them in its finest sable cloaks, as was befitting their stations.

Across the graveyard, Azrael threw Samuel against a crumbling crypt laced with dead ivy; the impact cracked the mortar under Sam's rock-hard body. But as Samuel slowly straightened from the crumbling indentation behind him, a moaning rose from the ground of the graveyard. It was a whistling, screeching kind of moan that caused Eleanore to duck her head and wish her hands were free to cover her ears.

The wailing, moaning din grew in volume and Azrael looked around him at the gravestones and matted, muddy earth.

Eleanore looked up to see Jason smile a broad, white grin.

Samuel spoke, moving away from the wall behind him and straightening his clothes as he did. "Like I said, Azrael, they know you're here. They know who you are." He looked down at the ground and the faint mist that was now rising from each grave. He smiled. "And they're not happy to see you."

The sound crescendoed and the mists coalesced and darkened and floated toward the tall, dark form of the one who had seen their father's fathers to their graves. It was like a dam of spirits had broken and the flood was rushing toward the former Angel of Death.

Samuel turned to Jason then and raised his hand. Before Eleanore knew it, Jason raised his other hand toward his master and the world melted around them.

"Why do you do this to yourself, Sam?" She sounded like weariness itself, her tone so soft, her voice so mournfully tender, that for just a moment, Samael regretted having brought her to that stage. But the regret was fleeting and flighty and left on the same fickle wings on which it had flown in.

"It's in my nature, Lily." He shrugged, gave her a sidelong glance, and then turned back to finish preparing the drink he had been making for Eleanore Granger—who waited with Jason in the sitting room next door. "It's who I am."

"No, it isn't."

At that, he smiled. He spared her the mirthless chuckle, however, and simply shook his head. "You'll never give up, will you?"

"Nor will you," she retorted. She stood from where she'd been sitting on the couch across from the bar at which he stood. "Such self-destructive behavior." She made her way to the bar beside him, and without looking at him, she began to pour herself a drink. "Thousands of years, and I am the only one to have glimpsed the side of you I've seen," she said softly. She glanced up at him over her shoulder, and he met her dark gaze. "You torture yourself," she told him.

"Someone has to do it." His smile was self-deprecating and entirely charming. Then he grew serious and his gaze narrowed. "How are you feeling?'

For a moment, Lilith appeared nervous under the weight of the question. Then she put down her freshly poured drink without taking a sip. She straightened her shirt and looked down at the marble counter of the bar. "Better. I heal quickly."

"Yes, I know," Sam said, cocking his head to one side and studying her more closely. "I never would have sent you otherwise."

She said nothing, and avoided meeting his gaze.

"Gillihan insisted on seeing you one last time before he left with the contract," he told her, watching her closely to see her response.

She blushed, if only slightly, and looked up at him in surprise. It was answer enough for him. His smile became one of dawning roguishness. "You're in love with the Guardian."

"Enough," she insisted softly. "What is it exactly that Max will learn once he studies the contract, Sam?" she asked, changing the subject. She paused and sighed, turning the stem of the wineglass in her fingers. "What have you done?"

Now Samael smirked, turning away from the bar with two drinks in his hands. "Stipulations, my dear. Details." He shrugged as he made his way to the door at the other side of the room. "Contracts are serious business. Uriel knew that going into it."

"You gave him little choice."

Samael stopped and shot her a dark look over his broad shoulder. His tone was very low when he replied, "There is always a choice, Lily."

The sun was coming up on Wednesday morning. He could sense it; there remained less than an hour of night. Azrael had grown accustomed to its coming and going and what it meant. But there was a vampire among them now who had never before experienced a dawn through a vampire's eyes. Az could effortlessly read Uriel's thoughts and emotions; it had been easy when Uriel was only an archangel. It was even easier now.

Uriel had always regarded the day as any human

would. It was simply the sun—it existed and it did its thing and that was that. But now, as the new vampire noticed its creeping rays slithering toward the horizon like tentacles of an angry god, he was fully aware of it in a way that no normal mortal could possibly comprehend. It was, in all of its gigantic, gaseous glory, *certain death*. And he felt as if it were coming for him.

"I haven't much time," Uriel said. His eyes were on the window and the thick curtains that hung over it. They were black and velvet and behind them were the protective wooden slats of venetian blinds. Beyond the blinds and the window they covered was a court-yard underground. This was Azrael's wing of the man-sion, as far from the reach of daylight's glowing orb as possible. And it wasn't enough for Uriel. He was still so new.

"I know," Max said, glancing up. "I'm working as fast as I can." The guardian watched his charge with a wary, careful gaze. Uriel had been warned by his brothers and by Max, as well, not to attempt to go after Eleanore on his own. He was not used to being a vampire and couldn't be trusted not to lose control and hurt her.

Azrael could feel the wrath that surrounded the for-mer Angel of Vengeance like an invisible, pulsing shroud. What they suggested may have made loads of sense, but it was clearly driving Uriel mad.

Max returned his attention to the task before him. In front of him rested a thick slab composed of some com-bination of marble and limestone. It resembled an altar, minus the candle wax drippings. On top of it rested, un-scrolled, the contract that Uriel and Samael had both signed.

On the other side of the altar, Gabriel and Michael watched Max closely, their handsome visages shadow-crossed, their jaws tight, their voices silenced.

Across the room, hidden in the shadows and leaning against a carved stone wall, Azrael waited. He was still weak. Samael's spell had taken him by surprise and drained much of the strength out of him. The Fallen One had called up the spirits of the dead that had not yet moved on—and they'd gone after Azrael. Their bitter essences had speared through him and about him, angrily devouring the life force from him they so desperately yearned for. Az didn't have a lot of life force in him to begin with. He was a vampire. The spell had left him weak beyond measure. And it had allowed Samael to escape with the archess.

But Az had since fed—twice—and now the darkness licked his wounds. He watched in silence and knew what they were all thinking. He carefully gauged Uriel's every heartbeat, his every tightened fist, and every impatient flexing of muscle within his tall, toned body.

He was paler now, Azrael noted. Uriel now resembled his infamous portrayal of Jonathan Brakes much more closely than he did the alias Christopher Daniels. Az had to smile at that.

"There." Max's shoulders slumped, just a little, signaling that he was finally relaxing in his effort to cast the spell that would disentangle the knotted web of lies Samael had cleverly forced upon Uriel. He waved his hand over the contract.

The black ink on the document began to rise into the air above the altar, its inkiness unwrapping from the paragraphs on the page. It hovered above the stone slab and, as the archangels and their guardian looked on, every letter of every word revealed itself to be composed of not a single stroke of a pen, but of many. Each letter was composed of several other letters—several other words—so that hidden within the very language of the contract was another contract. And another. Promise upon promise, layered so deceptively they would never have been seen with an unaided eye.

"I suggest you read it carefully," Uriel muttered.

Max blinked and turned to him, his eyes wide.

Uriel glanced at him. "That's what he told me." His green eyes glittered darkly. "Before I signed."

"Yes, well ..." Max turned back to the hovering phrases, and shook his head. "Samael is very good at what he does."

"So what now?" Michael asked, his blue eyes on the tiny print that continued to unravel from the blood-signed document.

"Now I read it carefully." Max smiled wryly. "It'll take me some time." He turned to Uriel. "In the meantime, you sleep. Samael won't hurt Eleanore. We've proof more or less to that extent right here before us." He waved dismissively at the unwrapping contract. "God only knows what the man is really after, but he appears to want her heart, not her body."

"You mean not *only* her body," Gabriel corrected.

Uriel's eyes sparked dangerously and began to glow. A very low, ominously deep growl rumbled through the stone chamber and caused the flames on the sconces to flicker unsteadily.

Gabriel's silvery gaze moved from his brother's burning jade-green orbs to the fangs that were so pronounced in Uriel's warning snarl. "Right," he muttered softly. "Sorry."

Max broke the tension then, as he was so accustomed to doing. He stepped back from the altar and turned to the shadows from where he knew Azrael looked silently on. "How are you feeling?" he asked.

Azrael could see himself through his guardian's eyes. Gold eyes reflected in the darkness and there was a stillness in the shadows around him, predatory and dangerous. "Better," he said softly.

"Good," Max said, nodding.

I will have to force him to sleep, Az told Max then, using his telepathic abilities. He was referring to Uriel. *He's set on going after her right away.*

At that, Uriel cocked his head to one side and offered Azrael a somewhat cruel smile. He may not have had the use of his vampire telepathy because of the bracelet he wore, but it was as if Uriel had read Az's thoughts anyway.

Azrael stepped out of the shadows, studying his brother carefully.

Samael knew Uriel too well. There was more of Jonathan Brakes in him than anyone had thought.

CHAPTER TWELVE

Eleanore glared up at Samuel Lambent from where she sat on one of his plush couches in his office in the former Sears Tower. She had materialized in this room along with him and Jason after Sam had magically whisked them out of the cemetery. She was no longer cuffed. What was the point? She knew she wasn't going anywhere.

"You're Samael," she hissed accusingly. She'd figured a few things out over the last few hours. "You're the archangel that Uriel was talking about. You're the one who caused the archesses to be dumped down here all those years ago."

Samael smiled down at her, his stance calm, his hands in his pockets. "I won't deny it."

"You did something to Uriel, didn't you?"

Samael turned and gave her a sidelong glance. "He did it to himself," he said, matter-of-factly. Then he stepped away from the couch to move around the coffee table behind him, his attention on a window set into one wall. The sun's morning rays were peeking through the shutters, warming the air. He stopped before the window, allowing the light to bathe him in its glory. "He signed the agreement. A deal is a deal."

"You turned him into a vampire."

At that, Samael smiled to himself, but said nothing.

"What do you want from me?" she asked, her teeth set on edge.

Samael turned again and looked at her long and hard. Eleanore wanted to be brave beneath such attention, but he was . . . well, he was too beautiful, his gaze unconquerable. In the end, she managed to pull her own eyes from his and look at the coffee table. It was all she could do to keep from being sucked into the crackling storms of his eyes.

"I was hoping you would consider making a deal of your own."

That got her attention. Eleanore's head snapped up, her eyes finding his once more. "With *you*?" she breathed. "You can't be serious."

"I generally find that I am rarely anything *but* serious," he told her with a hint of a smile.

"Mr. Lambent—"

"Sam."

Eleanore blinked. The alias thing was ridiculous with this bunch. She would never be sure exactly what to call any of them. She pressed on. "I would very much like to know what kind of game I've found myself in the middle of. I don't know what kind of pact it is you have with Uriel and his brothers, and I don't know where I fit into it all. But frankly, it's pissing me off."

Samael studied her closely. She could feel him taking everything in, from the top of her head to the tips of her boots. It unnerved her to no end, but she ruthlessly forced herself not to back down. *Be brave.*

He left the window and came to stand before her. To her credit, she didn't shrink from him.

"You want the entire truth?" he asked her.

"Please," she said, meaning it from the bottom of her heart. She was so tired.

"Very well." He told everything then. He retold the story that she had already heard from Uriel and his brothers—how she and three others like her had been created, long, long ago, as soul mates for the four arch-angels.

He told her about the revolt and how she and the others had been "discarded" by the Old Man. "Anything to keep an uneasy peace in a place where such a thing was merely a mask for irresponsible power and hindered desires."

He even told her about his deal and the contract with Uriel. The only thing he *didn't* tell her was why he had demanded the deal in the first place. That, apparently, was his business and his alone.

"You used me," she told him. "To trick Uriel into serving you."

"I may have," he admitted easily. "I am not always proud of the things I do, Eleanore. But I do them anyway." He walked once more to the window and peered out over Chicago. "It's who I am."

"And what kind of deal is it that you want from me?"

Samael blinked, looked down, and then, after a moment of consideration, he turned away from the window and moved to a large oak desk that rested in front of a set of massive bookcases loaded with books. He picked up a piece of paper from the desk and then reached for a fountain pen that stood upright in a marble holder in one corner.

"I want the same thing I have always wanted," he told her as he brought the paper and pen around the desk and set them down on the coffee table before her. "I want to win."

What the hell does that mean? Eleanore thought. She gazed down at the paper. It looked to be a fairly old and yellowed parchment piece, but was completely blank. The pen was equally strange to her. It looked to be made of something like quartz crystal, clear and glittery and beautiful.

Not quartz, she realized. *It's one solid diamond.*

With wide eyes, she glanced up at Samael, who was taking a seat on the couch opposite from her. He watched her steadily, not saying anything.

"It has no ink," she said. The pen was see-through, and focusing on its lack of ink took her mind off its general purpose.

"It doesn't use ink," he told her, his tone low, his voice a wicked, evil caress.

"I still don't know what you want from me," she choked out.

"I want your word that if Christopher Daniels—Uriel," he clarified, his eyes glinting with silver, "does anything to hurt you in the next seven days, you will come to me."

Eleanore blinked. "What would Uriel do to hurt me?" Images of the archangel with glowing red eyes and prominent fangs floated before her mind's eye.

"It can't be easy going through the changes his body is making," Samael said. "There's so much to take into consideration." He leaned back against the couch and shrugged. "Whereas daylight was once nothing more than illumination for him, now it will be deadly. Then there's the feeding," he said and his gaze cut to her. His voice had dropped subtly, meaningfully. "He will need to do it nightly—and he will need to learn how to prevent himself from killing those he feeds from. It can be very tempting to take things further than strictly necessary."

Eleanore digested this and found that the more she imagined Uriel sinking his fangs into someone's throat, the dryer her mouth got.

There was a brief flash of light in front of her and Eleanore gasped and looked down to find a tall glass of ice water sweating on the coffee table before her.

"It isn't poisoned, so please drink," Samael said.

Eleanore realized that this meant he had been reading her mind, and that he was most likely still doing so.

But she also realized it would be pointless to ask him to stop.

She took the glass and drank. It felt wonderful going down, cold and thirst-quenching, and it seemed to fortify her enough that she could ask her next question. She set the glass back down, now half-empty, and said, "You think that Uriel is going to kill me?"

"No." Samael smiled a wry smile. "No, Eleanore. If I did, there would be little use in my asking you to come to me should he harm you. However, I wouldn't put it past him to take more than you're willing to give."

Eleanore felt herself flushing once more as Samael's gaze burned into her from where he leaned so casually against the back of the couch. She looked down at the coffee table and self-consciously hugged herself.

"Agree to this one thing, and when the week has ended, I will release Uriel from his curse."

This drew her attention to him once again. "And if I don't agree?"

"Then he will remain trapped in his new form for the rest of eternity. Who knows? Perhaps he will get used to it one day."

Eleanore ran a hand through her hair and then over her eyes. There was no easy way out of this for any of them. There was too much to contend with. Contracts, deals, vampirism curses . . . She and Uriel still had each other to contend with, on top of it all. That was enough on its own. Could she grow to love him, as she was meant to as an archess?

I certainly already lust after him, she thought wryly.

It was the very basis of her existence that was bothering her the most. Learning that she was an archess was one thing; it explained so many questions she'd had all her life about why she was different. And finding out Uriel was supposed to be her soul mate wasn't so bad either; she had to admit, she felt attracted to him body and soul from the moment she'd met him in the flesh.

But learning that she had actually been created for the sole purpose of being his mate was something else again. Where was her free will in all of this?

It had been taken the first time Uriel had set eyes on her. Or perhaps it had been taken the first time her powers had shown themselves to the world and she'd instantly gone into hiding. Or maybe it had been taken the moment of her creation, and she had never had it to begin with.

She was not free. She never had been. And she resented it.

"I can give you freedom," Samael said then.

Eleanore looked up at him, eyes wide. "What?"

Samael took a quick, thoughtful breath and stood. He paced to his desk, turned, and leaned back against it, his arms crossed over his chest. "Eleanore, you must know in your heart that I can give you anything you desire."

Oh no, she thought. *Be strong, Ellie, be strong.*

But his smile was tender and his gaze made her feel weak. "You need but trust me." Then, without warning, he disappeared.

Eleanore stared in surprise at the spot where he had been only moments before. And then she became instantly wary. Slowly, she stood from the couch, her dark blue eyes scanning the four corners of the large, opulently furnished study. She slowly searched the shadows, her breath quickening once more, but found no sign of him.

He was simply gone.

She turned back around to face the coffee table only to find it had disappeared and Samael was standing a mere few inches away, watching her with that careful, calculating gaze.

Oh Christ, she thought frantically, and placed her hand to her chest. *He's scary as hell, but so gorgeous . . . and so close . . .* Her heart was racing.

He smiled down at her, no doubt reading her thoughts.

"Give me what I want, Eleanore, and I will reciprocate. It's that simple."

He raised his hand to gently cup the side of her face. She suppressed a shiver at the contact. He was so warm and that warmth suffused her upon contact, the way a sunbeam through the window in the winter could chase away a deathly chill.

"Give me this small boon. All I ask is that you trust me." He drew nearer and Eleanore's breath hitched. He lowered his lips until his next words caressed her ear. "And come to me."

He laid the gentlest of kisses against her earlobe then, causing a hard shiver to course through her slender form. "You have everything to gain," he whispered, so soft, so warm.

And nothing to lose . . .

The thought went floating, unchecked through her mind. She didn't know whether it was her own but she didn't care. She was under his spell, whether he'd done it on purpose or not. He was simply too perfect. Too beautiful. Too warm and tall and hard and strong and persistent and gentle and dangerous. *So wonderfully dangerous.*

She tried to nod, and didn't know whether she'd succeeded until he was gradually pulling away just enough for her to open her eyes. He had one of her wrists in his hand, his fingers curled around her in a gentle but firm grip. In his other hand, he held the pen; it glimmered in the sunlight coming through the window and sparkled in her eyes.

"Let me make this easier on you," he told her, bringing the inside of her wrist to his lips, where he gently laid a kiss over her pulsing vein. She watched in fascination as he pulled back and a small droplet of blood welled up from the place he had just kissed.

There was no pain. She was just bleeding.

"The pen requires the blood of each contracting party."

He then lowered the tip of the fountain pen to the blood and deftly filled the interior compartment with the red, precious fluid.

Once it was filled, he turned and set the pen down on the coffee table as it reappeared, still holding her arm firmly in his fingers. Then he faced her once more and loosened his grip on her wrist, running his thumb gently over the tiny wound he had created. It disappeared, leaving her flesh once more unmarked.

Eleanore's knees felt weak, and he must have known it, because he took her other wrist in his hand as well and guided her back down onto the couch. As she sat, he knelt before her, maintaining eye contact.

"Eleanore, will you promise to come to me should Uriel do something to hurt you within the next seven days?"

She hesitated. But then she realized there was no backing out now. Uriel was a vampire because he'd made a deal to protect Eleanore. The least she could do was return the favor and try to get him out of the mess she'd inadvertently placed him in.

And . . . it was more than that.

She didn't only feel she owed him. She *wanted* to help Uriel. In the normal scheme of things, it wouldn't make any sense. They'd only just met. But this wasn't the normal world. This was a world of archangels and their soul mate archesses. It was *her* world—and Uriel was at its center. If there was even the slightest chance that this deal with Samael would put an end to the pain she had seen Uriel enduring in the garage in the mansion, then it was worth it to her.

All Samael was asking was that she allow him to protect her. That she trust him. What could be the harm in that?

She looked up into Samael's eyes and swallowed hard, nodding once.

"Say it, Eleanore," he instructed calmly, his gray eyes glittering darkly.

She blinked rapidly and licked her lips. "Yes," she said. "I promise."

With that, Samael smiled a winning, beautiful smile and gently placed the now ruby-red diamond pen in Eleanore's hand. Its sharp fountain tip bubbled slightly with a tiny red drop, ready to be put to paper.

Samael stood and backed away from the table so that Eleanore had a clear view of the ancient parchment atop it. It was no longer blank; black lettering was scrolling itself onto the page even as she watched. The words were written in what she knew simply from the sight of it was a very old language. Ancient.

Like Sam.

When it had finished scrolling, a pair of signature lines appeared at the bottom of the page. One was for her.

Samael waited patiently, but Eleanore knew that if she didn't do it now, she would lose her nerve. So she slid off of the couch and onto her knees in front of the coffee table. Then she placed the pen on the line and signed her name.

She expected something to happen then. Perhaps lightning would strike her or maybe she would spontaneously combust. Instead, all that she heard was a gentle rustling beside her as Sam moved to the other end of the coffee table and knelt as well. He held out his hand, palm-up, and she realized that he wanted the pen.

She handed it to him, noticing that it was no longer red, but once more crystal-clear and empty. Samael took the pen from her, his fingers brushing over hers as he did so. She shivered and pulled away, looking at the floor.

What have I done?

When she heard the sound of scratching on parchment, she looked up to see that he was signing his own name, and once more, the pen was red. He'd taken his own blood and she hadn't seen it. She was grateful for that. Her stomach felt a bit strange at the moment. She was so unsteady, so unsure. . . .

When he'd finished, he waved both pen and parchment away and they simply disappeared. Then he stood once more, moved to her side, and offered her his hand. The expression on his incredibly handsome face was one of keen concern. "Are you okay?" he asked.

This struck Eleanore as odd. Why would he ask? Why did he care? He'd gotten what he wanted, hadn't he? She blinked up at him and then nodded once. "I think so."

"Then I will ask you for one last favor, Eleanore."

Oh no, here it comes, she thought. *The lightning . . .*

"The gala that Christopher Daniels must attend in Dallas is not until tomorrow night. I know you've agreed to go with him and I won't stop you. However, I also know that he's not the only one who poses a threat to you." Here, he paused, allowing the information to sink in. She realized it meant he knew about the men who had chased her for the better part of her life. "I am not sure you're safe in your apartment any longer. Please allow me to provide you with safe lodging until tomorrow." He paused again, allowing her to consider his request. Then he added, "I will make certain you're provided with food and clothing—and anything else you need or desire."

Why is he being so nice to me?

If it were possible, his stormy gray eyes looked sad then. Perhaps a bit weary. No—a *lot* weary. *He's exhausted,* she thought suddenly. The strong impression was there one moment and swept away with the next. Fleeting. She wondered if she had imagined it.

Reluctantly, she nodded. He was right. She couldn't go home.

He said nothing more. Instead, he released her hand and looked down at the floor. He seemed to be thinking deeply, the muscle in his jaw tensing and relaxing. "I'll have Lilith, my assistant, take care of everything."

"I have to call the bookstore," Ellie said.

"It's been taken care of," he replied.

With that, he turned away from her and strode to the

door of the office. Once there, he grasped the handle, turned the knob, and then glanced at her over his broad shoulder. He gave her a searching look and she wondered what it was he was searching for.

Then he opened the door and stepped out into the hall, closing the door behind him.

CHAPTER THIRTEEN

Michael watched with obvious keen interest as Max finally wiped his brow on the back of his sleeve and braced himself on the desk, letting his head drop in exhaustion. The blond archangel had been watching Max patiently as he'd worked. The contract and its unraveling, swirling, glowing words still rested before him on the polished oak surface of the desk, but the unscrolling had more or less stopped. It was now completely decoded.

It was quiet for a long while as Max leaned on the large desk, his head bowed, his eyes closed. It had taken just about everything out of him to unravel Sam's trickery.

Finally Michael spoke up, apparently tired of waiting. "Well? What does it say?"

Max raised his head to stare at him. "Nothing."

Michael frowned. "What?"

Max straightened once more, took off his glasses, and began to clean them with the hem of his untucked shirt. He was a mess. "It says nothing. Absolutely nothing." He sighed. He slipped his glasses back on and adjusted them. "Samael was toying with me."

Max took a step back and gazed at the glowing words that floated in the air, filling the space from the desktop to the ceiling in front of him. They hovered there in a vague paragraphic formation; there were thousands of them. And they meant nothing.

He ran a tired hand through his hair and turned away from the display to make his way to the liquor cabinet against one wall. "The only hidden obligation in the mess was the one that has already transpired," he told Michael calmly. "That being the one that gave Uriel his new vampire form. Everything else is non-sense." He pulled a crystal decanter from the top shelf, uncorked it, and poured a good amount of the brown liquid into a waiting crystal glass. "I suspect he was trying to keep us busy for a while. Either that, or this is simply his idea of fun."

He turned to see Michael shoot him a frustrated glare. "Knowing Sam, it was both."

Max grimaced as he swallowed a heady load of alcohol and gritted his teeth. He nodded and ground out, "Indeed." Max almost never drank; it just wasn't his thing. However, tonight the amber liquid was calling his name and since his guardian abilities allowed him to will away its effects with no more than a thought, he wasn't going to hold back.

"So what do you think he's been busy doing while we've been here decoding bullshit?"

"I'm sorry—'we'?" Max asked incredulously. He was very tired and was all out of social niceties just then.

Michael had the decency to look a bit guilty. He shrugged. "Sorry. I mean 'you.' "

"He's been up to no good, that's what," said Max. He was feeling the alcohol already; it was hitting him hard and fast. "Most likely involving Eleanore."

"Aye, that 'e has," came a new voice from the doorway.

He and Michael turned to see Gabriel saunter into the room, his expression bleak. "She signed a bloody contract with the bugger."

Max almost choked on his drink.

"What?" Michael roared.

Max hurriedly swallowed and cleared his throat. "How do you know this?" he asked, wondering whether he should sober himself up really quickly with a bit of magic.

"We knew she was in the Tower, so I waited outside since there's no gettin' in." Gabriel strode across the room to where Max stood and took the drink from his hand. He unceremoniously swigged the rest of the liquor in the glass and then handed the empty container back to Max.

Max shot him a dirty look, but Gabriel failed to notice—or to care. "Lilith came out and told me everythin'."

Max wasn't surprised. Lilith often helped the archangels when it came to dealing with Samael. It was simply part of who she was: selfless, brave, wise. It was one of the many things that Max admired about her.

"What the hell happened?" Michael asked.

Gabriel reached up to the top shelf of the liquor cabinet and took down the same bottle that Max had poured his drink from. With one hand, he positioned Max's glass, still in the guardian's hand, and with his other, he refilled it. Max watched him do this in irritation and vague bafflement. When Gabriel had finished, he returned the decanter to the top shelf and then once more took the glass out of Max's hand to throw back his head and swig its contents in one swallow. This time, when he returned the glass to his guardian's grip, Max's jaw muscle twitched. Gabriel gritted his teeth, belched, and turned away from the liquor cabinet to make his way toward the couches at the center of the room.

Max rolled his eyes and set the glass down on the countertop with an exasperated *thunk*.

"Gabe," Michael repeated, as calmly as he could, given the circumstances. "What the hell happened at Sam's fortress?"

Gabriel glanced at his brother and shrugged. "Wha' can I say? He offered her wha' we could no' give her."

"Which is?" Max asked, now completely sober once more. It was pointless to attempt insobriety around Gabriel. The archangel would always have him beat at that particular game.

"A lift to Uriel's curse."

Michael swore under his breath and Max found himself pinching the bridge of his nose to stave off an oncoming headache. "And what did she have to give him in exchange?" Max asked.

"Now, only you'll be able to figure that out, Max." Gabriel smiled a lopsided smile before he plunked himself down on one of the plush leather sofas.

"Meaning you have to ask for her contract as well," Michael clarified. "The devil only knows what may be in Eleanore's agreement."

"Well put," Max agreed somberly. Samael was an archangel, but Michael and his brothers had long since taken to referring to him as the Dark Prince and every other nickname that came with the title. And after all, why shouldn't they? Samael was dangerous and devious to the extreme. The names fit.

Max had never felt so tired. Once more, he ran a hand through his hair, realizing that he'd picked up on the habit from one or more of the archangels. It seemed they all did it. "I'll see what I can do about getting a copy. In the meantime, where is she?"

"She'll be stayin' at the August," Gabriel supplied in his lazy, drawling brogue.

"That's a relatively new hotel," Max pondered. "In Vegas." He frowned. "I expect she felt safer staying away from Texas at this point."

"Indeed," Gabriel agreed.

Michael made a derisive sound. "Only Samael would consider Sin City a safe alternative to Texas."

"Mr. Farnsworth, I'm afraid a deal is a deal."

Lilith paused outside of Sam's office in the Tower. It was open and she had a clear view inside. He was on the phone and his back was turned toward her so that he could gaze out the window of the sixty-sixth-floor corner space. He was fond of the view; it seemed to put his mind at ease. She didn't bother knocking; she simply slipped inside and waited for him to finish.

Samael chuckled low in his throat and Lilith paused in her quiet travel across the room. She didn't like the sound of that laugh; it was one of his more dangerous tones.

"Listen to me now, Farnsworth."

There was a pause. Then Samael continued. "You wanted *Comeuppance* to make a certain amount of money. It has done so. I kept my end of the bargain. It's time for you to keep yours."

There was another pause, and then Samael began to turn in his swiveling leather chair. "That's what I thought. See you soon, Mr. Farnsworth." He set the phone down in its receiver and glanced up at Lilith. "You told them."

"Yes," Lilith admitted right away. "It was better for her."

Samael's lips curled into a small smile. "Oh, without a doubt." He sat back in his chair and steepled his fingers in front of him. "It matters little," he said.

"I bet." Lilith's gaze narrowed. "You got what you wanted from her, didn't you?"

"Not entirely," he said. "But it'll do for now."

Lilith sighed, suddenly feeling very tired. She'd been feeling that way a lot lately. It was this world. It would take the strength out of the best of them. She was in awe of the human population; she had been for a very long time.

"Sam, tell me that you didn't destroy that woman," Lilith finally sighed. She was too weary to make small talk anymore. She wrapped her arms around herself as if to stave off a cold wind. It brought her some amount of comfort.

Samael was quiet in his chair. Then he stood and closed the distance to the window, pressing his palms to the glass. "I asked for a promise, Lily. Nothing more. I give you my word."

"You didn't weave a thousand lies into her contract?" Lilith asked, incredulous.

"No."

Lilith blinked. She straightened, letting her arms drop to her sides. She was confused, to say the least. She knew that Samael had asked Eleanore Granger to come to him if she and Uriel fought—or some such nonsense. But she had assumed that there was more to the contract than met the eye. Could Samael truly mean that there was nothing more to their agreement? That her *trust* was all he had requested of the archess?

Samael lowered his hands and turned away from the window. He fixed Lilith with a steady, unreadable gaze. "No one in this world trusts me, Lily," he said, again using the more personal nickname he sometimes called her by. Then he laughed softly, the sound self-deprecating and quiet. "For good reason, no doubt." He shook his head. "Not even you."

Lilith wasn't sure what to say. His words took her slightly by surprise. For one thing, they were true. Oh, so very true. Not one soul in the universe trusted Samael. They hadn't trusted him for two thousand years. And though he was also right about there being good reason for such distrust, she was jarred to hear him admit it. What must it be like to exist without the trust of man?

"Is it so wrong for me to want this *one thing* after two thousand years?" he asked her then.

It was a long while before Lilith could respond, and the silence permeated the room, its walls, its book-filled shelves, and was punctured only slightly by the sound of jet planes and helicopters from beyond the window's thick pane.

When she did finally answer, it was without voice. Lilith simply shook her head. Once.

And called it good.

If Eleanore hadn't been so weary, she would have been incredibly impressed by everything Samael had done for her over the course of the day. His private jet had flown her to Vegas in a little less than two hours. And then, when his limousine had finished transporting her to the August hotel on the Strip and she'd entered her suite, it was to find a closet full of clothing and shoes waiting for her.

They were all brands she loved. There were Frye boots, Dr. Martens, Converse sneakers, Ed Hardy jeans, T-shirts, and leather jackets, Victoria's Secret *everything* . . . all in her size.

On the table was a feast of foods from chocolate-covered strawberries to expensive cheeses and crackers and there were cold drinks in the minifridge.

But perhaps her most amazing find of all was the thing that was lying in the middle of the massive king-sized bed in her room.

It was her Fossil purse—and inside it, everything that she had left behind when she'd vacated her car right after the accident on Slide Road, which was only yesterday morning, but seemed like an eternity ago. Eleanore had no idea how Samael had managed to get it out of her car in the angels' mansion. She would have thought the ever-changing magical building was impenetrable. Regardless, there it was. She had her driver's license, her credit cards, her cell phone—everything.

She chalked it up, again, to the magic that had become her life and then she showered and changed into some of her new clothes.

She enjoyed hotel rooms. It was bizarre for a person in her situation, forced to move around as much as she had. But she couldn't quite explain it. She loved that "free" feeling of being able to go anywhere in the world and know that wherever she went, she could just get a room at some hotel or motel or hostel or bed-and-breakfast—and she would have, at the very least, a bed to sleep in.

She also loved seeing new places, which was lucky for her, since she had little choice in the matter. She'd never been out of the country, but she had been all over the US. She had literally traveled from sea to sea, and hotel rooms had long since become like second homes to her.

It was dusk now on Wednesday afternoon, and she gazed out of her floor-to-ceiling windows onto the ever-brightening neon circus that was the Strip below. She thought of Uriel and wondered what he was doing at that moment.

Uriel awoke from his sleep much like he always did—slowly, gradually, and not at all as he had expected a vampire would.

"Humans have it wrong." Azrael spoke from where he was sitting, Indian-style, on top of a table a few feet away. He was watching Uriel with keen, glittering eyes. "We don't die during the day. We don't stop breathing, and our hearts always beat." He smiled, flashing fangs. "We're just night owls."

"I'm hungry," Uriel stated simply as he shoved himself up and off of the cool, stone bed he'd spent the day on. He'd tried a normal bed first. But his body had been stiflingly hot; it had craved the coolness of the marble in this chamber that Azrael had created long ago, and for the very same reason.

"And that's another thing." Azrael chuckled. "We get really crabby when we don't eat."

Uriel raised a brow and smiled wryly. "So what's next?"

"We eat," Azrael said with a shrug, suddenly leaping to his feet on the table in one strong, graceful movement. The torches in their sconces along the wall flickered with the sudden turbulence of the chamber's cool air.

"You pull that shit onstage much?" Uriel asked, realizing that he didn't often catch his brother's performances as the Masked One.

"Occasionally." Azrael smiled.

"I can see why you've made such an impression," Uriel muttered, swinging his legs over the edge of the stone slab and hopping down. His body moved differently in this state. It seemed to blur into each action, moving at a much greater speed than normal.

"Why doesn't the bracelet stop me from moving like this?"

"Your ability to move quickly is no more a vampire power than the ability to run is a human power. It's simply part of your vampire physiology," Az explained.

"This is going to take some getting used to," Uriel said as he stared down at himself.

"Nah." Azrael jumped down from the table, blurring in the air as he did so. It was like watching a movie, but without the screen. "It's reflex," he explained. "It won't take long at all."

Uriel blinked and Azrael was suddenly standing directly in front of him, less than a foot away. The tall, dark archangel gazed steadily at him with those eerie golden eyes. "Now follow me. I'm initiating you."

"Sounds very eighties vampire gang," Uriel retorted dryly.

"And what better place to be a Lost Boy than Sin City?"

"Vegas? You're taking me to Vegas for dinner?"

Azrael laughed. "Nope," he said. He waved his hand at a tall, dark wood door in a stone wall of the chamber. The door and wall surrounding it shimmered, waving in and out of existence like some Hollywood special effect. Then it disappeared completely and a warm, noisy darkness was revealed just beyond the opening. Azrael turned back to Uriel, his smile as wickedly sharp as ever. "We just woke up, remember? It's breakfast."

Uriel chewed on his cheek. "Right," he said. This was definitely new. It would seem that Azrael was a different person if you caught him at night, on his own turf. Doing his own thing. He even *joked*. Azrael never joked. He was Death, for crying out loud. But right now, the tall, dark archangel was smiling, and there was a lightness to his step he didn't normally display.

Uriel realized then that he didn't know his brother very well at all. How many years had it been since the two of them had held a real conversation with each other? Much less done anything together—anything at all? It had been years. *Thousands* of them.

Well, that's about to change, Uriel thought. Whether they wanted it or not, they had been thrown into the roles of teacher and student. And, strangely enough, teaching seemed to come naturally to Azrael. He led without pretense and even seemed to be enjoying himself. Wonder of wonders.

"Are you ready?" Azrael asked then.

Uriel turned to study the dark opening in the chamber wall. He knew enough about the way the mansion worked to know that the portal Azrael had opened most likely led directly into the city of Las Vegas. Probably, it opened into a back alley somewhere. Or an abandoned warehouse.

He nodded once and watched Azrael step into the darkness. When Uriel followed on his heels, a warm breeze welcomed him, along with the sound of wailing sirens, muffled dance club music, and an argument between two drunk lovers down the street.

"Ah. Vegas," Azrael said as they stepped out of the alley and onto the sidewalk, taking in the atmosphere. They didn't worry about the portal to the mansion behind him. The multidimensional house knew how to take care of itself; the opening was already gone.

"There." Azrael nodded toward a pair of women halfway down the block. They were young—most likely no more than twenty to twenty-five years old. They were scantily clad, one in a leather miniskirt, the other in tight jeans and a pair of teetering heels.

Neither was to Uriel's taste, vampire or not. He shook his head and shot Azrael a sidelong glance. "No, thank you."

"Not the prey, genius," Azrael scolded. He pointed

higher to a spot above them in his field of vision, raising his hand so that Uriel followed the line of sight to a group of men standing up the street on the corner, half-hidden in shadow. "The predators."

Uriel's gaze narrowed on the group of men. There were three of them, their faces covered in scruff and grime. All three were slightly toasted, and if the smell he picked up from this distance was any indication, they were also high on something quite nasty.

"That's the smell of meth," Azrael told him. "They're far gone. And they're waiting for those two women to head straight for them."

Uriel was accustomed to acting on instinct. It was part of being an archangel. However, this time, when he sensed the danger and felt the evil intent on the desert breeze, the power he automatically called for wasn't there. It didn't answer.

Uriel frowned and looked down at himself, and as he did, he caught the glint of metal around his wrist.

Beside him, Azrael shifted. "You did put it on yourself, so it's up to you to take it off." Azrael nodded toward the powerful gold wreath that bound Uriel's powers within his body. "But you should wait until you feed to do it," he said soberly. "Once you take it off, the influx of your power will assault you and make it exponentially more difficult for you to accept the change that is trying to take place in your body. It may overwhelm you. And it will probably hurt." Azrael's tone was low, his words somber, and his golden eyes began to glow slightly with the weight of his warning.

Uriel clenched his teeth and fingered the golden band around his wrist. "I can do this without my powers, I presume?" he said, nodding toward the trio of drugged-out miscreants down the street.

At this, Azrael smiled again and laughed darkly. "But of course. Like I said, it's in your physiology. You're a hunter now; this is just reflex." He turned to focus his ever-intensifying golden gaze on the men who were un-wittingly waiting to become prey themselves. "It just makes it more fun."

"Very well." Uriel left the bracelet alone and nodded at his brother. "After you."

Azrael blurred into motion without warning and Uriel was momentarily left blinking at the suddenly empty spot where the archangel had been standing a millisecond before. And then something inside of him slid into place. The click as it connected was nearly audible; at once he simply knew what to do. As Azrael had said, it was a reflex.

Uriel's vision changed. The scents in the air became visible trails that led in different directions. His hearing sharpened. He could make out the sound of beating hearts up ahead. Two belonged to the young girls. Then came the rapidly erratic beats of the abused hearts of the men ahead of them.

It took a precious few of those wild heartbeats for Uriel to catch up with Azrael at the mouth of the alley where the men stood.

A few more and Azrael had dragged two of the men backward into the waiting darkness. Uriel took care of the third. He wrapped his strong arm around the man's neck and jerked him into the dank, smelly alleyway so quickly that both of their bodies blurred in the action. The man never knew what hit him.

Uriel's fangs found purchase in the side of the man's neck. He fought past the urge to pull away when salt met his tongue and the stench of alcohol and unhealthy bodies filled his nostrils.

Azrael's influence was instantly in his head. *It is sustenance, Uriel. And you've saved more lives here than your own.*

Uriel knew his brother was right. They were still archangels, after a fashion. In a way, it was still their job to deliver whatever kind of justice they were capable of.

But it tasted like crap and, frankly, Uriel was sick to

death of being an archangel. For once in his long-suffering existence, he would have preferred to be on the taking side of things instead of on the giving. He drank because he had to. The blood would keep him alive. But as he swallowed, he closed his eyes and imagined something else. It wasn't this man's blood he wanted to taste.

At that moment, he would have given almost anything to be drinking from Eleanore instead. The scent of her blood had been a siren song to him. It still was. In fact, the memory of her temptation was so starkly clear, it was almost as if he could smell her there in Vegas.

Which was impossible, of course. He really had it bad for her. He needed Eleanore as he needed nothing else in the universe. She completed him; she was his other half. The missing part of his soul.

With that thought, Uriel withdrew his fangs and tossed the now-unconscious man to the ground at his feet. Azrael followed suit a second later. The third man, Azrael had simply knocked unconscious in order to get him out of the way. The three would-be rapists now lay unmoving on the alley asphalt, surrounded by cigarette stubs, empty plastic water bottles, and straws from mixed drinks that were sold up and down the strip.

They wouldn't be harming anyone that night.

"Help me hide them," Azrael instructed. Uriel helped him drag the bodies behind a nearby Dumpster, where the men would sleep out the remainder of the night.

It seemed almost pointless to ask, as he could not have cared less either way, but Uriel found himself asking anyway. "Will they be okay?"

"They're not dead. In the morning, they'll wake feeling less than fantastic." Azrael smiled. "And I've added a dream or two to their memories."

"Oh?" Uriel turned a questioning gaze on his brother. Azrael had long had the ability to influence mortal dreams. Along with a host of other abilities, the power had come after many years on Earth and was now considered by the archangels to be part and parcel to being a very old vampire. Uriel was suddenly very curious as to just what the Angel of Death had done to these three troublemakers.

Azrael grinned. "They won't be wanting to rape anyone anytime soon," he said, his gold eyes sparking with dark mischief. "Not now that they've experienced the nightmare version themselves."

Uriel's eyes widened, but he couldn't keep the smile from his lips. Azrael clapped a hand on his back and turned away to lead them out of the stinking alley. As Uriel followed him out, he focused his attention on his own body and the changes it was continuing to make even now. The blood he'd taken was fueling his senses. His range of hearing had increased; he could make out a conversation that must have been taking place close to a mile away. And was that a shower running? A toilet flushing?

His sense of smell had increased as well. But it seemed like his unconscious desire for Eleanore was overriding it; he could swear he still scented her on the wind. Not just her blood, either. He could smell her lavender shampoo, her cinnamon breath. Even the gentle, clean scent of her skin.

Christ, he thought. She was filling him up inside. He couldn't get her out of his head and suddenly it felt as though his awareness of her might drive him mad.

But then Azrael was roughly shoving him back into the darkness of the alleyway shadows, one hand pressed solidly to his broad, thick chest.

"What the—"

"Quiet," Azrael hissed. "She can't see you here. Not yet. Not like this."

"Who?" Uriel whispered, too distracted by his thoughts of Eleanore to be as confused or irritated as he probably should have been.

At this, Azrael's hand slipped from Uriel's chest and he turned to face his brother, his stark amber gaze pulsing with warning light. "You're not going to believe this," he said softly, taking a step back so that Uriel had a clear view of the street beyond.

The slender profile of a woman with long black hair instantly caught his attention.

Azrael nodded at the dawning comprehension he must have seen in Uriel's face. "It's your archess."

CHAPTER FOURTEEN

It took a few seconds for Uriel to gather his wits about him and realize that his fantasy was actually reality. Eleanore was the last person he had expected to see in Las Vegas that night, but he was almost more surprised by the fact that he had known she was there all along.

"I thought she was with Samael," he muttered under his breath. He was simply thinking out loud. Had she escaped? Had Samael let her go? What the hell was going on?

"Gabe found out that she was here, and Max told me to bring you when you woke up," Az told him calmly. "I just thought we should have breakfast first."

"What hotel is that?" Uriel asked, his voice stronger this time.

"The August."

Uriel glanced around the hotel's entrance at the plethora of overly handsome men mulling about it and moving in and out. "What's with all the beef?" Uriel asked, feeling his irritation rise.

"The August is supposedly where performers prefer to stay while in town."

That would explain it. These men were probably magicians, jousters, dance instructors—you name it. But it only managed to quell a little of his mounting anger.

"How the hell did Eleanore manage to choose *that*

hotel, out of every hotel in Vegas?" he asked with irritation.

"She didn't choose it. Samael did."

As far as Uriel was concerned, that clinched it. "I'm getting her out of there," Uriel said with finality. He wasn't asking for permission in this, and as far as he was concerned, Azrael could either help him in his endeavor, or get the hell out of his way.

"Clean yourself up first," Azrael said as he turned to face him. "You're wearing someone else's blood."

Uriel looked down to find that he was right. He had disliked the flavor of the drug addict's blood so much that he must have inadvertently pulled away, allowing some of the red liquid to coat his chest.

He took a deep breath and let it out in a heavy sigh. He could head back to the mansion and change there, but he didn't want to waste the time. He could buy another shirt—but again, that took time. And the salesperson would undoubtedly question the blood.

On the other hand, he could simply transmorph the shirt and be done with it. Of course, that was a supernatural power and he would have to remove the bracelet if he wanted to use it. Which he wasn't at all certain he wanted to do.

Being an archangel, in and of itself, was like walking around with a constant buzz. The power hummed through his veins on a near constant level, and somehow, he'd always managed to keep a lid on himself.

Add to that power the influx of the hunger and the high of vampirism, and it was too much. Azrael had managed to survive the combination. But he was the only being Uriel knew of to do so, and Az was most definitely special. Uriel didn't feel ready to be put to the same grueling test.

"Do it quickly and then put it back on. You need to learn how to control all of your powers together anyway," the archangel said out loud. Then, mentally, Azrael added, *But keep yourself collared around Eleanore, Uriel. You don't want to frighten her.*

Uriel nodded his assent, and very quickly he pulled the gold bracelet off his wrist. It came away with a white flash and Uriel's eyes instantly went black from corner to corner. He could actually see it.

For a moment, he seemed to be floating outside of his body, looking down on the scene in the alleyway. He was watching himself, seeing himself through his archangel eyes, as he often did with mortals in order to judge what kinds of souls they possessed. He could see himself standing there with pitch-black demonlike eyes, his hair unnaturally darker and a touch longer, his skin paler, his fangs fully elongated, his long-sleeved thermal shirt covered in someone else's blood.

He was a little terrifying to behold.

And then, as if caught in some gravitational pull, Uriel was sucked back into his body and instantly overcome by the tremendous power running through his veins. He felt it all there—ready to use, calling to him. Every ability he possessed was amplified. And with this amplification came the piggybacking desire to fuel it. With more blood.

Focus, Uriel. Control it. Change your fucking shirt, and put the goddamned wreath back on. Now.

Azrael's voice found its way into Uriel's head, commanding him from within. But Uriel had a hard time paying attention. He wanted to run, to jump, to fly, to throw a freight train into the starlit sky—things he normally could not or would not do. He wanted to use his telekinesis to hurl cars across the street, knock buildings into one another, break something just to hear it shatter. Or to hear it scream.

Uriel!

His head snapped in Azrael's direction, his vision a strange, dark red.

Think of Eleanore.

Azrael forced the thought through him and Uriel

could almost feel the words scrape the walls of his consciousness. It hurt. But it also helped. Uriel closed his eyes and reined himself in. It was like grabbing a whirlwind of pixie lights and forcing them to come closer—within reach. He managed it, but barely.

When he did, his vision changed and he could safely assume that his eyes no longer looked black from corner to corner. He wasted no time in reaching into that vortex of lit-up abilities to pull out the one power he needed to clean himself up.

Within a few seconds, the blood was gone, his clothes were new, and he was slamming the bracelet back down onto his wrist. When it solidified into a solid gold wreath once more, the craziness left his blood, his heartbeat ceased roaring in his eardrums, and he no longer felt like rending something limb from limb.

He took a deep, shaky breath and looked over at his brother.

"You did well." Azrael nodded sagely. "She's made it into her room," he said, turning to peer at the hotel across the street once more. "Give her a few minutes. Then . . ." He glanced back at Uriel and smiled. "Good luck."

E: It's not what I expected, I guess.

A: How so?

E: Oh, you know. . . . I got here and thought the big-city thing would be fun for a night. But it's just packed and expensive and sort of smelly. But most of all, it just seems . . . I don't know. Plastic.

A: Oh, tell me about it. There's nothing sadder than a fake Statue of Liberty in flashing neon lights. Awe-inspiring on so very many levels.

E: Lol. Exactly.

Eleanore shook her head at the screen.

A: Listen, girl, I gotta go. Just take it easy for the night. Stay inside and watch the SyFy Channel. Stargate should be on tonight. I know how you lust for Daniel Jackson and his big, massive, pulsing gray matter.

E: *smiles* Right. Take care, Angel.

A: You too, sweetie. Xoxo

Eleanore signed off and closed the chat box. Then she leaned back in the reclining desk chair. With everything going on, she should have felt exhausted, but instead, she felt . . . buzzed.

She thought about Kevin, the crush she had told Uriel about in the garage before he became a vampire. She was fifteen when she met Kevin, just months before that fateful day with the man and the needle. Kevin was a senior at the local high school in the Connecticut town she was living in at the time.

She hadn't know anything about the boy because she was homeschooled, and she'd never met him personally, just watched him from afar. Every morning, he waited on the corner of the block for the bus. He stood out from the others because he was taller and more built and seemed older.

Most seniors drove themselves to school. But he always took the bus, his hands casually tucked into the front pockets of his jeans. And he filled those jeans out nicely. He wore tight T-shirts and she could tell, even from where she watched through the slats in her venetian blinds, that he had a few tattoos. She liked the tattoos. They made him seem tougher and she secretly liked them on the tougher side. In movies, she always fell for the bad guys. And, though she'd never actually dated anyone, she could imagine that dating a "bad boy" would be more fun, if shorter-lived, than dating a "good boy." She just wasn't stupid enough to mention as much in front of her family.

The boy was quiet. He kept to himself. She never saw him talk with the others who were waiting for the bus.

Then, one day, he turned to face the window. She wasn't able to move back in time to avoid being seen, but she reared away from the window, dropping the blinds, her hand to her heart. After a few seconds of calming her breath and steadying her rapid pulse rate, she chanced another peek through the slats.

The boy was holding up a sign he'd made on a blank page in his spiral notebook. He'd written in thick, black ink.

I'm Kevin. What's your name?

For the next two months, Eleanore had found it difficult to concentrate on anything but Kevin. They exchanged notes through the window, though they never spoke.

It wasn't that her parents were prison wardens and kept her under lock and key. They simply all agreed that it wouldn't be a good idea to become too friendly with anyone just then; Eleanore was entering a difficult stage. Her powers were inadvertently affected by her body's changes, and sometimes they were quite difficult to control.

The Grangers couldn't afford to take chances. They had grown increasingly worried that someone with ill intent had noticed Eleanore's abilities and was watching them.

So Eleanore watched Kevin from the window, and he smiled at her from the bus stop. His smile always filled her with butterflies.

That was how Eleanore felt now. She was distracted and antsy and a little high on endorphins and adrenaline. There were far too many tall, handsome, powerful men in her life at the moment. They occupied her days and nights, if not in person, then in thought.

Especially one in particular. She allowed her mind to wander to that first fateful moment in the bookstore, when Christopher Daniels had pinned her to the counter and leaned in.

Uriel.

Getting past security had been a breeze in his new vampire body. Despite the hotel's lavish decor and plethora of guards, Uriel had made it to the top floor of the highrise hotel with no problems and without being seen.

Now he stood before Eleanore's door and moved the bunch of red roses into his left hand. He raised his right to knock—and then he stilled. His head cocked slightly to one side. He could hear her beyond the door. But it wasn't just her movement and the shuffling sounds her clothes made or the soft creaking noises her chair made when she no doubt swiveled in it. It was that he could hear her breathing. He could even hear her heart beating.

Even with the gold band around his wrist, he could smell her as if he'd bent to inhale the scent of her hair. Lavender. He could time the beats of the pulse in her throat. And he could imagine what it looked like . . . inviting and tinted slightly blue beneath the taut porcelain of her flesh.

He lowered his hand and closed his eyes. Azrael was right. He was a hunter now; it was a part of him. Maybe this wasn't such a good idea.

And then she sighed softly and it sounded so sad, so lonely, his eyes flew open once more, his heart at once aching. The call of that loneliness hardened his resolve and he raised his hand and knocked.

He could hear her pulse jump, her heart racing, forcing the blood to rush rampantly through her veins. He smiled a slow smile, unable to help himself. That blood was as much a call to him as anything else. He wasn't surprised when she stopped moving and didn't answer the knock. She was being careful. But he was being persistent.

He knocked again and his smile broadened. "Knock,

knock," he added, at once giving himself away. He was pleased to hear that her heartbeat kicked up another notch. "Let me in?" he requested softly. Then, in a slightly deeper tone filled with amusement, he added, "I won't bite." It was what he had said to her outside of her apartment several days ago. It held a lot more meaning now.

He heard her moving then, quickly making her way to the door. She obviously peered at him through the peephole. "That was a lot funnier and a lot less meaningful the first time you said it," she told him, mirroring his thoughts.

He chuckled, his body thrumming to life at the simple sound of her voice and the hopeful fact that she was teasing him. But she made no move to open the door. He shifted from one foot to the other and considered his options. He could always break the door down. Vampires didn't actually need any kind of invitation to enter a dwelling as myth would have people believe. And even without the magic that the bracelet held in check, his vampire body would be through the door and on the other side in the blink of an eye.

But getting into the room wasn't the goal here. Getting into Eleanore's heart was. He tried another tactic and wiped the smile from his face. "You may as well at least open the door, Ellie," he told her, his tone calm and reasonable. "Think about it. If I truly posed a threat to you, would a door stop me?"

She was quiet, hopefully mulling his words over. After a few long seconds, she softly admitted, "Probably not."

Again, he smiled, but he ducked his head so that she couldn't see it through the peephole. It was important in that moment for him to keep the sheep suit on a little longer. Several more tense seconds passed and then Uriel heard the chain in the lock. A latch was thrown and the handle turned and Uriel looked up to find himself staring into a pair of wary indigo eyes.

A chord of shock vibrated through him. *So beautiful,*

he thought. Was it always going to be like this? Would he be stunned by her every time he laid eyes on her?

She slowly opened the door wide and gazed out at him, her bottom lip caught tight between two rows of perfect white teeth. He glanced at the pouty pink flesh, captured so tight, and thought about how it would feel trapped within his own teeth. The image made him ache and his muscles flexed of their own accord. He was lost for a while in his constant, returning desire for her, and it momentarily threw him for words.

Her perfect brow furrowed and her gaze narrowed.

Uriel realized he'd been lost and quickly pulled himself together. He felt thorns in his left hand and remembered the roses. He cleared his throat. "Truce?" he asked as he tentatively held them out for her.

Eleanore looked down at the roses and contemplated them in silence. Then, slowly, she took them from him and brought them to her nose. She inhaled and her lovely face unwound into an easy, natural smile. Uriel couldn't use the vampire ability he'd gained to read her mind while he wore the bracelet, but he didn't need to. He could see her thoughts written clearly in her expression. She loved the roses.

"I wanted to get you lavender," he told her. "I know you like it." Her hair always smelled like lavender, tempting and clean. He caught a hint of it now, in fact, and it made him yearn to run his hands through her silky strands and bury his face in it. She looked up at him expectantly, her eyes shining brightly. Again he cleared his throat, his body aching for her as it never had. "But no one in Vegas sells it," he continued. "So I went with something that smells almost as sweet."

Her smile broadened and she ducked her head. "I love them," she said quietly. "They're beautiful." She gazed down at them a moment more and then seemed to catch herself. She straightened, her smile faded, and she struck him with a suddenly guarded expression. "But I still want to know how you found me," she told him. "And . . ." She paused, looked at the floor, toed the doorframe in the carpet, and looked up at him once more. "And I want to know what you want from me."

What I want . . . Uriel could have growled with the hunger he felt when he thought about what he wanted from her. If she had the slightest idea, she would slam the door shut and bolt it. And then call the Marines.

Instead, he concentrated on forcing the fangs that had erupted in his mouth to shrink once more. And he shoved his hands into his pockets to keep them busy. "The truth is, I had no idea you would be in Vegas tonight," he said. "I woke up and had to . . . eat." He glanced at her nervously and then quickly averted his gaze. "Azrael brought me here."

"Then—" She broke off, and he looked up to study her face. He could almost see the wheels spinning in her head. "Azrael knew I was here, didn't he?"

Uriel nodded. There was no point in denying it. "Did Samael hurt you?" he asked then, surprised by his own question. It must have been burning in the back of his brain for him to suddenly blurt it out. But he found that even as he focused on the subject, his blood felt colder in his veins. His eyes felt hotter and his teeth throbbed in his gums.

Eleanore looked up at him in sudden silence, her own dark blue eyes widening slightly. He was tempted, then and there, to yank the band off of his wrists so that he could read her thoughts. There was fear in her eyes. And something else.

But she swallowed hard; he could hear it pushing past her tight throat, and she shook her head. "No," she said. "He didn't hurt me."

He didn't believe her. Not for a second. There was something she wasn't telling him. But there were no markings on her body that he could see and he would know if she were in pain; he would be able to smell the cortisol and adrenaline flooding her system.

All he could smell right now was the lavender in her

hair, the cinnamon on her tongue, and the heady scent of roses.

He cocked his head to one side and leveled his jade-green eyes on her once more. She fidgeted and captured a lock of her hair between her fingers in nervous agitation. "Uriel, can you read my mind now?" she asked. "I mean, now that you're a vampire?"

He smiled and shook his head, holding up his wrist. "Not with this on."

She glanced at the bracelet and he saw the memories flood her features. She was still angry about what had happened at the mansion. "I'm sorry, Ellie," he told her honestly. "Max suggested I keep it with me." He'd taken the bracelet as a precaution, but when it came down to it, he knew in his heart that he had hesitated in using it because he would never be able to force Eleanore to do anything against her will. "I never would have used it on you," he admitted. He prayed that she could see the urgency in his eyes. "I hope you believe me."

She studied him closely and he found himself unaccountably nervous under the scrutiny. Finally, she wiped her palms on her jeans and nodded. "I believe you."

Relief flooded him, fueling his courage. "May I come in, Ellie?"

She swallowed hard again. "I don't know," she said. "If I let you in, can you control yourself?"

No.

"Yes," he said, holding up his wrist once more. The gold band gleamed under the hall lights. "And I'm properly collared."

She smiled at that, her beautiful face cracking a true grin. His stomach fluttered, his muscles tensed, and his heart melted.

"All right," she said, stepping back out of the way. "You can come in."

Uriel bit back his smile of triumph and stepped into her suite. Samael had provided her with a corner suite; it was extravagant in the extreme. He could smell the lingering scent of strawberries and chocolate, wine and cheese. The air felt filtered and recycled to the point of sterilization. The carpet was plush, the colors muted, and the fixtures marble. Vases of fresh mistine orchids decorated every table surface.

His gaze narrowed on the flower vase nearest to him. They were Samael's doing.

Behind him, the door clicked shut and Eleanore sniffed the roses again. In a burst of vampire speed and before she could turn back around to face him, Uriel grabbed the vase of flowers, took the orchids out, tossed them in the nearby receptacle, and then held the vase out toward Eleanore.

"I'm going to put these in some water," she said as she turned to face him. And then she frowned. "Where'd you get the vase?"

"Does it matter?" he said with one of his disarming smiles.

She gave him a quizzical look and then shook her head a little as if she didn't really want to know.

Ellie took the vase from him and turned her attention back to the roses. "Not that putting these in water will help any. I may be able to heal humans, but I have a black thumb with plants." As she said it, her grip tightened on the roses as if in frustration.

He almost heard the thorn pierce her flesh as it slid in. He certainly heard the thump of her heart beneath the stab of pain. And he could instantly smell the blood.

She glanced down at the welling blood, shook her head in mute irritation, and strode to the bathroom.

Uriel stood in the middle of her hotel room, his heart hammering, his blood roaring in his ears. The scent of her blood was all around him. The roses had been a mistake; what had he been thinking? The slightest possibility that she would slice herself open was beyond dangerous for him.

Right now, it was all he could do to prevent himself from having his way with her. He could take her by surprise. He had strength and speed on her. It would be so easy to throw her on the bed and hold her down while he sank both his cock and his teeth into her gorgeous, delicious body.

Get ahold of yourself! He pressed the palms of his hands into his eyes and turned toward the window, trying to focus on the sounds and sights and smells beyond the glass. *You need control,* he told himself. *Get control. Get control. . . .*

"Would you like to go for a walk?" he asked, his voice tight, his forehead beading with sweat as he fought with his urges.

"Where did you want to go?" she called from the other room.

Uriel took a deep, penetrating breath and let it out slowly.

"Uriel?"

After two more deep breaths, he felt a semblance of calm returning and straightened to face the bathroom. He shoved his hands back into his pockets and made his way to the bathroom doorway. *I'm in control,* he thought, as he leaned his shoulder against the doorframe and watched her tend to the flowers.

"Have you seen the lights on Fremont?" he asked. His tone was low, his voice still much tighter than he'd have preferred it to be.

"No," she admitted, arranging the bouquet on the right-hand side of the marble counter. She then turned toward him and waited for him to move out of the way.

He remained where he was. He really didn't want to move. She was trapped in front of him and he liked it. *I'm wearing the bracelet,* he thought grimly. *And I still can't control myself.*

Eleanore's pulse ratcheted up a few notches. He could hear it. He knew he was spearing her with a hard look and he could tell by the way she looked at him that she noticed every one of his muscles was bunched beneath the material of his thermal shirt.

His body felt as if it were preparing to pounce.

She tore her gaze from his chest and crossed her arms over hers in a defensive gesture. Something in his eyes must have been scaring her. Not that he could blame her. He could imagine he looked pretty scary right about now.

A few long seconds ticked slowly by and, finally, he obligingly moved out of the way. It wasn't easy. She slowly slid past him, stiffening slightly as her body brushed by his. Electricity buzzed between them, thickening the air and holding her momentarily in place. Her breath caught softly and he'd never been so tempted in his life to reach out and grab something. He wanted to kiss her again. He'd have given his right hand for it in that moment.

But he let her go. This was a tentative time. Her trust needed to be earned again. *Sheep suit on,* he told himself. *Keep it together, Uriel.*

She moved past him and out into the main room of the suite and Uriel followed closely behind her. "Then I'll take you," he said, referring to the light show on Fremont Street.

Eleanore spun to face him. Of course, she knew he was referring to the lights on Fremont. But she didn't miss the double entendre. He could tell she knew exactly what he'd been thinking.

"Sounds good," she choked.

She turned away again and, with hands that shook slightly, she grabbed her purse. She pulled out her wallet and removed the money, her driver's license, her credit card, and the room key. She shoved these things into the deep inside pocket of her zip-up hoodie and then pulled the hoodie on.

They left the hotel room and waited for the next elevator going down. There were three other people already inside when the doors slid open. Two were an elderly couple who looked very well-to-do. The third was a young woman, possibly in her late teens or early twenties, dressed in a sequined tank top and black silk miniskirt and wearing enough makeup to supply three stage performers. One of the first things Eleanore noticed about her was the abundance of goose bumps across her chilled flesh. Even in Vegas it was too cold at night in November for a tank top and no jacket.

But Eleanore quickly forgot about the goose bumps when the girl's eyes widened in obvious recognition.

"Christopher Daniels!" she half whispered, half shrieked.

Eleanore found herself wanting to disappear. *Oh no,* she thought. *Not again.*

She tried to step back, but Uriel's strong hand found her elbow and steered her onto the elevator. At the same time, he flashed a pearly white smile at the young woman and greeted her kindly.

"Are you in town filming?" the girl asked. Her eyes lit up. "Are you in costume? You look so much like Jonathan right now! What an amazing makeup job! Your skin looks so pale and your eyes so strange." She reached up, as if she were going to touch him, and then caught herself and pulled her arm back down. "*Beautiful* but strange!" she repeated, then laughed nervously and began fishing around in her sequined purse.

"You have to give me an autograph, please, it would mean so much, it would be the best thing to happen to me in Vegas. I mean, wait until Maria hears about this, oh my gosh—Christopher Daniels in my elevator! Are you staying at the August?"

Eleanore was getting dizzy listening to the girl. She could only watch in wonder as the girl hopped from one question to the next, all the while rooting around in her purse for pen and paper.

The wealthy elderly couple in the elevator watched in silence as well, their facial expressions never changing.

"Oh no, I can't find anything to write on. I could have sworn I had at least some rice paper in here for my pores, but no, nothing, I don't know what I'll do if I can't get your autograph. Maria will never believe me—"

"I think I have a solution," Uriel said, his deep, charismatic voice easily overriding hers.

The girl blinked and smiled a brilliant, expectant smile as Uriel shrugged off his leather jacket and held it out for her. "Take this," he told her. "It's got my name scribbled on the label, so no need to sign anything." He smiled a completely disarming smile at the young fan, and a part of Eleanore melted right then and there in the elevator.

The girl stared openmouthed at the jacket and didn't seem to know what to do.

"Go on," he told her gently. "I was rather warm anyway. I can always get another one." He chuckled softly, maneuvering her so that he could slide the jacket over her cold, bare arms, then stepped back.

The girl positively swam in the leather, it was so big on her, but the look on her face was of such grateful adoration, Ellie actually felt sad for her.

"I . . . I don't know what to . . . I mean . . ."

"Think nothing of it," Uriel insisted. "Have a nice time in Vegas."

The elevator dinged and the doors slid open and Uriel wasted no time in grasping Eleanore's arm once more to pull her out of the elevator beside him. He said nothing as he steered her through the crowd in the lobby, past slot machines and men with radio communication devices in their ears and women dressed in uncomfortable, revealing uniforms, carrying trays topped with drinks and poker chips and dollar bills.

Eleanore noticed none of it. She kept thinking of the look on that girl's face when Uriel had handed her his jacket. It wasn't what she had expected. Not of him. It made her realize she didn't know him very well at all.

Ellie barely had time to look around, he spirited them through the lobby so quickly. But it didn't matter. At the moment, it was Uriel that had the bulk of her attention.

What he had done in the elevator had admittedly left her a little breathless. She couldn't imagine any other star doing something so selfless. Not that she knew any of them personally. Except for the Masked One.

The moment Uriel had taken off his jacket and draped it over the girl's shivering frame, a part of Ellie had melted. She'd felt as suddenly warm as the girl must have, wrapped snuggly in Uriel's kindness.

Uriel finally moved them through the large double doors at the entrance and out into the Las Vegas night. The temperature had decreased quite a bit since Ellie had arrived that afternoon. That happened in the desert; once the sun went down, the thermometer plummeted a good twenty to thirty degrees. It had been seventy earlier that day, but now bottomed out in the high forties.

On the sidewalk, he stopped and turned toward her. "Are you warm enough?" he asked.

"Yes," Eleanore told him truthfully. In fact, she felt flushed. She gazed up at him and offered him a sincere smile. The gesture seemed to take him by surprise. He blinked, his gaze dropping from her eyes to her lips and then back.

She almost laughed. "What you did back there was incredibly kind," she told him.

Uriel's brow furrowed. "Kind?" he asked, clearly confused. "What do you mean?"

"It was a very selfless thing to do, giving that girl your jacket like that."

At this, he looked positively bewildered. He blinked several more times, his frown deepening. And then he slowly turned to face her fully and gently took her by the upper arms. He shook his head. "That shouldn't mean anything, Ellie. I gave away something I will never miss. To me, it meant nothing—"

"But to her, it means everything," Ellie finished for him. "Don't you see? You really made that girl's millennium. And you certainly didn't have to."

Uriel seemed to be out of words. For several long seconds, his intense green eyes skirted the planes of her face, that same surprised expression softening his features. And then, finally, he cupped her face and moved closer. "If I had known it would make you look at me the way you are now, I would have done it days ago."

CHAPTER FIFTEEN

After all that, Uriel thought. *Wars and battles and earthquakes and floods* ... nothing he had ever done had made him feel as good as he felt in that moment, standing there on that sidewalk, his precious archess smiling up at him with what he could have sworn was pride.

He had never seen anything so beautiful. Two thousand years' worth of experiences on Earth and he had never laid eyes upon something as stunningly gorgeous as the smile she now wore. It was like the sun on his soul.

He could hear her heart beating hard and steady behind her ribs and scent the slight hormonal change in her bloodstream. She was excited. Her gaze flicked from his eyes to his lips and back again and he knew that she was wondering whether he was going to kiss her.

Oh, yes, he thought. *Nothing could stop me.*

As if she could sense his sudden, hard determination, her pupils expanded, her lips parted, and he heard her breath catch. The effect this had on him was instantaneous. His fangs erupted in his mouth, his vision sharpened, and he heard his blood rush through his eardrums.

"I'm going to kiss you, Ellie," he told her suddenly, speaking to her as if they were the only two people in Las Vegas at that moment. It was a warning; he was a vampire now and things were different. He was a hunter. She was his prey.

He used his gentle grip on her face to hold her still before him as he closed the small gap between them and leaned in. "Stop me now," he whispered. "You won't get another chance."

Eleanore said nothing and he felt her shudder against his hard body. He could wait no longer. She shuddered once more as his lips found hers.

He wanted to be gentle; she deserved as much. But when the first butterfly-soft touch of his lips against hers sparked with electricity, it ignited something volatile inside of him. She moaned against his mouth and Uriel nearly lost control. He moved in for the kill, deepening his kiss with the ferocity of the need riding him. He felt her stiffen slightly when her tongue brushed the tips of his very sharp fangs, but he held her fast, unwilling to let her slip away.

In the next instant, she was melting against him, giving in to his demands and moaning against his lips. He could hear her heart racing, like music for his deadly dance. And he could smell her. . . . She was wet for him.

It took every bit of strength for him to suppress the growl that the evidence of her desire ripped from deep within him. He wanted a bed. He needed more of her. . . .

"Holy shit! It's Christopher Daniels, girls!"

Eleanore went stiff in his embrace at the intruding voice and Uriel's monster instantly reared its ugly head. He felt her begin to try to pull away, and he tightened his grip on her. It was instinctive. She'd awakened something within him; he needed her so badly in that moment, it was everything he could do not to tear the bracelet off of his wrist, wrap his arms around her, and take her to the skies with him until they were alone and he could throw her down onto a rooftop, rip her clothes off, and slake his pain with her pleasure.

She had opened up to him so easily. . . .

Uriel ended the kiss, slowly pulling away enough that he could open his eyes and peer down into hers. He was met with a stark, dark blue gaze and an expression that bespoke of both yearning and fear.

She was shaking as badly as he was. He could see, hear, and smell the effect his kiss had had upon her. She wanted him as much as he wanted her. And now she was frightened because of the people behind them and their dangerous attention. He knew she didn't want to be seen with him, that she didn't want to be in the limelight because she believed there were bad men after her. He could see the fear wrap itself around her, chilling the heat he had given her only moments before.

"Oh my God, you're right," whispered a second voice. "Chris, I need your John Hancock, man!"

"Dude, do something vampirey for us!" came a third command.

There was a shuffling and giggling sound behind him and Uriel caught the scent of mixed alcohol and undigested onion ring on the breeze.

This was not some innocent little girl in an elevator, flustered and embarrassed. This was an intrusion, as far as he was concerned, and it was hurting Eleanore.

They were drunk. He hated sloppy drunks. His fangs were fully developed now behind his closed lips and he could see the reflection in Eleanore's eyes when his own gaze began to shift, taking on a reddish, angry hue. His blood began to roar inside his veins. This time, when the growl made its way from his chest to his throat, it was not a growl of desire, but of wrath.

Eleanore's eyes widened. The color drained from her cheeks.

"Uriel, no—what are you—"

He turned away from her then, and her protest fell short. He focused on the group of teenagers that had gathered behind him. One boy, possibly twenty years old. Three girls. One was the boy's sister; he could tell by the scent.

All were loaded beyond their ability to stand upright without swaying.

One of the girls had extracted a cell phone from her purse and was clearly switching it to camera mode. Righteous fury for Eleanore's sake swelled within Uriel.

"Aw, man, you look just like Brakes right now!" the drunk boy exclaimed, pointing at Uriel as his eyes glittered with inebriated brightness. "Britt, get a pic quick! I *love* vampires, man! Can I have your autograph too?" He was looking down then and feeling the front of his jacket as if he was certain he'd left a paper and pen in a pocket somewhere for just such an occasion.

"So you like vampires?" Uriel asked quietly, his deep voice carrying easily on the cool air of the night. All four of the drunk group seemed to still, as if suddenly unsure.

But then the girl with the camera phone giggled and nodded emphatically as the camera phone's shutter closed several times, capturing both of their images.

"Absolutely!" she exclaimed. "I would let Jonathan Brakes take a taste of me any day." She lowered both her phone and her head a touch and gave Uriel an unabashed coy look.

"Really?" Uriel smiled a small smile, turning to fully face the group and finally releasing Eleanore. "Are you certain of that?" he asked then, feeling the strong urge to show her exactly what it would feel like to be eaten by a vampire.

"Oh yes," the girl breathed.

Uriel grinned then, flashing his fangs.

The girls in the group gasped and the boy backpedaled. "Oh shit!" he said, feeling for the support column behind him as he'd temporarily lost his balance.

Uriel took a slow, menacing step toward the girl, who had frozen in place even as the rest of the group was moving out of the way. She gazed up at him in wonder, but there was more than a touch of real fear in her eyes.

"That's . . ." She swallowed hard, not able to so much as blink as Uriel took another step toward her. "That's an a-amazing makeup job, Mr. D-Daniels," she stuttered. But he knew that she was aware, somewhere deep down, that it was no makeup job.

"Uriel, please—leave her alone." Eleanore's hand was suddenly on his arm, gripping him as tightly as she could, given that his biceps was so much larger than her hand.

The touch was grounding enough, however, that Uriel realized what he was doing. He stopped moving and blinked. He glanced down at the slim fingers on his arm, their grip so desperate.

Then he took a deep breath and let it out through his nose. Without looking back up at the young girl, he took her phone from her hand and crushed it. Then he addressed her, his tone cool and commanding. "You shouldn't take pictures without asking. Now go back home where you belong." He paused, looked up, and then added, "And don't drink anymore. You can't handle it."

"Y-yes, sir," the girl stammered. Her entire demeanor had changed by then. She was no longer turned on, no longer nervous. She was simply terrified—and very much under Uriel's vampire influence.

He gave her mind one final push and she turned and fled across the circular drive of the August, leaving her friends to straighten up and stumble after her.

Eleanore's hand slipped from Uriel's arm, leaving him feeling as if he had lost a part of himself. He turned and met her gaze, noticing when she flinched from the look in his eyes.

He tried to rein it in. Again, it was difficult.

Eleanore's lips were red and swollen from his kiss and her blue eyes were so large and bright in her beautiful face. Her long raven-black hair was caught in a desert breeze and invited his touch. He wanted to fist his fingers in it and hold her down.

"Are you okay?" she asked, closing the distance between them and reaching for his hand.

He blinked, surprised. He had been concerned about her, and yet she was the one to ask him if he was okay. She was very brave. He looked down at her hand where she wrapped it firmly around his, and he squeezed it back.

Almost immediately, he felt his fangs receding. He felt his ire draining away. His vision cleared, no longer tinted red, and his body slipped from monster mode. He couldn't believe it. He hadn't had the strength to do it alone—but Eleanore had managed to bring him back under control in mere seconds.

He glanced up at her, once more meeting her gaze. "Ellie, how do you—"

She interrupted him with a gentle but firm finger laid over his lips. "I'm so glad you didn't eat that girl." She smiled a wry smile and looked as though she were about to laugh.

Uriel's eyes widened. She was *joking* about it. He stared down into her glittering eyes, and as she bit her lip to keep from laughing, the final threads of tension slipped away from him. He found he could not hold his own laughter inside.

She laughed with him and then asked, "You think she'll have nightmares about Jonathan Brakes now?"

He smiled and shook his head. "Who knows. I guess I lost a fan, didn't I?"

Eleanore shrugged. "Probably not. She'll wake up with a massive headache and a vague recollection of having gone to the movies to see *Comeuppance*. That would be my bet."

Horns honked on the road beside them and sirens began to wail a few blocks away. Uriel looked up to see the neon lights flashing pink and yellow and he grimaced. He had never been fond of Las Vegas. But for the fountains at the Bellagio, the place was just too gaudy for his liking.

"Do you have your heart set on seeing those lights at Fremont?" he asked her softly.

"Not really," she admitted with a guilty shrug. "I don't think I'm much of a Vegas fan."

He smiled. "Me, neither. The whole thing's a bit too plastic for my tastes."

Eleanore blinked up at him, pausing at his description. She seemed pleasantly surprised at his admission. Then her smile was back, bigger than before. "I agree," she said.

"Excellent. It's settled, then." He turned, still holding her hand, and began to lead her away from the hotel, toward an alleyway a few blocks down.

"Where are we going?" she asked, after they'd gone a block.

Uriel considered making her wait to find out and just surprising her, but it occurred to him that she may not like the place he had in mind. "How do you feel about the West Coast?"

"The West Coast?" she repeated, clearly confused.

"Yes," he chuckled. "California. Oregon. Somewhere in between."

"There's nothing in between," she said absently, blinking up at him.

"Ellie."

"I've only been there once. A little city called Trinidad was my favorite. It's a ways north of San Francisco. The beach was amazing; probably the most beautiful place I've ever visited. Why do you ask?"

"I'd like to take you there. I know someone in San Francisco who owns a clothing store. I thought maybe . . ." He paused, considering the best way to broach the subject of the gala tomorrow night. Then he straightened and said, "I had hoped you would still consider going to that gala in Dallas with me tomorrow night. And that you would allow me to buy the dress you'll need in order to go." He wasn't used to asking people for permission. It was strange how important it suddenly was that he tread gently and win this woman's full compliance. It meant everything to him that she accept him and that she not pull away.

"The gala?" She seemed to be talking to herself now, mulling everything over in her mind. She surprised him by smiling. "I would love to go with you, Uriel. As long as you promise not to eat anyone in the interim."

Uriel couldn't let that one go. "Anyone?" he asked, feeling his hunger for her rise again at the very thought of "eating" her.

Eleanore blinked and blushed furiously. "Well, I mean . . ." And then she let a breath out in a frustrated whoosh and simply punched him in the arm.

He laughed as they reached the alley.

"Then it's settled." He faced the dark length of the alleyway, located the rusted warehouse door he wanted, and waved his hand at its graffitied surface. Luckily for him, the ability to open a portal through the mansion was tied to the mansion and its recognition of him as one of the four favored archangels and not his own supernatural abilities or the bracelet would have held it in check. He turned to Ellie. "This portal I've opened will take us back to the mansion, and from there we can go anywhere. Just stay by my side."

It rippled before them and then vanished altogether. Beyond was the elegant foyer of the mansion. They both stepped through and then Uriel waved his hand again, opening a portal through a door on the opposite wall.

Uriel felt the change in the air as soon as the second portal opened up. It was salty and thick with fog and the sound of seagulls split the night. Waves crashed somewhere nearby.

"Is this Frisco?" Ellie asked.

Uriel was right behind her, gently urging her on and through the opening. They stepped through and Eleanore looked behind them. Uriel followed her example, turning to look as well. They seemed to have stepped through the crumbling facade of an old lighthouse. Only the door was really still intact. The mansion's portal closed behind them.

Uriel bent to whisper in her ear. "We're in Trinidad." The gesture sent a shiver running through her slim form and he smiled. "You said it was the most beautiful place you'd ever been. So I brought you back."

He gave her a gentle nudge toward the beach surrounded by cliffs of dark rock. A thick, souplike fog sat not too far out on the water, like a giant white god, waiting to come and cover the shoreline and cliffs with its massive, shapeless body.

For now, however, the reflection of the moon on those grounded clouds provided enough light for Eleanore to see her surroundings. Not that it mattered for Uriel. As a vampire, he would have been able to see everything around them without any light at all. *A silver lining*, he thought.

He stood behind Eleanore and scanned their surroundings. He had been all over the world countless times, but he had to admit that this beach was beautiful beyond description. He couldn't blame Eleanore for loving it as she did. A quick glance at her rapt, jubilant expression and he knew he'd made the right choice.

"I've got a lighter," he said. "Help me gather some wood and we can start a fire."

A few minutes later, they'd gathered a good amount of driftwood and piled it in the middle of a circle they had created out of worn, shell-fossiled stone. They stacked it from the tiny kindling-sized sticks, up to a handful of larger pieces at the top. Uriel took out the lighter and held it near the smaller pieces until a few of them caught flame and sputtered to life. The driftwood was still a little damp and his ability to manipulate the flames was currently trapped by the bracelet he wore. The fire would have sputtered into embers and then gone out altogether if it weren't for Eleanore's ability to control fire as well.

She caught the flame and concentrated on it, forcing

it to eat the ends of the other pieces of wood until they dried out and the fire was well on its way. By the time she released it from her control, it was clear to him that she was feeling a tad drained and more than a touch hungry. He heard her stomach growl.

"Sit down," he told her, wrapping his arm around her waist and gently drawing her down on top of his lap as he lowered himself to the sand. "Are you okay?" he asked her then, wondering if she'd truly worn herself out with the fire.

"Yeah." She nodded. "I'm just a little drained."

Drained . . . He couldn't help it that the first thing he pictured was his own teeth sinking into her neck. And speaking of drinking blood . . .

"You're starving," he told her then, whispering the words so close to her ear that she was helpless to stop a shiver.

It would have been impossible for Uriel not to notice. She was sitting between his legs and her back was pressed up against his chest. His arms were wrapped gently— but firmly—around her. He could sense everything about her now. He could hear her heartbeat as it sped up at his nearness. He could smell the shampoo in her hair and the slightest tint of adrenaline in her blood.

The image of him taking her was back, but stronger this time, and he felt a warning throb in his gums. "I know of a place not far from here. I can take you to eat. They're open late."

"We can walk?" she asked.

"No." He paused, considering his next words and his own thoughts carefully. "We would fly. But . . ." He licked his lips and glanced down at the gold band around his wrist. "But I'm not sure it's such a wise idea, now that I think of it." Flying was a supernatural ability that came with his newfound vampirism. The bracelet held it in check.

Eleanore turned in his arms and peered up at him. Her expression was a mixture of bewilderment and confusion. "You could honestly fly me somewhere? Like Superman?"

Uriel couldn't help but smile at that. "Yeah," he said. "Like Superman. And Jonathan Brakes," he added, his grin broadening. Luckily, he'd been able to keep his fangs in check.

"Why wouldn't it be a good idea?" she asked.

His grin faltered as he studied her face. He didn't miss the disappointment that furrowed her brow and flickered in her eyes. She wanted to fly. He'd never have imagined that about her. There was so much to learn. . . .

If he could give her that one thing—what would it do for them?

Now Uriel wanted to take her to the air more than he had ever wanted to do anything for anyone in his extremely long existence. "Never mind," he said, smiling confidently. "It's a good idea," he told her. "It's a very good idea."

They stood and he took hold of the bracelet, but paused a moment in quiet reflection. "Eleanore, no matter what happens, whatever you see—don't run from me." He knew instinctively that if she did, he would give chase. He was a hunter now. And like all born hunters, he would automatically pursue anything that ran from him.

"I can handle it," she said bravely.

This is insane, he told himself then. He looked down into Eleanore's dark blue eyes and thought of everything she meant to him. He had searched for her for two thousand bloody years. Through wars and famine and hardships that most people could not imagine. She was the other half of his soul. What he felt when she was near was unlike anything he had ever experienced with another woman. With no other being, period.

If he changed and couldn't control himself, he knew he would use all of his power to seduce her senseless, screw her brains out, and nearly drink her dry. And when she came around—if she came around—she might not forgive him. Was he willing to risk everything between them just to take her flying?

I may never get another chance, he thought. *I may always be a vampire. I may never be cured. I might have to wear this bracelet forever.*

With that thought, Uriel yanked on the gold band around his wrist. It came away from his arm with a bright, decisive flash.

CHAPTER SIXTEEN

E leanore watched as the bracelet dissolved, flashed out of existence, and then reappeared in Uriel's grip, no longer wrapped securely around his wrist. She looked up to find that his head was bowed and his eyes were closed. His lips were pressed firmly together as if he were in pain. Or possibly concentrating.

Eleanore couldn't take the tension. "Uriel?" she asked softly, taking a tentative step toward him. "Are you okay?"

She stopped in her tracks as his lips parted, revealing long, gleaming white fangs. Then she gasped as he raised his head and opened his eyes. The gorgeous light green of his irises was no longer visible. It had been swallowed up entirely by a deep, bottomless black that claimed his eyes from corner to corner.

Uriel settled this unnerving, unnatural gaze upon her and smiled.

It was not a reassuring smile.

No matter what happens, whatever you see—don't run from me. . . . Those had been his words.

"Uriel . . ." *Oh God,* she thought. Run was exactly what she wanted to do. It was instinctive. When a predator with big, sharp teeth pins you in his crosshairs, you run.

But he'd warned her not to. And somewhere in the tornado of Eleanore's thoughts, she knew he was right. Running would only make things worse.

He took a step toward her. It was a determined, deceptively calm prowl.

"Oh, Uriel," she breathed, feeling dizzy with fear.

"Yes, Ellie?" His voice sounded like satin and it slid around her like a silky vise, squeezing her will within its dark influence. It sapped her strength to move away any farther.

"Snap out of it!" she told him—begged him—not even sure what she was saying. She was grasping for words that would bring back the Uriel that had been holding her only moments ago.

He continued to advance. Her instincts told her to step back, but she remained stubbornly frozen in place. As she watched him come nearer, an idea flashed through her head. *He calmed down when I touched him,* she remembered. Outside of the August, when he'd gone into monster mode on the teenagers, it had been Ellie that brought him back to himself.

Another step. He was closing the distance between them.

Eleanore swallowed hard and tried to take a calming breath. "I know you aren't going to hurt me, Uriel," she said, shaking her head once for emphasis. "I trust you. You're stronger than that. You're an *archangel*." Against every defensive fiber in her being, she took the final step forward herself, closing the gap so that they stood toe-to-toe and she gazed up into his eyes. "You're not a vampire."

Uriel seemed to pause, staring down at her through those black portals, studying her carefully. But she couldn't tell what he was thinking; his eyes were so alien to her—devoid of color or emotion.

"Please remember who you are," she whispered, slowly reaching up to place her palm against his cheek. "And who I am."

Uriel could feel it again. But it was stronger than before. It was surging through him unchecked, beckoning him to use it. It was an angry sort of power, like a monster caged and starved and tormented through the bars—then suddenly unleashed upon the world that had imprisoned it.

At inception, he had scented Eleanore's blood, like desire and need and want all mixed together and bottled into a perfume. And she was there, standing before him, defenseless and beautiful, wind-blown and a touch cold, her skin ever so slightly dampened by the salty mist in the air. She was temptation in human form and he had never, *ever* felt so hungry.

She'd spoken his name—breathed it in fear—and at first it only fed the fire in his blood. But then she'd told him to snap out of it. She'd told him that she trusted him. And, though the curve of her chin and the beguiling tilt of her neck was very nearly killing him, she'd told him to remember who he was.

Who *she* was.

And he couldn't help but do as she commanded—because she was his archess. She had been made for him and, if you discounted the sequence of events, then in essence, he had been made for her as well. He could never hurt her.

She raised her hand and touched his cheek and the monster inside of him backpedaled into its cage, leaving him stunned and ... something else. He couldn't put a name to it. But it was staggering.

He could only gaze down at her as his world slowly turned from red to the normal nighttime hues it had been cast in before he'd pulled off the bracelet. His vision changed. His blood stopped rushing. The need within him tamped down and receded to a dull, insistent throb. It was not exactly comfortable—but it was the same aching need he always felt when he was near Eleanore.

He could handle it.

His canines receded to their normal size. He shuddered once beneath her touch and then lifted his own hand to cover hers on his cheek. "I'm sorry," he said softly. "Did I scare you?"

She smiled at that. He'd obviously scared the hell out of her. But she was brave. She was so, so brave and she amazed him to no end.

"Only a little," she fibbed, shrugging it off. "Are you okay?"

"Yes," Uriel said. "But it seems you're always having to ask me that. You deserve better."

"What's better?" she asked.

"This." And suddenly, his arms were snaking around her waist and he was pushing off of the sandy beach and taking her up with him.

Eleanore screamed. The world was falling away, vertigo rushing in to take its place, and everything blurred into one dizzying, terrifying motion as Uriel spun toward the heavens, holding her so tight that his embrace felt like a steel seat belt, strapping her body to his.

She shut her eyes against the unexpected change, clinging to the archangel with every ounce of her strength. She wondered if she was going to faint.

And then, just as suddenly, the wind ceased lashing her hair against her face. Her stomach dropped back out of her throat, and the air stopped biting. Eleanore was surrounded by silence, all-encompassing and vast. There were no seagulls, no waves hitting the shore. There was nothing but the sound of her trembling breaths, in and out in a nearly hysterical rhythm. Several seconds of this passed before she dared open her eyes.

Her face was pressed to Uriel's chest. She'd buried it there in fear.

She chanced a movement, pulling her head away to look up and over the hard swell of his biceps. Darkness spread into the distance, curving against the horizon just enough that she could tell the Earth was, in fact, round. The ocean was endless beneath them, dark and foreboding and, perhaps, bottomless.

Far, far below was the tiny white strip of beach they'd left behind. Their campfire was but a speck of beckoning warmth. The surf looked like a slow-rolling string of froth, moving lazily toward the shore. Over the water, the white wall of fog waited patiently, and small dots of black dove in and out of the mist— seagulls, playing in the night, their cries silenced by the distance between themselves and the angels that hovered above them.

"So now it's my turn to ask," Uriel whispered, his lips caressing the curve of her ear. "Are you all right?"

Eleanore slowly blinked as the stillness around them gradually calmed the frantic beating of her heart. They hovered in the air, separate from the rest of the world, apart from the chaos that existed on the ground. And little by little, Eleanore realized how perfect it was. How peaceful.

"Yes," she whispered, giving him a small nod. "It's so quiet." She turned in his embrace and looked up at him. She could barely see him in the darkness and his frame was outlined by the moon, making his expression a secret. But she caught a glinting in his eyes, flashing green as emeralds, and it reassured her.

"You won't let me go?"

Very softly, he said, "Not for anything."

A breeze picked up again, gentle and tentative. She could tell that he was slowly lowering them back toward the ground. "Where are we going?" she asked.

"Up the beach. Here, let go of my shirt and take my hand."

Eleanore glanced down at his offered hand. His other arm was still wrapped securely around her waist. She thought of Superman and how he had taken Lois Lane flying above Metropolis with nothing more than a grip on her fingers. She smiled a nervous smile and pried one of her hands out of the back of his shirt so that she could lay it across his palm.

His fingers closed tightly, possessively, over hers.

"Now let go with your other hand," he whispered, his words once more caressing her ear.

"No way."

He chuckled, the sound sending delicious shivers down her spine. "Trust me, Ellie."

"Uh-uh." She shook her head.

"You'll regret it later if you don't take the chance right now," he told her softly. "You trusted me enough to stick around when I took off that bracelet. If I didn't hurt you then, why would I hurt you now?"

He had a point. But it didn't matter.

"I can't," she told him.

There was a brief moment of silence as he seemed to be contemplating something. Then, in a more serious tone, he said, "I can help you."

Eleanore looked back up at him, trying to meet his gaze.

"I can make you relax. If you let me inside . . ." He leaned down and laid a very gentle kiss on her forehead. "In here."

"You mean hypnotize me?"

He laughed at that, loud and clear. It was a delicious, rumbling sound. "Yes. Basically. But only if you want me to."

Eleanore considered it. "You won't make me do a strip tease for you or cluck like a chicken, will you?"

Again with the laughter, this time a low chuckle that warmed her abdomen—and places lower down. "That I can't promise. I like chickens."

Eleanore shot him a sideways glance. "Okay. But just relax me a little and that's it."

"Yes, ma'am."

Eleanore thought he would allow her time to prepare, but almost at once, she felt his presence within her mind, and not just her mind, but her body. It was like being infiltrated by gaseous morphine or Valium, mixed with a heavy dose of some kind of aphrodisiac. Words whispered in her ears, but she couldn't make out what they were. They were indistinct and sent shivers through her—delicious, decadent shivers. Moisture pooled shamelessly between her legs. She couldn't help it.

She was incredibly turned on.

Eleanore closed her eyes, unable to suppress the moan of slow, catlike pleasure that escaped her throat.

"Let go now, Ellie," he said, his voice carrying easily over the influential whispers caressing her body and mind.

Eleanore could not help but obey. She let go of him. She felt his grip on her hand, tight as ever, but it was the only part of them still touching.

"That's it," he told her. "Now open your eyes."

Again, she obeyed. Then he turned out toward the long line of beach beneath them and began to soar above it, taking her with him. She squealed with surprise when he dove closer to the ground until they were skimming a mere few yards above the surface.

Eleanore knew that her eyes were saucerlike and her smile a mile wide. She could feel it, ear to ear, as the ground rushed by beneath her and her arms stretched out on either side of her. She became the flying Ellie that she'd always been in her dreams. It was wondrous; there was no discomfort, no fear, no pain. There was only the night and its endless ocean and its frothy waves and the way they all raced by underneath her. She felt as if she could reach down and run her fingers through the water like the fin of a shark.

They dove through a bank of fog and came out the other side damp and breathless. Eleanore became transfixed with the reflection of the moon on the water. She wanted to follow it, to keep moving, to keep skimming there just above the ocean, and Uriel seemed to know this, because he let her.

He never once loosened his hold on her hand. He simply guided her toward all of the places she wanted to go.

She laughed out loud when they buzzed past a small

pod of sea lions on an outcropping and the creatures barked back in surprise.

Eleanore forgot about everything in those precious moments. She left it all behind. There were no contracts, no men with needles, no worried parents, no dead-end jobs, no dangerous fans with cell phone cameras—not up here with Uriel and the night and its salty wind.

The night wore on and, eventually, Uriel began to lower them back down to the ground. He drew her close as they neared the paved asphalt of a bed-and-breakfast parking lot. When her feet touched down, it was with a gentle tentativeness, as she was wrapped tightly in Uriel's embrace.

They gained their legs beneath them and gravity worked once more.

Eleanore gazed up into Uriel's stark green eyes, which she could now see very clearly beneath the porch lights of the bed-and-breakfast. She wanted to tell him so many things. She wanted to thank him, especially. But she also felt breathless and high and fantastic and—because his influence had yet to drop away from her, she felt flushed. She yearned for him.

She wanted to kiss him again. She wanted to show him just how much she'd enjoyed the flight.

Something orange, like fire, flashed in the green of Uriel's eyes and his hand slid up her back, pulling her harder against his chest.

And then her stomach growled. *Loudly.*

She blinked.

Uriel closed his eyes, as if composing himself. And then he opened them again and pursed his lips to keep from smiling.

"Inside with you," he said. "There will be plenty of time for other matters after you've had a decent meal."

Sam finished reading the last of Juliette Anderson's file and then gently set it down on top of the coffee table in front of him.

She was a very interesting young woman. Born to twenty-two-year-old Abigail Anderson and twenty-five-year-old Scott Anderson in Sacramento twenty-five years ago. She was unlike Eleanore Granger in that her powers had not materialized until just recently. She was very lucky in some ways; she'd had a relatively normal childhood and had been able to go to college. However, she was unlucky in other ways. Samael's men reported that she was frightened of her new abilities. She felt alone; even her parents were unaware of her double nature.

She was a beautiful woman. As an archess, that was to be expected. The folder he'd perused contained various photographs, taken at different angles. She had a wealth of shining brown hair that fell in thick waves down her back. Juliette, or "Jules" to her friends, was a fair amount shorter than Eleanore, coming to a very petite five feet and three inches, but within her tiny frame was a vortex of strength, energy, and power. Her beautiful hazel eyes glowed with it, as well as with kindness. According to her file, the woman volunteered for numerous charities and freely donated money and personal belongings.

She was lovely, inside and out. But Samael suspected, as well, that it probably made it that much more difficult for the new archess to maintain a low profile. People noticed women like her.

Just as they had always noticed Eleanore.

And speaking of Eleanore . . . Samael leaned back in his chair and laced his fingers over his stomach. He wondered how she and the new vampire were getting along.

He, of course, hoped it wasn't that well. But, whether it was or not, it hardly mattered. The gala was tomorrow night. The archangel and his soul mate would most assuredly be in attendance.

But they wouldn't be alone.

Not by a long shot.

*   *   *

General Kevin Trenton appeared quite young to be a general. But he was not like most men. He was ... *different*. He always had been.

Right now, it was his own different nature that he pondered as he watched the recorded footage of Eleanore Granger healing a man and his daughter immediately following a car accident in a small town in West Texas.

It had taken precious time and resources to locate the footage. According to his men, despite the fact that the accident scene and subsequent healing had been messy, evidence of the event turned out to be nearly nonexistent.

Kevin wasn't happy. This cover-up meant that someone was looking out for Eleanore. Someone else out there was thinking along the same lines that Kevin had been thinking for years.

Granger was a very special woman. She had something that Kevin and his men didn't have—had never possessed—and desperately wanted. Her need to heal her fellow man had come naturally to her. And it was that healing ability that had drawn him to her all those years ago.

Eleanore Granger needed to be brought in. There was no more time to waste. He had tried to capture her after a lucky flux had located her in a mid-Texas town called Rockdale, where several of his men happened to be stationed, but somehow she'd escaped him.

Her ability to elude him was positively bewildering.

Kevin wasn't certain what Christopher Daniels had to do with Eleanore, but he suspected that the actor was not all he seemed to be. Furthermore, Kevin was fairly sure that Daniels, too, had something to do with the temporal fluxes his team had been charting all over the planet.

It all centered on Granger. He needed to get his hands on her.

Christopher Daniels had a promotional event in Dallas to attend tomorrow night. Kevin knew that Eleanore would be accompanying him. With luck, a careful plan, and a good number of skilled men, Granger would be under his control by Friday morning.

Uriel had never been forced to exercise as much control over himself as he had tonight. First the kiss in front of the hotel. Then the stupid fans. Then he had taken the bracelet off.

He was going a little batty on the inside. On the outside, he was calm, he was in control, he was understanding and gentle, but he had no idea how he was holding it together as well as he was because, frankly, Eleanore was making him crazy. If he hadn't had two thousand years to learn to exercise immense control over his own body, he would have a painfully raging hard-on at the moment. Luckily, all he had was a throbbing gum line and a pair of fangs that would not totally disappear.

He managed to hide those fairly well, making certain that Ellie couldn't see his face when they were pronounced. But how long would he be able to keep this up?

Christ, he thought, as he followed her through the front door of the bed-and-breakfast. He could smell her arousal. He knew she was wet with desire for him. He'd known it from the moment his influence had coiled inside of her, releasing the need she kept so carefully in check. He knew he was subduing her, breaking her will, and though he hadn't meant to do it, there was a part of him that was anything but sorry that he had. It had caused his own monster to awaken, rear its head, and sniff the air. His gut had clenched, his jaw tightened, his hunger spiking hard.

He had given her a taste of something she had always yearned for and, in return, she'd felt true happiness. Somehow, it made him love her even more.

Love her?

He could hear that her heart still beat rapidly in her chest and he couldn't help it when his gaze slipped to the curve of her taut ass in those tight jeans, swaying gently as she walked ahead of him.

He swore under his breath and bit back his groan.

He watched as she tentatively placed a slim-fingered hand on the wall and peeked her head around the corner of the entry hall into the foyer. The hair slipped from her neck when she did, exposing the long, slim column of her throat. He bit back another groan.

And there it was.

Fuck me, he thought. *I do love her. I love everything about her.* It didn't exactly come as a surprise to him. She was his archess, after all. But he'd existed for countless generations and had never known love before this. It was a new emotion for him, and it was bewildering in its own right.

There was a woman wiping down a coffee table in the room beyond. Uriel instantly caught her gaze and, in a most nonangelic way, he immediately subjugated her mind.

The woman smiled warmly at Eleanore and put her hands on her hips. "Oh my goodness! Look at you two; you're soaked through. Have you come from far?"

"Sort of," Uriel said, playing along with ease. He was good at acting. "We were wondering whether you had a room available and we're also hoping it isn't too late to get a bite to eat."

Bite . . .

"Of course we have a room!" the woman chirped happily. "In fact, our corner suite on the second floor cleared out this morning and won't be booked again until Thanksgiving! You're welcome to it; it's already been cleaned and prepared." She bustled past Eleanore to a small writing desk against one wall, where she extracted a few forms from a folder and handed them to Uriel.

"My name's Tilda, by the way," she said as she handed them the forms. "If you'll just fill these out real quick, I'll go ahead and put some soup on the stove. Minestrone all right with you?" she asked.

"That would be fantastic," Eleanore said with a grateful smile.

A half hour later, Ellie had finished her meal in the bed-and-breakfast's dining room and the two of them headed to their room on the second floor of the inn. Eleanore's heart was beating fast by the time she followed Uriel up the stairs. During dinner, she had confessed to him that she needed to talk. Though she'd been having a fantastic evening, she knew she had to tell him about her contract with Samael.

The room they had procured for the night was actually two separate rooms, joined by a long hallway that sported an enormous bathroom. The bathtub was more like a hot tub, complete with jets and nooks in the marble for placing cold drinks. There was a fireplace in the master bedroom, and Tilda had already started a fire for them. It burned low, crackling warmly and lending a comforting glow to the rest of the room.

But it was the view that people were paying for with this suite. One side of the master bedroom was lined with floor-to-ceiling windows and a set of sliding glass doors that led out onto a balcony. The sound of the surf was clearly audible, as were the cries of seagulls and the barking of sea lions somewhere in the distance. Even at night, Eleanore could tell that it would be breathtaking in the morning.

"Did you enjoy your dinner?"

No, Eleanore thought. *I spent the whole meal worrying about what was going to come afterward.*

"Yes," she fibbed. "It was good soup." At least *that* was true.

Uriel was still watching her closely. He nodded once and lowered himself into a large leather chair that sat across from the master bed. Then he rested his long, booted legs on the coffee table in front of him and speared her with a hard look. "Now talk."

"I'm scared," she told him honestly. "This has been

such a wonderful night, Uriel. You've . . . you've shown me so much. But I'm afraid." She shuddered, a chill working its way through her body.

He did not fail to notice it, but the hardness in his gaze also didn't let up. "What are you afraid of, exactly?" he asked softly.

"I don't want you to hate me."

"I could never hate you, Ellie," he told her calmly. "So you can stop being afraid of that right now."

Eleanore slowly lowered herself onto the edge of the bed and stared into the fire. "Fine. What's done is done." And though she knew it was foolish to have made such a deal with such a man, she also knew, in her heart, that she had done it for the right reasons. She had done it in the hopes that Samael would cure Uriel of his vampire curse. To her, that was a noble motive. She only hoped Uriel would see it that way as well.

"Yesterday, I signed a contract with Samael," she said, deciding to just let it out all at once. She didn't look up at Uriel to see his reaction. Instead, she gazed steadily into the fire and didn't even move. "The deal was that I would come to him for protection if, at any time in the following week, you did anything to . . . to hurt me." She swallowed, fighting past a lump that had formed in her throat. She was beginning to tremble, but she forced herself to go on. She still didn't look at Uriel. "In exchange, he agreed to free you from your vampire curse at the end of the week."

The room was silent but for the sound of the crackling flames and the seagulls and surf outside the windows.

Eleanore wondered whether she should look up and meet Uriel's gaze. She considered it. She considered pleading for understanding or forgiveness. But a part of her—the stubborn part—also felt that she shouldn't need forgiveness in the first place. After all, she wasn't the only one who had made a deal with Samael.

The silence continued to stretch until Eleanore was

so nervous, she was certain she was going to break out in hives.

"Did he hurt you?" Uriel finally asked, his tone eerily calm.

The question surprised Eleanore, but she still didn't look at him. She shook her head.

Again, he was quiet for some time. And then, "You did this for me?" he asked.

Eleanore nodded, keeping her eyes stubbornly trained on the crackling hearth.

Suddenly, Uriel blurred into impossible motion, carrying with him a burst of wind that rushed through her hair and sent the fire into a frantic, crackling fit. Eleanore shut her eyes as her hair whipped at her face. She felt strong arms at her waist lifting her, but she had no time to cry out or object before she was taken at breakneck speed through the air and shoved up against the wall. There she was pinned beneath a tall, hard body.

Uriel's dark vampire power was instantly penetrating her mind, flooding it with desire. Her lips parted, a moan of harsh longing climbing her throat, but it was never given voice, as Uriel's lips crashed down hard against hers, claiming them in brutal subjugation. He delved deep, with no hint of gentleness, and she could feel his fangs, fully elongated and sharp, threatening at the tip of her tongue.

A rush of trepidation fought to climb up her spine, but Uriel shoved it back down, ruthlessly smothering her in her own desire.

He reached down with one hand, his palm sliding along the side of her waist. He held her body against the wall with the weight of his own and wrapped his other hand gently—but threateningly—around her neck. He squeezed, a show of ultimate control over her, as the fingers of his other hand found the hem of her T-shirt and shoved it up, exposing the taut flesh of her abdomen. His fingernails raked across her skin, drawing a gasp of desire from somewhere deep within her, which he swallowed as he continued to kiss her harshly, drinking her in.

I want you, she heard him breathe into her mind.

She was befuddled and hot, feverish with confusing desire. She could not reply, but she found herself arching against him when his fingers headed south, ripping open the front of her jeans so that he could shove his hand under the lace band of her panties.

God, I need you, Ellie....

He was all around her. Encompassing her, bringing her to terrible, delightful, agonizing life. Her nerve endings cried out for him—to stop? To go on?

He found the soft curls between her legs and tightened his grip on her throat.

She was on fire.

I love you, he told her then, as his fingers pressed on, invading her, parting her, and sinking deep.

Then take me.

CHAPTER SEVENTEEN

Uriel was mad with lust. He was angry as hell at what Sam had done to his archess. He was so furious that, at Eleanore's words, his world had once more painted itself red. But his wrath was for the Fallen One, not Ellie.

His own spiking adrenaline had set off fireworks within his body. First came the anger, then the fierce jealousy that another man had gotten to Ellie in any way, then the pride and awe that she would do such a thing for him. That deeper, more heartfelt emotion was what really did it for him. Desire leapt to life like a bonfire, consuming his entire being, until all he knew was that he wanted Eleanore, needed her, and had to have her, or he was sure he would die.

Very slowly, he withdrew his fingers from her tight moistness and had to suppress a growl of mounting insanity when she actually moaned her disappointment. She was not herself, he realized. He had taken her over, body and mind, and she was a slender, wanton vessel of desire beneath him.

It was all he could do not to fist his hand in her hair, yank her head back, and sink his fangs into her throat.

"Christ, Ellie . . ." he hissed across her lips, and then nibbled gently at them, his fangs piercing her slightly before he moved to her jaw line. His grip on her throat tightened, just a little, before he slid his hand away and replaced it with his mouth.

Eleanore gasped when his teeth scraped across the side of her neck.

Uriel nibbled at her throat, his hot breath threatening, and then, as he pressed his body firmly against hers, barely leaving her room to breathe, he growled low in his throat and straightened, capturing her gaze in his once more.

With a roar of raging need, he pulled back and shoved himself from the wall, taking her with him. Coherent thought all but left him as he turned to the bed and threw her down onto her stomach in the center of the mattress.

Eleanore gasped and cried out, clearly struggling to make sense of the sudden movement, scrambling to get her hands and knees beneath her.

He didn't give her the chance. He was on top of her, pressing her into the quilt before she could gain any leverage.

"Uriel!" she cried out, and he again combed her mind. Her need was still there, her desire still hot and wet and demanding, but he was frightening her. He was all hard angles and unrelenting strength to her—and strange, dark eyes. A part of her coiled with fear, at once unsure and unsettled. Another part of her relished in the domination, wanting more.

He gave it to her.

"Don't fight me, Ellie," he hissed in her ear as his hands found her wrists and pulled them together, pinning them above her head in one taut grip against the mattress. "Just give in to me and let me lead."

Trust me, he told her firmly, lodging the command deep within her thoughts. It stilled her beneath him so that the only part of her that moved was her chest, rising and falling in quick, fierce succession with each desperate breath.

Uriel's self-control was gone. There was nothing left in him but a dominant vampire, an archangel who needed his archess, and a determination that forced his will upon the woman trapped beneath him. He would ease this transition for her in the only way he now could. He would give her the pleasure he felt himself and hope against hopes that it was enough.

He could have ripped her clothes off of her then and destroyed them. He could have morphed the material and made it fall away. He possessed powers that normal men did not have at their disposal and, if he'd chosen to, he could have laid her bare to his touch with no more than an impatient thought and flash of will.

But Eleanore was enticing in the extreme and there was no way Uriel was going to deny himself even the smallest pleasure when it came to bedding her. Her boots, he did flash away, as they would only slow him down. But the rest of her, he would damn well undress himself.

In one clean movement, Uriel shoved his hand between her taut stomach and the mattress, and fisted his grip around the top of her jeans. Uriel yanked on the material, shoving them and her white cotton lace underwear over the tight, round swell of her bottom.

Eleanore cried out at the sudden exposure, undoubtedly unused to baring herself in such a manner to anyone at all.

Uriel leaned in to chuckle in her ear. She shivered as he continued to strip her, his strong hand moving under her T-shirt, shoving it upward as he went. When he reached the underwire of her white lace bra, he fought the urge to wrap his fingers around it and rip it clean away from her body. That might cause her too much pain. So he forced himself to unclasp it, his arm beneath her, his body still holding her down on the bed.

Once he'd removed her bra, Eleanore shivered, her breathing ragged. He had her fully at his mercy now and the knowledge that she was aware of her helplessness made Uriel's rock-hard dick throb so that it pressed painfully against his jeans.

"I'm going to let you up. Don't try to get away, do you understand?" he whispered harshly in her ear.

She hesitated in answering, her desire fighting with her natural instinct to flee. Uriel's hand was out from between them and once more wrapped around her throat in a flash. He used it to pull her up and against him, squeezing in warning.

"Do you understand?" he demanded again, his lips at her ear.

"Yes," she gasped, and he could scent that more wetness flooded her in response to his domination. She trusted him and wanted him to take over as much as he did. "I understand."

He released her and moved back enough for her to find her hands and knees. She raised herself to a kneeling position and straightened.

"Raise your arms over your head."

She did as he said and he yanked her shirt up and over her head, taking her bra with it. As soon as it was off, he pulled her against his chest, his hand spanning across her midsection and sliding up to cup her firm, supple breast.

She moaned and arched into his hand, pressing her flesh against his palm. Uriel's teeth ached in his gums. His vision began to change yet again, darkening and hardening into sharp angles and deep contrasts.

"Grab the rail of the headboard," he told her, letting her go and pushing her forward.

She seemed confused at first, so he took one of her hands in his and wrapped it around the metal railing himself. She followed suit with the other on her own. He could hear her heart hammering away, sense that her own need was driving her as much as his was driving him. He could also smell her blood, mingled with the scent of her desire, and it practically begged him to do what he desperately wanted to do.

Once she had the railing in her grip, Uriel shoved her jeans to her knees and lifted her with a strong arm around her waist, yanking them and her underwear the rest of the way off of her.

She was naked before him, vulnerable and wet and waiting—his archess, with her knees slightly parted, her back arched, and her hands firmly gripping a metal railing in front of her. If he could have waited, if he could have taken the pressure, he would have remained where he was, his eyes burning her image into his skull so that he would never, ever forget this moment. But he *couldn't* wait.

Not anymore.

With that simple flash of thought, he sent his own clothes away. As if he hadn't been hard enough before, the release of pressure on his cock allowed more of his blood to flow into it, nearly driving him mad with throbbing need.

He clenched his fists against the near pain. He wasn't a small man. Add to that the fact that he was an archangel and formed of what the Old Man had considered perfection, and Uriel had a feeling that, like it or not, this was going to hurt Eleanore.

But it couldn't be helped. Nothing in the world could have stopped him from taking her then. Not able to stand being apart from her any longer, Uriel leaned forward, pressing his chest against her back. He ran his hands over her small hips, up her tiny waist, and to the swell of her ribs and her round, perfect breasts.

Eleanore moaned again, and with hard eyes, Uriel watched her fingers slip a little on the railing.

"Don't you dare let go," he growled, and she jumped, gripping it tighter. Then he moved up and pulled her taut against him, until she could feel his hardness pressing between her legs. Eleanore tried to lurch away then, almost releasing the railing once more. Uriel held her fast, bearing his teeth as another growl made its way up his throat.

His dick pulsed hot and heavy and brick-hard and Uriel's tight grip on Eleanore's waist guided her back toward him until its tip nudged at her opening. She made a small, gasping sound and shook her head, her raven hair cascading over her shoulders in blue-black rivulets. He removed one of his hands from her waist and fisted it in her hair, yanking back on it hard to expose her throat to him.

She gritted her teeth as he simultaneously rose up and shoved partway into her. She shuddered violently as his member breached her outer lips and slipped inside.

Uriel watched her face as he took her, a feeling of victory riding him. He loved the way she bared her own white teeth and squeezed her eyes shut at the pain and pleasure he was causing her. He loved her racing pulse and her rising and falling breasts and the way she obeyed him and had yet to let go of that railing.

He lowered himself until he could once more whisper in her ear. "I'm going to take you now the way I've wanted to take you since I saw you that night in the bookstore," he told her, keeping his grip on her hair tight so that she couldn't pull away. "I'm going to take you hard and fast," he promised her. "Because you're mine, Ellie." He almost growled his ownership. "And you always will be."

With that, he covered her mouth with one hand and thrust forward, holding her still as he did so. In one clean, driving shove, he ripped through her virginity and rendered it in two.

Eleanore screamed into the palm of his hand and Uriel held her there against him as she came down from the sudden, piercing pain. At the same time, he reached out with his vampire powers and flooded her with more of the pleasure she was already drowning in. Within seconds, she forgot about the pain and he removed his hand.

But his grip remained tight in her hair and, as he drew back and then drove forward again, all the way to the hilt, he lowered his mouth to the side of her neck. With his free hand, he parted her curls and pressed in on her clit, eliciting a low, mewling moan from deep in her throat.

He pulled back—and shoved forward. And did it again. And again.

Eleanore nearly let go of the railing at the sheer force with which he now plunged into her, but the innocent, captive part of her continued to heed his warning and hold tight. He had to smile at that, a dark, smug, male satisfaction fueling the strength in his veins. It wasn't until he exposed his teeth and pricked them threateningly at the taut flesh of her neck, that she finally let go of the headboard and grabbed his thighs behind her. He grinned as her nails dug deep, drawing blood.

"Mistake, Ellie," he purred in her ear, almost chuckling the reprimand. He gave her no time to ponder his words before he raised his head, opened his mouth wide, and then sank his fangs deep into her neck.

Again, Eleanore cried out, but this time, Uriel let the cry fill the room and the darkness beyond. If anyone heard, he would deal with it later.

He held her there in his vampire embrace, his cock deep inside of her, his teeth buried in her throat, and he pulled slowly against her skin, swallowing with barely tamed inhuman hunger as her body gave up its blood for him.

He drank sparingly, not wanting to drain her, and it was like holding a fire at bay with gasoline; it was nearly impossible to stop the heat from spreading and engulfing him.

All of you, he thought distantly as he moved inside of her, back and forth, urging her on to her own forbidden ecstasy. *Give me all of you. . . .* She tasted like heaven, the way he would imagine ambrosia to taste—sweet and seductive and quenching. He brushed his fingers over her sensitive clit and then pressed, over and over again, teasing and taking, as he claimed her.

Eleanore moaned and gasped and sighed, and he smiled against her pierced flesh as he felt her press unwittingly into him. She wanted more—so he gave it to her. With more force now, he propelled them on. A brief brush of her mind and he knew that she was in pain as well as pleasure. And he knew that she liked it that way.

The animal in him reared its head again and he pulled more fiercely against her vein, drawing her blood into him with renewed vigor. At the same time, he took her down to the bed, shoving her forward beneath him as he kept both teeth and cock firmly lodged inside of her, maintaining his claim on her body.

She hit the mattress and he released her hair, quickly grabbing her wrists and pinning them once more to the bed above her.

He drew out, nearly all the way, only to drive into her with ruthless force, shoving his rock-hard need so deep that she cried out once more. He was pitiless, ramming her over and over again in this same brutal manner.

He felt her climax building; then, as she tensed beneath him in a kind of shuddering and tightening that started in her stomach and worked its way down, until she was gripping his dick with unbelievable tightness.

Lightning crashed outside the windows, bathing their carnal act in electric, blue-white light. Thunder followed quick on its heels, drowning out the sound of Uriel's own guttural cry as he ripped his fangs from Eleanore's throat, dug his fingers into her wrists, and exploded inside of her.

Lightning split the sky a second time. And then a third. Hard, driving rain slanted onto the tin roof of the bed-and-breakfast, drenching the establishment in a strange, sudden downpour.

The bed stopped rocking. The fire had burned down.

And Uriel slowly—oh so slowly—lowered his lips to Eleanore's neck, tenderly kissing the wounds he had placed there. She shivered and sighed.

He drew his archess into his arms, rolling onto his

side so that her back was pressed against his chest. She shuddered and, because he was still buried deep inside of her, he felt the aftershocks of her climax with blissful rapture. He closed his eyes and breathed her in, scenting their sex, her hair, the ash from the fire, and her blood.

He could hear that her heart beat steady, strong, and calm. Her breathing had slowed into a gentle, sated rhythm. He absorbed all of this, taking in everything with careful attention. He was in heaven. No. It was better than heaven. He never wanted to move from that bed. His strong arms trapped Ellie's slim body against him and he never, ever wanted to let her go. Not for anything.

Thunder rolled in the distance. The rain poured on.

CHAPTER EIGHTEEN

Lilith peered out her window at the garden that was drained of color in the moonlight. She hadn't been able to sleep. There was something in the air tonight making her restless; it was an unsettled vibration that she couldn't quite place. She hadn't slept a wink all night, and she found that she kept fidgeting.

She turned away from the window, and with a simple thought, her nightgown transformed into a silk skirt, a silk blouse, and a pair of simple, low-heeled pumps. Then she left her rooms and headed down the hall toward Sam's quarters.

Halfway there, she paused in her tracks. Here, the vibration became worse, more erratic, more troubled. It felt now as if the very atmosphere had become apprehensive.

Oh no, she thought, her mind doing circles around the implications. Samael was a very, very powerful creature, and when he got mad, it was a very powerful kind of fury.

The corridor up ahead seemed darker than it should have, even at night. It was as if a pall had fallen over the area. Perhaps it was this, combined with the tension in the air, that had brought Lilith to a halt.

She swallowed hard and reached out with her mind, frightened of what she would find when she brushed whatever it was that was lurking in the rooms beyond that dark stretch of hall ahead.

She wasn't disappointed. For the dense, heavy fore-boding that stirred at the edges of her mental feelers was nothing if not evil. It was the very essence of wrong-ness. It was Samael at his worst.

She wondered what had brought about this change. Only a few hours ago, he had been speaking with Jason in hushed but relaxed tones. He was carefully planning their arrangement for Christopher Daniels's gala. And though Lilith had objected to their behavior enough that she'd stayed well away from their scheming, she had been grateful that he was at least calm and in control.

Now, however, there was that dreadfully familiar feeling in the air that reminded her of unholy ultima-tums and fallen angels.

Oh, Samael, she thought ruefully. *What have you done?*

With more courage than she would have thought she possessed, Lilith took a deep breath, squared her shoul-ders, and made her way down the dark hall.

Eleanore's body felt heavy. It was as if every inch of it were weighted down, forcing it to press hard into the mattress beneath her. Gravity held her captive, draining her strength, and made it difficult for her to open her eyes. She normally didn't feel this weak unless she had been using her powers. What was wrong with her?

She forced her eyes to open anyway, blinking against a blurry grayness, and tried to get her bearings.

She was naked, in a bed, in an unfamiliar room. There was a sliding glass door in front of her, and beyond that, there was fog. It was nothing but a wall of dense white.

Where am I?

She frowned and tried to move. She was instantly as-sailed by a deep soreness. It permeated each muscle, and between her legs, there was an ache that she had never before experienced. Her breath caught when she felt her very pulse down there, hot and swollen. And then

Uriel shifted behind her, his arm nudging gently against her hip where it was draped heavily over her body.

Memories began to rush at her, like floating photographs and cut scenes from a movie. Within a few still seconds, she remembered where she was.

And what had happened the night before.

Her neck and face flushed pink, her mind reeling at the memory of what had transpired. *Oh my God,* she thought, recalling Uriel's fingers buried deep inside of her—and then other parts of him later on. She stifled a moan, a shiver, and closed her eyes against the need that was already burgeoning within her once more.

It wasn't natural. It couldn't be normal for her to want to be taken again. And that was what he'd done—taken her. She remembered the look in his vampire eyes—the feel of him smothering her with his pleasure, desire cascading over her until she felt she would die if he didn't . . . if he didn't . . . if he didn't *fuck* her.

Oh Christ, she thought, her insides writhing with the plethora of mixed emotions riding her. She remembered Uriel's teeth in her neck, his hard heat so deep inside of her, and his thrusting that was anything but gentle. It had hurt.

It had all been painful.

Eleanore recalled her promise to Samael. It was a deal made in blood. If Uriel had hurt her, did she need to go to Samael now?

No.

She did not. Not this time. Because the pain had also been pleasure.

The realization of *why* her night with Uriel did not necessitate her running to Samael for protection was nearly more shocking than what Uriel had actually done. She couldn't count this as an attack; she couldn't claim that Uriel had caused her any undue suffering because, the hard truth of it was, Eleanore had *wanted* Uriel and the volatile, violent nature that came with his vampire form.

He'd done everything she had secretly needed him to do—everything she'd yearned for. How could he have known? Had he even been aware that each time he had taken over and forced more submission into her trembling form, he was only fulfilling her dearest, deepest secrets and desires?

Eleanore shuddered as she recalled the many times she'd brought herself to orgasm while alone—in her shower, in her bed, even in the car once while stuck in traffic. She was a sexual creature by nature, but had never been able to explore that side of herself with another person.

Last night, Uriel had somehow been able to see right through her to give her what she needed. She'd never had an orgasm like the one he had brought her to. And she wanted more. Right now, in fact. In that rented bed in that quaint two-story cottage on that cool, foggy shore.

She was actually wet for it; she could feel Uriel's warmth at her back, his strong presence wrapped around her. She could sense her own naked vulnerability, and even the throbbing soreness of the bite marks on her neck was turning her on.

She glanced down at the strong, well-muscled arm draped possessively over her and thought of Uriel's whispered words.

I love you.

Had she imagined those words or had he really projected them into her mind? If he hadn't, then she was losing it. But if he *had* and he'd meant it, then . . .

Her eyes trailed over the handsome planes of his sleeping face. With her fingertips she gently touched his cheek and brushed them over his lips. *He's so perfect,* she thought. *And he's mine.*

And then she almost laughed. She let her hand drop and shook her head. *I'm hopeless,* she thought with a slight smile. *He's obviously exhausted Let the poor boy rest.*

She glanced across the room at the windows again and pondered the color of the fog. It had to be very early morning, perhaps just after sunrise. The sky was thick with the soup of grounded clouds. She could barely make out the edge of the balcony just beyond the glass doors.

Very slowly, so as not to wake the archangel beside her, Eleanore slipped her small frame out from beneath his heavy arm and rose from the bed. Uriel frowned where he lay in the center of the mattress, but he didn't wake. He seemed deeply under and barely stirred as she padded across the room toward the adjoining bathroom.

Once there, she closed and locked the door behind her. She needed a long, hot shower.

"Something is wrong."

Michael looked up from where he was seated at the table, dressed in the blue uniform of an NYPD officer. "What do you mean?"

Max frowned and put down his coffee cup. "I don't know." He couldn't put his finger on it. There was a sour taste in his mouth, though. The air felt strange; as if it were charged with some kind of negativity. There was a churning in his stomach that he'd never felt before.

"I think it's Uriel," he finally said.

Michael put down his own coffee cup and narrowed his gaze. "Az said he was doing well when he left him with Ellie."

"I know, but . . ." Max shook his head, took off his glasses, and rubbed his eyes. He could always tell what was going on with his archangels. He was their guardian; he was connected to them in an indelible way. And right now, he kept seeing Uriel's face in his mind's eye. There was fog around him, but as Max concentrated, the fog lifted, revealing the rising sun over an ocean of blue.

He froze. He straightened and pinned Michael with a stunned look. "He's in trouble."

"Where is he?" Michael asked, pushing from the table to stand.

"The West Coast," Max replied, also standing. "Give me a few seconds and the mansion will take us there."

Clever, Uriel. Very clever.

Uriel frowned in his sleep, uncertain whether he was hearing someone speak to him, or if it was his own voice that was floating around in his head.

I'm impressed, brother. You managed to get what you wanted, didn't you?

Now Uriel's blood began to run cold. He recognized the voice. Samael was speaking to him, but Uriel couldn't seem to open his eyes to face the Fallen One. He couldn't wake up. He felt strangely heavy and sedated.

You had fun torturing your archess. I'm obviously jealous. However, though you caused her a good deal of physical pain in your ... methods, I can't take her from you. You only did as she desired. There was a sharp spike of unfathomable envy that prickled at Uriel's skin. *And that doesn't count.*

There followed a stillness, filled with electriclike loathing and a simmering desire for revenge. Uriel recognized *that* well enough. He was the former Angel of Vengeance, after all.

But, of course, Samael continued slowly, *you knew that.*

What's happening? Uriel thought. He couldn't get his bearings. He had no idea where he was; everything was dark around him and his brain felt clouded. He again tried to wake, to rouse himself and come into something solid. But his world would not cooperate.

Laughter. Low and ice cold.

Tsk, tsk, Uriel. You can fight me all you want. But you're a vampire now. How soon you forget your new weaknesses. There are some things, little brother, which you most assuredly cannot fight.

Fear, real and hard and life-threatening, lodged itself

in Uriel's gut. It churned there, burning up his mind even as his form—wherever it was—went numb with a cold certainty. Death was beyond this wall of black around him. Death awaited him.

All he would have to do is open his eyes.

Close, Uriel, but no cigar. Death does await you, but it isn't your sleep that holds it at bay. It's your archess who unconsciously keeps you safe. She doesn't even know that she protects you. She has no idea that it's by her own instinctive will that clouds surround your chamber, blocking the sun from your sleeping form.

Shock ramrodded through Uriel at Sam's words. He remembered everything in that split second—the night before, the taste of Eleanore, his delicious, perfect claiming of his beautiful archess.

And then he remembered the room and its many windows that looked out over the ocean and the open sky beyond. He'd fallen asleep without a care—and forgotten all about the impending morning and its very bright, very deadly sun.

There was more laughter, evil and dark and all around him.

I suggest you wake soon, little brother. Because I can control the weather as well. And I've never been fond of cloudy days.

With that, Samael's presence slipped from his mind and Uriel's heartbeat ratcheted up to a hard-drumming, painful degree.

Wake up, damn it! Fight this!

He knew from one night's experience that vampires did not actually become comatose during the day, and yet he couldn't fight the sleep that had been draped so heavily over him.

It was Samael's doing. The Fallen One had some sort of power over this cursed form. It made sense, being that Uriel was a vampire by Samael's will alone.

At the edge of Uriel's senses, there was the slightest prickling of pain. It was so distant, it was barely noticeable. More like a tingling, really. But it was foreboding in the extreme and Uriel became more desperate.

He imagined his body moving, his fingers twitching, and reached out with every ounce of his power to rouse his slumbering body from where it rested, so helpless and immobile, on the mattress beneath him. He failed.

The distant tingling at the edges of his body spread to a slow-growing burn.

Eleanore shut off the stream of water in the shower and ran her hands over her head, shoving her hair out of her eyes. She stepped out, wrapped a towel around her, and started to pat her long hair dry with another one.

The bathroom was thick with steam and the mirror was fogged up, but her gaze was caught by a stream of light from beneath the bathroom door.

For some reason, it gave her pause. She frowned at it, feeling as if it were out of place. *It shouldn't be there,* she thought warily. She didn't know why, but she strongly felt as if the light were wrong.

She threw off her towel and quickly pulled on her jeans and T-shirt, leaving her undergarments on the floor. Then she opened the door and stepped out into the room beyond.

It was too bright. Daylight flooded the room, no longer kept at bay by a thick blanket of fog beyond the second-floor balcony. Eleanore's gaze automatically fell on Uriel, his strong body immobile and half-covered by the sheet on the bed. He was on his back, deep in sleep, his handsome face pale, his lips blanched, his hair longer and darker than it had been before the curse.

The curse, Eleanore thought numbly.

A single, überbright stream of light had crept at an angle across the carpet and made its way to the bed upon which Uriel lay.

Realization hit her like a sledgehammer, and she barely suppressed a cry of alarm when she saw the stream of light had run its course, from the tips of Uriel's fingers to the palm of his outstretched hand, and the wrist and forearm beyond. Everywhere it touched, it left a scorch mark, deep and black and smoking. The smell of burnt flesh registered in her brain at the same time that she hit the mattress and was covering Uriel's body with her own.

She tried to bring the clouds back, tried to call up a storm with her powers, but the weather wouldn't answer her. She drew Uriel's arm across his chest and tried to roll him off of the bed, but he was too heavy—uncommonly so. It was as if he were weighted down by some unnatural force.

She sat back a little and tried to use telekinesis on him, hoping to move him in that manner instead. No doing. He wouldn't budge.

The sunlight crept up her back; she could feel its heat through her thin T-shirt. It outlined her shadow across the far wall.

Desperation wrenched a half sob, half cry from her throat. She needed help in moving him. She took a chance and called out. "Is anyone out there?" She hollered the question at the door, hoping against hope that someone would hear her. "Somebody please help me!" she called. "Hello!" she tried one last time.

Where was Tilda? Where were the other bed-and-breakfast tenants?

She couldn't move from where she was or the sun would hit Uriel again. *Think, Eleanore! Think!* She racked her brain.

Inspiration struck her at the sound of a Harley's engine on the road that ran along the front of the bed-and-breakfast. She remembered the Harley she'd lifted and shoved into the window of the garage in Uriel's mansion.

She could do the same thing now, only in reverse. She turned to spear the table against one wall with a determined glare. The table began to rattle—and then it lifted from the floor and floated toward the window, turning on its side as it neared the sliding glass doors. Eleanore concentrated on laying the table against the window and managed to block a small amount of the sun. However, light poured in over the top of it and she realized that she needed more furniture.

She lifted a chair next—and then another one. But balancing them all was beginning to be a problem and she could feel that the stream of sunlight was now on her shoulders. She was running out of time. A weakness was stealing over her. She was getting tired.... Uriel had taken a fair amount of her blood and this use of her power was draining her.

Come on, Ellie! Think, damn it!

Her gaze drifted over her lover's features, so cold and so handsome. He was dying there in that bed; she knew it. He would die, his gorgeous body eaten up by the daylight because there was nothing to protect him from it but a flimsy little sheet....

The sheet!

Eleanore cried out with frustration that she hadn't thought of this before and instantly focused her attention on the blankets and towels in the rooms of the suite, instead of its heavy furniture.

A flurry of different materials sailed across the room toward the tall windows and drew themselves across the glass. She blocked out the sun a little more with each layer she added to the makeshift curtains. As she worked, she couldn't help but curse Tilda just a little for not providing the huge glass doors with blinds of their own. But she wasted little time on her anger; she was feeling very tired as it was. The important thing was to protect Uriel from the direct sunlight until she could figure out how to move him.

When the sun was completely blocked, Eleanore slumped forward a little and bowed her head. But she couldn't let go yet. She had to maintain her concentration or the blankets would fall.

"Uriel!" She grabbed his broad shoulder and shook

hard, trying to wake him. He barely moved beneath her ministrations; his body was like iron, heavy and solid beyond logic. "Uriel! Please wake up!"

She pressed her fingers to his neck and felt the pulse there. It was weak and erratic, but at least it existed.

The corner of a few sheets slipped at the window and Eleanore closed her eyes.

Oh God, she thought. *I need help. What the hell do I do?*

She was on the verge of tears when the door burst open and Michael, Gabriel, and Max Gillihan rushed into the room.

"Ellie!" Michael cried.

"Uriel!" Max echoed.

Eleanore let out a sob of gratefulness at the sight of them and hurriedly got off of the bed as they rushed in to surround the sleeping figure.

"I can't move him!" she wept, still trying to concentrate enough to keep the window blocked. She was ready to fall, she was so exhausted now. Max looked from her to the window, noticed the drapes, and cut his gaze to her once more.

"You're doing great, Ellie," he told her quickly as he brushed by her to rush to the window. He held the corners of the blankets up manually and turned to the archangels.

"A little help!" he called out. "Eleanore's about to drop."

Gabriel glanced up, took in the situation, and his silver eyes began to glow. Eleanore could feel a shift in the air as he began to use his powers. The light behind the sheets darkened, continuing to fade until it was naught but a faint grayness, almost as dark as the wall itself.

The sheets dropped to reveal windows that looked as though they had been painted in thick gold paint. Whatever it was, it blocked the sun. She pulled her gaze from the strange windows to where Uriel lay on the bed.

Michael had his arms wrapped around the top half of

Uriel's body and Gabriel had his legs, but both men were still having trouble moving him.

"It's Samael," Michael said.

"I know," Gabe replied.

"Sam, you've had your fun, now lay off!" Michael bellowed into the air, his blue eyes flashing for a moment with unnatural sapphire light.

Eleanore's eyes widened as laughter filled the room like thunder, low and otherworldly—and cruel. She closed her eyes then and shuddered as it brushed her body like the tips of warm fingers, running along the back of her neck. A sapping kind of warmth followed after, rushing over and through her, making her even sleepier and draining what was left of her strength.

She leaned back against the wall behind her, trying to focus on what was happening in the room. It was so hard.

Beyond the bed, Michael and Gabriel could now lift their brother's body enough for them to move him. They wasted no time. She watched as they rushed him to the door—and just beyond that, she could see that a portal to the mansion had been opened up.

Max crossed the room in two long strides and took Ellie's arm in his hand. As he muttered something under his breath about "Samael's infernal influence," he pulled her from the wall and half carried her toward the portal after the others.

"See that she gets through; I'll stay behind to deal with this mess," Max told them hurriedly. He gave her a well-meaning shove forward and she stumbled through the opening.

When the portal flashed around her and closed off their passage behind them, Eleanore's legs finally gave out. Someone caught her easily on the other side, wrapping her in a strong embrace and lifting her from the ground to hold her against his chest.

They were in an underground chamber of sorts; a

stone platform was raised at the center of the room and lit torches lined the circular wall.

"Rest your head, Ellie," her savior whispered in her ear. It was Azrael, and without realizing she was doing so, she obeyed him, laying her head against his shoulder and closing her eyes. Tears slid free as she did so.

Please let him be all right. . . .

"Wha' the bloody hell do we do now?" Gabriel cursed.

Eleanore opened her eyes and focused on him and Michael. Uriel had been laid on a stone altar. It looked like an altar to her, anyway.

He was so still and pale. Like a sacrifice.

"He'll need blood," Azrael told them calmly, his voice rumbling in his chest near Eleanore's cheek. It was the kind of voice that nearly hurt because you feared you wouldn't hear it again soon enough. It was that voice, of course, that had made her a fan of Valley of Shadow and the Masked One.

Gabriel and Michael both looked at her—and she could feel their gazes slide to the mark Uriel had already left on her neck.

"Not from her, he doesn't," Michael stated flatly.

"No," Azrael agreed easily. "From me."

Michael and Gabriel both blinked, their expressions horrified.

Azrael, however, wasted no time. He strode toward Michael, closing the distance between them. "Take her. I have no time to explain. He needs blood, and once more, human blood will not do."

Michael came forward, taking Eleanore from his brother's grip. "You've never given anyone your blood before," he said. "Are you sure about this?"

"No," Azrael admitted. He rolled up his sleeve and approached the stone platform where Uriel lay.

"Then let one of us do it instead," Michael said, allowing his voice to carry in the semidark chamber. Azrael froze beside the platform and then slowly turned to meet his brother's gaze.

"It will hurt," Azrael told him simply.

"I'll bloody well do it," Gabriel volunteered, coming forward before anyone could stop him.

Both archangels turned to watch as the former Messenger rolled up the sleeve of his left arm and held his other hand out toward his brothers. His jaw was tight and he sighed impatiently. "Well?" He waved his fingers as if waiting for them to hand him something. "I'll need a boggin blade, then, won't I?"

CHAPTER NINETEEN

Once Azrael handed the wicked-looking dagger to his brother, Gabriel wasted no time in slicing a clean line across his wrist. Ellie flinched as the blade sliced clean through his flesh and a line of crimson rose to meet it. But she was so weak, it was all the reaction she showed.

Gabriel held his wrist out beneath Uriel's unconscious nose. For a moment, nothing happened. Uriel's strong body remained motionless, splayed out where it was upon Azrael's altar. And then, without warning, Uriel shot forward, blurring into motion as he gripped his brother's forearm, bared his fangs, and sank them deep into Gabriel's wrist.

Eleanore had never seen Uriel like this, and the ferocity with which he ripped into his brother's flesh and fed on him was highly unsettling. The tight, pained expression on Gabriel's face left her feeling queasy. She sat up in Michael's arms and he allowed her to stand on her own feet. She was wobbly, but numb enough that her muscles worked on their own.

Gabriel gritted his teeth as Uriel clamped down tight and greedily drank. Eleanore's stomach tied itself in more and more knots as the scene unfolded before her. As she had always been able to do with someone who was in pain, her healing instinct kicked in and she could sense Gabriel's discomfort as if she were feeling it herself.

Each pull for Gabriel felt as if combs of needles were scraping the insides of his veins. Each swallow felt like a sharp stab of steel pikes in the muscles of his arm. And the pain was spreading.

"Easy, Uriel," Michael whispered, his voice reflecting the bewildered, somewhat disgusted awe with which they all watched one brother feed off of another. "He's taking a lot," he said, his brow furrowed with worry. "Uriel, take it easy!"

"He doesn't hear you," Azrael told him flatly. "And if he did, he would not care. Nothing either of you say to him will make him stop."

"Bloody Christ, this hurts," Gabriel said tightly, as sweat broke out on his brow. "Did it hurt you like this, Ellie?" he asked, his voice reflecting a world of hurt.

She felt her face flush with embarrassment, but it was no secret Uriel had bitten her. There was a very real bite mark on her neck as proof. She glanced at Uriel and then back up at Gabriel and she shook her head. "No," she told him, honestly and somewhat breathlessly. She was still so weak. "It didn't."

"This is different," Azrael told him. "You're his brother and you are very, very old. Your blood is not meant to be shared." Azrael cut his eyes to Uriel. "And Uriel is close to death. He is unable to make this easier on you as he undoubtedly did for Eleanore."

"Did it feel like that for Lilith?" Michael asked.

There was a short pause in which Azrael's expression was dark but unreadable. "I believe it felt worse."

Eleanore turned away from Azrael to look back at Uriel and Gabriel once more. From the pale tinge to Gabriel's handsome face, she wasn't certain how much more of this he could take. Just when she was certain he would not be able to stop himself from either falling or pulling away from Uriel, Azrael stepped forward and placed his hand on Uriel's shoulder.

"You must stop, Uriel."

Eleanore watched as Uriel ignored him and continued to drink. Gabriel gritted his teeth and sweat broke out along his brow. Eleanore found herself chewing on her lip, her stomach cramping with tension.

And then something strange and dark passed between Azrael and Uriel; it was like a flitting shadow or shroud that skirted from Az's tall, dark form and blanketed Uriel before disappearing entirely.

And Uriel froze. He straightened and his eyes flew open, flashing like emerald lightning.

"Let go," Azrael commanded. His voice sounded different. Deeper.

Uriel released his grip on Gabriel's arm and withdrew his fangs.

Gabriel took a step back, no doubt earning a good deal of respect from Uriel and his brothers by not instantly falling to his knees with the weakness and pain he must have felt.

"Uriel?" Ellie's small voice sliced through the silence of the chamber, at once claiming Uriel's attention.

His green eyes cut to her where she was still standing beside Michael. Uriel's form blurred into motion and then came to an abrupt halt a few feet in front of them. The sudden movement took Ellie's breath away once more, surprising her enough that she found her hand pressed to her heart. But his handsome face was no longer composed of hard angles and hunger. His eyes looked normal. And she couldn't see his fangs.

Eleanore stepped away from Michael and approached Uriel. "Are you okay?" she asked, not really knowing what else to say. She was exhausted and wrung out by the morning's events and she could feel a new, more volatile strength coming from her archangel. She wasn't sure what to think of it, but she was glad—really glad—that he wasn't dead.

Uriel's eyes cut to hers and his features relaxed, his expression softening. "I'm fine," he said softly, almost whispering it. "You saved my life, Ellie."

Eleanore looked down at the ground, recalling the

clouds outside and the way they'd blocked the sun and then the furniture and drapes she'd cast across the window's surface. She supposed he was right. More or less.

Uriel turned to address Gabriel, who stood across the room and looked more than a touch pale. "You both did," Uriel said.

Gabriel immediately looked away, his silver eyes flashing in the darkness. He was too proud to cradle his arm, but Eleanore knew that it hurt him very badly. The cuff of his sleeve was red with blood. The Scottish arch-angel glanced back at Uriel once, and then away again. He nodded. It was his version of "you're welcome."

Michael made his way to Gabriel's side and, before his brother could pull away, he placed his hand to Gabriel's chest. A brief flash of light later, and Gabriel was healed. The knife cut and the double wounds on the inside of his arm were gone.

"He's gone too far this time," Michael said then, letting his arm drop and turning to face Azrael and Uriel. His gaze skirted over Eleanore as well. "Samael could have killed you today."

"I'm aware," Uriel said.

"You may be aware," said Max, who suddenly appeared through a new portal, stepping into the room as it closed behind him. "But you aren't taking it seriously enough."

"Oh?" Uriel asked, raising a brow.

"You went to sleep without protection and failed to set an alarm," Azrael told him, his tone as calm as ever, but hinting at disapproval. "If I were Samael, I'd have done the same thing."

"I'm going to kill him," Uriel said then, his tone tight with pent-up anger.

"No, you aren't," Max told him simply. "But if you go to that gala tonight, Sam will be there. And I think we can be certain that he's done playing nice."

"He'll get nothing by killing me," Uriel said. "The

contract was for my eternal services. It'll be hard to serve him if I'm dead."

"He isn't trying to kill you." Max shook his head, his tone weary. "Can't you see that? He was well aware that we were coming for you this morning." Max's gaze cut to Eleanore. "He was also well aware that Eleanore would protect you, and he let up on his control over you. He doesn't want to kill you, Uriel. I can't say for certain, but it seems to me that he just wants you to lose. My guess is he wants you to fail in the one thing you thought you could acquire before he could."

With that, Max's eyes cut to Eleanore once more—as did everyone else's.

"Well, Sam's all but attacked the both o' them, hasn't he?" Gabriel pointed out. "It's no' likely she'll accidentally fall in love with the arsehole now, is it?" Gabriel shrugged. "I don' see wha' you're afraid of."

"Like I said"—Max sighed—"I have no idea what Samael is really after. But he's immortal. And as long as Eleanore is kept from Uriel, then he has all the time in the world to bring whatever twisted plan he has to fruition."

"You're saying he's going to try to separate them," Michael said. "At the gala."

"No." Max shook his head, turning to meet Michael's gaze. "He won't try. We're talking about Sam here. He'll succeed."

"Then you can't go." Michael turned to Uriel. "You should stay here within the mansion. It's the one place in the universe where he can't interfere."

"That isn't going to happen," Uriel told them. "I won't allow us to become prisoners because of this."

"You're risking a lot, Uriel," Max warned.

"We always risk a lot, Max. Existence is risky. Life is a battle—you know that." He paused and looked down at Eleanore. He caught her gaze and she lost herself in his emerald eyes. "And I owe Eleanore a dress."

"What?" Michael and Gabriel asked simultaneously.

"I'm taking Ellie shopping," Uriel announced. "I have an engagement tonight and a lot of people are counting on me to show up. The money goes to good causes and I've already given my promise. Promises should mean something, gentlemen," Uriel told them softly, but with conviction. "Especially for us."

Max sighed again. "What a time for you to start accepting your responsibilities. But the truth is, it would be hell to deal with the consequences of not showing up tonight."

Michael and Gabriel turned their wide eyes on him now and stared at him as if he'd turned traitor. The guardian turned his hands up and shrugged. "He's right. They can't stay trapped in here forever."

"No' forever, but for a bloody while at least!" Gabriel insisted.

Azrael hadn't spoken for a while, but now he cocked his head to one side, directing his gold eyes at Uriel. "What did you have in mind?"

Michael and Gabriel both gaped at their enigmatic, long-haired brother. He ignored them and watched Uriel, his expression unreadable, but his eyes simmering with mischief and curiosity.

"Well, it's day here, obviously," Uriel fielded slowly.

"Almost noon," Azrael supplied, the slightest hint of a smile curling the corners of his lips.

"But it's night in Paris."

Azrael's smile broadened and he was suddenly flashing fangs. "Ah, Paris." The archangel grinned. "It has been far too long."

Uriel's brothers would only agree to the outing on the condition that they all go together. Eleanore was torn about this.

On the one hand, she sort of wanted to distance herself from them. She felt a little crowded and overwhelmed and she wanted time to sort things out. On the other hand, she was admittedly grateful for the extra protection. The archangels and their guardian seemed to surround her, on all sides, at all times. It was like she was a wolf pup in a pack; the hunters and warriors enfolded and encircled her to protect her.

She was grateful for this, but not because she was afraid that Samael would separate her from the herd. No. Something else had occurred to her while she listened to the discussion in the underground chamber at the mansion. She wasn't sure whether the possibility had suggested itself to any of the other angels, but if it had, they were choosing not to say anything about it.

If Samael truly wanted to prevent them from being together, the easiest way to do that would be to kill her. It had already been decided that Sam wouldn't want Uriel dead—after all, the Fallen One wanted the former Angel of Vengeance as a servant. At least that was as close as anyone could surmise.

However, there was no reason for Sam to want Eleanore alive. He stood to gain nothing from her continued existence. And that chilled Eleanore to the core. She found that she couldn't stop holding on to Uriel. Not that he seemed to mind at all. When the portal in the chamber had opened once more, this time taking them through a door in a back alley in a street of Paris, Uriel had reluctantly released Eleanore. But she'd hurriedly claimed his hand with both of her own. And instead of the surprise she had expected to see on his handsome features, she'd noticed a smile; he tried to hide it by turning away to lead them through the opening. But she'd seen it there.

He was happy.

She supposed that was a good thing, at least.

It was just after sunset in Paris, and in November the air was quite cold. Between the four archangels and their guardian, they'd managed to fashion warmer clothes for Eleanore, which of course made her ask why they couldn't make her a dress for the gala too.

"That's not as fun," Azrael had said.

"And it isn't the point," Uriel added. "I owe you this."

After stepping out of the alleyway and strolling the fairly busy streets of the beautifully lit up city for about a half hour, Max directed them into a bakery and ordered several pastries for Eleanore, one for himself, and a sandwich and a bottle of wine for Gabriel. Michael decided on an apple, and of course, Azrael abstained.

"You're missing out," Max told him.

Azrael only smiled and shook his head begrudgingly.

"I grew up here, you know," Max told them. The brothers rolled their eyes. "In a little *appartement* a few blocks down that way." He gestured down the lamp-lit street. "*Ma mere* made these same *Brasiliennes* and *brioche aux sucre*." He sniffed the pastries in his hands and grinned.

This confused Eleanore until Uriel leaned down and said, "It's just Max being Max. He does this everywhere he goes."

All of the archangels spoke perfect French, it seemed. Eleanore remained mute and bewildered.

Once they'd eaten and "Christopher Daniels" and his entourage had politely shooed away a few European fans, they went about finding a dress. Azrael took off on his own, disappearing into the Paris contrast of electric light and damp shadow as if he were nothing more than vapor.

Eleanore wanted to hurry. She felt conspicuous and spoiled, and she was more than a little worried about Sam, for all of their sakes. But Uriel insisted that she take her time, that she relax, and that she pick out something she truly loved, no matter what the cost.

It was hard for her to concentrate.

So it was with little surprise that she eventually felt Uriel's vampire influence slip over her body and mind. She was almost angry about it. Almost. But once the anxiety lifted and her chest became unconstricted, she realized she was actually incredibly grateful. He must have known how scared she was. And it softened her heart to know that he cared enough to help her in this manner.

Her fear had been knotting up her stomach and giving her a headache and utterly ruining what was her first visit to France. Despite a lifetime of travel, it had all been within the US, as having to create passports only drew more attention to you. That was something Eleanore's parents avoided at all costs.

"There."

Eleanore was pulled to a stop, Uriel's grip tight on her wrist. She looked up to find that they had stopped before a shop window. It was the Maison Lavonde and there was only one article of clothing in the window—a dress.

Crimson red satin.

Eleanore gazed at it, stunned into silence. There was no way in hell she was going to try that dress on—much less buy it. It was probably the single most gorgeous dress she had ever seen. Lavonde was known for red-carpet creations that people talked about for months afterward. Sometimes years. This dress was no exception. In fact, it had to be Lavonde's most breathtaking design ever. And it also had to cost more than Eleanore's MINI Cooper.

"No way," she whispered. She'd meant for it to come out with a bit more force, but her throat was dry.

Gabriel and Michael were already making their way into the shop, completely ignoring Eleanore's objection. Max strolled a little ways down the street to lean up against a streetlamp.

Uriel stood behind Eleanore and bent to whisper in her ear. She could feel him strong and solid and warm at her back as he gently pressed into her. "Yes," he said softly. "At least try it on."

"It's probably the kind of thing where, if you take it off of the mannequin, you have to buy it."

"Nonsense," Uriel said, nudging her toward the door.

"Or I'll ruin it just getting it over my head. I think it's a size two. I'm not a size two."

"In you go."

"They don't like Americans. They probably won't allow an American woman to wear the dress."

"After you," he said as he held the door open.

"I bet you have to be famous to go in here," she tried desperately as he reached around her waist and ushered her inside. "I'm not famous!" she finished.

"I am." The door closed behind them and Uriel brushed past her to meet the shop attendant, a small man in Armani with piercing black eyes, slim fingers, and a permanent expression of judgmental distaste. Eleanore disliked him on the spot.

But when the attendant caught sight of Christopher Daniels, his expression changed instantly. He was now the very image of congeniality and humble subservience. Eleanore's gaze narrowed. *Elitist prick.*

After a brief discussion between the two, the attendant smiled warmly at Eleanore and then bustled to the window, where he gently removed the dress from the mannequin and then expertly draped it over his Armani sleeve. He sauntered to Eleanore, his warm smile still in place, even if it didn't quite make it to the black of his eyes.

"If you will please follow me, miss, I will show you to a fitting room," he said, in an accent that was a surprisingly good imitation of American. He walked away, heading to what must have been a dressing room in the back and Eleanore cut her eyes to Uriel.

"You look as if you're about to pass out, Ellie," he told her gently, his smile the genuine article.

"Do I really have to do this?"

"No," he said, then leaned over to whisper in her ear once more. "But if you don't, then I'll hypnotize the sales attendant, send my brothers outside, and take you into the back dressing room myself."

Eleanore's body went rigid with a combination of lust and heat and trepidation.

Uriel pulled away slightly and met her gaze. "Come to think of it, maybe I'll do that anyway."

Eleanore swallowed. "Off to try on the dress now," she quipped as she spun away from him to cross the shop. Eleanore slid past the attendant while he held the door open for her.

"I set a pair of shoes out for you there, on the settee," he told her. "Press the call button if you need any assistance."

Then he shut the door and she was alone. She turned to face the long, luxurious red gown that hung so gracefully, so perfectly on the hanger. *I'm alone with a dress that costs* . . . She glanced at the tag on the inside of the gown. *Holy fuck!*

She dropped the tag with a frustrated gesture and looked from the dress to her reflection in the mirror. *I'm a mess,* she thought. *Look at my hair!* The cold damp in Paris had brought out its curl and it had quite a bit more body than she was used to. Her nose and cheeks were slightly red, but the rest of her face was too pale, especially in contrast to her blue-black hair. And her eyes were utterly enormous in her head. She looked vaguely like a ghost.

She was sure that she couldn't possibly do justice to the dress.

"Put it on, Ellie," came the command from the other side of the door. "Last warning."

"I'm putting on the damn dress!" she hissed at him.

He chuckled, the sound deep and promising, and then she could hear his footsteps wander back down the hall toward the front room of the shop.

Uriel entered the front room and Gabriel looked up from where he was seated in a plush leather divan. Michael glanced over from the edge of a counter. Both men smiled at the look on Uriel's face.

"Shut up," Uriel said.

"Can I get you gentlemen a drink?" the assistant asked in French. "A glass of Romanée Conti or Pétrus?"

Gabriel stood and made his way to the assistant, coming to a towering stop before him. He had a good foot on the small salesman. The assistant looked up and wasn't sure whether to be turned on or terrified. Gabriel took a wad of big bills from the inside pocket of his leather jacket and peeled off a good number of them. Then he took the sales assistant's hand and slapped the bills into his palm. "Take something to the man outside in the three-piece suit leanin' against the lamppost," he told him in English.

The assistant swallowed hard and Uriel could see sweat breaking out along his brow. He nodded quickly and stuttered, "Y-yes sir. Right away." He pocketed the bills and then reached behind the counter, where he extracted a bottle of fine, expensive French wine and a single crystal goblet.

Uriel watched as the assistant went outside, allowing the glass door to close behind him. Then he turned raised brows on Gabriel, who was no longer paying attention. He and Michael were both staring, wide-eyed at something over Uriel's shoulder.

Uriel turned to see what they were gaping at.

Eleanore had emerged from the fitting room. She moved slowly into the overhead lights of the shop, and as she did, the lamplight caught the satin luminescence of the crimson gown and instantly awakened Uriel's senses.

To say that the dress was stunning would have been a gross understatement. At once, Uriel could feel his jeans becoming tighter. The gown clung to Eleanore like a second skin, making it at once clear that his archess wore nothing beneath it. The color was like blood, stark and enticing against her perfect, milky-white skin.

It came to a mere few inches above the floor, but a slit that ran along one side exposed Eleanore's long, lean leg to the men's gazes. Her feet were strapped into silver high-heeled shoes that were designed to subtly and cleverly bring to mind bondage and restraints.

Her shoulders were bare, as the dress's long, satin sleeves began at her upper arms, like a red carpet to the gorgeous expanse of flesh that was her collarbone and décolletage.

Uriel could barely breathe. He felt tight inside, as if someone had him in iron bands. Distantly, he was aware of the shop's door opening behind him, and the bustling sound of someone quickly entering.

"My God," the assistant whispered in French after a sharp intake of breath. "She is breathtaking. . . ."

Eleanore smiled nervously, flashing perfect white teeth. "Well?" she asked softly, demurely, her fingers gently brushing the fabric of the dress before she shrugged. "How do I look?"

He could hear her heart hammering behind her rib cage. She was terrified.

Uriel tried to answer, but had not yet found his breath before Michael spoke up from behind him. "Like you'll launch a thousand ships," he said softly.

"At the very least, start one hell of a fight, lass," Gabriel added, with deep appreciation.

"The dress was made for you," the assistant added with a helpless, gentle gesture. "That is obvious." All hint of phony pretense was gone from his expression and tone.

Eleanore was finding it hard to breathe. It wasn't that the dress was too tight, though it did fit snugly. It was the way they were all looking at her. And their words— she'd never been complimented in such a manner. *No* woman had ever been complimented in such a manner, she was certain. It was that—and the fact that Uriel had yet to speak. He was simply staring at her with slightly wide eyes so dark, they were nearly black. Their pupils had expanded, once more eating up the jade in his irises.

Hunger, she thought, her pulse kicking up another notch. *That's what that look is.*

"You are beautiful," he finally said, his voice so soft it was almost a whisper. "Now take off the dress."

"Right," Gabriel said from behind him, jumping into action. "I think it's time we step outside for a bit."

Michael needed no further hints. He strode quickly toward the door, grabbing a surprised sales attendant by the elbow as he did so.

"Why?" Why did he want her to take off the dress? Eleanore asked, her voice also a whisper.

Uriel took a step toward her and she stopped breathing just as the shop door closed once more, leaving the two of them alone. "You look like a goddess in that dress," he told her. "I would hate to see it damaged." Another step and he was closing the distance between them. "But I need it off you right now."

Ellie began to tremble. Images from the night before shot through her mind's eye, flushing her warm and sending heat between her legs. She was shaking, not from fear, but anticipation—delicious and terrible. She had no idea what to say or what to do and she couldn't move anyway. "But the windows . . ."

Uriel bent and, in one strong, fluid motion, he lifted her into his arms and cradled her against his chest. Then he strode with her down the hall toward the fitting room, leaving the empty shop behind them.

CHAPTER TWENTY

"**Y**ou're making me nervous," Ellie scolded as she fidgeted in the seat across from Uriel. It was Thursday night and they were alone in the back of a shiny black stretch limo; Max was driving.

"You were already nervous."

"Well, you're making it worse." Eleanore turned her face toward the window, uncrossed her legs and recrossed them, then wrapped her arms around her middle. "Stop looking at me. Just look out the window or something."

Uriel's deep chuckle regained her attention. She cut her eyes to him to find him smiling broadly. "Not likely." He shook his head.

Eleanore huffed in frustration. The man was insatiable. He'd just taken her against a wall in a dressing room in Paris less than three hours ago and, already, he was burning a hole through her with those hungry eyes.

It didn't help that no matter how Eleanore sat on the seat in front of him, the provocative slit in her brand-new Lavonde gown afforded him a clear view of most of her bare leg. He, on the other hand, was dressed from head to toe in black—black jeans, black motorcycle boots, a black long-sleeved shirt, and a black leather sports coat—as was befitting a vampire.

And she felt like vampire bait.

Eleanore gritted her teeth and forced herself to stare out the window at the neon signs and streetlights that blurred as they passed by. The reception hall where the gala was to be held was a relatively small venue known as the Quixotic World Theatre House in Dallas. Max had explained to her that it was a Gothic-inspired, chandelier-lit building with a red facade and black and gold veined marble flooring. Apparently, it was private and quaint in its own way, but perfect for a vampire-actor and his Brakes Flakes fans.

The building held booths and tables inside but there were so many guests, the outside patio and garden had been expanded into the street, which was blocked off for the event. This left a lot of possible ground to Samael and his men.

They could come from anywhere.

Because of this, Max had decided that it would be a good idea to arrive at the hall early and scope the place out. Michael and Gabriel had gone ahead, in the guise of security, to field the attendants and news crews and get the lay of the theater's neighboring areas. Azrael would be watching the proceedings from a vantage point high above the chaos, as only he could do. He would be perched on a neighboring building's roof. At least, that was what Eleanore assumed he'd meant when he told them that he would be their eyes in the sky.

Max also hired extra "muscle" to beef up the security ratio of the crowd. Ellie knew very well that this would do no good against Samael and his minions, but that wasn't the point. Sunlight Cinematics, the company that owned the rights to *Comeuppance*, had publicized the charity event to kingdom come, so it was going to be beyond packed. The point was to waylay any extra trouble where it might lurk—and to give Max some semblance of control over what was nearly a hopeless situation.

Ellie was stoic as her thoughts turned dark and she wondered just what Max and his archangels were planning to do if Samael popped himself into existence behind her and shoved a magical dagger through her heart.

Eleanore shared this concern with Uriel.

"It occurred to us," he said, "but we dismissed the possibility. Samael doesn't want you dead."

"What makes you so sure?"

"It's simple," he said. "If he wanted you dead, you would be."

Eleanore could say nothing to that. She only hoped he was right.

Uriel reached across and took her hand in his, squeezing it gently.

The car turned a corner and slowed to an idling stop behind a limousine that was emptying itself of passengers. Eleanore could see them through the window to Uriel's right. One was the actor who played the enemy of Jonathan Brakes. The other was the actress who played Brakes's love interest. Both were making their way through a boatload of excited fans crowding at the ropes along either side of the red carpet.

"I can't do this," Ellie said, not meaning to voice her thoughts out loud. She was at once overwhelmed by the throng outside the car door and unsure of what part she was to play in all of this.

"Yes, you can," Uriel said gently, giving her hand another squeeze. Then his jade-colored eyes flashed with something impish. "Besides, you wouldn't deny the Global Fund for Women its hefty donation by deciding to become a no-show and forcing me to become a no-show too, would you?"

Eleanore blanched. "That's the charity this event is sponsoring?"

He nodded.

"Oh jeez." Eleanore rolled her eyes and ran a nervous hand over her face. She was lucky she never wore makeup or it would have smeared. She sighed and her voice came out shaky. "Fine," she croaked.

The glass that separated the passenger seats from the driver's section slid down. Max turned and draped an arm over his seat and offered her a reassuring smile.

"You'll be fine, Ellie. We're watching you carefully. No one will even touch you. Now, are you sure you know what to do?"

"When we get out, Michael and Gabriel will escort me into the building while Christopher Daniels over here signs autographs and talks to the press."

"Yes. And not that Mike or Gabe would allow you to, but if anyone tries to ask you any questions, don't stop and oblige them," Uriel added.

Eleanore didn't like this. She understood how important it was to keep promises and support charities and all of that, but this could still be considered a brand of insane. Plus, by being rushed from the limo to the security of the building, she felt like some sort of "secret" that the famous actor was keeping. She had no doubt that the crowd would put two and two together and realize she must be the "Ellie Granger" that he'd asked out on national television. At the very least, they would expect her to stop, smile, and introduce herself like a normal, sane human being.

"What are you going to tell them?" she asked. "When they ask about me?"

"You'll tell them she's an old friend who's camera shy, then move quickly on through the crowd," Max informed him brusquely. "Just get yourself into the building as fast as inhumanly possible."

Uriel sighed. "Right."

Max turned back around just as the car in front of him pulled away from the curb and he was able to inch forward into its place. Uriel sat back and reluctantly released Eleanore's hand. Immediately, her fingers curled into fists and her nails dug into the skin of her palms.

"Showtime," Uriel whispered with a glance at the throng outside the windows. The car came to a complete stop and a tall man in a tuxedo and white gloves opened the limo door.

Uriel stepped out first and stifled the urge to put his

fingers in his ears as the crowd went absolutely wild. His hearing was sharper as a vampire; the adoring din actually hurt his eardrums. But he plastered a smile to his face and took a minute to wave at his fans. Then he turned and reached back into the car to offer Ellie his hand.

Ellie stared at his hand, her eyes bright and wide with trepidation. She swallowed hard and he could hear it, despite the roar of the crowd. He was simply that tuned in to her.

"Ellie, take my hand, baby," he said softly, hoping his voice would assuage some of her fear. She looked up into his eyes and he thought of how much he loved her. As if she could see that love transferred there in his gaze, she offered a small, brave smile and took his hand.

Protectively—possessively—his fingers closed over hers and he gave her a gentle tug to help her out of the backseat. When her long, bare leg and the hem of the gorgeous red dress were revealed to the flashing camera bulbs and the mob of fans, a hush fell over the crowd. He couldn't blame them. She was a goddess. He felt a smile of pride tug at his lips.

She slowly stood and straightened beside him, her dark blue gaze skirting across the faces of the crowd. They were in awe of her. He could hear their hearts beating rapidly, hear their gasps, see their dropped jaws and wide eyes. Ellie wasn't immune to the attention either; she blushed furiously beneath their scrutiny and he felt her tense beside him.

He leaned over and whispered in her ear. "That's my girl."

When he pulled back, it was to find Michael and Gabriel in front of them, both dressed in SWAT-like attire from head to toe. "Come with us, lass," Gabriel said as he and Michael moved to flank her on each side and Uriel reluctantly released her hand.

The hush that had fallen over the crowd lapsed into a

murmur of whispers and then a din of shouted questions. The questions were directed at all of them— Christopher Daniels, the "beautiful lady in red," and even her "bodyguards." Once Max stepped out of the vehicle as well, they were also directed at him.

No one answered, of course. Michael gently took Ellie's elbow and he and Gabriel ushered her forward. Uriel noticed her vague unsteadiness at first, but she dutifully forced one leg in front of the other and managed to make it halfway down the red carpet before something shifted in the air.

Uriel felt it a half second before it went down.

BANG. A gunshot, loud and clear. There was no sound on Earth like it.

The crowd fell into an eerie, sudden hush, and Ellie was immediately surrounded by a wall of muscle. A split-second later, someone screamed. Shouts rang out and were joined by a second *BANG.*

Uriel rushed forward and grabbed Eleanore's arm, jerking her back. She gasped as he lifted her into his arms and shot at an impossible speed toward the doorway of the building ahead.

He wasn't thinking. He was simply acting. His body had become a vessel of pure animal instinct. His mate was in danger; he needed to protect her. Outside, he could smell the iron tinge of blood and the tangy overlying notes of fear. Adrenaline was thick in the air as Uriel swept Eleanore up into his arms. More shots rang out and the atmosphere thickened with the scent of blood and fear. Uriel's brothers remained beside him as he headed with lightning speed toward the theater.

"Where are the shots coming from?" Michael asked.

"I canno' tell," Gabriel replied.

"Uriel, put me down!" Eleanore was digging her fingernails into the muscles of his biceps as he shot them both through the doorway and into the darkness beyond. Her eyes were wide. "Someone's hurt! I can feel them!"

Uriel set her down between a table and a booth seat and they both hunkered down together. Michael and Gabriel split up then, leaving the two alone. "You can't go out there," he told her.

"There's more than one!" she screamed, unable to help the pitch of her voice.

She was desperate; he could see the set of her jaw and the glint in her indigo eyes. Uriel knew that several people had been shot. That much was plain to him. He could tell by their scent that they were young. Two women, one man.

"They're dying, Uriel!"

She was right about that, too. He could hear their heartbeats—single them out from those other, rapidly beating hearts around them as they slowly waned, denied the blood they needed to pump through the veins of their torn bodies.

"Michael!" Uriel bellowed, wondering where exactly his brother had gone. Most likely, he and Gabriel were outside, trying to figure out who had done the shooting.

But Uriel had a sinking feeling. He knew the shots had come from several directions.

He also knew that this was not Samael's doing. Guns were not the Fallen One's style. Samael had most assuredly had something planned for this night, but whoever these shooters were, they had beaten him to the punch.

Uriel, is Eleanore safe?

Azrael was communicating with him. He probably already knew, just by sensing her heart rate and biorhythms, that she was fine. But he needed to establish a link.

She's fine. But she wants to heal whoever was injured. Who's been shot?

Two teenage girls and a camera man. However—
BANG, BANG, BANG!

Uriel could not make sense of the cacophony outside the doors of the building. People were racing inside now, rushing toward bathrooms and trying to dive behind tables and booths, as Uriel and Eleanore had done.

Who the fuck is shooting? he called out to Azrael.

I can see no one. I see no armed men, no guns. The bullets are literally coming out of nowhere.

Azrael's mental voice was as calm as his spoken voice usually was, but there was an undercurrent of urgency and frustration as well.

BANG!

This time, the sound of the gunshot came from inside of the building—and Uriel looked up in time to see one of the women who had raced through the door go flying face-first into a nearby table. Her own blood preceded her, fanning out across the tablecloth and wax candles like a Gothic display.

The shooter was inside now.

Uriel looked from the fallen woman to his archess, who was even now rising from her crouched position in order to run to the victim's aid. He wasted no time in grabbing hold of her arm and jerking her back down beside him. "Ellie, no!" he yelled.

"Uriel, let me go, for God's sake. She'll die if I don't heal her!"

Uriel blinked. It struck him then—in that moment. The shootings were random and vicious and supernatural in nature. There seemed to be no reason for them—and no logical explanation for their existence. They achieved nothing.

Unless you were trying to get someone with healing powers to separate herself from her protector and then drain herself by healing as many people as possible.

Oh my God, he thought, his horror matched only by the depth to which his feelings sank. *Whoever is doing this is after Eleanore.*

He knew what he had to do. If he wanted to keep her safe, it was his only option. He only hoped that she would forgive him. Eventually.

"I'm so sorry, Ellie," he said. His tone had lowered and he wasn't certain that she heard him over the sounds of screams and sirens.

But then, with teeth gritted and eyes darting to the injured woman, Eleanore shook her head and asked, "Uriel, forgive you for wha—"

He never gave her the chance to finish her question. Instead, he reached out like lightning and grabbed the hair at the back of her head. Then he jerked her forward into his embrace and simultaneously yanked her head back, exposing her throat. His fangs erupted in his mouth and, a split heartbeat later, they were plunging into the side of her neck.

He didn't bother with the pleasure this time. That was not the point. This time, he needed her to feel the pain and *only* the pain. He needed it to hurt, in every sense of the word. It was, quite probably, her last hope.

Eleanore's slim form went rigid in his arms and Uriel's heart broke. He felt it; a very real pain in the hollow of his chest. She didn't even scream. When true pain overtakes a person, it can steal their breath from their lungs, taking their voice altogether.

Please forgive me, he repeated desperately, sending the thought into her mind even while he knew that he shouldn't. It would be best for her if he showed no emotion, no remorse; if he simply took and gave nothing back. He had to really *hurt* her if he wanted Samael's contract with her to kick in. But, though he was able to bring himself to hold her still, to pierce her flesh, and drain her nearly dry, he could not keep from doing this one tiny thing. He could not keep his pleas from her mind and from her soul.

I love you, he told her. *Forgive me.*

The gala had officially begun and Samael smiled at the knowledge that he would be fashionably late. However, he turned in surprise from where he had been adjusting his cuff links in the mirror as the air in his master bedroom shimmered and began to hum. The vibration had a familiar ring to it—a delicate, female kind of buzz.

It can't be, he thought. But he was wrong this time, because as it turned out, it *was*.

He turned toward his king-sized bed, where the shimmering air lowered, warped, and then flashed a blindingly brilliant white. He squinted slightly, and when the flare died down a young woman lay on his bed, her unconscious form sprawled delicately across his black satin comforter. She was dressed in crimson and her very pale skin contrasted starkly against the dark, shimmering material.

"Ellie," he whispered.

He made his way to the side of the bed and looked down on her unmoving form. She seemed not to be breathing, but two terrible, deep wounds in her throat continued to bleed as he watched. Her life's liquid pumped ever so weakly from the puncture marks, slowly drenching the quilt beneath her.

It meant that her heart was still beating.

Samael knelt beside the bed and took her chin in his hand. He gently turned her face toward him and gazed upon her closed lids. Her long lashes brushed the tops of her cheeks. She looked innocent.

He placed his palm to her chest, closed his eyes, and concentrated. A rare and incredible power eased itself from his form into hers. It repaired the damage to her throat, mended her broken artery, and even replaced what blood had been lost. Not all angels could replace blood. Just him, in fact. But, then, he had many powers that the other archangels did not possess.

Samael leaned back then, and once he felt her pulse begin to beat steady and strong beneath his palm, he removed his hand from her chest.

It had been a very long time since the Fallen One had bothered to bring someone back from the brink of death. And yet now, with Eleanore Granger, it seemed the natural thing to do. To not heal her would have been unthinkable.

In fact, bringing Ellie to the brink of death in the first place was unacceptable. And he could not fathom why it had been done.

For a moment, he watched her sleep, his gaze sweeping over her slumbering features to the curve of her chin, her long graceful neck, and décolletage—and the slim gorgeous body beyond. Then his gaze flicked back to her eyes. With sudden, hard determination, he mentally delved past them, going deeper. Within the confines of her brain, he scanned through her memories, rifling through her thoughts and sifting through the events of the past several hours, searching for what reason there could possibly have been for Uriel to attack her.

When he heard the shots and felt the instant fear and saw the confusion from Eleanore's perspective, Samael understood.

It all made sense now.

Uriel hadn't hurt her because he'd *wanted* to. And he hadn't lost control, which was what Samael had assumed happened, considering the sight of Eleanore in that red satin gown. Instead, Uriel had attacked her in order to save her. He'd known that she would have no choice but to keep her end of her bargain with Samael. And he also assumed that, knowing Samael, there was most likely a stipulation within the contract that would magically whisk her away from Uriel the moment he hurt her.

Luckily for Eleanore, Uriel had been right in his assumptions.

Uriel fell slightly forward when Eleanore suddenly shimmered and popped out of existence in his arms. Then he shoved himself back against the wall behind the table and forced himself to stay calm.

She was with Samael now. And though he trusted Samael about as far as he could throw him, Uriel knew that she was safer with the Fallen One than she was anywhere else in the world at that moment.

Uriel took a moment to push away the dizzying swell of power that rushed through him as Eleanore's blood mingled with his own in his veins. But along with the ebb of power came a hearty dose of fear for what he may have done to her by taking so much.

However, this, too, he pushed away. It could do him no good to dwell on it. What was done was done.

The important thing now was to find out what the hell was going on and deal with it. Uriel shifted fully into vampire mode. At once, he was moving so fast that his body became blurred to the people around him. He came to his feet and searched his surroundings for any sign of familiar faces.

Scores of people had entered the building and were now crowding the bathrooms in order to escape the gunshots that seemed to be coming from all directions. Someone had dragged the injured woman down from the table and moved her aside. From the sound of her heartbeat, she was still alive, but barely.

Outside, the sirens were drawing nearer, but some of the people in the crowd had become hysterical. Others were in shock. Uriel focused outward and shot out a telepathic call to his brothers and his guardian. There were several beats of silence, in which Uriel had the new and disturbing sensation that he was alone—that his "family" was no longer in existence. But then he sensed a familiar, heavy presence brush his mind and the fear was gone.

I'm here, Uriel, Azrael told him. *You've done the right thing with Eleanore. I'm afraid we are battling something we cannot easily defeat.*

That's not possible, Uriel thought back, as he blurred across the room and shot out the front door in between two press members who were hiding against the walls on either side.

It is. Azrael said. *Michael and Gabriel have already fallen.*

Uriel stopped in his tracks, his breath taken from his lungs, his world knocked out from beneath him.

What?

Max took them back to the mansion. I do not know if our enemy will be able to follow him there, but he had no choice. These men are not human and I have never before encountered anything like them.

Where are you? Uriel called out, hard rage and fear rocketing through him. He didn't understand. Nothing was more powerful than an archangel. Nothing!

There was no answer from Azrael, however.

Uriel called out to him again.

Still nothing.

Uriel stood in the middle of the sectioned-off street and turned in a quick circle. All around him, people had hit the deck when the first bullets were fired. Some were injured. A few had been shot; others had been wounded by trampling and panicked attempts at escape. The sirens were just down the block now. The injured might survive.

Suddenly, a hard spike of sound and sensation ripped through Uriel's mind and body.

Uriel!

It was Azrael. It was a warning—and a cry for help.

Another shot rang out through the air, but this time the bullet found its mark in Uriel's chest.

The impact was impossibly violent. Uriel had been shot many times in the past. He'd lived through countless wars. He'd suffered spear wounds, knife wounds, arrow wounds, gunshot wounds, grenade blasts, shrapnel injuries, concussions, fractured bones, and every other known manmade injury.

But no human could forge a weapon like this. Uriel looked down to find that his chest cavity had been turned black as night. His heart felt heavy and cold and—*wrong*. Then, before his eyes, he saw his body shimmer and shift. He felt sick.

He had never felt sick before. Not like this. He doubled over to vomit, but nothing came up. Instead, he fell forward, onto his hands and knees amid the terrified stares of his various adoring fans.

He tried to breathe, but his lungs would not expand. His entire midsection had been turned into one immobile, solid mass. It was as if he'd been petrified. The world tilted around him and became fuzzy around the edges. He toppled onto his side and gazed up at the streetlights and the stars in the dark sky beyond them.

A face moved into view, coming into brief focus.

The face was smiling down at Uriel. It was a handsome face. It blurred and Uriel's world went black.

CHAPTER TWENTY-ONE

Whoomp...
Whoomp...

The sound was low and slow and hollow and it surrounded Uriel on all sides. It was all there was in his world at that moment—just the sound. It came again. And again.

Whoomp...

And then, finally, the sound was not alone; it was paired with a faint reddish light that expanded and contracted. Once. Twice. Three times. Four.

Then came the third sensation. When it arrived, Uriel instantly wished that it hadn't and that he could remain in the world of sound and sight alone.

"It hurts, doesn't it?"

The voice was so loud, it echoed in Uriel's ears and filled in the spaces in his brain.

He tried to speak, but failed. He couldn't feel any part of his body but his chest, and that was in agony.

"I know," the voice continued. "An unfortunate side effect of shard guns is that they do not kill their victims. Death, in this instance, is the preferable choice for the one who has been shot."

Shut up, Uriel thought. The man's voice was driving him mad. Or maybe it was the pain. His chest was desolidifying, and as it did, he felt as if he'd been drowning and was now coming up for air. The moment when his lungs finally expanded after having been denied air for far too long was so intense, it almost knocked him out again.

"Not to worry," the man said. "It's almost over."

He was right. Uriel hated that he was right—whoever he was. He hated the fact that the stranger knew what was happening and was so obviously in control. It only added to Uriel's suffering.

"In about thirty seconds, you'll be capable of speech, which is good, because I have a number of questions to ask you." There was a scraping sound, like someone moving furniture across a concrete floor. Then there was a bright whiteness behind the red glow that had been ebbing and receding behind Uriel's closed lids.

Now he could feel that he was bound; his wrists were manacled and the metal was biting into his skin. At the moment, the sensation was not painful enough to override the throbbing in his chest.

He inhaled and exhaled, and with each breath that felt like nerve gas in his lungs, he became more aware of his position. He was not lying down, but was propped up in a vertical position. His booted feet were not touching the floor. His entire weight rested on the metal of the manacles around his wrists.

They were hurting a little more now, even as his lungs and heart began to hurt less.

"Is the pain passing?" the man asked.

Uriel knew that he expected an answer; it was a test to see whether he was yet capable of speech. But he didn't exactly feel like cooperating with his captor. He remained silent.

"Very well. I'll assume that you're ready to talk."

The light intensified and Uriel found himself blinking rapidly. His eyes were open now; light flooded in, blurring his vision and spearing his head with a new pain. His tongue was dry and felt overly large in his mouth. And there was that wooziness again. It was an entirely new and highly uncomfortable sensation for the archangel.

He thought of the weapon that they—whoever *they* were—had used on him and his brothers. What the hell could possibly have done this to them?

"How many of your kind are you aware of here on Earth?" the man asked.

Uriel could make out a vague outline of his captor now. He was tall and muscular; in the darkness his outline looked like Azrael's. His hair was black, but cut short. If Uriel had to guess, he would say this was the same man who had stood over him outside the theater just before he'd passed out.

Uriel continued to ignore the man. He concentrated on his body instead. It was hard to do otherwise. He was getting what he knew humans called a full-fledged migraine. Though he had never personally suffered one before, it was easy to recognize. It shot through the right side of his brain and there were only so many kinds of headaches that could hurt this much.

"I had thought we were alone here," the man continued, almost conversationally. His tone had dropped and his voice was softer now, as if he were reminiscing. "For so long, we've been alone. Then came Eleanore . . . and now you." He took hold of the back of a metal-backed chair, spun it around, and then sat down, draping his arms carelessly over the top. "So I'll ask you again. How many of you are there?"

"Billions," Uriel replied, deciding that the man could go and fuck himself. "Billions and billions of us." His voice cracked a little as pain punished him for speaking.

His captor laughed. It was a deep, genuine chuckle of amusement.

"I take it the other three at the gala were your comrades," he ventured, ignoring Uriel's smart-assed response. "And, from their descriptions, I'll even wager a guess as to their names—and yours."

He stood then and Uriel got a better look at him. He was, indeed, as tall as Azrael, looking about six feet and five inches. He appeared to be around thirty years of age. He looked strong and hard, and there was an edge to him that reminded Uriel of a human dagger.

He was dressed in combat boots, black army fatigue pants, and a black T-shirt that stretched taut over his arms and chest. There were no markings anywhere on his clothing or body that gave away who he worked for or where, in the world, Uriel was at that moment.

The man moved around the chair and came to stand in front of Uriel, who was strapped to a thick metal "X" using welded-on restraints. They must not have been normal iron or steel; Uriel had already attempted to transform them, to bend them, and even to break them with his mind. His powers were useless against them.

"You're the four favorites, aren't you?"

It wasn't a question. Uriel didn't bother to respond.

The man went on, undaunted. "The blond was Michael," he stated, his gaze locking on Uriel's and holding it fast.

Uriel noticed that his blue eyes were, curiously, as blue as Michael's. Uncannily similar.

"The Old Man's number one is easy to recognize. There's a sense of seriousness about him that borders on comical." The man's expression was not quite a smirk. It was more a small smile of genuine amusement.

Uriel could see that this man had charisma in spades. There was a spark to the blue in his eyes, a charming and intelligent bent to his features. Uriel assumed he was the leader. Of *what*, he had no idea.

"The one with the brogue is Gabriel, I'd wager. The Old Man's Messenger *would* be the one to acquire a discernible accent. And, by process of elimination, that would make the dark one who gave us so much trouble Azrael." The man looked down, clasped his hands behind his back, and turned away to pace slowly across the small metal-lined room.

Uriel was alert enough now to take in his surroundings. No windows. One door. Everything was constructed of the same metal that bound him to the cross. One table. One chair. One ultrabright lamp—and his black-clad captor.

"And you, of course, are the Angel of Vengeance. Or, should I say *former* Angel of Vengeance?" He turned and leveled a somewhat weary, knowing smile on Uriel. "Which is it, Uriel?"

There was a long, silent beat where neither of them spoke, and their gazes could have burned each other to ash.

"Who are you?" Uriel finally asked. He was no longer able to contain his curiosity.

The man ignored his question. "How did she get away from us tonight?" he asked. His tone had lowered a touch; the question was obviously important to him.

Uriel swallowed past the dry, painful spot in his throat and thought of the horrible thing he'd done to his archess. If this man wasn't aware of what had transpired, then there might still be hope. It was possible that he didn't know about Samael at all.

"I didn't expect you to tell me," his captor said. "But I assume it has something to do with another of her abilities. It must have been how she avoided us in Rockdale, as well."

Uriel frowned. Rockdale? *What's he talking about, now?*

"She is, indeed, an amazing woman. There's so much we could learn from her."

"Who the *hell* are you?" Uriel asked again, this time fairly growling with the pent-up wrath he was feeling. Pain was edging his words, making them sharp, and reducing him to his basic instincts. He needed to know who his enemy was.

So that he could kill him later.

The man's blue gaze narrowed slightly. He watched Uriel for some time, as if carefully considering his reply. Then he took a quick breath, let it out with a sigh, and leaned against the metal table, his arms crossed over his broad chest. He stared down at the floor as he quietly spoke. "We're a practice round, I guess you would say. I'm a rough draft." He laughed bitterly, if softly, and Uriel's stomach dropped, his world once more falling out from under him. Somehow, he knew what was coming next.

"There was something the Old Man saw in you that he did not see in me. Nor in my brothers. We were incomplete, the lot of us. Not quite right. I was the first."

Uriel swallowed and licked his dry lips. "The first what?"

"The first archangels. He *tried* with us—but got it right with you. We were disposed of." He glanced around and gestured to the room, as if gesturing at the entire world beyond. "Sent *here*." His eyes narrowed then and he cocked his head slightly to one side. "Tell me—what's your excuse? We heard rumors that the four of you had come to Earth. But we dismissed it as nothing more than gossip. Until now."

Uriel could barely digest what he was hearing. There were other archangels? Before he and his brothers? *Imperfect* archangels?

Disposed of?

It was incomprehensible. The Old Man had punished Lilith by sending her to Earth. And he'd sent the archesses to Earth in order to protect them. Uriel and his brothers had elected to come down and look for them. Samael had chosen to follow them down. But the Old Man hadn't ever *disposed* of anyone or *destroyed* anything. He wasn't like that. Not really.

Was he?

It was something Uriel could not wrap his head around. Why would the Old Man need a rough draft?

"What do you call yourself?" Uriel asked.

"Kevin." The man laughed softly. "At least now I do. General Kevin Trenton," he supplied coolly. "But I was once known as Abraxos."

Kevin . . . Uriel's brow furrowed as memories flitted through his head. Eleanore—standing beside the door to the garage in the mansion, telling him about her first crush. A boy on a street corner. It had been a boy with black hair and blue eyes . . . tall and strong. A boy named Kevin.

Kevin Trenton.

Jesus, he thought. "You're the kid she fell for in high school. The kid on the street corner," he gritted. But how could that be? If what this man was saying was true, he was an archangel. Archangels were never children.

"You were a boy . . ." He grimaced as a sharp twinge in his chest arrested his breath.

Kevin chuckled. "It's good to know her memories of me are fond. Do you think I might have looked something like this?"

There was a brief flash, like a grayish lightning-fast fluctuation of space and time. Uriel blinked, losing sight of Trenton for a moment. When he reappeared, the general was no longer the tall, broad man that he had been a moment before. He was a teenager, still tall, but less muscular, and with a boyishly handsome face that bespoke of an innocence that was in sharp contrast to the tattoos laced across his forearms and biceps.

He can change forms, Uriel thought, his spirits sinking ever more by the second. *Oh fuck . . .*

Kevin flashed again and was once more an adult.

This was too much for Uriel. It was too much information, too much power, too much bad news. It wasn't a human altercation—a war, a battle, a robbery, a rape—something he'd dealt with for thousands of years and had protocol for. This was different. Kevin and his men seemed all but invincible. If they were all like their leader, they were doppelgangers with magical weapons that could take down the very Knights of Heaven.

He couldn't process it all. Nor did he want to try. Right now, his bleeding wrists were throbbing and the muscles of his arms and chest were aching. He had no idea what had happened to his brothers or whether or not they were even alive. And Eleanore was with Samael— that, alone, was too much to digest. He was in no mood to consider the philosophy of creation and the reason behind everything that happened and did not happen in this utterly confounding universe.

All he was sure of—all he could even begin to understand—was his love for Eleanore, and the fact that the man in front of him was after her for some reason.

"What do you want with her?"

Kevin considered him for several beats. Then he pushed off of the table, shoved his hands in the pockets of his fatigue pants, and paced slowly around the room. "My kind possess many very valuable talents." He glanced at Uriel over his shoulder and shot him a smile. "As you can see."

He turned back and continued. "Part of what originally scared the Old Man was the amount of power he'd given us." He paused, fell quiet for a moment, and then went on. "However, we have never been able to list the ability to heal among our attributes. I'm sure I don't need to tell you how precious a skill it is to be able to heal wounds and sicknesses, even as we are."

Here, he stopped again, turned, and stared at the wall adjacent to Uriel.

Uriel wondered what he was looking at until Kevin pulled his right hand out of his pocket and waved it at the wall. The metal surface began to ripple like water. Uriel blinked, unable to hide the fact that he was, indeed, impressed.

The silver-gray wall disappeared and when the shimmering-rippling ceased, in its place was a scene in a playground, as if Uriel was watching it through a window.

Several children were spinning on a small merry-go-round, holding on to its metal bars. A little girl was swinging alone on the swing set not too far away. She had raven-black hair and porcelain skin. She could not have been more than six or seven years old, but even at her very young age, Uriel recognized her as his archess.

"Twenty years ago, I was passing through a play yard. I was unnoticed by the children there. This was what I saw."

Through the window to the past, Uriel watched one of the children on the merry-go-round let go of the metal bar she had been holding on to. As a result, she went careening off of the surface and flew through the air to land awkwardly on her side and roll to a stop several yards away.

There were screams from the other children, and then a stunned slowing down of the spinning merry-go-round as they tried to climb off. The little girl did not move from her crumpled position on the grass and dirt.

Then Eleanore Granger was jumping off of her swing and running to the little girl.

Uriel knew what was coming.

Eleanore knelt beside the unmoving child, placed her hand to the girl's back, and then closed her large, dark blue eyes. Within a few seconds, there was a warm glow emanating from beneath her small palm. The glow spread as the children behind her stood in stunned silence and watched.

Uriel wondered where her parents were. Surely, they would have stopped this from happening if they'd witnessed it.

The child on the ground stirred and rolled over and Eleanore lifted her hand, straightening to rest back on her knees. There was a quiet conversation between the two children then, one Uriel could not hear.

"The little girl is asking her if she's an angel," Kevin said. He let the scene play out for a few seconds longer, and then waved his hand once more, dispelling the image.

"What would you do to her?"

"That depends," Kevin replied easily. "We would prefer that she join with us and pass her DNA along naturally. A new race of beings possessing a mixture of our abilities and hers would be unstoppable."

Uriel realized, then, that Abraxos had no idea Michael also possessed the ability to heal. As far as Kevin Trenton knew, only Ellie possessed that power. And the general planned to bed her—and allow his men to do the same—with the hopes of passing on whatever gene it was that gave her that ability.

Uriel had never wanted to kill a man so badly in his entire existence.

"If that fails, we can take the DNA straight from her veins and experiment with it until we have the results we need."

Uriel imagined Eleanore strapped to a hard white-sheeted bed with needles in her arms and he knew that what he was seeing would destroy her.

Kevin stared at the spot where the image of Eleanore's past had disappeared and said, "She's not an archangel. I can tell that much." He turned to face Uriel and pinned him with blue eyes so intense they nearly glowed. "So what is she?"

"Bite me," Uriel ground out, trying the metal around his wrists once more. His efforts did nothing but cause the manacles to cut into his skin, releasing more of his precious blood.

"Apparently, that's your job now," Kevin said. "I have it on good authority that you've made some sort of transformation." He grinned, flashing straight white teeth. "You liked your Hollywood character that much?"

Uriel didn't answer. He tried to enter the man's brain, but was blocked. He tried to use telekinesis to throw him into the wall. It didn't work. He tried to set him on fire. That didn't work either. He tried to transform him into something small and amphibian. But Kevin remained Kevin and Uriel was starting to feel tired.

"It's all right." Kevin gave a small shrug and slowly paced toward Uriel. "I can wager a guess as to what she is."

Uriel held his breath.

"She's an archess, isn't she?"

This time, it *was* a question, but Uriel still wasn't going to answer it. However, he knew his silence was as good as an affirmation.

"That's what I thought." Kevin nodded, smiling a strange, somewhat sad smile. "I know of their existence through a sort of . . . *celestial grapevine*." He laughed, the sound deep and genuine. "Believe me when I tell you that archangels aren't the only creatures the Old Man has disposed of on Earth."

The laughter trailed off and Kevin's expression became serious. He locked eyes with Uriel and his gaze narrowed. "I assume you believe her to be yours."

Uriel gritted his teeth. "There's no doubt," he ground out.

"Oh?" Kevin looked bemused. "I met her long before you set eyes upon her, archangel. Purely by accident. Who's to say she wasn't, in fact, meant to be mine?"

"You're delusional."

Again, Kevin laughed. "Maybe. But then, you and I both know that the Old Man is not the most powerful force in the universe. Only I'm wise enough to admit it and you're still a stubborn fool." He turned away, walked to the table, and leaned against it a second time, his hands shoved casually into his pockets once more.

"No, Uriel. The Fates are stronger. And the Old Man has made mistakes before." He leveled that sapphire gaze on Uriel again. "And it doesn't matter. My men and I need Eleanore one way or another. Therefore, now that I know exactly what she truly is, I fully intend to test my theory. After all"—he smiled a devastating smile and Uriel was reminded of his costar on *Comeuppance*, the one who had played his enemy—"I was her first crush."

"Touch her and I swear on everything unholy that I will kill you."

"Yes, of course." Kevin waited several beats. Then he shook his head. "Do you really believe that I'm going to let you live long enough for you to pose any kind of competition, much less *threat*, to me?"

Uriel felt his gaze burning as his vision turned red.

"You're only alive now because I need you in order to get to her." Kevin stood and strode casually to the metal door, which clicked open as he neared it. "When Eleanore Granger is in my possession, you will have outlived your usefulness."

He pulled the door open, stepped through, and shut it behind him. Uriel rested his head against the metal "X" that had become his prison and closed his eyes against the pain.

Max watched as Michael pushed himself up onto one elbow on the cushions of the couch and blinked hard, trying to clear his vision. It was the same thing Azrael had done an hour before. The former Angel of Death was the strongest of the four; his body had repaired itself first, but it hadn't been pleasant to watch.

Gabriel, who had been hit twice in the chest with the strange weapons, had yet to awaken. He still lay sprawled and seemingly lifeless on the second couch in the mansion's living room.

Max Gillihan was more worried about his charges now than he had ever been. Uriel was missing. Eleanore was with Samael. And Gabriel's chest was black as night and hard as stone. Max honestly wondered whether the Messenger Archangel would ever move again.

Max knelt beside Michael and caught his gaze. "Can you hear me?"

Michael grimaced and held up a finger, unable to speak, then curled in on himself in pain. Azrael had been in agony as well; it seemed to be what happened when they came out of the cursed state the strange weapons had put them in. It didn't kill them. It just ... petrified them, or something akin to it.

Michael groaned low in his throat and then the groan turned into a growl of rage. Azrael had been furious as well. Neither archangel had taken well to being felled by an attack.

"Who—the—fuck—"

"We don't know," Azrael replied calmly. He had healed completely and now stood in the archway between the dining room and the meeting room, his tall, broad frame outlined by the low light behind him. "But whoever it was has captured Uriel."

Michael's gaze cut to him.

"Michael, are you well enough to heal Gabriel?" Max wanted to waste no further time. Michael was the only one among them who possessed the ability to heal, and Gabriel didn't seem to be coming out of this on his own. It might just be a matter of time before he did, but then again, time might take him from them altogether. Max would rather be on the safe side.

Michael looked over Max's shoulder to the unconscious form of his brother, sprawled lifelessly on the couch opposite him.

"His injuries are greater than ours," Azrael said.

Michael slowly angled himself to a full seated position, his brow sweating with the pain it caused him. Then he closed his eyes, took several very difficult, deep breaths, and got to his feet. A few stumbling steps across the gap between the two couches and he was once more falling, this time to his knees beside Gabriel.

"Gabe ..." he gasped, as he shoved Gabriel's shirt open to reveal his blackened chest once more. It looked bad—as though Gabriel were a Michelangelo sculpture constructed of some black marble; a statue of an archangel, and not the archangel himself.

"Christ," Michael whispered, shutting his eyes and shaking his head. At once, he pressed his right palm to his brother's rock-hard chest and Max watched him sit back on his heels to concentrate.

The warm light that peeked from beneath his hand grew from a soft glow to a radiant, blinding flash. When it at last died down, Michael was hunched over, his eyes shut, his body utterly exhausted.

Gabriel's chest was no longer black—and best of all, it was moving up and down.

He's breathing, thought Max, feeling vastly relieved.

It was clear that Michael was drained. He had never had to put forth so much effort to heal someone before. His face was pale, his tall form slumped, his breathing slow. He was nearly unconscious again. But he had healed his brother.

"You did it," Max exhaled, only then realizing that he'd been holding his breath. He hurried to the couch and knelt down beside them both. "He's breathing." He placed his hand on Gabriel's wrist and felt the pulse there. *Finally.*

It was as if he were back from the dead.

He turned his attention to Michael, who had yet to say anything further. His eyes were still closed, his head bowed, his strong body hunched over.

"Are you all right?" Max asked.

A single nod was his only reply.

"Someone is coming," Azrael said then.

Max turned to face him.

The vampire archangel was striding gracefully toward the archway that led to the foyer and the door beyond. "It's Samael's servant," he added, just before disappearing through the exit.

"What?" Max asked in alarm. He stood, and with one final worried glance at Michael and Gabriel, he hurried to follow Azrael out of the living room.

Az reached the door, grasped the handle, and opened it. On the threshold stood Jason, Samael's right-hand man. Max greatly disliked him. On the outside, he was a fairly handsome, well-dressed man of perhaps thirty years. Max knew something quite different to be underneath the attractive facade.

"I won't mince words or waste anyone's time," Jason said, clasping his hands behind his back. He was, as always, dressed impeccably in an Armani suit and tie that flattered the blue of his eyes. "You already know that Miss Granger is with us. Lord Samael wishes to bring the archess here. In light of the situation, he feels he has much to discuss with the four of you."

"He knows what has occurred," Azrael stated.

Jason nodded. "Indeed. And I think you will agree this calls for cooperation."

"What a coincidence," came a gravelly, weakened voice from behind Max. He turned to see Michael standing in the archway behind them, leaning up against the wall. "Sam is so very good at lending help to those willing to pay his price."

Jason met Michael's gaze and held it. Their mutual unmitigated hatred and distrust was clear.

"In this case, Michael," Max said with a sigh, "Samael might be right. We are fighting something we can't defend ourselves against, let alone comprehend. And they have Uriel."

"What does your master want, exactly?" Azrael asked, always the one to cut to the chase.

"He wishes permission to enter the mansion. If you won't agree to this, he has acquiesced to meet with you in a public place. However, if you choose the latter, be aware that your proceedings may not be as private or protected as you desire."

"Son of a bitch," Michael whispered, closing his eyes as he leaned back and ran a rather shaky hand through his blond hair.

"I'll bloody well agree to that," came yet another gruff voice from behind them all. Michael and Max turned to find Gabriel pushing himself away from the wall on which he'd apparently been leaning on his way to the foyer. He looked terribly weak, horribly pale, and his silver-gray eyes were strikingly bright in his face, as if he were feverish. There was a slight sheen of sweat along his brow, dampening his shaggy black locks. "But the wee shite's go' Ellie. And whatever we're up against feels like the bubonic plague in a bloody bullet."

"You look like hell," Michael said softly, almost teasingly.

"I need a drink."

Max turned from the two archangels to face Jason once more. "We have no choice in this instance. When would he like to meet?"

"Now," Jason replied simply. "All you need do is invite him in."

At this, Max's eyes cut to Azrael. The archangel had to be invited?

The corners of Azrael's lips turned up ever so slightly. "Humans have their myths confused."

"How long would the invitation last?" Max asked him.

"A night," Azrael supplied. "Most likely the day as well."

Max sighed and turned to spear Jason with a hard look. "The invitation is for your master—not for you."

"That's okay," came yet another voice from behind the group in the foyer. Michael and Gabriel were instantly straightening to their full heights, their bodies in alarm mode as they spun around to face the intruder in the living room.

"He doesn't need an invitation from you," said Samael, from where he sat back in one of their plush leather recliners, his legs casually crossed at the ankles, his charcoal-gray suit the very image of perfection.

"That was fast," Max said under his breath.

Samael's smile was all-knowing and lightning flashed in the depths of his stormy eyes. A moment later, Eleanore appeared beside him, still dressed in red satin, a veritable goddess of crimson temptation.

"Eleanore!" Max rushed toward her.

"Max," she said, hugging him. She straightened, looking over his shoulder. "Michael, Gabriel, Az—you're all right." Relief flooded her features, but guilt clouded her eyes and the fidgeting of her fingers in her gown gave away her feelings of culpability.

"Ellie, this is *not* your fault," Max instantly told her, taking her hands in his. He could see the stains of tears on her porcelain cheeks. "Christ, Eleanore you can't blame yourself for this."

"Yes, I can," she whispered, her eyes down-turned. "Those men are after me. And they hurt all of you and—now they have Uriel." Her voice cracked as she finished, and Max pulled her into his arms again.

"This wouldn't be your doing, would it?" he accused as he locked eyes with Samael over Eleanore's shoulder.

Samael shrugged innocently. "On the contrary. I have already tried to convince her that she's not to blame. If I were to place responsibility anywhere, it would most likely be with the Old Man."

"Oh, here we go." Gabriel rolled his eyes and dropped hard into another plush love seat, his body clearly exhausted with the effort of standing.

Jason disappeared from the threshold of the mansion, and in a greenish grayish flash, reappeared behind Samael's chair. No one was surprised. Obviously Samael had pulled his servant inside.

Azrael calmly closed the door and joined them in the living room. "What is it you wish to discuss?" he asked, no hint of emotion showing on his stark, handsome features.

Samael turned his gaze on the dark archangel. "While Eleanore was mending, I read her thoughts and scanned her memories."

No one was surprised by this confession, though a general tensing of muscles around the room gave away the fact that they were no less irritated by it.

"It seems that while you and I were having it out in a cemetery in Texas, a group of men were in the process of tracking Eleanore's progress across the country." He laced his fingers over his stomach and continued. "I don't know who they are. But they apparently cornered her in a parking lot outside of a grocery store just before she eluded them and managed to make her way to the graveyard."

Eleanore slowly pulled away from Max and ran the back of her hand over her eyes. "They were dressed in lab coats and black fatigues. Some had needles filled with a clear liquid," she said softly. She gave a small shudder and Max could see a tremor make its way through her slender frame. "I recognized them. They looked like the men who came after me when I was fifteen. My family barely escaped."

The group digested the information for a moment. "You think these are the same men who attacked us at the gala and abducted Uriel?" Michael asked.

"Almost certainly," Sam said.

"Do you have any idea what kind of weapon it is they're using?" Max asked.

Samael considered this. "Honestly, no. But if it's capable of taking out the four of you at once, then we have much to be concerned about."

"What do they want Ellie for?" Michael questioned.

"I'm afraid I can't be certain of that, either. I know little more than you do in this case. However, if I were to hazard a guess . . ." He shrugged. "As an archess, Eleanore possesses many enviable abilities. They might want a number of things from her. Perhaps they want her to join them in some fight. Or they want to determine a way in which to reproduce her powers and create them in others. The possibilities are many."

"Well, on the one hand, this is good news." Max sighed. "It means they'll keep Uriel alive long enough to barter with him."

"Speaking of which," Azrael said, "we have company."

Max frowned, his brows drawing together in utter confusion. "That's impossible. No one knows the location of the mansion." He blinked then, considering something, and added, "No one human, anyway."

There was a knock at the front door and it reverberated through the room like a tidal wave of doom.

"In that case, I think we can assume one thing for sure," Michael said.

Everyone looked at him.

"Whatever we're up against isn't human."

CHAPTER TWENTY-TWO

"Geneeneral, I have the colonel on the phone for you."
Kevin took the receiver and placed it to his
ear. After a few seconds, he nodded. Then he returned
the phone to his captain and strode across the room to
the door. The invitation had been delivered. All that was
left to do now was wait—and plan.

Kevin had a few more questions he wanted answered.
Another conversation with his special prisoner was in
order. He left the room and made his way down the hall
toward the holding cells.

The archangel Uriel had been released from his
bonds in the interrogation room and allowed his own
private cell. Of course, he was still secured and there was
nothing in the cell but its four walls and floor. It was
constructed of the same materials as the interrogation
room. Uriel was going nowhere.

Most likely, at this moment, the general had one very
angry Angel of Vengeance on his hands.

"General." As Kevin reached the cell, the men on either side of the door greeted him and stepped aside.

"Any trouble from our guest?" asked Kevin.

"No, sir. Nothing we couldn't handle."

The door clicked open and Kevin peered into the
grayness of the room beyond. He listened. Shallow
breathing came from its corner. He adjusted his vision
and Uriel's tall, bent outline became clearly visible.

"No need to stand on my account. Please sit before you fall down."

"If you've come to torture me, at least do it in silence. I really can't stand the sound of your voice," Uriel rasped.

Kevin stepped into the room and allowed the door to close behind him. It clicked shut and the lock slid into place.

He took in the archangel's physical state: bloody lip, bloody nose, black eye, cut on the forehead, bruises forming everywhere. His men had been having fun with their prisoner. No doubt it confused Uriel that he could not defend himself against them. The manacles around the archangel's legs were lined with the same metal that he'd been strapped down with on the interrogation table. It was a metal that Kevin had created centuries ago when he'd discovered that the alloy prevented an archangel from using any of his supernatural abilities.

"It's a shame you've had to suffer so much. If only Eleanore were here." Kevin moved through the room to stand before Uriel, who was leaning against the back wall, his clothing tattered and torn and soaked with both blood and sweat.

The archangel eyed Kevin through wary—and weary—eyes.

"She could heal you," Kevin finished.

Uriel threw back his head and laughed, the deep, barking sound bouncing and echoing off of the walls around them.

Kevin stopped in his tracks. The laughter was Uriel's only reply. Not that Kevin had expected anything more. But it would have been nice, for once, not to have to do things the hard way.

Lightning coursed across the dark night, thunder chasing on its heels with dogged determination. It shook the windows in their panes and created a chaotic background music to the conversations taking place within the mansion.

The storm was Eleanore's doing, Though she'd had years of practice controlling the weather, it reflected the turmoil inside of her now no matter how much she tried to calm it. And she wasn't the only one upset. Everyone in the mansion's large kitchen was agitated to some degree.

Everyone, that is, except one.

Samael alone appeared calm. He was the eye of the hurricane, and he remained collected and in control. It was unnerving and felt a little like sitting in a living room with a disturbingly composed dragon.

When the knock had come at the door less than an hour before, Azrael had opened it to find a sealed envelope on the doorstep. An ultimatum had been delivered: Eleanore for Uriel, or Uriel would die and Eleanore would be taken, one way or another.

The ultimatum had set off a domino-like tremor of anger through the room. Not one of them was under the delusion that their enemy intended to turn Uriel over to them alive, no matter what the paper might read. If Michael, Gabriel, and Azrael had any hope of seeing their brother alive again, the fact was they needed Samael's help. Nothing brought home that realization more than the fact that the enemy had found the mansion in the first place. Such a thing was supposed to be impossible.

No one in the mansion was reacting particularly well to the night's developments.

Gabriel's reaction was the most impressive. He'd gone through a six-pack in forty-five minutes and had nearly carved a trench in the floor where he had been pacing back and forth, furiously running his hand through his thick black hair, his silver eyes flashing with obvious wrath.

Max handled it differently, preferring to remain in his role of caretaker than to break down and show any real emotion. He had instructed the archangels to create new clothing for Eleanore so that she could get out of the Lavonde dress and be more comfortable. Then he brewed a pot of tea.

Michael, for his part, had taken up residence in a seat across from Samael at the dining room table. Jason, as usual, was standing, and was watching Ellie's storm through a large window several discreet steps away from his master. Azrael had gone out to find a "meal." Eleanore was under no delusions as to what that meant.

The men who had Uriel wanted to make a trade at two a.m. in a field outside of Dallas. They had an hour and twenty minutes to go and virtually no workable plan as to how to retrieve Uriel alive. Eleanore's skin felt prickly. Her face felt hot and her body felt cold. She was terrified.

Many people made it a policy never to deal with terrorists or hostage takers. It wasn't a good idea to allow the enemy any kind of control over you. Everyone in the mansion was aware of that. They were all well aware that agreeing to anything the kidnappers proposed would be as good as saying, "You win. You're stronger than we are. Take what you want; we can't stop you."

But their enemy's weapons were superior, their powers were greater, they knew about the mansion and those inside it—and they had Uriel. They were holding all the cards.

"You can't place any confidence in such an action," Samael said, in response to something Michael had just suggested. "We don't know what powers they possess. We don't even know what they are."

They had been tossing ideas back and forth for the last forty minutes, and with each passing second, Gabriel and Max became more agitated. Samael, on the other hand, simply remained the poster boy for handsome, confident serenity. From the look on Michael's face, Eleanore surmised the man had never hated Samael more.

"Then wha' the bloody hell *are* they?" Gabriel finally shouted, slamming his fist down on the table as he shot out of his chair to take up pacing once more. "Will someone just fucking *tell* us already!"

"They are called Adarians," came an unexpected female voice from just beyond the archway that led to the living room and foyer.

Everyone in the room spun to find Lilith standing beside the fireplace, her hands calmly clasped before her, her wealth of dark hair pulled into a loose bun that allowed wisps of it to fall and frame her delicate features.

"Lilith," Max said, clearly surprised, as he came to his feet.

"Max." Lilith nodded at him. "Michael, Gabriel, Azrael." She greeted them all in turn and then settled her dark eyes on Eleanore. "Archess," she said, smiling kindly and bowing her head ever so slightly.

Eleanore blinked, surprised by the gesture. But she was saved from having to respond in any way by Samael's deep, sexy voice slicing through the silence.

"Lilith, what are you doing here?" There was an edge to his words that hadn't been there before. It was the first break in his calm facade that any of them had witnessed thus far that night.

"I'm *helping*, Sam," Lilith said. "As you should be."

To this, Samael said nothing. But his storm-gray eyes darkened and the lightning that crisscrossed the sky outside was reflected in their shadowy depths.

"As I was saying," Lilith continued, undaunted by his dark look. She moved away from the fireplace and Max simultaneously moved around the table, drawing closer to her. Eleanore noticed that Samael had straightened in his chair as if he, too, were ready to stand.

"The men who have Uriel are the Adarians. They are, for lack of a better description"—she paused and met each of their gazes before she finished—"archangels."

Stunned silence followed this proclamation. Archangels? The idea was impossible.

Michael and Gabriel stared at Lilith in shock. Max

was pale. Azrael was still as a statue, which Ellie knew only meant that whatever surprise he was feeling, he was hiding as masterfully as always.

Samael was the only one among them who did not look astounded. Instead, his expression was one of barely contained fury.

Lilith went on. "You didn't know of their existence because the Old Man did everything he could to hide their creation from you. You were made long after they were disposed of."

"Lilith." Samael's voice was so low, so deadly in its warning that the Fallen One drew every pair of eyes in the room.

However, Lilith ignored him once more. "Their name was given to them by their creator after their disposal, and means 'the first,' though they were obviously not the last of their kind," she continued. She had come to a halt near the archway that led to the dining room, and she drew no closer. Instead, she glanced once at Samael, who speared her with a hard gaze, and then she pulled her eyes away to look at Max.

"There were twelve Adarians created before one was fashioned that the Old Man was not unhappy with. The thirteenth Adarian did not appear to be as powerful as the others, or as concerned with his own welfare and interests. Up to that point, the Adarians had proven themselves to be selfish, and the combination of their egotism and immense power troubled the Old Man. So the first dozen were cast down. However, the thirteenth Adarian—"

"Lilith, that is *enough*." Samael rose from his chair then and lightning struck directly overhead, its thunder shaking the very foundations of the mansion.

"Oh my God," Eleanore whispered, her hand at her throat in an unconscious protective gesture. She stared up at Samael in wonder. "The thirteenth archangel—the thirteenth Adarian—is *you*."

Another stunned moment of silence followed, and

then Gabriel turned his silver gaze on the Fallen One. "You *knew*," he accused with a hiss. "You bloody well knew who they were this whole fucking time."

Samael met his gaze and held it. He didn't confirm it. But neither was his silence a denial.

Michael must have sensed what was coming a half second before it happened, and he shoved his body into motion in an effort to stop the impending trouble.

Gabriel was rushing for Samael, a blur of tall, dark male, and Samael was turning to meet him head-on. Michael moved so quickly, he seemed to almost blink out of existence from where he was standing to reappear between Gabriel and Sam.

"Stop!" He turned and barked the order at Gabriel, allowing his otherworldly command to boom through the room and echo off the walls.

Gabriel came to a sudden halt, his silver eyes glowing eerily in his tanned, handsome face. "Get out of the way, Mike, or I bloody swear I will take you down along with 'im," Gabriel growled.

"Enough, both of you." Max waved his hand forcefully and a surge of hardened air separated Gabriel from Michael, shoving them both back until Gabriel slammed into the counter behind him and Michael hit the wall. Both men landed on their booted feet, teeth bared, bodies primed for battle.

Eleanore backed up into the kitchen that adjoined the dining room. She didn't know what to make of any of this. But she knew that the fact that Samael had kept the truth from them was not just selfish and wrong, it was dangerous. She had no idea why he wouldn't share what he knew, especially since he had come to them in a kind of truce. But she knew she couldn't trust him—ever.

Samael's tall, strong form had never appeared more like carved steel. He turned away from the two brothers and focused his attention on Lilith. "You believe you've helped, but as you can see, you've only complicated matters." His expression was calm once more, but behind that cool and unruffled exterior was a tumultuous temper.

"So you would like to believe, Sam," Lilith said. "But you and I both know that isn't true. And you know that Uriel will die unless his brothers understand and can prepare for what they are up against."

"Why would you want Uriel to die?" Eleanore asked softly. She couldn't help it. None of this made any sense. "If Uriel dies, then you'll lose him as a servant. I thought that was what you wanted," she accused.

Samael turned those intense charcoal-gray eyes on her and she swallowed hard. There was more than just anger in their stormy depths. There was something covetous there as well.

"Don't look at her like that!" Gabriel bellowed. "She's no' yours!"

He launched himself from where he was standing against the counter in the kitchen. He and Samael hit so hard, so fast, the impact created a flash of power that rippled out like circles in a pond. Lightning and thunder once more shook the mansion. Eleanore was forcefully thrown back, but Max managed to catch her in his arms before she hit the wall behind her. He set her on her feet and rushed toward the two struggling archangels, as did Michael.

But before either of them could interfere, Azrael's tall form shifted where he stood in the shadows on one side of the dining room. Eleanore looked up to catch the briefest flash of an image overlaying the vampire archangel. It was blurry and indistinct, but she could have sworn she saw the outline of what looked like a dark figure in robes, carrying a scythe.

And then it was gone and Azrael's gold eyes were glowing like suns and his fangs were bared and there was a sound wave of power swelling outward from his corner of the room.

The wrinkle in space slammed into both Samael and

Gabriel, separating them with hurricane force and throwing them both across the rooms of the mansion. It was an immensely focused wave of power and, miraculously, hit no one else. Gabriel went sailing through the air to slam into and then through the wall on the left so that he landed in the hallway on the other side. Samael came within a foot of hitting the living room wall to the right before he stopped, straightened in midair, and gently landed on the carpet beneath him. However, his glowing eyes were anything but gentle.

The storm raging outside had now given birth to a wind so strong, it sounded as if they were about to be hit with a class five tornado.

"Azrael is right," Eleanore said. "This needs to stop." Hers was a voice of reason in what had become a mansion filled with raging testosterone. "We haven't much time," she continued, as she made her way to the dining room table and began to pull out a chair.

Max seemed to shake himself and leapt into gentlemanly action, moving forward to take the back of the chair from her hands and scoot it out for her. She offered him a small, grateful smile and sat down. Then Max turned to Lilith and pulled out another empty chair. He gestured that she should sit as well.

Lilith sat down and Max joined them.

In the dining room, Samael snapped his fingers and the torn and slightly ruffled suit he'd been wearing a moment before was instantly replaced with a suit and shirt of pitch-black. His charcoal-gray tie matched his eyes. As he made his way to the table and gracefully took a seat across from Eleanore, she had to admit that it was an incredibly sexy look on him.

Samael caught her gaze and he held it fast; there was no way he'd missed her appreciation. Eleanore blushed furiously and forced herself to pull her attention from the Fallen One and back to the task at hand.

She could hear Gabriel coming up from behind and

could see Michael joining them as well as she turned to Lilith and asked, "How do we get Uriel back alive?"

"Finally," Lilith said, smiling warmly at her. "A reasonable angel."

"I'm no angel," Eleanore quietly insisted.

"Yes, you are," said every man in the room.

"All right, big guy," the guard said as he gave Uriel's chains a jerk and, with the help of two other guards, brought Uriel to his feet. "It's time to move out." The guard flashed a nasty, brilliant-white smile. "The rabbit's nearly in the wolf's den."

Uriel slowly raised his head and peered at the guard through the tops of his green, glowing eyes. The man was caught, if only for a moment, in the hatred of that burning, emerald gaze. For a millisecond, uncertainty flashed in his own light brown eyes. But then it was gone, and the guard was once more barking orders to the other members of his security detail.

Together, they moved Uriel down the long, metal-lined corridor and through a metal door that led outside. The moment the door opened, sheets of rain slammed into the group, slanting out of the darkness of the pitch-black night. The guards seemed to be expecting it; they weren't surprised by the lightning that split up the sky with blue-white fractures that looked like spiderweb cracks on an ebony vase. They were unfazed by the thunder that seemed to rumble at a loud and constant drone.

Uriel, on the other hand, hadn't known it was storming. The tiny cell he'd been locked in had been deep underground and pain had been his constant companion, blocking out all other sensations. The rain surprised him now, as he raised his face and tasted it in the drops that entered his mouth and nose. As they moved him from the nondescript building where he had been kept to the van that awaited them, the rain washed over him, a cool salve on his torn flesh and weary muscles.

His body was exhausted.

The general's men possessed truly malicious powers. They were all supernaturally strong and they had all been trained to hit where it hurt. But a few of them had the vile ability to simply cause pain with no more than a touch. Or a glance. One of them had demonstrated his aptitude for causing someone to bleed through the pores, soaking Uriel's shirt with the blood he desperately needed to remain within his vampire veins. Yet another possessed the ability to enter Uriel's mind, flashing torrid, sickening images of Eleanore, tied down and suffering through all manners of torture, each of them blatantly sexual.

Their combined manipulations over the past several hours had drained Uriel both body and mind. He had tried to defend himself so many times, but he failed and in the end, he was left devoid of strength or power. He couldn't even fix his clothing, and should he ever see Eleanore again, he desperately didn't want her to see him covered from head to boot in his own blood.

He had never felt so helpless—so hopeless—in his entire, long life.

But the rain . . . Maybe it was his imagination; maybe he was delirious and his mind was playing tricks on him. But he could have sworn that the rain was taking the pain away. It felt different; it felt *good*. In the fever of his weary brain, it reminded him of Ellie.

Uriel glanced down at his torn black shirt and noticed the rain washing the blood off of him in pink-tinged rivulets. The red streams were becoming clearer and clearer with each passing moment. He caught a glimpse of his skin and, to his blinking surprise, he didn't see the cut that had been there moments before.

It was gone.

"Get him in quick," a guard ordered. Uriel was shoved forward until his shin hit the van's doorframe and he fell onto his manacled wrists and across the metal floor. The handcuffs once more bit into his skin, but this time the metal scored fresh slices into his flesh. Which meant that the wounds he'd had before had healed.

Again Uriel blinked, astonished. He could barely fathom how this had occurred. Somehow, the storm that raged outside had healed him. At least to some physical extent. He was still drained of precious blood—and as a vampire, that was particularly dire.

But the cuts and bruises were gone, and the few bones they'd managed to break felt as if they'd mended. He wondered if the guards had noticed his miraculous recovery.

Uriel thought fast. In an effort to keep his mending hidden, he curled in on himself, as would a man in great amounts of pain. Someone standing above him laughed. Another man snickered. The door to the van slid shut.

His captors made a few rude comments about "vengeance" and "comeuppance" and the van started up and pulled out of the empty, private lot. Uriel lay still and listened to the sound of the tires on the wet asphalt and the rain pelting the van's roof. His mind was spinning in a mad, frantic attempt to formulate some sort of plan.

He had no idea where they were going. He only knew that, wherever it was, the men who held him prisoner, along with their general, were positive Eleanore would be waiting for them there.

If Uriel's attack on her had indeed sent her to Samael, as he'd planned, then she wouldn't be alone. Samael might not care what became of Uriel, but he sure as hell cared about what happened to the archess. Archangels were a dime a dozen to Samael, but an archess was precious.

And his brothers . . . Would they be there? Were they even alive?

Uriel's chest felt tight at the thought, but he shoved his doubt away and forced himself to think positively. *They are alive.* He would know if they weren't.

In which case, it was possible that they might be able

to help. Not probable, but possible. All it would take was a little cooperation between them—and Samael.

Uriel closed his eyes and forced his negative thoughts away. It was a long shot. Like rain healing your wounds. *There* was something that didn't happen every day.

It's Ellie.

The thought struck him from nowhere, but it echoed in his mind clear as a bell. Eleanore was causing the storm. She must be somewhere nearby. She had called up a gale—and, somehow, it had healed him. *She* had healed him.

As impossible as it seemed, he knew it was true. And whatever the reason, it only strengthened Uriel's resolve to be free of these monsters and save Eleanore from the fate he'd endured for the past several hours. He would not let them touch her. She was more precious than the sun and moon. And she was his alone.

From beneath the cover of the arms he had folded over his face and head, Uriel opened his eyes and glanced quickly around the van. There were three men in the back with him. All were armed with the strange, horrible guns. Uriel's wrists and ankles were still bound with cuffs made of the same metal as his cell and prevented him from using any of his supernatural abilities. And he desperately needed blood. Now that the rest of his body was healed, it was easier to feel the gnawing pain in his gut that told him he needed to feed—and soon—or he would die.

Think, Uriel. Think! He shut his eyes again and saw the van's interior behind his closed lids. Three men. All armed. He envisioned them all, their positions, their weapons. His powers had not yet worked against any of these "first" archangels. He knew that well enough now not to waste his energy even trying. If he was going to defeat them, he would have to do it without any supernatural ability.

Like a human.

Think like a human, he told himself. *Think.*

*   *   *

"So let me get this straight," Eleanore ventured, licking her lips and drawing the glances of several of the men around her. Not that she noticed. She stared at the table-top as she concentrated, her focus one of stark determination. "The boy I communicated with through my bedroom window when I was a teenager isn't actually named Kevin. His name is Abraxos?"

Lilith nodded. "Yes, though he does go by Kevin for the most part these days. He has changed his name many times over the years, as you can imagine."

Eleanore nodded her understanding.

Lilith continued. "At first glance, and to an outsider, this appears to be some kind of military operation as he has colonels, lieutenants, and captains working beneath him. But most of them aren't even human, much less belonging to any army on Earth. The ones that *are* human obviously come and go. They act as servants to the Adarians—pawns, if you will. But they do so of their own free will and usually for the rewards that come with the service. The general has amassed a hefty amount of wealth over the years. Not one of his human soldiers has ever betrayed his trust, and I'm sure you can guess why; it would be suicidal. The rest of his men are Adarians. All of them, human or not, are aware of what he is and are loyal to a fault."

"So what are their weaknesses?" Michael asked, a tad impatiently.

Lilith thought carefully. "They can't heal themselves, so if they're injured, they have to heal at a normal, human rate."

"But Samael can heal," Eleanore said with a slight frown. "I don't understand."

"He was determined different from the other Adarians for several reasons," Lilith explained, as if Samael were not actually sitting there with them at the dining room table. Much to everyone's surprise, though, Samael simply sat back in his chair, crossed his arms over his chest, and listened quietly as a small smile curled the corners of his lips.

"There are a few powers that the Adarians possess that Samael does not. And vice versa," Lilith said.

There was a brief moment of silence after this, and then Michael leaned forward on his arms and laced his fingers together on the tabletop. "So they can't heal themselves, they can't control the weather, and they can't read people's minds. So far, this is a list of *non*-powers, not a list of weaknesses. What the hell can we do that will actually *hurt* these guys?"

"Gold."

The room went still at the single word Samael uttered. He smiled at the response and exchanged a knowing glance with Lilith.

"Come again?" Gabriel said, his voice gruff with the anger he'd managed to keep in check for the past half hour.

"Gold is caustic to the Adarians," Lilith said.

"You mean in the way that silver is caustic to werewolves?" Eleanore asked.

"Silver is not caustic to werewolves," Azrael told her gently. "Again—humans have their myths confused."

Eleanore supposed she shouldn't be surprised by anything at this point.

Michael turned his gaze to Lilith. "So gold will harm them. And all it has to do is touch them?"

"I believe so. Mind you, my knowledge of the Adarians is limited," Lilith replied.

Max sighed heavily. "So we need a boatload of gold and we need it fast. You'd best get to work, boys. We're supposed to meet the Adarians somewhere just outside of Dallas in little more than half an hour."

"No problem," Azrael, Gabriel, and Michael all said at once. The three archangels turned to face the living room behind them and, as one, they focused on the coffee table at the center of the room.

A flash of light, a buzz in the air, and the oak coffee table was solid gold.

Eleanore's eyes widened. She remembered the thick gold "paint" that Gabriel had created over the window in the bed-and-breakfast in Trinidad. Now she realized he had actually turned the window to gold. "Ok*aaay*," she whispered. "Why isn't every piece of furniture in your house made of solid gold, then?"

"What, like a King Midas kind of thing?" Michael asked, turning a friendly smile on her. "Not our style. Besides," he went on, shrugging his broad shoulders, "gold is cold and hard and blinds the crap out of you when the sun catches it."

"So we have our gold," Max said. "Now we need to figure out what to do with it."

"I say we try this out right now and see if it works on Adarians like he says it will." Gabriel cut his eyes to Samael and narrowed his gaze. Then he reached his hand out and a carving knife from the kitchen countertop slid from its resting place in a wooden receptacle and flew into Gabriel's grasp. Another small flash of transformative light and it, too, was solid gold.

"Control yourself, Gabriel," Max warned, coming to his feet to stand between the two archangels. "We don't have time for this."

Gabriel shot Samael a warning look of pure silver and the golden carving knife flew back to its place in the block.

Max turned to face Samael. "For hand-to-hand combat, solid gold bends too easily. We need weapons constructed of some kind of alloy; I would say ten carats or less?" He looked to Lilith for confirmation and, after brief consideration, she nodded.

"Good. Can the four of you handle that while I speak with Eleanore?" His gaze slid from Sam to Michael and his brothers.

He didn't wait for them to reply, but instead he of-

fered Eleanore his hand. She looked up at him with uncertainty. Then she took his hand and he led her out of
the dining room, through the living room, and into one
of the long hallways beyond.

Once they were alone in one of the guest rooms, Max
closed the door behind them and waved his hand over
the face of it. It rippled slightly and then settled back
into place.

"What did you do?"

"Soundproofed the room. I don't want Samael hearing what I have to tell you."

Eleanore fidgeted nervously as he turned his full attention on her.

"If what Lilith told us is true about Samael and the
Adarians, and I have no reason to doubt her, then Samael is incredibly powerful, Ellie. More powerful than
we had imagined. If he's determined that he'll claim you
as his own archess, then you and Uriel both have a terrible fight on your hands." He shook his head. "A fight
you have almost no hope of winning."

"Why are you telling me this?"

"Because it's a possibility." He waited a moment before continuing. "It's also possible that it's not you in
particular that Samael is after. It's possible that he has
his sights set on an archess in general. You're just the
only one we've managed to find so far."

"Okay . . . *and*?" Eleanore hedged him for his point.

"In that case, his plan might be to stop the bonding of
at least one of the archangels. I'm not sure why, but I get
the feeling he doesn't want all four of them to find and
claim their archesses. A part of me dearly hopes that this
is the case, because it would mean that once you are
fully bonded with Uriel, Samael will let you go in favor
of hunting down another archess."

Eleanore considered his words, her stomach turning
somersaults. She didn't know what to do. How was she
supposed to bond herself to Uriel? "What do you need
me to do?" she finally asked.

"I want you to search your true feelings, Eleanore," Max said, cupping her cheek gently with his palm as his eyes peered deeply into hers. "Because when the time comes, you are going to have to make a choice—and you're going to have to make that choice very clear. It isn't as easy as proclaiming your love in three little words. I hope you didn't think it would be."

Eleanore frowned. "Well . . . yeah. I guess I sort of did."

Max smiled and shook his head. "Do you have any idea how many lies have been told using those words? Countless. It's number one on the top five million lies list and has been since time immemorial." He chuckled softly and Eleanore found that she couldn't help but smile as well, even though her heart was sinking into her stomach.

"But that's what Uriel did," she said softly. "He told me he loved me."

Max nodded. "Uriel truly loves you. He has from the moment he set eyes upon you, Eleanore. His devotion to you was never in question. But *you* are a being of free will and you haven't been searching for your angelic mate for the duration of your life, as he has."

Eleanore swallowed hard and shook her head, shrugging once more. "What am I supposed to do?"

"Just remember, Ellie," Max said as he let his hand drop to his side. "Actions speak louder than words. They always have and they always will. You will know what to do when the time comes." He offered her one last tender smile, winked at her, and then waved his hand over the door. It rippled once, clicked open, and Max left the room.

Eleanore watched him make his way down the hall toward the family room until he disappeared around the corner. Then she turned toward the large French windows against one wall and gazed out at the wet, waiting night. Lightning flashed and thunder rolled, echoing the tempest of emotions wreaking havoc with her heart and soul.

"Max Gillihan is a wise man," came a cool, deep voice behind her.

Eleanore spun to see Samael standing just inside the room, tall and strong and impossibly handsome in his sable suit. His charcoal eyes met hers and darkened. With a casual flick of his wrist, he waved the door shut. For the second time that night, Eleanore watched it ripple under a silencing effect.

"Now that he's had his say, it's time that I have mine."

CHAPTER TWENTY-THREE

Samael looked down at the floor as the door's lock slid telekinetically into place. He casually slipped his hands into his pockets and seemed to be contemplating something deeply as he began a slow pace toward Eleanore.

A sharp, intoxicating mixture of fear and anticipation shot through Eleanore and she found herself taking a step back.

Sam's stormy gaze lifted instantly, cutting to her with hard precision and holding her in place. His expression was more determined than she had ever seen it.

"Ellie," he began softly, "I'll be honest with you. Gillihan is right. I do want an archess of my own," he told her, still coming ever closer in slow, deliberate steps across the carpeted floor. "And I do have my reasons."

She could no longer retreat; he was holding her in some sort of thrall.

"He's also correct in assuming that I possess . . ." He stopped a foot away from her, looked her up and down, and recaptured her indigo gaze. "Formidable power," he finished.

Then he cocked his head to one side, his charcoal eyes glittering as he studied her features. "I am a king among angels, Ellie. And I could use a queen. What do you say?"

Eleanore swallowed hard and did not even try to

hide the fact that her breathing had become ragged and her body trembled.

Samael closed the final distance between them and Eleanore gasped at his sudden nearness. He smelled divine; it was the scent of expensive cologne, and something else, something seductive and heady—*power*. His tall, broad form, so expertly draped in fine, tailored material, was overwhelming. He was so intense, so vividly potent. She could feel his power all around him, and it was surrounding her as well.

He raised his hand and slowly captured a lock of her raven hair to rub it admiringly between his thumb and forefinger. "You know in your heart that I can give you anything you desire." He dropped her hair and Ellie felt his hand snake around her waist to press gently against her lower back. She could barely breathe now.

"I want Uriel," she said.

Samael was not fazed. He chuckled softly, using his hand to pull her body against his. "And you can have him." He grinned. "Be mine, Eleanore, and Uriel will become my servant. If you join me, he will serve you as well. You can have him whenever you like." His white smile was devastating. She couldn't tell whether he was joking or not, but she was lost in that smile and the pure predatory nature of it.

Eleanore closed her eyes. She was not sure it was the safest thing to do while she was in the Fallen One's arms, but it at least allowed her an escape from his hypnotic gaze. It gave her the slightest bit of room to think.

"You were going to let him die," she accused softly.

"Marry me and I will make certain he lives."

Eleanore's eyes flew open and were immediately caught once more in his. She peered long and hard into that stormy gaze, as if searching for some sign that what he said was true. "You can save him?" How could he be so sure? The Adarians were a small army of intensely powerful archangels. Could Samael truly promise such a thing?

His smile and the lightning that flashed so resolutely in his gaze were all the answer she needed. He could do it. He could do anything. He was Samael.

"Consider something, Ellie," he continued. His free hand rose toward her neck and she tried to pull away, but his arm at her back prevented her escape. Deftly and gently, he encircled her throat and caressed the curve of her chin with his thumb. "I know what you like. I know what turns you on." Using tender, but persistent strength, he tilted her head to one side, exposing the column of her neck to his gaze. Ellie once more closed her eyes. "And in a week's time, your precious Uriel will no longer be a vampire. A deal is a deal, after all."

He bent over her, lowering his lips to her ear. "Tell me, Ellie, will you still enjoy his company so much when he doesn't bite?"

Fight him, Eleanore. Get away from him! Her mind screamed at her, but her body remained captured in his thrall, her legs weakening, her head spinning end over end. He drew her against him with more persistence. Her breasts pressed against the hardness of his chest and she felt his breath on the taut flesh of her neck.

His teeth grazed her there.

Eleanore's breath caught in her throat and her hands flew up, her fingers gripping the hard muscles in his arms beneath the fine material of his suit.

Stop, she thought, because she couldn't say it out loud. *Please stop.*

"Do you really want me to?"

His hand slid beneath her hoodie and T-shirt at her back to meet smooth skin. His teeth trailed a threatening path up her throat to the curve of her ear, where he nipped gently. A wave of piercing pleasure rode through her, making her wet and drawing a moan from somewhere deep in her throat.

No ... yes!

She wanted him to stop—she really did. But he was confusing her, tying her in knots inside, befuddling even her mental responses to his damning questions. He was far too good at this. No one was better at seduction than Samael.

And yet there was a part of her, somewhere in the vicinity of her chest, that was hurting in a way that was not at all pleasurable. Even as Samael sent bliss coursing through her body, an aching emptiness yawned open in her heart. It felt wrong.

Uriel.

She thought of him giving his jacket to his fan in the elevator. She saw him wink at her from the other side of a door. She remembered the way he'd first felt, so close to her, as he'd trapped her against that customer service desk in the bookstore less than a week ago. And her emptiness grew.

You have feelings for him. Samael spoke in her mind, his voice echoing in the chambers of her consciousness. *This much is clear. So save his life, Ellie. Surrender to me.*

No, she answered. She had no idea where the strength to deny him had come from, but there it was. She could not give in to Samael. She knew deep down that Uriel would rather die than have her sacrifice herself in order to save him. And though it tore viciously at some part of her to act on such knowledge, it gave her the will to withstand the Fallen One once more.

No, she repeated, this time truly meaning it.

Sam stilled over her, his mouth at her throat, a menace unmoving. His grip on her did not lessen, however, and he was still in her head.

You would make such a rash decision on his behalf? he asked softly. There was a darker rumble to his words now, one laced with peril. *You would doom him to death for the sake of your uncertain romance?*

He will not die, Eleanore told him.

I won't let him, she thought. This time, the thought was meant for her alone. It was an affirmation, a promise to herself.

He heard it all the same.

Samael drew back and looked into her eyes. She straightened as he released her from whatever spell he'd had her under, but his hand remained around her neck, an ever-present reminder of his dominance.

"Such determination," he whispered, his thumb caressing the side of her throat. "You truly are a fascinating woman, Eleanore."

Ellie swallowed and forced herself not to give in. Not to back down. A little more of his influence slipped away from her, but she knew it was his doing, not hers. He was going easy on her, letting her go.

"What a waste," he said then, removing his hand and taking a full step back. His retreat produced a dichotomy of regret and relief so strong, it nearly buckled her knees.

Eleanore wrapped her arms around her stomach and implored him with her eyes. "Will you let Uriel die?" she asked, not caring that she sounded desperate. She *was* desperate. And he knew it.

"What happens to your archangel is not my doing," he told her, his tone soft, even as it was hard.

"But you just said you could save him!" Eleanore insisted.

"Be careful, Ellie," he warned then. The lights in the bedroom flickered. The air around them felt heavy and hot. "Do not test me," he said. His charcoal-gray eyes lightened into a platinum so stark that they seemed to glow. She watched as he took a step backward, and then another, his eyes never leaving hers.

"So that's it? I won't be your whore so you're going to pout and let Uriel die?" *Oh my God,* she thought suddenly as realization piggybacked on her words. *Did I seriously just say that?* Eyes wide, breath quickening, she found herself stepping back as well. *I am so dead.*

But instead of the wrath she fully expected from the formidable archangel, she was greeted with a long, stone-cold silence. Samael pulled his gaze from hers and looked at the floor as he once more put his hands in his pockets.

"I could never kill you, Ellie," he almost whispered. "Not ever. But hear me well," he said as he looked back up and captured her gaze a final time. "I'm not known for my kindness." He waved his hand at the door and it rippled and then settled back down. "I'm a determined man and accustomed to getting my way."

With that, he opened the door and left the room.

Eleanore stood still and quiet for several long minutes. Then she ran a shaky hand through her hair, took an equally shaky breath, and lowered herself to her knees on the carpet. She felt weak and emotionally exhausted.

And she couldn't stop thinking about Uriel. And what the Adarians were doing to him.

Ellie closed her eyes and lowered her face into her hands. She remembered the teenage boy from the street corner all those years ago. He had been so handsome, so tall, with eyes of piercing blue.

Kevin. The first archangel ever created. And now he was probably torturing Uriel and she was about to go up against him and his men in a strange, bloody battle with no determinable outcome.

He loves me, she thought suddenly. *Uriel loves me.* She was a woman so fortunate that she had the unconditional devotion of one of the four legendary archangels. How often did something like that happen?

Four times, apparently, Ellie thought, at once smiling to herself. It helped break the darkening mood she'd found herself in. *After me, there will be three others. Maybe . . . Maybe, if I can make it through this alive, and Uriel and I can figure things out between us—then I can help the others. Somehow.*

Eleanore pondered that for a moment. It was a bolstering thought. She took a deep breath, this one far less shaky than the last, and she got to her feet. As she did, she shoved her hands into the pockets of her hoodie and the tips of her fingers brushed against something cold, smooth, and round.

The bracelet.

It was the binding bracelet she had snatched from Max Gillihan after she'd struck him with lightning what seemed like ages ago. Every time she changed clothes, no matter where she went or what she did, she somehow managed to keep possession of the strange, beautiful article of jewelry.

It went from an inner fold of her red gown to the pocket of her fleece hoodie despite the fact that Michael had fashioned these clothes for her out of thin air. It was as if the bracelet were a mythical boomerang—it always returned to her.

Like Thor's hammer, she thought to herself.

She drew her hands back out of her pockets, leaving the bracelet there. Then she left the bedroom, feeling a little better than she had two minutes ago.

Uriel watched the three guards through the slits of his jade-colored eyes. They had no idea he was observing them. As far as they were concerned, he was curled in on himself, badly injured, and most likely unconscious.

He used their misperception to his advantage and took the opportunity to hastily formulate a plan. Several minutes went by, in which Uriel mentally measured distances, figured probabilities, and slowly and carefully flexed each of his muscles to make certain his bones had indeed been mended and that his limbs were working properly once more.

He could tell what kind of road they were on by the vibration of the tires on the tarmac. By the time they had taken an on-ramp and the van increased speed onto a highway, Uriel was ready to move.

Hoping he was right about the dispositions of these men, Uriel pretended to cramp up tighter and made sounds as if he were going to vomit. The nearest guard was seated close enough that his boot wasn't far from Uriel's chest. Uriel leaned a little toward him, using all of his acting ability to make it clear that he had no control over the bile that was now rising up his esophagus and would most likely project, cannonlike, all over the guard's leg.

Just as Uriel expected, the guard pulled his leg back and kicked Uriel square in the chest, sending him flying across the van. Uriel twisted a little in midair, again making it look as if he had no control over his movements. By the time he hit the guard on the opposite side, he was facing him.

On impact, Uriel snatched the hand gun from the Adarian's unsnapped holster. Then, with skills honed by thousands of years of battles and wars, Uriel landed on his feet and spun, aiming the shard gun at the guard who had kicked him. He fired once, got the Adarian in the chest, and then quickly leveled the weapon on the second guard, who was too taken by surprise to react. He pulled the trigger a second time and struck his target on mark. Another split second and he was whirling once more to face the guard whose gun he had taken. The gun went off a third and final time and all three Adarians were on the floor of the van.

Their chests were expanding in petrified blackness; their hands were claws that clutched and tore at their clothing. Within a few seconds, they slipped into unconsciousness.

Uriel stood alone at the center of his fallen enemies and lowered his weapon. It was fitted with a strange sort of silencer and had not at all sounded like the guns that had struck him and his brothers down at the gala.

With a sharp glance at the front of the van, where the driver continued to maneuver the vehicle as if he had not heard the commotion, Uriel bent to his knees and searched the body of the guard closest to him. He was looking for the keys to the manacles that still bound him. He'd had time to figure out that they kept him from using any of his supernatural abilities.

However, the keys weren't on the first guard. Or the second or third guards. Which meant they were either with the driver—or with the general. Uriel was seriously hoping for the former rather than the latter.

He dropped the gun he'd been holding, presuming that a good amount of its ammunition had been spent, and took the two unfired weapons from the other fallen guards. Then he drew up the archangel who had kicked him, yanked his handsome head back by the hair, and sank his vampire fangs into the man's thick corded neck.

The blood was slow to come, as there was stone in the guard's veins, spreading in a sluggish petrifaction. But what Uriel managed to get was incredibly powerful. It was not sweet and intoxicating in the manner that Eleanore's blood had been. There was no erotic note to it that fired his blood and forced the animal in him to awaken with dire, untamable need. It was only sustenance. But it was very old blood, and very potent, and Uriel hoped that if he tried hard enough, if he wanted it badly enough, and if he concentrated deeply enough, he might be able to absorb a bit of the power that came with that blood.

He *wanted* the Adarian's abilities.

Uriel blinked in surprise when he felt a change in the sensation of each pull and swallow. He was doing it. He was absorbing the Adarian's abilities. He briefly wondered why it hadn't happened with Eleanore. Then again, he hadn't wanted to take Eleanore's powers when he'd bitten her. He'd only wanted to give her pleasure or send her away. He assumed now that if he drank from her while attempting to absorb her healing ability at the same time, he would be capable of doing so.

Apparently, you just had to want it badly enough.

Uriel drank more quickly when he realized that one of the powers he was absorbing from the Adarian was a sort of immunity to shard guns. Even as he drank, he noticed the Adarian's body beginning to restore itself.

Uriel took his fill from the guard, then let him drop before he unloaded the remaining blasts from the first shard gun he'd used into the guard's body. That would buy him more time.

Then he moved on to the next unconscious Adarian. He was fairly certain he hadn't managed to kill them, but in the space of a few precious minutes, he had absorbed the supernatural abilities from all three of them, restoring the precious liquid that had been stolen from his own veins and restocking his own store of power.

Now to get the keys.

Uriel picked up the gun that he had discarded earlier and aimed it toward the right rear of the van. He tried to judge where the wheel would be spinning beneath it and aimed. Then he braced himself against the wall of the vehicle and pulled the trigger. As he'd hoped, there was a strange thumping sound as the tire went flat. The van did a jumping-grinding routine and veered to the right. Uriel presumed the driver took his foot off of the gas in order to slow down.

He lowered his weapon. He'd successfully blown the tire. That would at least get them to the side of the road.

When Eleanore reentered the living room, it was empty. She frowned and moved through it and into the dining room, but that was empty as well.

On the otherwise empty table, there was a full and steaming cup of tea. It was honey-chamomile-vanilla, from the smell of it. Her own special brew. She picked it up and turned it around in her hands, allowing its warmth to sink into her fingers and palm. It was light with soy creamer, which she loved, and could also smell. She knew it had been made for her.

She took a sip. It was really good and it warmed her as it went down, chasing away the chill that came with the questions she had been pushing away all night.

Will I ever see him again? Are they going to kill him?

"Are you all right?"

Eleanore lowered the cup of tea in her hands and turned to face Azrael, who stood in the archway that led to a series of hallways and rooms beyond the dining room.

"Yes," Eleanore replied, nodding. "Thank you for the tea."

"Think nothing of it. I had a feeling that after such an encounter, you would need something to calm your nerves. I apologize that we left you alone with him," Azrael said calmly. "One of Jason's abilities is that his form can be molded by his master," he explained as he shoved his hands into the pockets of his black jeans and leaned his left shoulder against the wall. "When Samael's scent was suddenly *not* his scent any longer and Jason was nowhere to be seen"—he smiled and shrugged—"I knew Jason was masquerading as the Fallen One as a diversion. The only reason Sam would have for wanting to disappear for a while is *you*."

Ellie smiled a small smile, took another sip, and swallowed. "You were right." Then she put the cup down. "Where is everyone?"

"In the garage. They're nearly finished building the weapons we'll use against the Adarians."

"Gold grenades?" Eleanore hedged, only slightly joking.

Azrael smiled a dazzling, white, and fang-filled smile that lit up his eyes. "Clever girl," he said. "In fact, yes. Among other things."

Eleanore blushed a little beneath the compliment. She looked at the wall and bit her lip before saying, "Well, I figured that swords probably wouldn't be the way to go against ancient angels using shard guns." She could hear his soft chuckle and couldn't help but look over at him.

He was still smiling at her. "You assumed correctly." He pushed himself up off of the wall and strode gracefully toward her. He was so tall. . . . What was he? Six foot five? Six foot six? And draped in the color of night, with eyes so stark they nearly glowed, even when he wasn't in full vampire mode.

"You were very strong in there. Not many people can stand up to the Fallen One as you did."

Eleanore didn't know what to say to that. He was complimenting her again, but it was embarrassing, too. It meant he knew what had happened between the two of them, despite the fact that Sam had soundproofed the room.

She tried to duck her head, but his finger at her chin prevented the movement. He caught her gaze once more and held it tight. "We'll bring him home alive," he said softly. "I promise."

Eleanore felt a weight lift from somewhere in the vicinity of her chest. With those few spoken words, Azrael had managed to reach in to where she hurt the most and ease the yawning, empty pain.

"I'll hold you to that," she whispered.

"All right, kids." Max appeared in the doorway carrying three black military-style sacks over his shoulder. "It's showtime."

Ellie and Azrael turned to face them as the other archangels appeared behind Max. Both Gabriel and Michael wore double shoulder holsters, outfitted with hand guns, and God only knew what was in the black packs they each carried. They were identical to Max's.

Eleanore could see that on their arms, they wore bracers composed of leather with strips of gold sewn into the outside. Around their necks were what looked like torques also made of gold. They moved into the kitchen and Max handed Azrael the second of the three he carried. Then he turned to Eleanore.

"I have a few things for you as well," he said, handing her a pack of her own. "We'll fill you in on what they are and how to use them once we get to the trade site."

"We're leaving now?"

Max nodded. "I want to get there early so we can see the lay of the land."

Eleanore looked toward the doorway, which was empty, and noticed that Samael and Jason had not come into the dining room. "Where are—"

"They'll meet us there," Max told her. Then he turned to face the dining room and raised his right hand. His palm began to glow and a portal swirled to life within the living room. "It's time to go."

Abraxos, also known as General Kevin Trenton, narrowed his gaze on the back of the van ahead of them. The right rear tire had blown out with no warning and the driver was pulling over. He had communicated as much over his radio.

Kevin gave his consent and the driver followed his order, but the general didn't like it. It made no sense. The tires on his vehicles were all new. He and his men were very good at tending to every little detail in every operation. The tire should not have blown. Either something in the road had caused it to give—or there was a problem with their prisoner.

"Pull in behind him," he ordered to his own driver. Then he turned to the men in the back. "Keep your weapons trained on the van. Shoot anything that comes out of the back without warning." They nodded their assent and pulled their weapons.

Kevin waited until the SUV came to a complete stop behind the van. Then he pulled his own shard gun from the holster on his thigh and got out of the vehicle. He waited for the driver of the van ahead of them to get out and come around to the back, but after several long seconds, the driver's door still hadn't opened.

And then, suddenly, the van's engine was revving. Kevin's eyes widened when the back right wheel shimmered, rippled, and then exploded in a quick burst of light. He shielded his eyes with his arm and, when the light subsided, he saw that the tire was repaired—whole—as if it had never blown.

"Code red!" he yelled into the receiver of his radio and broke into a run toward the van. However, the van squealed forward, its tires leaving black smoke in their wake before he could get to it.

Kevin shot back to his own vehicle and issued the command to follow. In a few seconds, the van had made it off of the median and back into traffic and Kevin's black SUV was speeding up behind it.

Uriel knew that he could use one of the van's doors to open a portal into the mansion now if he wanted to. The strange metal cuffs were off and he could feel the swell of his power, plus the powers of the men he had drained, rising inside of him. However, opening a portal in the middle of the night and in the middle of an interstate was dangerous enough; humans could get hurt. Doing so with a team of Adarians on your tail was even worse. For all he knew, they would follow him right through the portal and into the mansion.

As both a vampire and an archangel, he could fly out of there, but he was betting at least some of the Adarians could fly as well. And they outnumbered him almost ten to one.

So Uriel did the only thing he could think of. He knocked out the driver, got behind the wheel, and started driving.

He knew the general and his men would follow him. With any luck, he could pull the evil convoy away from the interstate and to some place more private. What he would do then, he had no clue, but he was working on it.

On either side of the highway, gigantic metal windmills split the sky, turning more quickly than normal beneath the building storm. The Dallas area was full of wind turbines, the tops of which periodically lit up in synchronized red lighting to keep low-flying planes away from them. He shot them a glance and then turned back to the road.

And then it hit him.

He looked back at the turbines. Some were spinning faster than others. In fact, they seemed to speeding up alongside him—as if he were drawing nearer to the heart of whatever storm was building in this area.

With a newly determined grip on his steering wheel, Uriel took the van in that direction. A mile and a half down the road was a turnoff. He veered right, glancing in the rearview mirror. On cue, the black SUV behind him veered right as well, as did another SUV behind that one.

Uriel glared at the reflection. He was impressed that they hadn't shot at him yet. He guessed they didn't want to chance killing him. Kevin Trenton wanted his prisoner alive; Uriel was the man's only bargaining chip and he really wanted to get his hands on Eleanore. The thought forced Uriel's fangs to erupt in his mouth, but this time he was hungry for one man's blood in particular.

No matter, Uriel thought grimly. It will all be over soon, one way or another.

He knew where he was going now. He knew what waited at the end of this trail of ever-more-quickly spinning windmills. The storm that grew and darkened ahead of him was no normal storm. It was born of the same woman whose magical rain had healed his wounds. And it was that woman that he drove steadily toward now.

Uriel hated the fact that he was leading the Adarians straight toward her. But he knew she wouldn't be alone. At the very least, she would be with Samael. With any luck, Uriel's brothers would be there as well.

And considering that there were nine Adarians and a handful of armed humans behind him who would do anything to take him down, he liked those odds much better than the ones he was up against right now.

"You're a stormy woman, Granger," Gabriel muttered beneath his breath as he looked up overhead and into the nucleus of the whirling, building tempest around them. "Can you no' control that?" he asked, looking back down to meet her eyes.

She shook her head. "Sorry."

All around them, giants of metal groaned their anger

at being awakened so roughly. For as far as the eye could see in every direction, tall white bladed structures dotted the landscape, their tallest reaches flashing a slow warning red every few seconds. From a distance, they were rather beautiful—slowly spinning monuments to the ironic fact that Texas was number one in the country for renewable resource advances.

Up close, however, each turbine was ominous in its overwhelming size. The bases of the structures were more than fifty feet in diameter and, from what Eleanore had learned while living in Texas, the turbines stood more than two hundred and fifty feet high.

They had always frightened Eleanore. Their blades alone were longer than semitrucks and had to be transported individually over the interstates, draped in protective tarps until they reached their destinations and could be assembled. They spun so slowly downward, so portentously, that they could be viewed as nothing but threatening from someone as small as a human standing beneath them.

Now they sliced through the air as the dark sky turned yellow-gray with anvil clouds and lightning was caught by the lightning rods positioned throughout the fields.

"How much longer do we have?" Michael asked Max, shouting a little to be heard over the mounting wind.

"Ten minutes, give or take!" Max replied. "Now gather around!" He motioned for the others to pull in close and they did so. There was still no sign of Samael or any of the multitude of minions who worked for him. Eleanore wondered whether they would really show up as he'd said they would.

"Okay, here's what we know," Max began. "The Adarians can become invisible, some can fly, and according to Lilith, they have a host of abilities they can use long-range." He paused for a moment, glanced at his watch, and then continued. "For that reason, they're as dangerous at a distance as they are up close, if not more so. We need to get inside their personal space and take them down hard," Max said.

It was surreal for Eleanore to watch the man give such instruction. She was used to seeing him in glasses and a three-piece suit. Now, however, he was dressed in fatigue pants and a tight T-shirt and she could see he was actually quite built. He vaguely reminded her of *Stargate*'s Daniel Jackson, taken out of the library and placed on the battlefield. He didn't sound like a celebrity agent now either; he sounded like a drill sergeant, but without all the ridiculous swearing.

Max turned to her then and pinned her with a hard look. "Ellie, I need you to stay hidden. The moment they get their hands on you, our fight is over."

Alarm shot through her. "But what about Uriel?" she asked.

"Leave him to us," Michael replied firmly.

Lightning struck a rod somewhere very close and they all ducked a little, out of reflex, and shuddered under the booming thunder.

Max straightened and put a hand on Eleanore's shoulder. "Try to control your fears, Eleanore," he said. "You're not without recourse. In that bag, you will find grenades, an automatic pistol, gold dust blow guns, and three separate pouches of gold dust itself." He nodded. "That's why it's so heavy."

Eleanore nodded her understanding, though her stomach was officially tied in knots now. She was terrified that if Kevin didn't see her right away, he would just kill Uriel.

Remember my promise, little one.

Eleanore glanced up at Azrael, catching his gold gaze. He had promised that they would bring Uriel back alive. They stared at each other for a moment and then she nodded. Somehow, she believed him.

"We've come up with one final safeguard for you, Ellie, though we hope you won't need it," Max said then.

"What is it?"

"Armor. More or less."

Max pulled a small vial of what looked like shimmering lotion from his pack. "Put this on your arms and neck. It's embedded with gold dust and should act as a repellant of sorts should any of them get near enough to touch you."

Eleanore took the vial and shrugged off her hoodie. She popped the top off of the small container and wasted no time in pouring the solution into her hands and then spreading it over her exposed flesh.

"Lookin' good, lass," Gabriel said. He winked at her. She blushed and looked back down at her skin to see that it shimmered a little with a glow that reminded her of some sort of exotic tan. It was actually rather attractive. She sort of wished she had a few bottles of it in her apartment. Once she was done, she handed the vial back to Max and pulled her hoodie back on. The rain was beginning to fall now and it was cold.

Max turned to Michael and was about to say something when the sound of screeching tires reached their ears over the distant crack of thunder and the ever-more-steadily falling rain.

They turned to see headlights in the distance, three pairs.

"Crap," Michael muttered. Time had officially run out.

CHAPTER TWENTY-FOUR

The archangels had been around for a long time, and Eleanore was certain that when the bullets had begun flying several seconds ago, they had all known, instinctively, what to do. But Ellie was new to the trauma of being shot at, and other than her brush with terror at the gala, she had no experience on battlefields.

When a machine gun that she could only assume was like the shard guns that Lilith had told them about began kicking strange stonelike holes into the dirt in front of them, she'd screamed. It was only natural. There hadn't been time for her to hide before the attack was upon them. Everyone was moving and the world was a flashing chaos of gunpowder sparks and lightning and shouts and thunder.

Someone put a firm hand over her head and shoved her to the ground, rolling his body on top of hers.

He barked some kind of statement to someone else, though the sound of it was lost to her ears when lightning slammed into a turbine nearby, cracking her eardrums with a roar of thunder that was closely followed by the strange and ominous groaning of grinding metal. She tried to roll over and look up, but someone heavy was on top of her. And then that person lifted her by the wrist in a firm, viselike grip.

She was whirled around and quite unexpectedly, she was airborne. She tried to scream, but the sound lodged itself in her throat. She was only in the air a few short seconds before she once more hit the ground and rolled.

Again a body was on top of her, and the sound of bullets *thunk*ing against metal forced her eyes shut tight. The body atop her moved a second time and she was pulled up along with it. Then Ellie was shoved toward a white, windowless van. She stumbled and was caught. She was steadied and righted again, rushed almost violently along until, finally, she was falling to the prickly, gravelly ground behind the stalled vehicle. Peripherally, she noticed that it had four flat tires.

"Ellie!" Someone hissed the word by her ear, lifting her again until she was sitting. He grasped her head in his hands so that she looked into his eyes.

They were green.

"Ellie, are you all right?"

Eleanore stared up at him, not sure she should believe what she was seeing. "Uriel?"

"It's me, Ellie." He smiled, flashing those fangs of his, and brushed his thumb across her cheekbone. "I'm getting you out of here right now."

He removed his hand from her face and stood, taking her by her upper arm. Reflex kicked in and she grabbed his hand. "We can't leave!" She must have been insane to think what she was thinking, but there it was. She couldn't leave in the middle of the battle; she had to stay to heal those who were wounded. Max and Uriel's brothers were out there. She had to help.

But in a move so utterly unexpected it made Eleanore gasp, Uriel yanked his hand out of her grip and pain flashed in his green eyes.

Ellie looked down at his hand to find it burned dark red and blistered with fingerprint bands around its edges.

. . . gold is caustic to them. . . .

"Oh my God . . ." she whispered, remembering the gold-flecked lotion she had put on.

"Sorry, sweetheart," Uriel hissed, drawing her attention back to his face. He reached out like lightning and grabbed her upper arm where she was covered by her hoodie. "God isn't here." His gaze hardened, going from green to blue in the space of a single heartbeat.

Eleanore recognized those eyes. Even after ten years, she knew Kevin Trenton's handsome gaze as if she had peered into it only yesterday. It wasn't Uriel holding her at all. Lilith had said the Adarians could shape-shift. This was Kevin.

Rain was starting to fall now, and it made Uriel's grip on his enemy slippery. Through the contact he had on the archangel's throat, he felt surges of great power, yet untapped.

Uriel had fed three times that night and Eleanore's rain had healed him. Yet he wasn't certain he could survive the general's attack, much less get himself and Eleanore to safety.

He had hoped to have more time to plan an escape. But as soon as he had begun driving that van across the empty valley of space between him and his brothers, the gunfire started up. It wasn't long before he figured out that the first archangels were trying to prevent his progress to the other side. Within the space of seconds, he lost all four tires and, ultimately, control of the vehicle.

He'd slammed on the breaks and thrown open the door to drop to the ground beneath as bullets fanned across the makeshift battlefield. A shard gun blast hit him in the leg, began solidifying his calf muscle and knee, and then the Adarian's blood he'd taken had kicked in and reversed the process.

He managed to get his feet beneath him once more and start running toward his brothers when he was knocked to the ground and bowled over by one of the general's men. The archangel who tackled him was one of the men who had tortured him in his holding cell. He recognized him immediately, not only by the man's features, but by the fact that the enemy archangel instantly began forcing horrid mental images into Uriel's mind.

Uriel struck out with vampiric speed and literally ripped out the man's throat. The man's esophagus popped open with a whooshing sound and blood sprayed out with exuberant, tremendous pressure, nearly coating Uriel. He managed to duck and roll, avoiding the gory mess, and when he looked over his shoulder, it was to find the archangel toppling forward onto his face in the blood-muddied dirt. The Adarian did not move and no longer breathed. He simply laid there and bled to death.

They can *be killed by other archangels,* Uriel realized as he listened to the man's heart falter and stop.

Another shard bullet found Uriel's shoulder and he grimaced with the spreading rock-hard pain. But it, too, subsided and receded once more, leaving his flesh normal in the end. He shot to his feet and started toward his brothers a second time, using vampire reflexes to half disperse into green dust and dodge beneath bullets that flew in both directions.

Up ahead, Uriel could make out the fire-emblazoned outline of two tall, broad-shouldered men. He heard his name shouted on the wind. In another few seconds and two shard-blast impacts later, he'd made it across the space between them and was being shoved to the ground behind a turbine foundation beside Gabriel.

"Where is Eleanore?" Gabriel shouted, the expression on his face a stark mixture of confusion, fear, fury, and pain.

Uriel's heart shot into his throat and stayed there. He wasted no time in delving into his brother's mind, and Gabriel willingly let him in. It was within a few heartbeats that Uriel learned his brothers thought they had already greeted him, albeit quickly and amidst unfriendly fire, and had seen him take Eleanore out of the fight. Apparently, Uriel—or some being they thought was Uriel—had grabbed her, shouted a brief good-bye to the others, and taken to the skies. Gabriel was utterly mystified that Uriel was now back, and without Eleanore.

Kevin Trenton, Uriel thought coldly. The archangel had the ability to change form.

Once more, he was up and moving. This time, he shot up into the sky and evaporated into green mist, effectively avoiding any and all gunfire. It was more difficult to maneuver like this, especially in the storm that Eleanore had wreaked around them. The wind buffeted his particles, separating them until it took almost too much concentration to keep himself together. And it was harder to see. It was a sight of the mind and not of the eyes—everything was an afterimage, a negative of sorts, and it was like viewing impressions instead of three-dimensional beings.

Still, he was determined.

He found her below, beside the white van, standing with Trenton, who was disguised as Uriel himself. He homed in on her as if she were a lifeline and he was drowning.

He landed on the opposite side of the van and came around the corner to find her and Trenton face-to-face. The general was holding her fast, spearing her with an evil blue gaze.

"God isn't here," he said.

"No," Uriel hissed, drawing their attention. "But I am."

Kevin bared his teeth in anger, tossed Ellie unceremoniously aside, and braced himself as Uriel charged straight toward him. Lightning once more slammed into something nearby and actual sparks of electric fire fanned out into the night sky above them as he and Kevin met in combat.

Uriel could hear the horrid sound of bending, creaking metal and knew that the last bolt of lightning had done serious damage to a nearby turbine. But it was a passing realization and took a backseat to the battle at hand. He and Kevin now fought in a way that he had never fought another being. This was more than vengeance, which, in and of itself, was deserved. This was more than jealousy, self-preservation, and love. This was hatred, at its finest, at its core, and it fueled his body beyond all sense of pain, sound, or vision.

Trenton's face morphed before Uriel's eyes, taking on his own familiar, handsome, and detested features.

"You can't win, Uriel," Kevin growled at him through straight, white, gritted teeth. "You're outnumbered." He grimaced and grunted as Uriel slammed them both into the cement platform of a turbine. "Two of your brothers have already fallen. The third will follow in short order." It must have been difficult for him to speak through the limited air supply Uriel's tight grip around his neck afforded him. But he managed, perhaps fueled by the same kind of hatred that fed his attacker.

Uriel knew what Trenton was doing. Whether he was telling the truth or not, his words were a distraction, a warning meant to slow Uriel down, to give him pause, and make him unsure.

Beside them, a blade from the damaged turbine fell and its impact shook the ground and sent dirt flying into the air. Uriel paid it no heed. Nothing could have deterred him from what he was going to do next.

Heal this, Uriel spat at Kevin through a forced mental connection. Then he reared back, intent on ripping out the man's throat as he had the other soldier. But before his arm descended to its mark, it was grabbed by a pair of strong hands and jerked roughly back, forcing Uriel to lose his grip and topple.

It was another face he did not recognize that loomed into view on his left, and it was a power he had not yet encountered that slammed into him like an invisible brick wall, picking him up and sending him with crushing force into the stem of the same turbine that had lost its blade. Reinforced steel and concrete groaned under the impact, bending in on the crumpled indentation where Uriel's body had impacted it. Up above, the two remaining windmill blades tilted on their axis and began to scrape against their stem, now knocked out of their proper alignment. It sent sparks of heat shooting into the night and wrenched a shriek of scraping metal that sounded like a train wreck.

The turbine's going to fall, thought Uriel, as the soldier who had attacked him hit him with his wall of solid force once again. This time, the invisible field slammed Uriel farther into the turbine trunk, crushing him with immense, merciless force. Behind him, the turbine cried out its death throes and buckled. Uriel felt it give, curling over him like a massive, wilting metal flower.

He knew that he was trapped. He tried to evaporate into green mist, but failed. He tried to use telekinesis to make the giant windmill straight, and again he failed. It was as if the very force field that held him in place also trapped his powers within his body. Like a binding bracelet, but bigger. And invisible. And controlled by the enemy.

He could go nowhere as the metal giant above him bent in on itself and began its ominous, otherworldly descent to the ground below.

When Eleanore looked up from the ground beside the white van to find two Uriels fighting in hand-to-hand combat, a new kind of terror gripped her. She wanted to help the real Uriel, but was powerless to do so.

And then the turbine above them that had been hit with lightning stopped spinning altogether and began to groan in an entirely new and evil way.

She had looked up once more, her wide-eyed attention caught on the blade as it bucked, dipped a little, and began ripping from its casement where it was bolted onto the stem of the windmill, two hundred and fifty feet up. The sound had been horrible. It was what she would have imagined a plane crash to sound like, the death throes of four engines and three hundred people.

She had spun in place and begun running just as the

blade tore free of its bolts and soldering and began its strange, slow descent to the earth below. She'd known it was going to crush everything beneath it. She needed to get out of the way, but it was like she was treading water, moving in slow, sluggish motion through a dense atmosphere.

Behind her, the turbine blade hit and shook the ground. There was more terrible noise, the rending of more metal and the sound of something being crushed, and then lightning struck in several places all around her and Eleanore dove to the ground and covered her head.

Now her ears were ringing, her chest hurt, and there was no sense in the world any longer. Somewhere in her mad dash from here to there and back again, she had dropped her backpack filled with gold weapons. She literally had no idea what to do or where to go.

And then Eleanore felt arms slide around her, gripping her with an oddly gentle security, despite their strength. She uncovered her head and rolled over as she was lifted once more off of the ground.

Samael's storm-gray eyes were not their normal charcoal as they peered through her. They were platinum and glowing starkly in the handsome planes of his angelic face. Behind him, the darkness moved. Eleanore's gaze traveled to the shadows beyond Samael. It took but a few short seconds for her vision to adjust, and when it did, she found herself staring at a scene straight out of a Dantesque version of the apocalypse.

Rows of black-armored riders sat astride pitch-black stallions that pawed at the earth, causing sparks to fly where their hooves scraped the ground. There were dozens of them. A horse snorted and fire shot from its nostrils. Another whinnied, and fire erupted from behind its muzzled lips.

Long swords sheathed in black leather hung from the waists and backs of the horses' riders. From the gaps in their black-metaled masks, their red glowing eyes peered across the darkness and pinned Eleanore to the spot.

They're not human, she thought numbly. *Monsters. Demons. Dark Riders . . .*

"It's over, Ellie," Samael told her. She turned her attention back to him and knew that he commanded the strange, dark army behind him. They waited for him to issue orders. "Uriel and the others have as good as lost," he went on, his glowing gaze unforgiving. "Come with me. I'll take you out of here."

Eleanore shook her head.

The horses behind Samael pawed impatiently at the ground. The air felt heavy and the sounds of thunder and gunfire and groaning metal were drowned out by a rushing in her ears.

"Yes," Samael quietly insisted.

Again, she shook her head. Her heart felt like lead in her chest. Her stomach felt empty and bottomless and she was fairly sure that her soul had slipped through the spreading hole inside of her that led, undoubtedly, to Hell.

"N-no," she muttered, unable to think of anything else to say. She could not imagine Uriel dying. She could not imagine his brothers losing. She simply could not picture it—or, perhaps, she simply did not want to.

But Samael's expression told her everything she needed to know. It was both triumphant and repentant, pitiful and victorious. There was a firm resolve to the set of his lips, and it was matched by the unrelenting grip he had on her arms.

"But those riders . . ." Eleanore whispered, "you can use them—make them help!"

Samael shook his head. He did so, once, and a very real panic blossomed within her. In that moment, she saw the remainder of her life spread out before her. She walked the halls of Samael's infinite mansion alone but for the brief moments that she whored herself out to the Fallen One and his selfish desires. His queen. His concubine.

She saw a grave marker in the mists, dateless and barren, but for a single, ancient name. And she knew that she would never speak that name in earnest or in lust or in exasperation again.

Because he was going to die.

Unless . . .

"No." Eleanore spoke the word again, this time with conviction. "No!"

She jerked herself out of Samael's grip and lightning split the sky above them, so close that her hair stood on end and the air around her crackled menacingly. Ellie gasped and ducked, and on impulse, she jammed her hands into the pockets of her hoodie. Her fingers brushed cold, smooth gold.

Without thinking, she lunged forward, thrusting her body against Samael's. He wasn't expecting the strange move; his instinctive response was to wrap his arms tightly around her. Eleanore jerked the bracelet out of her pocket, turned in his embrace, and then slammed the bracelet down onto his left wrist. The gold band shimmered, flashed, and resolidified, now locked securely into place.

Samael pulled back and gazed down at the bracelet. Eleanore watched him, breathless, waiting to see what he would do. She expected him to strike her, and she tensed for the attack.

But Samael surprised her. Instead, he turned his arm over to see the gold glint beneath the flashes of lightning overhead. And then he smiled. It was a rueful and somewhat secret smile.

Eleanore had no idea what it meant—and she didn't care. She wasted no further time. "Save them, Samael, or I will never remove that bracelet and you'll be stuck without your powers forever," she hissed at him. It wasn't an empty threat. If Uriel died, she wouldn't care what happened to Samael. She wouldn't care what happened to anyone.

Samael glanced back up at her and the platinum fire in his gaze died down. "You continue to make an impression on me, Eleanore," he told her. Amazingly, she heard his voice once again over the cacophony of the battle. "However, I wonder what you expect me to do in Uriel's favor if I can't use my powers?"

"You have an army of—I don't know—Dark Riders behind you!" she yelled angrily. "Tell them to attack!"

Samael stared at her long and hard. He seemed to ponder something and Eleanore felt time being pulled from her grasp. Her temper flared. *"Now, damn it!"* she yelled again.

At that, Samael's smile broadened, stretching into a white grin. He lowered his arm, and with slow and casual grace, he turned to face the riders behind him.

I'm going to die, Uriel thought.

It was not the first time that week he had thought such a thing. But this time it was with the added unpleasantness of a bitter and tangy fear on his tongue. He knew that this particular death was sure to hurt. It was certain to be slow. He would be crushed to death—could a vampire even die in such a manner? Or would he lie there, dying and awakening and dying and awakening, over and over again in an eternal round of agony?

The force field was unrelenting; the archangel who pinned him stared him down through a haze of loathing. Uriel had no hope of dislodging it, and the turbine was bending low over him, shoving him slowly, relentlessly into the concrete platform on which he stood. He closed his eyes against his grim fate, desperately wanting Eleanore and her closeness and her healing touch more than he had ever desired anything in his life.

For the third time in the last several seconds, Uriel attempted to disintegrate into mist, but without success. The archangel soldier's power held Uriel's form together, forcing him to remain in his solid, pain-filled state.

Uriel gritted his teeth as his muscles screamed.

And then, suddenly, the turbine halted in its downward progress, groaning to a begrudging stop even as Uriel's legs began to buckle.

Uriel opened his eyes and gazed out into the night across from him to find a scene very changed from the one he had looked upon only seconds earlier. The archangel soldier who locked him into place against the turbine was under attack himself. Impossible though it was, Uriel watched as a black-armored rider on an equally pitch-black mount swung a sword that blazed with blue-black fire. The soldier ducked, rolled, and came to his feet, sparing a glance at Uriel and attempting to keep the force field up long enough for it to do its job and kill him.

But even as he did so, Uriel could feel the barrier slipping. And, at the same time, the turbine was no longer falling.

Uriel scanned the area and his eyes widened. Eleanore rested on her knees several yards away, her head bent, her eyes closed. She was obviously concentrating very hard. And her entire body was glowing with a strange and beautiful white light.

She couldn't take much more. She felt like the *Enterprise* after a horrible fight with the Romulans, every ounce of her energy and fuel and strength used up and shot out at some clever, dangerous enemy. And yet she pushed on. As she had on the street when those cars had crashed several days ago, she pulled strength from her own body now. It was sapped from her muscles, from her bone marrow, from her blood.

With each passing heartbeat, she felt a little sicker and a little closer to death. But the alternative was too horrible to allow. She could not live while Uriel was crushed beneath all of that metal—*crushed*. Like being swallowed by an ocean or steamrollered on concrete or flattened by a freight train.

No.

As soon as Samael had left her company to command his bizarre and wholly evil-looking troops in a rally against the Adarians, Eleanore had noticed the sound of a turbine falling. She'd homed in on the sound, running to follow it back to the turbine beside the white van that had already lost its blade.

The massive windmill was bending in on itself, crushing an immobile form beneath it.

Uriel.

Eleanore hadn't given it thought. She'd simply rushed toward him and began using her powers once more in an attempt to stop the turbine from falling any farther onto Uriel's trapped form.

And now, here she was. *Dying*. She was sure of it. The moment had long passed when she had taken and used the last of her stores of energy and converted it to telekinesis. There was nothing left inside of her from which to pull.

She felt light as air where she knelt there on the ground. She felt numb and weightless and empty, like a helium balloon. A part of her wondered whether she would begin to float away on the wind.

But the rest of her was still focused on that turbine—and the man trapped beneath it.

Her love. Her life. The other half of her soul.

It was as she stooped there on the wet ground that she realized there was no other man in the world who could make her feel as he did. And no other man in the world cared for her as he did. He had recognized her on sight. He rescued her from the crowd on the streets. He took her flying over the Pacific Ocean.

He would die for her. She knew that.

And in the end, Eleanore simply couldn't live knowing that she might have to go on without him. If he would die for her, then she would die for him as well.

So be it.

With no understanding of where the strength came from, Eleanore halted the turbine in its downward arc. She felt a new commotion stirring around her, but the light and numb body she now inhabited barely cared. She cared only that she was saving Uriel. Nothing else mattered.

Wings, Uriel thought in wonder. *My God, they're wings. . . .*

Behind Eleanore's glowing body, dual bluish whitish shapes had begun to take shimmering form. They were faint and transparent, reminiscent of the glowing after-image from a camera's flash. Or ghosts.

But as Uriel braced his legs beneath him and tried once more to evaporate into the mist that could finally escape, he watched Eleanore's blue shadows change. They solidified and darkened, taking on a midnight cast that reflected the flashes of lightning above in the same manner as her raven hair until, at last, the archess bore midnight-black, gossamer wings, folded neatly at her back. They were so large, Uriel could imagine them stretching to at least eight feet in either direction when extended.

The archangel soldier who had trapped him was suddenly struck broadside by his attacker's sword and the turbine pulled angrily upward, allowing Uriel to break free. The mighty metal flower screamed its anger at not being allowed to die and he knew it was Ellie saving him. Eleanore Granger, the archess who now glowed strangely in the lightning-scarred night and bore the very real, very physical wings of a mythical archangel.

Ellie.

Once Uriel was away from the cement platform of the windmill, he ran toward his soul mate, knowing only that he had to hold her—that he had to feel her in his arms, real and unimagined and precious.

He made it to her in the space of a millisecond and knelt, bending before her on reverent knees. But when he reached out to pull her to him, his arms coasted through her form as if she were not there.

He blinked, refusing to accept what had just happened, and tried again. And again, he moved through her.

"Ellie," he choked, trying to curl his finger beneath

her chin. There was nothing there for him to touch. She was visible, but intangible, and when she lifted her head to look into his eyes, he found himself drowning in pools of inhumanly glowing indigo blue.

You're safe, she thought into his head.

He fought back the madness that clawed at his brain and the agony that crept up on his heart.

Yes, he told her firmly. *You saved me.*

I tried. She smiled. But it was an exhausted smile, wan and faint and was gone nearly as quickly as it had come.

Uriel knew despair then, and he realized that he'd never known it before.

Don't leave me, he told her. He begged her. *I love you, Ellie. Please don't leave me.*

Eleanore was as pale as the moon. Her lips parted and Uriel waited on what he swore would be one of his last breaths, to hear her words.

At once, two voices reached him—one in his mind, the other out loud. Together, they softly said, "I love you, too."

CHAPTER TWENTY-FIVE

Uriel's mind rebelled; his heart cleaved itself in two. *No.*

"No, Ellie—"

When he reached out to attempt for the third time to pull her into his arms with the painfully numbing desperation he felt, it was to find that not only was she formless and ethereal—so was he.

His fingers trailed through her essence, leaving streams of their own molecular signature as they did so. He was dissolving, it seemed, breaking into fragments of what he was and dissipating into the glowing soup of shimmering substance that was once Ellie Granger.

He glanced up to capture her blue glowing gaze. Her look of relief was gone and had been replaced with one of confusion.

"What's happening?" she asked, glancing down at his quickly evaporating body. He could sense her distress. She had just saved him, and now he was disappearing before her eyes.

It was unsettling to him as well but not as much as, perhaps, it should have been. Because something inside his head seemed to . . . *remember*. It clicked into place.

As their world melted around them and the rest of the universe began to seem more and more unreal, Uriel realized that he wasn't afraid of this change. It was *supposed* to happen.

He'd been waiting for it for two thousand years.

"Uriel?" It was that echoing whisper again. Hollow and resonant.

"Close your eyes, Eleanore," he told her softly.

She frowned at him. But he smiled a reassuring smile and nodded. "Trust me," he said. "Close your eyes."

She did so. Her ethereal lids barely muted the blue-white glow of her otherworldly eyes.

Then he closed his as well and waited. *And waited . . .*

"Now open them, Ellie."

In the muted gray-white darkness that enveloped her, Eleanore realized that the world around them had gone silent. It was the kind of silence that pervaded on a snowy morning, muffled and absolute. She knew she was no longer on a battlefield in Texas amid fallen giants and petrified angels. There was no storm. No nothing.

If she hadn't just heard Uriel's voice, she would have thought herself well and truly alone. But he told her to open her eyes and she opened them to stare across at the man she loved.

He was solid once more and at his back was a pair of wings unlike any she'd ever imagined. They were black, but tinted green, the way a raven's feathers were tinted blue. They were enormous. Beautiful. Stunning.

As was his smile.

"Uriel?" she said, more to test her voice and the sound it made than anything else.

He laughed softly. "Are you okay?" he asked, at last cupping her cheek with his hand. His now solid touch was warm. It filled her with instant peace and reassurance.

"I'm fine." She smiled. "Nice wings."

"Yours aren't so bad either," he said, his emerald eyes sparkling. They matched his wings, she noticed. Perfectly. "Where are we?"

"Nowhere," he said. Then he glanced to either side of him, at the wall of foggy white that encompassed them.

"Not yet anyway." He looked back at her. "I think we're being given a choice."

"What kind of choice?"

"To leave Earth—or to stay."

Eleanore considered that for a moment. "You mean, we can"—she hesitated, as if saying it out loud was somehow different from experiencing it—"we can *die* and go wherever it is people go when they die . . . or we can go back to the way we were before?"

Uriel nodded, brushing his thumb against her cheekbone. The gesture was so tender, she closed her eyes again just to enjoy it.

"What about our wings?" she asked, her eyes still shut. She wasn't sure why she'd asked such a thing. There was no filter between her brain and her tongue just then, and she *liked* the wings. They felt natural.

He laughed again, a soft, easy sound. "I honestly have no idea. I kind of like them too."

She opened her eyes when she felt his fingers brush along the tops of her blue-black feathers. If someone had asked her to explain what it felt like to have a person touch her wings, she wouldn't be able to. It was like asking a mermaid to describe her legs.

But it felt good. She shivered.

"Yours match your eyes," he added.

She peered up at him and watched his pupils expand, eating the green of his irises. There was that telltale hunger again, that desire that never seemed to be far from his gaze when it came to her.

She swallowed, sensing his need and feeling it build within her own body as well.

"I have a family," she said. "I can't leave my parents. And knowing what we know now, we can help your brothers and their archesses if we stay—"

She broke off when he leaned in, his wings expanding, enveloping her in his tall, broad darkness. His lips slanted over hers with blatant yearning, pressing and opening and demanding. He stole her breath and, with it, every thought she had thought she possessed.

He pulled away, quickly and but for a moment. Long enough to mutter a few ground-out words between clenched teeth.

"We'll stay," he said.

As Ellie began to nod her assent, he kissed her again, and she felt the world change around them once more. It dissolved, shifted, and resolidified, and somewhere in between his subjugation and her surrender, sound crept in at the edges and a wet, muddy chill settled in beneath her knees.

At long last, Uriel broke the kiss.

"I thought for sure you weren't coming back," came a familiar voice.

Uriel hesitantly pulled his gaze from his archess and turned to see Michael and his brothers standing a few feet away. Behind them rested a tangled metal mass of fallen turbines and steel and concrete debris. The storm around them was lifting and drifting away.

The battle was over, apparently. And his brothers were still standing.

"We won?" he asked.

Max stepped up on the other side. "For now," he said. But then he smiled and his gaze drifted from Uriel to Eleanore.

"Nice wings," he said.

"I'll say," Gabriel added. "How're you plannin' on hidin' those?"

But no one had a chance to answer him before Azrael spoke up. "Welcome back, Ellie," he said softly. The corners of his mouth were turned up in a welcoming and warm smile. *Are you sure this is the choice you wish to make?*

Eleanore smiled back at him. *Yes,* she thought. *It is.*

Then it's good to have you with us. There was both relief and admiration in his mental tone.

She knew that it wasn't going to be easy, this life she had chosen. She was still an archess and she possessed the ability to heal. The Adarians would always be looking for her. And for the other archesses, she imagined.

And then there would be Samael to contend with.

But at least she knew what she had here. She had the archangels and Max. She had the mansion. And she had her parents. Together, they would be strong. They would figure things out.

With Uriel, she thought with a smile.

She turned away from Azrael and was once more caught up in her lover's covetous gaze.

Oh yeah, she thought. *We'll figure it out.*

EPILOGUE

It was several days before the mess of the gala and its aftermath had been cleaned up and order had been restored. The battle in the turbine field had ended when Samael's hellish army had overrun what was left of the Adarians. Though Michael, Gabriel, and Azrael had destroyed at least half of the ancient archangels with their gold weapons, quite a few still remained by the time shard guns had caused Gabe and Michael to fall.

However, nothing seemed to hurt Samael's Dark Riders. It was only a matter of time before the general and his men, including those who had been unconscious or seemingly dead at the time, disappeared, one wounded soldier after another, all of them using some kind of recall device to pull themselves off of the battleground.

In the wake of the fight, Max got busy re-erecting monstrous metal monuments, erasing memories, locating and destroying documentation, and perhaps most difficult of all, helping Eleanore smooth things over with her parents.

She had decided to come clean with them. When they heard what happened at the gala and saw footage of her racing into the building with the famous actor Christopher Daniels, they had become understandably terrified.

So Eleanore and Max were quick to locate them,

get them alone, and reassure them to the best of their ability.

They took it well, considering. Her mother cried for only a few hours and her father had to have only a few drinks. In the end, they spent the better part of three days talking with the archangels, learning about the mansion and the archesses, and coming to grips with the unreality of it all.

She was proud of them. She also supposed that it was the fact that they'd been aware of supernatural things for some time that allowed them to more easily accept this new information. They had raised a daughter who could manipulate the weather, heal wounds, and will SpaghettiOs into the shopping cart when Mom strictly forbade it.

So this was just one more impossibility for them that was not so impossible after all.

For Eleanore's part, and for Uriel's, they had learned to manipulate the structure of their wings. It was as easy as willing them away and then willing them back. The best part about them, of course, from Ellie's viewpoint, was that they were functional.

She could fly.

She and Uriel took their first flight together in the middle of the night, out in the vast expanse of the Nevada desert.

At one point, Eleanore landed on a cliff overlooking a canyon and sat down to simply watch Uriel fly. He was the very essence of grace. His wings were enormous, spanning ten feet in either direction, their feathers thick and dark, shimmering deep emerald like his eyes. There was just something unmentionably sexy about a man in tight, worn blue jeans, a tight black T-shirt that outlined his muscles, and a pair of massive wings at his back.

He's mine, she'd thought. *All mine. My angel, Uriel.*

Now, as Ellie sat back on the couch, alone in the mansion for the first time in nearly a week, she sighed. It was one of contentment. This was the first real peace she had known in her entire life. She understood who and what she was, and she knew where she belonged. There was definitely something to be said for certainty.

The fire in the hearth crackled and popped with a comforting welcomeness as Ellie opened her laptop, clicked on her browser, and established the familiar connection.

> E: So, guess what.
>
> A: Hey again! Long time no type! What am I guessing at here?
>
> E: Remember that business with Christopher Daniels?
>
> A: How could I forget?
>
> E: I'm marrying him.

There was a long pause where nothing happened on the screen. And then, suddenly, Angel's reply shot to life on the next line.

> A: You're shitting me, right?
>
> E: Never, A. I'm surprised you don't already know—it's all over the tabloids.

Eleanore laughed and shook her head as she typed this. It was true. Instead of the stiff downturn in popularity Uriel had predicted would arise from him hooking up with someone, the public had decided to love the new couple. They'd taken to calling them "Chrisellie."

> A: Holy crap. I need to get out more. Where are you doing this? When?!?
>
> E: Private ceremony

Eleanore was purposefully vague. She and Uriel were going to exchange vows behind closed doors. They didn't want the Adarians showing up and ruining the ceremony.

>   E: But I wish you could be here.

There was another pause, this one shorter than the last.

>   A: I can.

>   E: Come again?

>   A: Lol. Just have someone open a chat box during the ceremony. I'll be there in spirit. ;)

Eleanore laughed at the idea. And then she straightened. Actually, that was entirely doable.

>   E: You've got a deal.

>   A: Woohoo! I'll be there with bells on.

>   E: ☺

>   A: Hasta, chica. I have to head out. Congratulations and don't let the bedmates bite. xoxo mwah!

With a smile, Eleanore typed her own good-bye and closed the computer once more. Then she turned and gazed into the flames. She thought of the red dress Uriel had bought for her a week ago. She was going to wear a white version of it for the wedding.

A knock at the door pulled her from her thoughts.

And then it sent her heart into her throat. No one was supposed to know where the door to the mansion *was*, much less be able to knock on it.

She stood up and faced the foyer, beyond which the door to the mansion waited. She hesitated and pondered and curled her fingers into the material of her tunic-length T-shirt.

The knock came again.

Crap, she thought. What was she supposed to do? Max and Uriel were dealing with press releases for the sequel to *Comeuppance.* Michael was on duty in New York, Gabe had returned to Scotland the day before, and Azrael was in his underground chamber, sleeping.

She squared her shoulders and made her way to the foyer. She paused and called out, "Who's there?"

"It's Jason, Miss Granger. I've come to deliver a present from Lord Samael."

What? Eleanore's brows rose, her eyes widening. What on earth could Samael want to give her?

"I swear to you, Miss Granger, you are in no danger. You have my master's word that you will come to no harm."

Eleanore pressed her fingers to her eyes for a moment and considered the options. Jason wasn't likely to go away. And if Samael wanted to harm her, he would have done it long ago.

She took a deep breath, let it out in a sigh, then opened the door.

Jason stood there on the doorstep, dressed in suit and tie as usual. A Carpathian mountain range stretched out behind him.

"Miss Granger." He addressed her formally, nodded once, and held out a small black box with a red bow.

Eleanore took the box. "Okay, now you can leave."

He said nothing, but the corners of his mouth curled up ever so slightly. "As you wish." With that, he took a step back and vanished.

Eleanore quickly closed the door and then on impulse, she slammed the dead bolt home. She returned to the living room and set the box down on the coffee table, eyeing it warily.

She continued to eye it warily for several long minutes.

And then, able to wait no longer, she knelt down in front of the coffee table and pulled the ribbon loose. The top came away easily, revealing a black velvet interior—and a gold binding bracelet.

It was the binding bracelet that Eleanore had placed on Samael's wrist during the battle with the Adarians.

Ellie gingerly lifted the smooth gold ornament from its casing and turned it over in her hand, confusion marking her features. She'd been told that only the one who placed it an archangel's wrist could remove it. Yet here it was.

She gazed down at it for several more long moments—and then she blinked.

The entire time, she thought, the realization stunning her to the core. Samael was never bound by the bracelet. He helped them in that battle of his own free will.

There was a note on the bottom of the box. Ellie put the bracelet down and unfolded the note.

> *Dearest Ellie,*
>
> *Congratulations on your engagement.*
> *Consider this my gift.*
>   *—Samael*
>
> *P.S. Love the wings.*

Read on for a sneak peek at the next novel
in the Lost Angels series,

MESSENGER'S ANGEL

Available from Signet Eclipse in June 2012.

It was early Sunday morning and not a high-travel time; her car was empty but for her. She felt like Harry Potter when the trolley came by with teas and soups and biscuits for sale. There were no Bertie Botts Every Flavor Beans, but with a little effort it was easy to imagine that when she turned around and looked out the window, she would see the towering spires of Hogwarts rising over the hills in the distance. It was enough to take her mind off the attack she'd suffered and her burgeoning powers and what the hell they could possibly mean. At least for a little while.

But the sense of bereavement and haunted remembrance she experienced while traveling across Scotland was stronger on the train than it had been in the car. Perhaps it was because she had nothing to do but stare out the window at the passing countryside and its crumbling castle walls. Whatever the reason, though, Juliette remained nearly motionless as the world passed her by, and memories she knew she couldn't have assaulted her mind.

A flash of an ancient church, and a chill ran down her spine. A shadow fell across a painted red door, and Juliette felt sad. A path beckoned into the darkness through a tall wood, and she had the sudden urge to jump off the train and run down the trail. It was almost frustrating, the way the land made her want to remember.

"I see you feel a kinship with our bonnie Caledonia," came a deep brogue from behind her.

Juliette jumped just a little, and turned in her seat to find herself staring up at the man who had kissed her in the pub. The man who had saved her from the stranger. The man who had, until only a few hours ago, been in police custody.

Gabriel Black. True to his name, he was dressed in head-to-toe pitch, his wavy, raven locks blending in with the leather collar of his jacket. His silver eyes sparkled with secrets as they locked onto hers.

Juliette's jaw grew slack, and her tongue found itself knotted, useless, and mute. She caught a whiff of him, a scent like sandalwood and cedar and hearth-fire smoke, and images of her dream flashed before her mind's eye. Her fingers went limp on the tabletop, her legs pressed themselves together self-consciously, and her bottom lip began to tremble.

"B-Black," she whispered.

Gabriel smiled, and then, without being asked, he lowered himself into the empty space on the seat beside her.

His solid nearness washed over her like a blanket of intoxicating sexuality, and Juliette hurriedly scooted back a bit on the seat. She could go no farther when her left arm pressed against the cold metal beneath the coach window.

Gabriel watched her retreat, his eyes sparkling with amusement. "We need to talk, lass," he said. His accent had so much more of a brogue than that of most of the people on the Western Isles. By and large, Hebrideans sounded Irish and Gaelic. Black, however, sounded as if he'd come from all over Scotland; it was the timbre and lilt of his tone that bespoke of the land.

"A-About what?" Juliette asked. *The kiss? The man in my room? The fact that you were arrested?*

Gabriel's smile broadened, his silver gaze flicking to her lips and back again. Casually, he turned toward her, caging her with the hard mass of his body as he reached across the table and picked up her cup of tea. It was still steaming. Without taking his eyes off her, he placed it to his lips and took a sip. "You've go' good taste," he said as he put the cup back down. "Bu' then, you're a Scottish lass by blood, so I'm no' surprised."

"Look," she said, feeling a little dizzy. "I'm grateful to you for saving me from whoever it was that came into my room last night, but . . ." She lost track of what she was going to say when he reached over and nonchalantly took a lock of her long, thick hair and began rubbing it between his thumb and forefinger. "But . . ." She licked her lips, utterly distracted by the scent and sound and feel of him so close. The air around her felt too thick, too charged.

Somewhere in the distance thunder rolled, barely audible over the rhythmic sound of the train on the tracks. But Black's eyes cut from the hair in his hand to Juliette's eyes once more, and he cocked his head to one side. He said nothing, as if waiting for her to continue.

"But I don't know you and you're . . ." She trailed off again.

"I'm wha', Juliette?" he asked softly.

He knows my name, she thought. For some reason, she wasn't surprised. He seemed unreal, sitting there only inches from her, more solid than a sable-draped statue of bronze. He seemed impossible, like a superhero. Like a dream. *You're scaring me.*

Thunder boomed closer to the train, the storm obviously having moved in, as it was easier to hear over the metal slide of the rails. Something strange flashed in the light gray depths of Gabriel's eyes. He gently released her hair and leaned in a bit, closing the space between them. "You'll want to control that, luv." He smiled a decidedly dark smile. "Let it rage an' it'll drain your strength." He leaned in even farther so that Juliette's head bumped the wall behind her. "An' then how will you fight me off, lass?"

Juliette could barely breathe now. Her mind fought to process what he had just said, even as her body fought with itself over the effect he was having on her. Enough of his words got through that her blood pressure shot through the roof, and adrenaline poured into her bloodstream. "Control what?" she asked, her voice barely more than a whisper.

"The storm, Juliette," he replied. "It's one of your powers as an archess, is it no'? An' from the way it's growin' stronger by the moment, I'd wager it's a fairly new one to you."

Terror thrummed its way through Juliette's body, instantly chilling most of the heat Black's nearness had awakened. Her stomach turned to lead in her middle, and her heart hammered against the inside of her rib cage. "What are you talking about?"

Gabriel's smile never wavered. The pupils of his eyes were expanding, like those of a predator singling out its prey. "You know verra well, luv. An' I do, too. I know because I've been searchin' for you for so long, I've lost track o' the time."

The world blurred around them and melted into slow motion as Gabriel slowly raised his hand and cupped her cheek. At the contact, Juliette felt trapped and possessed and wanted and cherished and more beautiful than she had ever felt in her life. Even through the fear, her body was responding to his as if it wanted him more than it wanted life itself. His hand held hers as if she were a delicate treasure; she felt a tremble in his fingers, despite the apparent calm of his tone, and it echoed the chaotic beat of her heart—and the growing storm outside the train windows.

She wanted to close her eyes as he leaned a little closer; he was so close now, his next words whispered across her lips, a breath of mint and Parma Violets. . . . She loved Parma Violets. "You were made for me, Juliette," he said. His thumb brushed possessively, enticingly across her full lower lip. His gaze flicked to her mouth and back again; the silver in his eyes had become mercury, liquid lightning that reflected the gale building beyond the window. "How else would I know wha' I know aboot you?"

Juliette kept her gaze locked on his as she shook her head. "I don't know what you're talking about," she insisted stubbornly. He couldn't know. This was insane. She barely knew about her powers herself. "Please back off," she added, almost desperate now for him to either kiss her or disappear. One or the other—or she would pass out.

"Och. No, I canno' do that, luv," he told her with a single shake of his head. His thumb brushed across her lower lip again, and she shivered. "There are men after you, if you'll recall. The one who attacked you last night was no' the first of his kind to come after an archess. An' he won' be the last. You're no' safe alone, an' there's no' anythin' I won' do to keep you safe."

Juliette's gaze narrowed. "How do I know you didn't set up that entire scene last night?" she asked him. "Scumbags sometimes work in teams; one to play the bad guy—the other to 'save' the victim." She gritted her teeth, trying to believe her own words enough to deliver them with some conviction. "I'm not stupid."

"No, lass, that you're no'." He shook his head, clearly agreeing with her. His eyes still twinkled with some secret merriment, and it made him so handsome, she had never felt so close to losing control. She'd never thought herself the kind of woman who could lose her composure around a man simply because he was beautiful. Gorgeous. Godlike. But she may have been wrong. Because at that moment she wanted to kiss him—and do other things with him—so badly, her body was aching in the most embarrassing places.

As if her own need were a signal of surrender for the predator in him, Black's pupils ate up the silver in his eyes, and the sight of it made Juliette weak from the neck down. Before she could react, he was moving in for the kill, his lips slanting over hers even as his hands framed her face, claiming her for his.

God, yes . . . She was lost now; there was no coming back from this. Nothing else in life would ever feel so good. Juliette was instantly on fire; her heart was hammering, her body melting, her core throbbing as wetness wantonly gathered between her legs and her breath left her lungs. Her hands came up of their own accord and clutched at the thick black leather of his jacket, her fingers curling into the material as if holding on for dear life.

He was an expert kisser; he did everything right. He knew how to surround her, how to open her up and delve deep. He possessed her with that kiss, taking and tasting and destroying her defenses as if they were tissue paper. And then, suddenly, he went still above her. His body tensed, his hands slid to her hair and tightened their grip, and very, very slowly, he pulled away.

The moment his lips left hers, Juliette experienced such cold and emptiness, she actually shivered. It was like tasting despair, this abrupt separation. It *hurt*. But she retained enough control over herself to release his jacket and open her eyes.

When she did, she almost gasped at the change she saw in Black's expression. The lust and need were still there in that handsome face, but there was anger there now as well, stark and dangerous. His own gaze had narrowed, and lightning reflected in the molten silver of his eyes. His stubbled chin was set with hard determination. "Do no' move from here, lass. Stay in this seat until I return," he told her firmly.

Juliette was too stunned to react in any way. He must have taken it for acquiescence, because with that, he pulled back and in one fluid, graceful movement, he stood in the aisle on the opposite end of the table. Juliette sat up a little straighter in the seat as reality slowly flooded her world like a cold shower. She watched his tall, dark form take a step back and, in that brief moment of space and clarity, she entertained a hundred different thoughts. *He's crazy. This is nuts. He's dangerous. He knows. I have to get out of here. Wait until he's gone—*

As if he knew what was going through her head, Gabriel came forward to brace his hands on the surface of the table and lean in toward her once more. "Know this, lass: there is nowhere you can go where I will no' find you. Leave here an' I promise you'll no' get far." His eyes speared her like silver daggers.

She swallowed hard. He waited a moment more, trapping her in his metal gaze, and then he straightened and turned to stride down the aisle of the otherwise deserted coach. The automatic door opened before him. He stopped, turned to look at her over his broad shoulder, and captured her gaze with his. There was a world of meaning in the look he gave her. It was a brand of a look, hot and searing.

Then he turned back around and stepped through the plastic sliding doors and out of her line of sight. Juliette sat there in the seat, just as he had told her to, for several long moments. She couldn't help it. It wasn't that she was obeying his order; she simply couldn't move.

The first time he had kissed her had been heaven. He'd torn down her walls and breached her world with seemingly no effort at all. The second time he'd kissed her, he'd marched right into her castle and claimed it as king. She was ruined now. No man in the world would ever kiss her like that again.

Slowly, Juliette raised her fingers to her lips. She touched the swollen, sensitive flesh and closed her eyes. No matter how perfect the man was, he claimed to know about her ability to control the storm—which was throwing as big a fit as ever outside the windows now. He had called her something strange—an archess. And now that she'd said it out loud, the possibility that he had collaborated with the blond in her room to set up that kidnapping attempt just so that he could rescue her seemed much more likely.

She didn't trust Gabriel Black. She didn't trust anything about him—not his tall, hard body or his piercing silver eyes or his incredibly handsome face or his accent, which melted the bones in her body. She didn't trust the graceful way he moved or the sexy way he smelled or the subjugating perfection of his damnable kiss.

She *definitely* didn't trust the kiss.

Juliette's fingers trembled on her lower lip. "I have to get out of here," she whispered to no one.

As if the train had heard her and decided to become her partner in this venture, it slowed as the next station drew closer. Juliette lowered her hand and scooted to the end of the seat to peer down the length of the aisle. The doors on both ends were shut tight, and though she detected movement beyond them, it was blurred and indistinct; passengers disembarking in the neighboring coaches.

Without giving it further thought, Juliette jumped off the seat, grabbed her carry-on bag from its place above her, and raced to the door on the opposite side from the direction Black had gone. It opened as she reached it, and she shot through it and off the train onto the landing.

Disoriented, it took her a moment to figure out where she was. There weren't many big cities or even towns in Scotland, and this certainly wasn't one of them. A sign inside the station house marked it as the Muir of Ord Railway Station. So she must be in Muir of Ord. Wherever that was.

At least she knew it was somewhere between Ullapool and Inverness. She was in the Highlands. This was where her mother's side of the family, the MacDonalds, was from.

Now what? Her mind did summersaults inside her skull. She needed transportation, she needed a map, and she needed to get away from the train and its windows as soon as possible. Her feet moved of their own accord, eating up the ground at a desperate pace as she made her way off the landing, down the ramp that took her from the station, and around the brick building. She would ask the station manager or director or whatever he was called for help. But first she would hide.

The women's bathroom was as good a place as any. She would wait there until the train took off again. It was a shitty plan, but it was better than no plan at all.

Gabriel's blood was on fire in his veins; he'd never felt like this before. Juliette was ripping him apart inside. He'd felt her give in to him. He'd won her surrender with his kiss and he knew that if he'd wanted to, he could have taken her right there on the seat on the train. Not that he would have. Well, maybe.

But then he'd felt something else. It was a vibration in the air, a thickness to the atmosphere, charged and negative and wrong. And he would recognize it anywhere. The Adarian was on the train. Not only was he on the train, but he had been in that coach with Juliette, invisible and lying in wait like an unseen serpent. He might have even been sitting across from her—watching her all along.

Gabriel wasn't sure why he hadn't sensed it at first. It might have been that he was so focused on Juliette, nothing else registered. It might have been that the Adarian was so good at hiding, Gabe hadn't felt the change in the air until the man moved right by him.

That he had felt. It was a shift in the air, like sandpaper molecules of oxygen and carbon dioxide scraping along his flesh and soul as the Adarian moved past him and down the aisle.

He had no idea what the man was waiting for. He could only guess that the Adarian hadn't attacked Juliette outright because there would be no easy way to get an unconscious body off the train without being seen. And then Gabriel had shown up and most likely thrown a wrench into the Adarian's plans. He'd left the coach while Gabe and Juliette were kissing. And now he was somewhere—somewhere on this train. And Juliette was alone in her car and Gabriel wasn't an idiot. He knew she would try to escape. He knew that once he gave her enough space to think, she would come to her senses and a good, hard, healthy fear would set in. She had no reason to believe that his intentions were pure. She was right about the way some men set women up with the good-guy, bad-guy routine. Michael had come across many a rape scenario in his line of duty as a cop in New York, and he'd shared enough of those stories over the years.

Men could be monsters. And Juliette had a good head on her shoulders. She would run. He'd seen the thoughts in her eyes as he'd left her. He could threaten and try to scare her all he wanted, but it wouldn't work. In the end, she would flee.

At least there was nowhere she could go on a moving train. She was too smart to try to jump off, and the doors wouldn't open in that fashion while the train was moving anyway. For the moment, she was stuck, giving him the time he needed to track down the Adarian.

What was confusing Gabe, however, was the apparent absence of any of the other Adarians. Where was the General? Why hadn't Abraxos made his infernal appearance yet? What the bloody hell was going on?

Gabriel strode through the aisles of the train, honing his senses for that familiar spark of negativity that would tell him the Adarian was near. He cursed his luck that just as he was finding the woman he had searched two thousand years for, his enemy had found her, as well. At least he didn't have to deal with Samael the way Uriel had when he'd found his archess months ago. Small blessings.

Nonetheless, the Adarian's intrusion was like watching the Roman army lay siege to Gabriel's homeland. She was his—and *only* his. It was time to deal with the intruder once and for all.

Gabriel ignored the stares he got as he passed through the compartments. He was too focused to pay them any heed. But the farther down the train's length he got, the more agitated he became. The air was clean of the feel of the Adarian. There was no static, no thickness, no wrongness—not like there had been in Juliette's cabin. Where had the intruder gone?

And then something niggled at the back of Gabriel's brain—and the train began to slow. *No.*

Gabriel stopped in the aisle and turned to face the direction from which he'd come. The LCD screen at the end of the car read "Muir of Ord," and a few people were grabbing for their luggage. Gabriel broke into a near run, brushing rudely by the people who had claimed space in the aisle. The doors opened for him as he neared them and he shot on through.

But by the time he reached Juliette's car, the train had been stopped completely for several seconds and his fears were confirmed.

She was gone.

HEATHER KILLOUGH-WALDEN

Always, Angel
A Novella of the Lost Angels

**A prequel to the Lost Angels series—
available as an eSpecial***

When four female angels were created for the four archangels, a chaos spurred by jealousy erupted, and the archesses were secreted away to Earth. The archangels followed, prompting a search that has lasted millennia.

The Culmination is about to begin. Angel knows it the moment the first archess is discovered—and she's far from happy. Inextricably bound to the archesses, Angel won't be able to hide her true nature once each archess is found by her fated mate. Once her nature is revealed, the man Angel so desperately craves, but can never have, will discover her—and every realm will pay the price.

**Available online wherever books are sold or at
penguin.com/especials**

S0308